TAPPING *the* BILLIONAIRE

BILLIONAIRE

Bad Boys

BOOK ONE

max monroe

Tapping the Billionaire
Published by Max Monroe LLC
© 2016, Max Monroe

ISBN-13: 978-1532946776
ISBN-10: 1532946775

Editing by Indie Solutions by Murphy Rae
Formatting by Champagne Formats
Cover Design by Perfect Pear Creative
Proofreading by Silently Correcting Your Grammar
Photo Credit to David Vance Photographer

DEDICATION

Fuck you very much, Leslie.
You always manage to ruin everything, but you didn't ruin this.

Disclaimer: You are NOT the Leslie we're talking about. No, really. You're not her. We swear. It's another Leslie. One you don't know and have never heard of. Camp Love Yourself Scout's honor.

INTRO

I'm Kline Brooks.

Harvard graduate.

President and CEO of Brooks Media.

Net worth: $3.5 billion.

Devilishly handsome. How do I know this? I was prom king two years in a row.

Highly intelligent. Proof? I can solve any Rubik's Cube, in front of your face, with *magic* fingers.

Certified master of female orgasms. My fingers, my tongue, my cock—I can make you scream, *"I'm coming!"* before you even realize I've removed your panties with my teeth. Not the almost orgasms that spur a pathetic moan and half-ass whimper. *No.* I'm talking toe-curling, back-arching, earth-shattering *O*s that will leave your voice hoarse, your body shaking, and pack a punch so powerful you'll be left a sliver of intensity short of unconscious.

Am I piquing your interest?

Should I mention my cock is the kind of cock that's actually dick-pic worthy? I'm not talking an average six-inch shaft. I'm talking big.

Thick. Smooth. And hard. Especially when there's work to be done.

Or maybe all I've done is turn you off. Are you thinking I'm like every classless man out there who's literally a disgrace to my gender?

The type of spineless dicks who won't call the next day. The guys who specialize in late-night booty calls but refuse to take a woman out on an actual date. Yeah, you know exactly who I'm talking about. Those idiots who have women thinking staying single for the rest of their lives is a better alternative than dealing with the bullshit that's running rampant in the dating world.

Well, I'm not that kind of guy.

I say what I mean and mean what I say. I don't kiss and tell. I call the next day. And if I'm interested in a woman, I *will* take her out on a date. I'll open doors for her. I'll pull out her chair. And I'll never be the kind of horny bastard who texts dick pics—unless the right woman begs me for them.

Bottom line, **I'm a gentleman**. I prefer monogamy to serial dating and fucking my way through New York City. I've spent the past few years avoiding the kind of women most would label "gold diggers" and trying out a couple of girlfriends in between. I've looked for the kind of woman I want, but lately, I have to admit I haven't put in as much effort. My focus has been on my company—building it to what it is and then keeping it that way, not only for me, but for all of the people who work so hard for me.

Until Georgia Cummings.

She's fiery, beautiful, has this sassy attitude that demands attention from everyone within her orbit, and is worth way more in value of character than I am in money.

I don't know how I missed her.

I don't know why it took me so long to *really* see her.

Two years, right there in front of my face as my Director of Marketing.

Maybe it's because I need to stop drowning myself in work so much. Maybe she didn't want to be seen.

No matter the reason, it only took one spur-of-the-minute decision for this remarkable woman to come barreling into my world.

I wasn't prepared for her.

And I sure as hell had no idea she'd knock me on my fucking ass.

Because the nice guy who believes in real love enough to build his entire fortune from a dating website?

That's me.

And this story?

Well, that's us.

CHAPTER 1

Georgia

*M*y eyes! Dear God, my eyes!

There were things in life that, once seen, were damn near impossible to forget. A bleach scrub…acid straight to the retinas… three hours of perfect porn GIFs…hell, even a lobotomy wouldn't remove those kinds of images.

Lucky for me, I had come across not one, not two, but *four* day-destroying pictures. Dick pics, to be more specific. And let's just say this latest one was *not* pic-worthy. Not by a long shot. Or a short shot, if I took size into consideration. This was the kind of pic that would leave any woman wondering why. *Why? Why would anyone want to advertise they were the owner of* this?

It was the gremlin of male members—and the sole reason my night had taken a turn for the worse. What was supposed to be a nice evening in, watching TV with my best friend and roommate, Cassie, had turned into a nightmare of pubes, wrinkled balls, and a crown that was not fit for a king.

I banged my fingers across the keypad with a response.

TAPRoseNEXT (11:37PM): Is that your dick? Really? REALLY?

TapNext was the latest and greatest dating-site-turned-app for single men and women to meet, chat, and, hopefully, find their next date. Generally speaking, it was a better alternative to nights out at a bar or club. Because, for me, those nights had the same ending—politely declining the thrilling (insert *heavy* sarcasm) offer of hooking up with some random dude at his apartment, one hell of a hangover, and weird guys with names like Stanley or Milton sending me texts for late-night booty calls for the next month. Which I *always* ignored.

My business card said *Director of Marketing, Brooks Media*. It was a hefty title for someone just starting out in their career, but I had earned it. I worked harder than anyone else in my department, and it also may have helped that the man who held the position prior to me had been fired after being arrested for picking up a prostitute in one of the company cars. Why he had even been driving a company car in the city was still confusing to me. Seriously, even hookers cabbed it in New York.

Since Brooks Media owned TapNext, it was easy to understand why I was well versed and highly invested in the app's success. It was a requirement when hired—all single employees had to create a TapNext profile. Staff were strongly encouraged to use the app and give honest feedback about their experiences. Profile names were kept top secret and on penitentiary-style lock-down with Human Resources. And feedback stayed anonymous.

Translation: *Don't worry,* **TAPRoseNEXT***, your boss doesn't know about your pervy play on words.*

At first, I'd felt it was an odd way to handle business, but after two years of working at Brooks Media, I'd found that my TapNext profile was a damn good way to do research and find promotional ideas.

My phone pinged with the offender's response.

BAD_Ruck (11:38PM): …

Did he just ellipsis me? Really?

TAPRoseNEXT (11:38PM): Creep Threat Level MOTHERFUCKING Red.

There was no immediate response, but the rest of my rant would not be contained.

TAPRoseNEXT (11:39PM): Don't any of you know how to start conversations anymore? Jesus.

Cassie sighed beside me. "Stop slamming everything around, Wheorgiebag! I'm trying to watch *American Ninja Warrior* and you're totally messing with my pumped up vibe."

I ignored her, still focused on finding a way to erase the offending images from my brain.

She peeked over my shoulder before I could pull my phone away. "Whoa. Whoa. *Whoa.* Is that *my* picture on *your* profile?"

Creamy, perfect-skinned thighs on display, she was bent over with her dark brunette head peeking through the space between her open legs. Her hooch just barely escaped making an appearance.

"Paybacks, Casshead."

"And what did I do to deserve being your pro-bono photo ho?"

I cocked an eyebrow. "Do I have to choose just one?"

"Go ahead, give me one example. I dare ya."

"College. Sophomore year. I told you not to post those pictures on Facebook, but did you listen? Of course not."

She grinned. "Ahhhhh, yes. I remember those. I thought you looked really cute that night."

"My head was in the toilet."

"But you had those cute puppy dog eyes going on." She glanced at my phone again, dusky gray eyes hitting the phallic bull's eye. "Holy hell, what is that? Is that Quasimodo's dick?"

I stood up from the couch and began to pace in front of the TV. "Four dick pics today, Cassface. *Four!*"

Cassie scrunched her face up. "And what? You were hoping for five?"

My expression was a combination of disgusted and puzzled.

"You know," she explained, "one to fill all the holes and one for each hand." Easy to interpret and equally graphic hand gestures matched her words as she spoke. "Although, I'm not sure I'd want DP from The Hunchcock of Notre Dame." One look at my face and she coughed out a laugh. "You're not really a prude, but right now, you're playing one on TV."

I groaned and gave in, planting my ass back on the couch and burying my face in my hands. "I guess it's because this profile is for work research. I have this unjustified sense that it should be more professional."

She shook her head and smiled, propping her mismatched-sock feet on the arm of our couch. "I gotta say, that wiener is pretty fucking awful. But, Georgie, you work for a company that specializes in an app called *TapNext*, not the White House."

After a brief beat of silence, we laughed at the same time, and I raised one eyebrow in question. "You're comparing *TapNext* to the *White House*?"

"You're right," she agreed. "Bad analogy. There's probably *more* dick pics there." A giant, mischievous grin consumed Cassie's face as she grabbed the remote.

"*Cassie...*" I pointed in her direction, but it was too late. She was already standing on top of our coffee table, using the remote for a microphone.

My best friend had this thing with making parody songs out of pretty much anything when inspired. And she didn't do it quietly. No way, quiet was not Cassie's style. She sang like she was Adele performing at the Grammys.

"I call this one *White House Lovin',*" Cassie announced.

I groaned but secretly couldn't wait to see what she would come up with. Think Kristen Wiig on *Saturday Night Live* kind of hilarious shit. That was Cass.

"Blue-dress intern, found my pants fast..."

"White House intern, it was a blast..."

She was singing her little heart out.

"This girl, she was crazy for D..."

Snapping fingers. Pelvic thrusts. Head bobs. Cassie wasn't missing a beat.

"Met the prez, down on both knees..."

One verse in and the dick pic bandit had been forgotten. I hopped off the couch and tackled her to the floor. She screamed. I laughed. And five minutes later, Cassie was back on the coffee table while I sang backup to the rest of her ridiculous song.

Tell me, whore... Tell me, whore...

Admit it, you're singing it too.

Later that night, once I had cozied myself in bed and was so very close to reaching that heavenly REM cycle, the ping of my phone pecked at me. I groaned my way out of Dreamland slowly. God, it was time to make some major life changes. For example, the alert settings for my TapNext profile in my phone. It was either that or murder, and I'm the kind of person who likes to dip a toe in the pool water to test it rather than cannonball my way in.

Rubbing a hand over my face, I forced my eyes opened and snatched the phone off my antique nightstand. I barely resisted the urge to slam it back down, thus breaking it into a million tiny pieces. Luckily, my rational thinking wasn't as sleepy as the rest of me and realized the amount of work that would result from such an impulsive decision.

Cleaning and shopping and transferring my contacts, oh my.

Yeah, *screw that.*

BAD_Ruck (2:09AM): It's NOT my dick.

It's not his *dick?*

What the double actual fuck?

No. Nope. This was *so* not the right time to deal with this bullshit. Not. Answering.

The sides of my pillow exploded upward with the force of my punch and made the perfect cushion for my face when it slammed down beside my hand. I had so much shit to do at work tomorrow, and dealing with **BAD_Ruck** and his proclivity for awful crotch selfies and unintelligible responses was not going to be on my agenda.

I was focused on getting shut-eye, confident that sleep and I would spoon the fuck out of each other until the sun rose the following morning. I channeled Buddha for my inner Zen, humming my way toward unconscious bliss. It was either that, or grab my vibrator and participate in a ménage à moi.

Thankfully, my return to sleep came easily that night. No hands-on approach required.

The next day, while I was getting ready for work, I decided to give **BAD_Ruck** a piece of my mind. I spit toothpaste into the sink, rinsed my mouth out with water, and turned off the faucet. Striding into my room with purpose, I grabbed my phone off the nightstand and sent the dick gremlin a response.

Suck. On. That. Buddy.

CHAPTER 2

Kline

TAPRoseNEXT (7:03AM): Then it's someone else's dick? WORSE. Threat Level EXPLODED.

"Good morning, Mr. Brooks."

"Good morning, Frank," I replied, picking my head up from the crime scene on my phone just long enough to meet his honest amber eyes before sliding into the soft leather seat of my Town Car.

Fucking Thatch.

I swear, somehow he took doing what would already be really fucking annoying and advanced it to the next level. If he didn't have the same ability with money, I probably would have dropped him by now.

To the bottom of the ocean. *With a cinder block attached to his ankles.*

She was right, of course. Sending a picture of someone else's dick *was* considerably worse than sending a picture of your own.

Especially this one.

Three rings trilled in my ear before his sleep-laden voice forced one hungover syllable past his lips. "'Lo?"

"A dick, Thatch? Really?" I asked immediately, pinching the bridge of my nose to stave off a headache.

No amount of lingering alcohol could stop his answering laugh.

His throat cleared a little more with each chuckle, and by the time he responded, he was speaking clearly. "You're the one using my picture for your profile, bro. It was only fair that I unleashed the gargoyle dick."

Gargoyle dick. Too fucking right. A winglike knob, a hunchback, and questionable coloring all lent themselves to his description. I'd left my phone on the bar without hawk-eyeing it for *two fucking minutes,* and the asshole had somehow managed to send one of the world's worst illicit pictures to some poor—now blind—woman in that time.

"That profile was only payback for the last awful thing you did to me."

"Which was?" he asked, altogether too amused.

"Who knows," I admitted, staring up at the passing high-rises and shaking my head. "I can't keep up."

"Then join in, K. Live a little, for fuck's sake."

The burgeoning sun glinted off of a pane of perfectly smooth glass at the top of a building and reflected a rainbow right into the window of my car.

"I'm living just fine," I argued.

"Yeah." He laughed and scoffed at once. "Say hi to Walter for me."

That was Thatch's version of calling me a cat lady.

"Hey, fuck you!" I said, only to be met with dead air. I pulled the phone away from my ear to discover he'd ended the call.

"Fuck that guy," I muttered, somehow calling more of Frank's attention to myself than I had with all the yelling.

"Sir?"

"No worries, Frank." I paused for a second and looked back out the window. "You wouldn't happen to know a hit man, would you?"

I glanced up front in preparation for his reaction.

"Um," he murmured hesitantly, flicking his eyes between me and the road in the rearview mirror. "No, sir."

I shook my head as I smiled, a brief chuckle tickling the back of my throat.

"Good. That's good," I remarked, just as we pulled up to the curb in front of my building.

Flexing the door handle in my hand, I shoved the door open with the toe of my shoe.

"Mr. Brooks," Frank started to protest, as usual, jerking into motion in order to hop out to help me, but I just couldn't get into the mindset where his *and* my time was well spent waiting on him to walk around the car just to do something my opposable thumbs and lack of paralysis made shockingly simple.

I smiled in response before he could get out, meeting his eyes in the rearview mirror before exiting.

"Have a good day, Frank. I'll see you at six."

With the slam of the door, I buttoned my suit jacket as I walked, twenty audible smacks of my soles eating up the concrete courtyard in front of my building in no time.

New Yorkers buzzed around me, continuing a marathon life that started the moment they opened their eyes. That was the vibe of this city—active and elite and totally fucking focused. No one had time for each other because they barely had time for themselves. And yet, each and every single one of them would still proclaim it the "best city on Earth" without prompting or persuasion.

As my hand met the metal of the handle, I surveyed the lobby of the Winthrop Building, home to Brooks Media, to find the front desk employees and security guards scurrying to make themselves look busy when they weren't.

I bit my lip to keep from laughing. I'd never been the kind of boss to rule with an iron fist, and not once had I uttered a word of micromanagement to loyal employees like the ones practically shoving their hands in their staplers in order to look busy.

But being CEO of a company of this size and magnitude had a way of creating its own intimidation factor, whether it was intended or not. And, sometimes, the weight of unintended consequences was heavier than gold.

"Morning, Paul."

He nodded.

"Brian."

"Mr. Brooks."

The button for the elevator glared its illumination prior to my arrival—more help from the overzealous employees, I'm sure—and the indicating ding of its descent to the bottom floor preceded the opening of the shiny mirrored doors by less than a second.

I stepped in promptly without another word, offering only a smile. I knew anything else I said would only cause stress or anxiety, despite my efforts to convey the opposite. For a lot of people, their boss was never going to be a comfortable fit as a friend—no matter how nice a guy he was. The best thing I could do was recognize, accept, and respect that.

I sunk my hips into the rear wall as the doors slid closed in front of me and shoved my hands into the depths of my pants pockets to keep from scrubbing them repeatedly up and down my face.

I rarely overindulged, so I wasn't hungover, but Thatch's antics, both in person and online, were wearing me out. It wasn't that I didn't think the gargoyle dick was funny—because it *was*—but it was really one of those funnier-when-it's-not-happening-to-you things.

In fact, that rang surprisingly true for most of Thatch's prank-veiled torture.

The direction of my thoughts and the weight of my phone bumping against my hand had me pulling it out of my pocket against my better judgment.

I hovered my thumb over the TapNext app icon.

With one quick click, I had the ability to make a bad situation worse.

The screen flashed and the app loaded as soon as my thumb made contact.

BAD_Ruck (7:26AM): Despite what the gargoyle dick conveys, I promise I'm NOT a sexual terrorist.

Clutching the phone tightly in my fist, I shamefully knocked it against my forehead multiple times.

"Fucking brilliant."

I should have just dropped it. Moved on. I didn't fucking know this woman, for God's sake, but I couldn't help myself. I couldn't stand for even my fake dating profile persona to be remembered like this.

Here lies this man to rest. He will be remembered: Sexual Terrorist, Social Media Nuisance, Unfortunate Genital Development.

The elevator settled smoothly to rest on the fifteenth floor, and as the doors opened, I stepped out. My receptionist stood waiting with a stack of messages, having been warned of my arrival by the staff one hundred and fifty-some-odd feet below.

Neat and conservative clothes encased her sixty-eight-year-old frame, and stark white hair salted its way through her dark mocha bun.

Her smile was genuine, though, years of age, wisdom, and experience coloring her view of her thirty-four-years-young "boss." When it came to the infrastructure and real office inner workings, she ran this show.

The ends of my lips tipped up, forming wrinkles at the corners of my eyes.

"Good morning, lovely Meryl."

She clicked her tongue. "You better find some other roll to butter up, Mr. Brooks. It may be early, but my allowance of saturated fats is all used up for the day."

"Geez." I winced, clutching my chest in imaginary pain. "You

wound me." A grin crept onto one end of my mouth and a wink briefly closed the eye on the same side. "And it's Kline. Call me Kline, for
shit's sake."

"Ten years. Same conversation every day for every single one of
them," she grumbled.

"There's a lesson in there somewhere, Meryl, and I think it has to
do with bending to my will." I took the messages gently from her hand
and bumped her with just the tip of my elbow.

"I'm consistently persistent."

"So am I," she retorted.

"Don't I know it."

"Four urgent messages from new potential investors on top, and
multiple urgent IT problems below those," she called to my back as I
walked away.

I shook my head to myself. Potential investors were always urgent.

Pausing briefly and turning to look over my shoulder, I asked,
"And *you're* giving me the messages from IT, why?"

Things like that normally came from my personal assistant.

"Because I am," she called back, not even looking up from her
desk. "And because Pam is at home with a sick baby."

I leaned my head back in understanding and bit my lip to stop a
laugh from escaping.

"Ah. And we all know the only soft spot in your entire body is
reserved for the babies."

"Precisely," she confirmed unapologetically, looking over the
frames of her glasses and winking.

I turned to head for my office again, but she wasn't done talking.

"But don't you worry—"

Shit. Anything that started with Meryl telling me not to worry
meant I should worry. I should *really* worry.

"Leslie's here to pick up her slack."

I shook my head. I didn't know if it was in disbelief or resentment, but whatever it was, I couldn't stop the motion.

Meryl's eyes started to gleam.

"And since *you* hired her and all, I figured you wouldn't mind taking her directly under your knowledgeable wing for the day."

Fuck.

I let my head fall back with a groan briefly before resigning myself to a day from hell and getting back on my way.

One foot in front of the other, I walked toward my doom, knowing the only people I had to blame, other than myself, were my family. And I couldn't even *really* blame them. I was an adult, a business owner, and the leader of my own goddamn life. It had been my choice to hire the airhe—*Leslie*—whether I had done it out of obligation or not.

Still. "Fuck."

"Good morning, Mr. Brooks," she greeted as soon as I rounded the corner, the last syllable of my name trailing straight into a giggle.

God, that's painful.

Her eyes were bright, lips pouty, and her forearms squeezed into her breasts. Her black hair teased and sprayed, several curls rolled over her shoulders and hung nearly all the way down to her pointy nails. And she eye fucked me relentlessly, pounding me harder with every step I took.

I plastered a smile on my face and tried to make it genuine. She was really a nice person—just devoid of each and every quality I looked for in both lovers and friends.

"Come on, Leslie." I gestured, turning away from her nearly exposed—completely office inappropriate—breasts and walking straight into my office with efficiency I knew Cynthia, my head of Human Resources, would appreciate.

The boss in me wanted to tell her to put them away. The man in me knew I wouldn't be able to do that without opening some sort of door for a sexual harassment suit. Situations like this were ripe for postulation.

"You're with me today," I went on, walking straight to my desk and shucking the suit jacket from my shoulders to hang on the hook to the back and right of me.

"Here," I offered when she didn't move or speak, holding the messages from potential investors Meryl had handed me not five minutes ago out to her. "Take these to Dean and have him make some precursory calls. He can schedule calls for me this afternoon with any of them that show signs of legitimacy."

A fake-lashed blink followed by a blank stare.

I even shook them a little, but she didn't respond.

Right. Small words.

"Ask Dean to call these people back. He'll know if it's worth my time talking to them, and if it *is*, I'm free to do so this afternoon."

"Got it!" she said with a wink, jumping from one heel to the other, spinning, and sashaying her way out of my office.

I wasn't a psychic, but one thing was increasingly clear—I was going to need to stop and buy an extra bottle of scotch tonight.

CHAPTER 3

Georgia

I dove through the subway doors mere seconds before they crushed me to my death.

Okay, maybe that seems a tad dramatic, but if you lived in New York, you'd understand the sentiment I'm trying to portray.

The subway waited for no one. It didn't care if you were the next big shark on Wall Street. If you didn't reach those doors in time, *fuhgeddaboutit.*

I loved my job. I loved working at my job, once I managed to get my "never on time" ass there. It was that whole getting out of bed thing that caused me the most grief. Morning person, I was not. My body preferred to wake up on its own time. Therefore, my snooze button was ridden hard and put away *extremely* wet.

Every day was a race against time, and today was no exception.

I found a seat across from a thirty-something-year-old guy whose nose stayed buried in a book. He was hot by all accounts—brooding eyes, red flannel shirt, beanie-adorned bedhead, and cheekbones that would make Michelangelo's David look soft.

His book: *Sex, Drugs, and Cocoa Puffs: A Low Culture Manifesto* by Chuck Klosterman.

I knew that book well. I'd fiddled around with it during under-grad at NYU. It was a handwritten bomb of pop culture references and reflections on pretty much anything that mattered to young peo-ple. *The Real World*, porn, kittens, *Star Wars*, you name it and Kloster-man discussed it. His witty take on American culture was supposed to be ironic in an existential kind of way. But I wouldn't say any of the topics were deeply examined, which was probably why the book had left me with a Tumblr-like aftertaste in my mouth.

Translation: *Total hipster.* Although insanely good-looking, this guy would probably end up an NYC transplant in Portland within the next year. But I wasn't ruling out seeing his gorgeous mug on one of my favorite Instagram accounts, *Hot Dudes Reading.*

Because who doesn't love seeing man candy nose deep in a book?

My ogle time came to an end as I jumped off at my stop. Brooks Media headquarters was located on the prestigious Fifth Avenue, smack dab in the center of Midtown. This part of Manhattan was the central business district of the city—hell, even the country. Name a successful business, and it was probably located here. And lucky for me, my apartment in Chelsea was only a ten-to-fifteen-minute sub-way ride away.

Doesn't explain why I'm running twenty minutes late.

Following the hustle and bustle of sidewalk traffic, I maneuvered past as many map-reading tourists as possible. Street vendors littered the sidewalks. A guy on a bike missed getting hit by mere inches, ele-gantly flipping the driver off over his shoulder.

It was a weekday in New York, and it was fucking beautiful.

I loved my city. I loved the ebb and flow of its many eccentric-ities. Heels click-clacked against concrete, headed for Fifth Avenue's upscale boutiques. Loafers tip-tapped their way toward the Financial District. Taxis honked. Delivery trucks unloaded their goodies with clashing bangs and swift maneuvers. It was the New York song and dance. Everyone was on a mission to start their day. And nothing would stop them.

I strode into the Winthrop building, the spacious lobby greeting me with its gorgeous marble pillars and floor-to-ceiling windows. It was breathtaking. The office space was just as exquisite—wide hallways, natural stone floors, and the perfect amount of light coming in through large windows and skylights. Brooks Media had definitely shelled out some cash for this prime piece of real estate. By all accounts, it was stunning.

"Morning, Paul. Morning, Brian," I greeted the front desk security guards.

"Well, hey there, pretty lady." Paul smiled. "I see someone is still having issues with getting here bright and early."

"Oh, shut it, Paul. Not all of us can look as good as you without a little work in the morning." I grinned and batted my eyelashes.

Brian laughed. "She's got your number, dude."

"I *wish* she had my number," Paul interjected. "C'mon, Georgia, let me take you out to dinner."

"We've been going through the same conversation at least once a week for the past two years, Paul. My answer isn't going to change," I called over my shoulder as I made my way to the elevator.

"It will change!" he yelled. "One day, it will change!"

The elevator pinged and I stepped on, giving Paul a little wave before the doors shut.

He was an adorable guy: mid-forties, hard-working, and sweeter than honey. But I didn't mix business with pleasure. And Paul from security wasn't my kind of guy. One day, though, he'd meet the right kind of lady who'd wash his socks and make him beer-cheese dip for Monday Night Football. He needed a woman who was just as good in the kitchen as she was in the bedroom. I could sixty-nine with the best of 'em, but I was useless when it came to home-cooked meals. Talented chef would never be on my résumé. My oven was better used for storing shoes.

"Well, look what the cat dragged in. Fashionably late today, Georgie?" Dean winked, passing me in the hallway.

Shit. My late arrivals were starting to mimic the walk of shame. I seriously needed to get my shit together.

"I was only trying to impress you with my new A-line skirt," I called over my shoulder, sashaying my hips a little. "Vintage. Vera Wang. How 'bout them apples, cupcake?" Should I have mentioned I found the skirt at a secondhand shop in SoHo? Designer digs were great, but I refused to pay designer prices.

"Someone is fierce this morning. Go on with your bad self, little diva," he teased, snapping his fingers. Dean was one of my favorite people in the office: hilarious, flamboyantly gay, and smart as a whip. What more could a girl ask for?

He turned in my direction, stopping in his tracks. "Lunch today?"

I paused at the entry to my office. "I'd kill for a chicken salad sandwich from the deli across the street."

Dean grinned. "No homicide needed. We'll grab it to go."

"Let's eat there. My office, quarter till one?"

He blew me a kiss. "It's a date, lover."

Another day, another dollar, yadda yadda yadda. My mantra, even though I would have preferred staying wrapped up in my comforter and sleeping until noon. Some days, adulting was too much responsibility. Get up for work. Brush your hair. Pay bills. It was an endless list of too many things and not enough time. The struggle was real, my friends.

But rent in Chelsea wasn't a Sunday picnic in Central Park. A two-bedroom space with an elevator and doorman was pricey. Bottom line, I *had* to adult. No ifs, ands, or buts about it.

I settled into my day, checking emails and making follow-up calls to a few marketing prospects. The TapNext app had skyrocketed in success over the past year. I'd developed an ad campaign that had brought in several companies wanting to advertise within the windows of our app. And these scrollbar ads had become quite lucrative for the company. Businesses not only paid us a nice advertising fee, but they also agreed to some form of promotion for Brooks Media. We scratched their backs, and they gave us a full body massage. Although I was no use in the kitchen, I was *very* persuasive in a board-room.

"Knock, knock," Leslie announced her arrival. Her curvy frame swayed into my office, seemingly aloof to the fact I was in the middle of a conference call with Sure Romance.

"Uh, Georgia, like, there's birthday cards you need to sign for people in the office," she continued, tossing the greeting cards onto my desk. They spilled over my laptop, stopping my busy fingers from making much-needed progress on the current contract I was discussing.

I held up a finger, pointing to the Bluetooth in my ear.

"Georgia? Hellooooo, Georgia?" she repeated, tapping the toe of her stiletto in six quick, impatient movements.

Leslie was a horrible nightmare of ditzy responses, poor time management skills, and cleavage-revealing tops. And she was new to the company. But *for fuck's sake*, how hard was it to see that I was currently in the middle of something?

"I'm so sorry, can you hold on for just a second?" I politely asked Martin, Sure Romance's Director of Marketing.

"You know what, Georgia? I've got about three minutes to get to another meeting. How about you make the changes in the contract and send them over to legal? Let's shoot for another call on Friday to review everything and find a middle ground we can both be happy with."

Goddammit. This, my friends, was a perfect example of how to lose valuable footing in a business deal.

"Sure thing, Martin. And since Mr. Brooks wants to be on that call Friday, let's plan on it being a video chat." My boss knew nothing about that call. But this was me calling Martin's bluff. My persuasion skills were top notch, but there was a reason Kline Brooks was President and CEO of his own company. The man could talk an Eskimo into buying ice.

"Oh, okay." Martin cleared his throat. "In the meantime, I'll try to get legal to review everything over the next twenty-four hours. The sooner we can sign off on this deal, the better."

Translation: I'd like to avoid a video chat with your boss.

"Perfect. I look forward to hearing from you." I ended the call and used all of my strength to plaster a neutral smile on my face as I looked up at Leslie.

"So, like I was saying, you need to sign these," she repeated, still clueless.

God, I didn't even care if I had resting bitch face. Hell, I wanted to active bitch face this chick so bad. She'd been with the company for a hot minute, and I was already done with her.

"Okay, Leslie. Just give me a second and I'll sign them so you can go about your day," I responded through a fake smile. I wanted to berate her. I wanted to let her know just how much her interruption could have screwed up an important business deal. But it would've been useless. My words would have gone straight through the giant hole in her head.

I gripped my pen, scribbling half-assed sayings about celebrating and happy birthday and have a great day. Five cards later, I handed them back to Leslie and sent her ditzy ass on her way.

I was twenty emails deep before another interruption peeked in my door.

Kline Brooks. He was the kind of man women fantasized about. A quintessential billionaire bad boy—styled, short dark hair, muscles for days, and a panty-dropping smile.

Except—he *wasn't.*

His smiles were genuine and his orders gently delivered. He kept to himself, from what I could tell, and didn't appear to sleep around. Despite his crazy good looks and net worth, I'd yet to see him land an "NYC playboy" spot on Page Six. I'd never seen him execute a salacious glimpse at a single employee—male or female. He was a mystery, hidden under all of that quiet direction with absolutely no chance of being uncovered.

As an employee, he wouldn't touch me with a ten-foot pole. Honestly, I wasn't sure he knew I had a vagina. He treated me as an equal and seemed to truly value my opinion on all things business and marketing. His eyes never strayed to my tits. His mouth never flashed a devilish grin.

And I stood strong in my beliefs that business and pleasure may as well have been oil and water. Kline was business, plain and simple.

Plus, he wasn't at all what I was looking for.

And yes, I can practically see the word billionaire flashing in front of your money-hungry eyes and feel the judgment rolling off of you in thick, disdain-filled clouds.
But this isn't actually about him. Not really, anyway.

Despite my inexperience with relationships, I knew myself enough to know I liked a straight shooter—both in conversation and the pun that intends. And I wasn't willing to settle—even if it was on a big, comfy pile of money.

Christ, there had to be a middle ground between soft talkers like Kline and dick pic bandits like **BAD_Ruck.** *Didn't there?*

"Good morning, Georgia," he greeted with that professional yet handsome smile of his. "Just wanted to check in and see how the Sure

Romance deal was doing."

"Even though I had to threaten Martin with your presence on a video chat, I think we'll walk out of the deal with a million more than we anticipated."

"Nice work. Keep me abreast on the progress and let me know if you need backup."

My mind went straight to the word *abreast*. I knew my boss wasn't referring to my breasts, or breasts in general, but I couldn't stop my thoughts from wandering there.

I doubted Kline Brooks had ever thought about my breasts.

That would have been weird, right?

There was no way he saw me *that* way. And of course, I didn't think about him like that either. But it didn't hurt that he was easy on the eyes. Well, not *my* eyes, but other women's eyes. I was sure he was easy on *their* eyes. My eyes *knew* not to look at him.

I wouldn't deny my eyes were thankful he didn't have a weird comb-over or nose hairs or crusty lips. But Kline Brooks was business, *not* pleasure. He wouldn't touch me, and I sure as hell wouldn't touch him.

"Georgia?" he asked, pulling me from my rambling inner monologue.

Shit.

"Sorry." I shook the awkward thoughts out of my head. "I will definitely keep you updated on the Sure Romance contract, Mr. Brooks. I'm planning on signatures being finalized by the end of this week."

"Good to hear." He rapped his knuckles twice against the doorframe in that way only a man can pull off. "Thank you."

And with that, through the glass walls of my office, I watched as Kline Brooks strode down the hall with purpose. I knew that look well. Either someone was ready for lunch or they were about two minutes late for a meeting.

Before I could resume the task of responding to the morning's emails, Dean walked into my office, a shit-eating grin plastered to his face. "Got a minute, sweet cheeks?"

"Of course." I shut my laptop, giving him my full attention.

He plopped his Prada-wearing ass in the leather seat across from my desk. Dean kept grinning like the fucking Cheshire Cat as he slid a Hallmark card across my laptop.

I raised an eyebrow. "Why are you smiling like that? It's creepy, dude."

"So, Tits McGee put this card on my desk," he sing-songed. "Of course, this was after she practically shoved her cleavage in my face." The wide smile turned to irritation. "That girl has about the worst gaydar I've ever seen."

"Aw, poor Dean. So attractive that single women are throwing themselves at him," I teased.

"Well, you're about to be thanking poor Dean here in a minute." He nodded toward the card. "Go ahead and read it, sassy pants. I think you might want to make some changes."

Huh? I glanced at the front, reading the sentiment. It was, by all accounts, a sympathy card. Someone in the office must have had a death in the family. I opened it and read through everyone's thoughtful responses.

I'm so very sorry for your loss, Mary. -Patty
You're in my thoughts and prayers. -Meryl
Please let us know if there's anything we can do. -Gary

My coworkers were really sweet. That much was apparent.

Lots of love and prayers being sent your way through this difficult time. -Laura
HAPPY! HAPPY! JOY! JOY! Have a great day celebrating! -Georgia

Oh, fuck.

I read it again just to make sure my eyes weren't playing tricks on me.

Shit.

Shit.

Shit.

My *Ren & Stimpy* reference wasn't all that funny when written in the center of someone's *CONDOLENCE CARD.*

"Fucking Leslie," I spat. "She threw a bunch of cards on my desk and said they were *birthday* cards."

Dean proceeded to lose his shit, his cackling laughs echoing inside my office.

I glared at him. "It's not *that* funny."

"Oh, hell yes it is. You referenced *Ren & Stimpy* on a sympathy card," he wheezed.

Seriously, fuck you, Leslie. Fuck you, hard.

I was convinced I could blame her for everything wrong in my life.

Lost my keys? *Goddammit, Leslie!*

Missed the subway? *Fuck you very much, Leslie.*

Another awful dick pic sent to my phone? *You're such an asshole, Leslie.*

I sighed. "I'm not even sure how to fix this."

"White out?" he suggested, still laughing like a lunatic.

"Please." I waved my hand at him. "Continue to giggle your ass off at my expense."

"This was literally the highlight of my day. When I read it, I about fell out of my chair from laughing so hard. Pretty sure everyone in the office heard me. Even Meryl was giving me the stink eye."

"Glad to know I'm brightening someone's workday."

He smirked, standing up and snatching the card out of my incompetent hands. "Let's just throw this card out. I'll have Meryl send flowers to Mary's house from everyone in the office."

I let out a breath of relief. "I'm in full support of this plan. I'll even chip in fifty bucks."

"Perfect."

"Hey, you're throwing that card out, right?" I asked before he made his way out of my office doors.

He only responded with a shrug and a few more cackles.

Dean was such a bitch. If I didn't love him so much, I'd have definitely disowned his designer-tag-wearing ass.

As his laughter faded, the annoying crescendo that signaled a text on my phone built.

I grabbed it quickly, knowing if I didn't read it now, I wouldn't remember it until the end of the day.

Cassie: I just watched the police arrest two guys for fucking right up against a wall on Broadway.

Not sure how to respond, I said the only thing that came to mind.

Me: Well, it is the Theater District.

I exited my messages, and before I locked the screen, I noticed the little red notification on my TapNext app. A message from **BAD_Ruck** from this morning made promises of sexual normalcy despite his indiscretions. A truce was in order.

TAPRoseNEXT (12:14PM): Awkward apology accepted.

His response came two minutes later.

BAD_Ruck (12:16PM): Thank God. Though, to be fair, your profile name really does nothing to discourage bad behavior.

CHAPTER 4

Kline

TAPRoseNEXT (12:19PM): Ugh. Don't remind me. I owe it mostly to a bottle of wine and an ill-advising roommate.

I chuckled to myself and then glanced at my watch, compelled to double-check the time even though the display on my phone told it to me just fine.

A pastrami and corned beef on rye from the deli on the corner was calling my name, yelling louder with each passing minute, but every single action of the day seemed to move as if it were coated in molasses.

"What are you laughing at?" Thatch asked from the screen in front of me.

I'd nearly forgotten I was on a video call with him.

"Your ugly mug," I countered, pointedly electing not to tell him I was having any further conversation with **TAPRoseNEXT.**

"This face? No way. This is my moneymaker, son."

"You sound like the biggest douche on the planet right now. Can we work, please? I'd like to eat lunch sometime this century."

"You and your delicate stomach."

"It's not fucking delicate," I argued grumpily. But he really couldn't blame me. I *was* hungry after all. "It's manly and it needs food on the regular. There's nothing wrong with that."

"Right. Now you're justifying your PMS symptoms—"

"Yes, Leslie?" I interrupted Thatch as she pushed open the door to my office.

"I just finished moving all of your meetings from this morning to this afternoon," she purred, smiling at me like I should praise her. *She* was the one who'd told Dean to schedule the investor calls for that morning rather than this afternoon, necessitating a schedule flip in the first place.

"Thanks," I said through gritted teeth. Catching sight of Thatch's "Duran Duran" face on the screen in front of me stopped me from rolling my eyes. Operation *Cockblock Hungry Wolf* superseded my needs.

"You can just leave the new schedule by the door and head to lunch," I offered, hoping she'd telepathically understand what I was trying so hard to communicate—*get out*.

She giggled.

Nope. Life wasn't that easy.

The tile of my office floor turned into a runway, her dramatic, foot-crossing steps designed to amplify the swing of her hips and elicit a man's attention.

And for any other man, it probably reached into his pants and hardened the attention right out of him.

I, however, was too busy cleaning up her mistakes and trying to finish a phone call so I could go to goddamn lunch.

Tits suddenly filled the frame of my vision, and I practically had to slam my head back into my chair to keep from eating them by accident.

No, I wasn't *that* hungry. That was how close she had placed them.

"Here you go."

"Yeah, thanks," I said, dismissing her and averting my eyes as much as possible. It wasn't a battle of wills, but rather, strictly a game of proximity.

The day I was willing to subject myself to that kind of pussy was the day my cock would rot off and my office would burn straight to the ground. I was sure of it.

Come hell or high water, I was done being this amenable to my mom's suggestions. Leslie needed to be gone by the beginning of next week. Soon, but not soon enough that I couldn't talk my way out of it at family dinner.

I watched as she walked, counting the seconds and praying he'd wait until she left the room.

"Ho-ly hell—"

"Thatch—" I attempted to interrupt, recognizing his tone from experience and knowing it would only lead to bad things.

"Where the hell have you been hiding that one?"

"Don't say another word," I warned, just as the door shut blessedly behind Leslie.

"Fuck me hard, fast, and dirty, Kline-hole. Did you see the tits on her? Seriously, let her know she can swaddle me up and ride me like a cockpuppet any fucking time she wants."

I picked up a pen and pretended to scribble on a piece of paper.

"Ride…you…like…a…cockpuppet. Got it."

The muscled chords of his throat flexed with a bark of laughter, and recognition of his absurdity flashed in his eyes.

"All right, point taken." He raised his hands and winked, his fingers in air quotes, mocking, "Business."

I didn't waste any time getting back to it. "I've got two investor meetings in L.A.—"

"And you want me to be there."

"Yeah."

He sat back in his leather chair and crossed his thick arms. "Done."

"You don't even know when they are," I pointed out. I reached forward and took hold of my mouse to double-check the timing, but he didn't wait.

"For you, my love, no time is a bad time." He blew me a kiss.

"Why do I put up with you?" I asked, sitting back again and raking a hand through my hair.

His response was immediate. "I personally think it's because you like a reminder of the fine male specimen you'll never live up to."

I shook my head and smirked, knowing I'd never be the six-foot-five monster he was and not struggling to swallow it even one little bit. My leaner but no less toned six-foot package hadn't failed me yet.

"I'll see you in L.A. tomorrow night, Adonis."

"No way. I'll see you here, at the airport, so you can hold my hand during—"

Raising my middle finger in salute, I clicked the button to end the call.

Thatch's ability to bounce back from a night out was almost unfathomable. I needed more than four hours of sleep, and I needed to do it for some other reason than being blackout drunk.

My best friend and money man could go several nights in a row without, it seemed, and holding his liquor had practically been his first childhood milestone.

Nights out were dwindling for both of us, though. My tendency to be "an old man," according to Thatch, and his secret rendezvous with every available pussy in Manhattan pretty much soured the deal.

It's not that I didn't enjoy nights out or the company of a beautiful woman. I loved women. I loved every fucking thing about them. I just didn't love the idea of having drunken sex with some chick I picked up at a bar. I wasn't a fan of Pussy Roulette, and when I ate one, I wanted to be able to remember the taste.

My phone rang on my desk as though the call had been put straight through without a heads-up from a lunch-eating Leslie. Normally, Pam rolled my calls to voicemail when she was away from her desk, sorting through them and passing along worthy callers upon her return.

Every ring made it that much more painfully obvious she was out, a duck-lipped, inexperienced seductress in her place.

"Brooks," I answered, putting the phone to my ear.

"Yo," Thatch greeted. "I forgot to ask. Do we have BAD practice tonight?"

I covered my groan. I'd forgotten about rugby practice.

That didn't stop me from busting his balls. "Yes, Princess Peach. We have practice every Monday night."

"Yeah, but with it being football season and all, I thought maybe Wes was busy cheerleading or whatever."

Wes was the third member of our bachelor trio and the owner of the New York Mavericks. We teased him relentlessly, but in reality, it was *cool as fuck* to know somebody who owned a team in the National Football League. A little sweet-talking got us tickets anytime we wanted and field time with the players.

"I take no offense, by the way. Princess Peach is a badass bitch."

"Most of their games are on Sunday. You know, like the one you talked me into going out to watch last night. I'll see you at practice tonight," I said, shaking my head at another ridiculous conversation.

"Geez, Diva. Eat a Snickers."

I pinched the bridge of my nose. "You know, you force me to say *fuck*, as in *fuck you*, way more than I ever dreamed in a business environment."

His answering chuckle was dry. "Just one of my many talents, K. Most of the others involve a lighter, a forty of beer, and my cock—"

I ended the call before he could finish.

Jesus. Is this guy really my best friend?

The short of it was, yes, he *was* my best friend. And I wouldn't change it despite his ability to produce migraines. I was never short on entertainment, that was for sure. But my well of patience had run dry for the day. Simple as that.

Standing quickly, before I could be interrupted again, I yanked the skinny end of my tie from its knot, unwound it from my neck, and hung it on the hook next to my jacket.

I dropped my keys with a clang into my pocket and slid my wallet snug into its spot in the one in the rear.

Retracing my steps from several hours earlier, I passed Meryl with a nod and escaped the building without having to do more than smile politely at passing employees.

The sun nearly blinded me as I pushed the front door open, and the sounds of an active fall lunch hour overwhelmed my office-trained ears. Horns honked and cabbies yelled and pigeons took off in a rush as a toddler ran screaming through the middle of them.

I popped the buttons on my sleeves as I walked, rolling them up to expose my forearms and bask in the dramatically warm weather, and faded into the crowd of pump-wearing women and suit-clad men.

Indian summer, I think they called it, the desertlike arid heat settling deep into my bones and radiating from the inside out.

I could see the sun and city from the wall-to-wall windows of my office, but my lunch hour was pretty much the only opportunity I got to *feel* it.

That was the real root of my grumpiness, I guess. I worked hard from sunup to sundown, and one simple hour in between was what helped keep a happy head on top of tense shoulders.

"Kline!" the owner of my favorite little mom-and-pop deli called as I pushed my way inside the door.

"Hey, Tony!" I answered, gently making my way through the standing-room-only crowd to shake his hand over the counter.

"Here, here," he urged, moving some old memorabilia to unearth the one empty seat in the place.

"No way," I denied with a smile and a shake of my head. "I'll wait for a table like everybody else. I could use the extra time to clear my head today."

"Sit, sit, sit," he said over me, his refusal to let me stand in the crowd and wait a regular occurrence. But he didn't do it because I had money. Tony didn't even *know* I had money. All he knew was I'd been coming in every workday I was in town for the last ten years, and I looked him in the eye and shook his hand every single time I did.

"Thanks, Tone." Giving in was the only option.

"We got a sandwich for you today, buddy," he said as I slid my butt onto the seat.

"I hope it's a pastrami and corned beef on rye. I've been fantasizing about it all morning."

"Ah," he said with a shout and a wink. "For you, I've got just the thing!"

And the truth was, he did—a warm smile, familiarity, and a genuine exuberance. Stuff I needed way more than a sandwich.

CHAPTER 5

Georgia

"Finally!" Dean remarked as he slammed through my door half an hour later.

I'd just finished finalizing and faxing the *original* Sure Romance contract. The one where a little quick talking had prevented Leslie's ill-timed interruption from ruining my life and dragging the company over a swath of hot coals. *The one I was shoving down Martin's throat whether he liked it or not.*

Meanwhile, my stomach was working on chewing a sandwich-sized hole through itself.

"I swear that evil trampvestite is the bane of my existence."

I raised a single, perfectly plucked eyebrow in amusement. If Cassie was the expert of parodies, Dean was the single-most talented nickname giver I'd ever encountered. No two people were alike and no name was deemed off-limits in the name of political correctness. Basically, Dean did the dirty work and I reaped the benefits.

"Trampvestite, huh?"

"Oh, yeah," he confirmed, pointing to his fluttering eyes. "Fake lashes to here." He held both hands out generously in front of his chest. "And fake tits out to there."

I didn't bother to conceal my laugh.

"She's had me running all over this goddamn place this morning, putting out fires and sweating through a five-hundred-dollar shirt."

"You know what will make you feel better?" I cooed.

His green eyes twinkled under the fluorescent lights. "Twenty million dollars and a private island with Brad Pitt?"

"A hot turkey sandwich."

"Hmm," he mumbled as he pretended to consider it. "I guess that'll work."

I slid the bottom drawer of my desk open with ease, yanked my purse out, and slammed it shut with a bang.

"Let's go. Feed me. Regale me with all of your tales of woe."

"She's been annoying you too," he argued as I slid my arm through his at the elbow.

"She has," I agreed. "You just play a much more convincing victim than I do."

A small blush stole through his cheeks, and he leaned down to smack a kiss on mine. Compliments always cheered him up.

"I've had more practice," he comforted me. Not that I *needed* to be comforted. This was still all about Dean and giving him what he needed. I didn't have a dick, but I could do drama.

"Ah, yes, the struggles of an attractive gay man."

"They're like wolves, Georgia! One innocent cherub like me in the club and they swarm like bees."

"Wait. I'm confused. Are they wolves or bees?" I teased as he pushed the button for the elevator.

"Shut your crimson lip-stain-covered trap!"

Perfect.

A distraction of *cosmetic* proportions.

"You like the color?" I asked as I backed into the rear wall of the elevator, propping my chin up on a posed hand and pursing my lips.

"Hmm." He pretended to inspect me, fluffing the hair on both sides of my head. Consideration turned into a quick smile, and a wink popped his left eye closed. "Love!"

"Thanks," I offered with a return grin.

While Dean proceeded to gab about his recent rendezvous with a cute bartender, I couldn't shake a question that'd been nagging me. I needed an answer.

TAPRoseNEXT (12:52PM): So, if that wasn't your dick, whose dick was it? I think I want to know the answer to this, but there's another part of me that's a little afraid…

BAD_Ruck (12:53PM): Afraid I'll reveal that I've got a stockpile of other dudes' dicks on my phone?

Hells bells, that answer was *not* reassuring.

TAPRoseNEXT (12:54PM): …

TAPRoseNEXT (12:55PM): For real "…" is the only response I have to that.

Okay, seriously, if he didn't respond in the next two minutes, my trigger finger was going straight for the block button.

TAPRoseNEXT (12:56PM): …! (If I could use shouty caps for ellipses, I'd be doing it RIGHT NOW)

BAD_Ruck (12:57PM): I don't make a habit of collecting other dudes' dick pics or taking my own. But I do have a friend (who's a bit of a prick) who loves "gargoyle dicking" people as a prank.

TAPRoseNEXT (12:58PM): My friend (who's pretty hilarious)

referred to the dick in question as, "The Hunchcock of Notre Dame."

BAD_Ruck (12:59PM): If I were the kind of guy who used text acronyms, I'd definitely be responding with LOL.

TAPRoseNEXT (1:00PM): Question: were you purposefully withholding important information to get me worked up?

We crossed Fifth Avenue, heading straight for my favorite family-owned deli. The sidewalks were bustling with energy, but **BAD_Ruck** had become quite the distraction. I only willed my eyes to look away from our message box to avoid being run over by a taxi or knocking over my fellow pedestrians.

Dean cleared his throat. "Excuse me? Are you even listening? Or am I rambling on about Sir Sucks-A-Lot for no reason?"

"*Sir Sucks-A-Lot?*"

"Jesus." He sighed. "What in the hell are you doing? Are you texting someone?"

I shrugged. "Just checking work emails." No way in hell would I give Dean any kind of ammunition regarding TapNext. I'd never live that down.

He stopped in the middle of the New York sidewalk traffic, nearly causing a woman with her dog to trip over the leash. "Work emails? You're so full of it."

Uh-huh. I hid the screen of my phone. "What? I've got that big deal with Sure Romance I need nailed down by the end of the week…"

"You're the worst liar. Seriously. It's like you're so bad at lying that I honestly wonder if you're doing it on purpose."

"I'm not lying," I said, fighting a smile.

Dean pointed to my mouth. "Says the girl who's notorious for smiling or giggling nervously whenever she's lying."

Shit. I covered my mouth.

"Honey, you are too much," he teased, placing his hand at the small of my back. "Now, let's get your lying ass inside that deli so I can fight the starvation that's threatening to take place."

"This place is insane," Dean whispered in my ear as we stepped in the door.

The restaurant was packed. Every table was filled, and the line to order reached the door. But I didn't care. My nostrils had already been seduced by the delicious aromas of freshly baked breads and soups. I'd wait two hours if I had to.

"I know," I agreed. "But it's like this all the time." My eyes scanned the tables for any open seats. "It looks like that woman in the corner is about to get up."

"Perfect. You grab it. I'll order," Dean suggested. "The usual?"

I cocked an eyebrow. "Like you even have to ask."

"Chicken salad. Lettuce. Light mayo. Hold the onion and tomato."

I nodded. "I swear if you didn't have an aversion to vaginas, I'd beg you to be my husband."

He smirked. "Plenty of women are beards to their fabulously gay husbands."

"Yeah, but we'd fight too much over our clothing budget. You'd shop us out of food and rent money."

"I bet you wouldn't be complaining too much when your curvy little ass was decked out in designer duds."

Laughing, I held up both hands. "Fine. You've convinced me. If I reach the age of thirty-five and neither of us is married, I'll be your beard."

"Fabulous." He winked. "Now go snatch a table while I grab the food."

Since Dean was a diva from way back, I did as I was told. I pretended to mosey around the joint, casually stopping to look at the memorabilia on the walls, but in reality, I was watching some woman with a red turtleneck and Crocs like a hawk. By the time she gathered her trash and was getting ready to hop to her feet, I had strategically placed myself a few feet away from her table, carefully planning my descent onto her chair.

The second Turtleneck's butt cheeks left the seat, I slid into her place with the finesse of a gazelle. Well, in my head, I looked like a gazelle. The guy whose head I nearly took off with my purse probably would've called it more *bull in china shop*, but whatever. Tomato. Tomahto.

My phone pinged inside the front pocket of my purse.

BAD_Ruck (1:12PM) Question: Is now the time to confess you're pretty adorable when you get worked up?

TAPRoseNEXT (1:13PM) Egging me on for your own amusement? That's not very gentlemanly of you.

BAD_Ruck (1:14PM) I can assure you, I'm a gentleman in all the ways that count.

TAPRoseNEXT (1:15PM) Are you flirting with me?

BAD_Ruck (1:16PM) If I am, is it working?

TAPRoseNEXT (1:17PM) A lady never kisses (or flirts) and tells.

BAD_Ruck (1:18PM) Neither does a gentleman.

TAPRoseNEXT (1:19PM): I think you might be BAD news.

BAD_Ruck (1:20PM): BAD in the best kind of way, sweetheart.
TAPRoseNEXT (1:21PM): You're definitely flirting with me,
Ruck.

BAD_Ruck (1:22PM): You've got a keen eye, Rose.

"I'm convinced. You're sexting someone."

I glanced up from my phone, meeting Dean's knowing look. "Don't be ridiculous. Why would you think I'm sexting someone?"

"The fact that you're smiling like a loon and haven't noticed I've been sitting here for a good five minutes with our food."

He had a point. I was too wrapped up in **BAD_Ruck**'s responses to notice anything else. I couldn't deny, the man intrigued me. But I also couldn't deny that if I didn't set my phone down and give Dean my undivided attention, it might be grounds for a full-on catfight.

TAPRoseNEXT (1:23PM): I've got a growling stomach and
an impatient friend who's staring at me from across the table.
Rain check (on the flirting)?

I set my phone on the table, eyeing the goodness set before me. The aroma of chicken salad and greasy French fries called my name. "This looks like heaven ready to explode in my mouth."

"That's what Neil said last night when he was taking off my navy Gucci dress slacks."

My hands stopped at the halfway point of sandwich-thrusting into my mouth.

"Simply stating 'my pants' would have been sufficient. And who the hell is Neil?"

"Sir Sucks-A-Lot," Dean said, taking a bite of his Greek salad. "And honey, those weren't just any pants. They were Gucci's twill blended wool. And they make my ass look fabulous."

"I guess that explains why Neil was taking off your pants in the first place."

Dean grinned. "Truer words have never been spoken."

A jolting bump forced the sandwich to fall from my hands and land half open on the kitschy diner table. *What in the ever-loving hell?* If Turtleneck was coming back for her seat, it was about to go down.

"Excuse me," was muttered over a man's shoulder as his dress-slack-covered ass—fantastic ass, mind you—moved past my chair and toward the doors. His face was too buried in his phone to realize he had just barreled through my lunchtime fun.

"*Jesus,*" I grumbled. "Does everyone in New York have to be so pushy? I mean, how hard is it to watch where you're going instead of knocking into everyone?"

Dean tilted his head to the side, eyes focused toward the front of the restaurant. "I think that was Mr. Brooks."

"What?" I turned in my chair and watched as my boss's tall frame walked out of the restaurant and onto Fifth Avenue.

An incoming TapNext message icon lit up my screen.

"Yep," Dean agreed. "That's definitely him. I'd know that body anywhere. Broad shoulders. Sexy forearms. Perfectly toned ass. The things I'd do to that man."

"Horny much?"

"Nah." He waved me off. "I'm still recovering from having all the horny sucked out of me last night."

"On that note," I announced, standing from my seat. "I think I'll go order another sandwich. Be right back."

"I'll be here, doll face."

While I stood in line, I took a gander at what else Ruck had sent my way.

BAD_Ruck (1:25PM): Can't wait. Enjoy your lunch, Rose.

Two things stood out in my mind.

1. I wanted to chat more with **BAD_Ruck.** Which was crazy, con-

sidering we had been introduced by a gargoyle of dickish proportions.

2. How had I not known Kline Brooks had such a tight ass? And more importantly, if his ass looked that good *in* pants, what did it look like without them?

CHAPTER 6

Kline

"I found the perfect date for you Friday night," my mom claimed in my ear as I walked out of my office to head home for the night.

I didn't even have to think about it.

"No."

I pulled the door shut behind me and walked slowly down the hall and around the corner to the main office space.

"She's twenty-nine, long dark hair, well kept and attractive—"

"No."

"Her name is Stacey Henderson. I don't know if you've been at any social engagements that she's attended in the past—"

Stacey Henderson? Oh, *hell* no.

She *was* well kept and extremely attractive. And an eleven in vapidity on a scale from one to ten.

"Mom. *No.*"

"She's really excited—"

"Mom—"

"Said she had just the thing to wear—"

"Mom," I snapped, finally speaking firmly enough to earn her attention.

"What?"

Excuse. I needed an excuse.

My marketing director's back and bright red hair caught my attention from across the office, and the words left my lips before I could think of anything else.

"I already have a date."

"Oh. Oh dear. Well, I guess I'll have to call Stacey and cancel, then—"

"Yes!" I agreed eagerly. "Cancel Stacey."

Her voice turned suspicious.

"Kline—"

"Gotta go, Mom. Have to touch base with my date."

Convince her to go with me.

"Kline—"

"Loveyoubye."

With a tap of my thumb, I hung up fast, hoping I wouldn't find myself in too much hot water for ending the call so quickly but desperate enough to end the conversation that I didn't care.

Thirty-four years old and, if anything, my mother was "mothering" me the most she had in my entire life. Wanting a respectable woman to take under her wing and claim as her own was a powerful motivator, apparently, compelling her to meddle like she'd never meddled before.

Most of the time I gave in, but living with Walter on a day-to-day basis was a pretty unforgettable lesson. The grumpiest cat in Manhattan—if not the world—lived with me, and it was all my mother's fault.

I don't want you to be lonely, she said.

We're traveling too much to take care of him, she said.

You'll love him, and he'll love you, she said.

Ah, to go back in time.

There were days I actually avoided going home—to *my* apartment—because Walter lived there.

But that was a subject for another time.

I crossed the office quickly, my shoes slapping out a muted rhythm on the marble tile and a whistled tune flying from my lips.

Georgia Cummings.

My employee and the cure for my Stacey Henderson-themed nightmares.

She'd been working for my company for a couple of years now, but as I approached, I realized I'd never actually *looked* at her in all that time.

A glance here, a smile there, a professional exchange every week or so. But I'd never studied her body the way I was now.

I knew I hadn't.

Because I sure as fuck would have remembered.

Petite in stature but curvy in shape, her body was a perfect pint-sized hourglass perched precariously on top of razor-thin five-inch stilettos.

Her goddamn calves looked like they had been carved out of granite, and the rounded cheeks of her ass grabbed on to my eyes and refused to let go.

She moved slightly as I got closer from behind, and she bent at the waist to do something in the filing cabinet in front of her.

The gloriously short filing cabinet.

I watched as she went about her business, wondering how I'd managed to so effectively blind myself to her. I worked really hard at treating every single employee with fairness and without prejudices. I could remember the looks Dean had given me when he'd thought I wasn't looking, and the friendly crinkles at the corners of Pam's eyes. *The devil was in the details*, my dad had always told me, and I did my best to notice them. Except for hers.

As I tried to picture her smile from memory—*and couldn't*—I knew all of my compartmentalizing engines must have been running at full fucking steam to protect me from getting into something I shouldn't.

But those engines weren't running now, the override switch turned and fully engaged thanks to Meddling-Mom-Maureen, and as the fabric of Georgia's creamy white dress pulled tight over her ass, alarms started blaring.

"My neck."

A sway of her tight-white-fabric-covered hips accompanied her off-key singing.

Something told me she didn't know I was standing behind her.

"My back."

More torture in the opposite direction.

"Lick my pussy—"

Ears bleeding. Pants tightening.

"—and my crack."

Holy. *Fuck.*

I had to stop her before it got even worse. *Better.*

Quickly, I shook my head to clear it and then reached forward to tap her smooth shoulder.

Hair flung out in an arc, she turned on her heel at warp speed, her eyes widening in horror as she pulled on a white cord to release an earbud from her ear.

"Shit."

I smiled. Her eyes widened impossibly further.

"Mr. Brooks. I'm so sorry." She clamped her eyes shut in shame. "I didn't know anyone else was still here."

Her face was mostly hidden in shadow as she tilted it to the ground, but I was still almost positive I saw her mouth the word 'shit' again.

"It's all right," I offered, and her head snapped up in question. I grinned slightly. "The singing and the shits. In fact, if you really need to, you can say it again."

Her face froze in shock.

"I can tell you want to," I prodded. "Maybe even three or four more times."

"Three. Four." She shrugged helplessly. "Forty, maybe."

"Forty shits?" I questioned, raising a brow in amusement.

"Depends on how much you actually heard, I guess."

I craned my neck to one side and back again.

"I'm not sure. I'm feeling particularly attuned to your neck and back, and, well, the rest I'm not sure I can say in an office environment."

"Oh my God," she cried and sank her face into her hands, embarrassment renewed.

"Definitely forty shits. Maybe even fifty."

I coughed on a chuckle before tucking it away, knowing it was the perfect time to get on with what I needed.

"It's okay. I know how you can redeem yourself."

Her gaze jerked up from the floor and her eyes widened with hope. "Yeah?"

"Tomorrow night. Go to the benefit for the Children's Hospital with me."

Horror contorted her face into a scrunched-up version of itself. Not *exactly* what I was going for.

"What? Go to the…with you… No." She shook her head frantically, desperately even, her bright red hair swinging to and fro before settling helplessly on the white fabric at her shoulders.

"No."

I had to admit, the double, *emphatic* nos threw me a little. It wasn't that I thought no one could turn me down. They could, and hell, they probably should. But they hadn't in a long time.

Not in a *very* long time.

"You're busy?" I offered as an excuse, hoping her visible discomfort was more about being caught off guard than anything else.

One slim wrinkle formed between her eyebrows, and the corners of her eyes seemed to pinch together slightly. "No. Not busy."

Ouch.

For the first time in quite a while, I struggled to find my words.

"I…uh…well. Okay."

She forced a fake smile in response.

And yet, I couldn't bring myself to give up.

Walking around her desk and into her space enough that she backed up a couple of steps, I leaned my ass into the surface behind me and crossed my arms.

She rubbed goosebumps from her arms in a nervous fidget.

"So, how definite is this 'no'? Is it an 'I'm mildly considering it, but I'm thinking no' or a 'not a snowflake's chance in hell no' or maybe somewhere in the middle where negotiation lives?"

She shook her head as if mystified and tapped the toe of her stiletto twice.

My gaze shot down the length of her legs and back again, only to find her bright cerulean eyes narrowed slightly at the end of my circuit.

"I'm not disgusted with you, if that's what you're asking, but negotiation isn't likely."

Jim Carrey inhabited my body and took over my vocal chords before I could stop him. "So you're telling me there's a chance?"

"What the hell is going on here?" she snapped softly at the ceiling, almost as if to herself. Her eyes jumped to me. "Why are you asking me out? Why now? None of this is making any sense."

The only thing I could do was give it to her straight. Whether it was a good thing or not, I never could stop the honesty. It was just my nature.

"Look. For some godforsaken reason, society has decided to care about my completely uninteresting life because I have money, and because tabloid fodder is way more important than donations or time volunteered, they want me to have a date at every function I attend. Normally, this wouldn't be an issue, as in they can go fuck themselves, but in another slap of fate, my mother has decided she cares. Wants a daughter-in-law and grandbabies and all that crap."

Her previously peachy-tan skin blanched white.

"But she has terrible taste, and though I know next to nothing about you, you're already guaranteed to be better than any of my other options."

"Gee, thanks."

"Trust me, I intended that as an insult to the others, not you."

"Right."

"I'm not trying to marry you, though I'm sure I'll enjoy our time together endlessly—"

"I'm sure."

I couldn't help but smile at her mockery.

"I'm trying to avoid ending up with another chattier, day-spa-loving version of Walter."

"Walter?" she asked with good reason.

"My cat."

Incredulity warred with confusion on her face, pulling her lips out flat to the sides and back again several times.

I knew I was talking her in circles. I just hoped her confusion would lead to grudging acceptance.

Just when I feared she'd chew her lip raw if she kept on at that pace for much longer, she broke the silence with one simple question. "Why me?"

Once again, honesty prevailed.

"Because you're here."

She pursed her lips around the sour of my words, but as I tore my gaze away to look into her bright blue eyes, I knew I wasn't done.

Not with her, not with this conversation, and not with being stupid for the day.

"And you're fucking beautiful."

CHAPTER 7

Georgia

"Beautiful?!" I shrieked, slamming the door to my apartment behind me. The walls shook from the undeserved abuse. "For fuck's sake, all it takes is one guy—who's never even been on your *let's get naked together* radar—to call you beautiful and you're acting like some desperate hussy! Really? *Really?* That's all it takes?" I dropped my purse to the floor and kicked off my heels. "Where is your pride, you stupid hussy! Where is your *fucking pride*?"

Cassie barreled out of her room like a herd of buffalo with a curling iron in hand and the cord trailing behind her, startling me enough that I slammed my ass into the counter of our island.

"Where's the stupid hussy?" she yelled, eyes manic and searching.

I rolled my own eyes dramatically, too pissed at myself to laugh at her antics. "You're looking at her!" I pointed at myself like a lunatic. "She's here! She's right fucking here!"

"Oh," she sighed, losing her aggressive stance, dropping the unlikely weapon to her side, and standing straight at once. "You don't count. I thought there was *actually* a stupid hussy out here you needed to be saved from. I was ready to throw down and beat some ass."

"Oh, I am a stupid hussy. A pathetic slut who's a disgrace to our gender. Trust me."

"Nooooo, you're not. You're a Wheorgiebag, but even that isn't a *real* whore. Whores have excessively loose vaginas. I'm talking big enough to store all of their whoring money, and yours has never even been open for business. Probably couldn't even fit a nickel."

She had a point. My vagina was sealed tighter than Fort Knox. A proverbial "do not pass go" zone for all cockbandits begging entry. It wasn't because I was a prude or saving myself for marriage. I had just never found the right guy I deemed worthy of thrusting into my goodie bag.

Maybe I was too picky. Maybe my sex therapist mother had driven me to insanity. Or maybe my expectations of waiting to do the deed with a man I had an actual connection with were unrealistic in this day and age. I mean, the plethora of dick and sac pics floating around social media could've been evidence of this.

Don't even get me started on the reaction I received from men when they found out I was a single, twenty-six-year-old woman with an unclaimed V-card. I might as well have told them I was a unicorn who could shoot sparkles out of my ass.

And it wasn't like I was averse to *all* sex. I was a big-time advocate for oral. Well, as long as there was a giving and receiving clause in the agreement. Call me crude, but if I'm going to suck it, you're going to eat it. Period. End of story.

Despite the shocked reactions and stigma revolving around being a woman who had made it through college with her virginity still intact, I stuck to my guns, refusing to just *give it up* to whoever was hard and willing. It wasn't a statement of abstinence or strong religious views. It was just me, being myself, and doing what I thought was right for me.

That's the most important thing when it comes to a woman's sexual prerogative. She should decide what she really wants without being influenced by social norms or penis peer pressure.

"You're doing it again," Cassie interrupted my thoughts.

I tilted my head, confused. "What am I doing?"

"You're doing that 'this is why I'm still a virgin' inner monologue thing. Do I need to turn on the fireplace for a bra-burning ritual? Or should we throw out the razors and let our pit hair run rampant?"

"You're a pain in my ass." I laughed. I couldn't help myself.

"I love you too, my beautiful, virginal best friend."

I ignored Cassie's shit-eating grin and strode for the fridge. Lord knew there was a giant glass of wine with my name on it.

"Let's hear it," she demanded, plopping down at the kitchen table. "Why are you a stupid hussy?"

Grabbing a bottle of moscato from the fridge, I filled a coffee mug to the brim. "I don't want to talk about it. It's too embarrassing."

"Uh-huh. Sure you don't. That explains why you were just talking *to yourself* about it." She eyed me with a pointed look. "Spit it out, Georgia Rose."

I shook my head, taking a giant swig of sugary wine.

Cassie stared.

I shook my head again.

Her eyes did that scary death glare thing where I started to be concerned for my well-being.

"Okay," I relented, holding both hands in the air like I was being held at gunpoint. "Okay. But you have to cool it on the creepy eyes first. You're wigging me out."

She smiled. "Works like a charm. Every. Single. Time."

I groaned.

"So," she encouraged, gesturing with her hand. "What has your panties in such a twist?"

"Kline asked me out."

"*Kline?* Who's Kline?"

"Kline Brooks…Mr. Brooks…" I offered, jogging her memory.

"Holy fucking goat scrotums! *Kline Big-dicked Billionaire Brooks?* Your crazy-hot, super-rich boss?" she continued before I could utter a response. "Say *whaaaaaaat?* How in the hell did this happen?"

"First of all, what do you mean by 'how in the hell did this happen?' I might be a virgin, but I'm not a two-bagger. I can look pretty when I actually take the time to brush my hair."

"Oh, cool your jets. You're gorgeous and you know it. Kline Brooks would be one lucky son of a bitch to score a date with you."

"And how do you know he has a big dick? You've seen him once. And it was a five-second 'Oh, that's my boss, Kline' conversation while we were walking across the parking lot. You haven't even met him in person."

"Five seconds is all I need." She tapped the side of her head. "You know my cockdar is off the chain. I can sense a giant swinging penis pendulum from at least ten miles away. It's a God-given talent, Georgie."

I choked on my wine. "Let's not bring God into this."

She raised an eyebrow. "God knows the G-spot needs a more than adequate-sized wiener to get the job done."

"I'm pretty sure that comment just got you wait-listed for heaven."

"Probably." She shrugged. "Tell me you said yes to Big-dicked Brooks."

"Stop calling him that!" I shouted, unable to hold back laughter.

"Oh, c'mon, Virgin Mary, you know your boss has that *'Hello, ladies, I'm packing'* swagger." She waggled her eyebrows. "Tell me you said yes to him. For the love of God, tell me you're going on a date with him."

"He's not my type."

"Georgie," she groaned. "He's handsome. He's successful. He's not propositioning you for a five-dollar blow job. What's not to like? I don't get it."

"Five-dollar blow job? What are you even talking about?"

"Obviously, *bad* propositions." She held out both hands, irritated. "Even the worst blow job—with teeth and chapped lips and poor suction—is worth more than five bucks."

I sighed. "Look, he has like eleventy bajillion dollars in his bank account. His suits cost more than our apartment. We are not on the same level. Not even close."

"First off, that's not a number. Secondly, who the fuck cares? Why are you judging him by his money?"

"I'm not judging."

She nodded, eyes wide. "Oh, yes you are. You're totally judging."

"But…he's…"

"Stop it." A stern finger was pointed in my direction. "Stop being judgy."

Was I really judging Kline by his money?

And more importantly, did he really have a big d-i-c-k?

"You're going on a date with him, aren't you?"

I feigned confusion. "I have no idea what you're talking about."

"You little hussy! You're freaking out because you said yes, didn't you?!"

Her evil, victorious laugh pushed me over the edge. "Fine!" I shouted. "He called me 'fucking beautiful' and I folded like a deck of cards. I might as well have lifted my skirt and spread my legs for him. I was pathetic. Like some swooning, teenage girl. I said yes because he tossed a goddamn compliment in my direction!"

"God, I'm sure it's going to be absolutely terrible for you. Having to go on a date with a rich, successful, gorgeous man who also happens to give you compliments." She feigned shock. "Oh, the humanity!"

I stared at Cassie for a good three seconds before her words sank in. And then, I couldn't stop myself from laughing after muttering, "You're such a bitch."

Maybe I was being a tad bit ridiculous over this whole scenario. It was just one compliment. And I only agreed to one date. How bad could it be?

Darth Vader's dark side ringtone filled the room, vibrating my phone across the counter.

Incoming Call Dr. Crazypants

"Ugh," I sighed. "It's my mom. Lord help me, I'm not in the mood for her randomness." I sent her call to voicemail, too tired to keep up with her rambling.

My mom, otherwise known as Dr. Savannah Cummings, was a force to be reckoned with. She spent her days counseling couples and her nights doing God only knows what with my father. Sex therapy was her game and bringing sexy back into the bedroom was her claim to fame.

And yes, I was well aware of the "sex therapist named Cummings" irony. My mother was too. Several years ago, she had made a point to use that satire to her advantage—on a *billboard*, hovering over a *main* interstate that led straight into *New York City*.

Her slogan: "Dr. Cummings wants you to *come*…visit her brand new office."

Needless to say, eighth grade was a pretty hard year for me.

Conversations with Savannah mostly consisted of small talk about my dating and sex life and her usual spiel about the importance of masturbation. *"Make sure you're masturbating at least once a day, Georgia Rose. It's imperative for your sexual health."*

My mother, the sex therapist, was a bit of a weirdo. But she was my weirdo and I loved her dearly. I just couldn't handle her open-ended questions and virginity interrogation at the moment.

I downed the rest of my wine and slammed it on the counter. "I'm calling it a night. I'll see you on the flipside, Casshead."

"Night, Wheorgiebag."

Without wasting time, I did the usual bedtime routine—face washed, teeth brushed, and comfy sleep clothes applied—and happily plopped my tired ass into bed.

But sleep refused to come.

My brain had reached the hamster-on-a-wheel stage of insomnia. Thoughts raced and unanswered questions refused to leave. I kept replaying Kline asking me out, over and over again. And all I could think was, why me? What made him all of a sudden show interest in me?

"And you're fucking beautiful."

I wasn't dealing with a shortage of self-esteem by any means. I considered myself an intelligent, attractive, confident chick. Now, I wouldn't go as far as saying I was perfect by any stretch of the imagination, but I knew how to highlight my strengths and downplay my weaknesses. Heavy makeup, spandex, and the color yellow were always a hell no. Long hair, red lips, and a pair of well-fitting jeans that accentuated my ass were always a hell yes.

My confusion over Kline asking me out wasn't about my attractiveness.

I'd never had a man like him on my radar.

We were total opposites.

He had a chauffeur. I took the subway. He wore Armani. I shopped at vintage, secondhand shops. He had enough money to invest in things like hedge funds and annuities. I had a fifty-dollar bond from 1996 that my grandmother had gifted me on my birthday. Fingers crossed that baby would gain another two dollars and twenty-five cents this year.

My life and his life were pretty much worlds apart.

Or was Cassie right? Was I judging Kline Brooks by the fact that he had more money than God? Or was I just freaked out over the fact that my boss, the CEO of Brooks Media, had asked me out?

My dating experiences hadn't been the best. They generally ended on epically bad notes. So, what would happen if Kline and I dated a few times and the shitstorm that was my overall luck with men took over?

Fuck.

I had to do something to take my mind off things. It was time to take things into my own hands. Literally. There was no sleep aid better than a climax-induced coma. Just one shot from the orgasm bottle and I'd be out like a light, racing thoughts and restless nights be gone.

Grabbing my vibrator, I lay back, spread wide, and pictured Chris Hemsworth in all of his Thor glory. I'd been on a recent Avengers kick—Captain America, Thor…hell, even Black Widow when I was feeling frisky. Scarlett Johansson in that black leather suit could make a lot of women switch-hit.

A few minutes into my fingerbating session, Thor's hammer was hard and ready. Things were feeling good. Real fucking good. Muscles were tight, fingers were moving at the perfect pace, and Amen for my vibrator, the glorious little clit tickler that he was. I was on the brink, white spots dotting my vision, and then, Thor and his hammer cock slowly morphed into someone else. Someone I had never fantasized about before.

Kline.

He was hovering over me, his hot, naked body mere inches from mine. That body—good God, that body. Lean, tight, toned muscles. So many fucking muscles. Washboard abs and that perfect V pointing right down to his…um…*yeah…Big-dicked Brooks.*

Hot damn, Cassie was right.

He had the kind of cock you could make a five-second GIF out of and never get tired of watching it on loop. I was convinced, somewhere down the line, Kline's dick had a great-great-great-great grandfather dick, and it was that exact shaft that had inspired some woman to pull down a guy's pants and say, "Oh yes, I need to suck on that." This was a history-making, Nobel Prize award-winning cock. The sole reason the blow job was an actual thing.

"I can't wait to taste you," he whispered, *sliding my panties down my legs.*

Yes. Hell. Yes. Taste me.

"God, you're fucking beautiful." He licked across my stomach.

"Your cock is beautiful," I said.

He kneeled between my legs. "Tell me how bad you want my cock, Georgia." Blue eyes scorched my skin as he stroked that perfect dick.

"Bad. So bad," I begged.

"Be patient, sweetheart." He smirked. "I can't wait to fuck you, but right now, I need your taste on my tongue."

Kline gripped my thighs, spreading me wide, while his head was between my legs doing everything a guy should know how to do with his tongue.

"Oh, fuck," I moaned, gripping his hair and following the movements of his mouth with my hips.

"Come for me, Georgia," he demanded.

And like a goddamn romance novel cliché, I came on command...*on my boss's face.*

I was panting. Drained. Sated. My muscles were lax, skin peppered with a sheen of sweat. I had thoroughly worked myself over. When I opened my eyes, I realized I had just gone to a place I could never come back from.

Kline Brooks had just been inaugurated into my spank bank rotation.

And he'd given me the best orgasm I'd had in a long fucking time.

CHAPTER 8

Kline

"So the Sure Romance contract went through as expected. Martin folded like a fitted sheet at the threat of..." Georgia recited as if rehearsed, her attention drifting from the lights overhead to the paperweight on my desk, out the window, and back again.

She'd been trying her damnedest not to look at me since she'd knocked on the door of my office two minutes ago.

"Wait," I interrupted, startling her enough that her eyes found my face. "Aren't fitted sheets hard to fold?" I kicked one corner of my mouth up in a grin, adding, "Mine sure as hell are. Is there some secret I'm missing out on?"

Bewilderment forced her eyebrows together and her plump bottom lip out.

I could see the thoughts race through her eyes one after the other, wondering what we were talking about and why we were talking about it at the same time she questioned the likelihood that *I* was the one who actually folded my sheets, rather than a maid, a butler, or several servants, perhaps.

Once she realized I was teasing her, the lines of her face transformed from confused to punishing.

"Sorry," I apologized, easing from a grin into a full-blown smile. "Continue."

"Right." She huffed adorably. "As I was saying, Martin…"

Her words muffled into a simple rhythm of soothing sounds as my concentration transferred to my thoughts.

Two years of listening to Georgia Cummings talk about product placement and commercial budgets didn't hold a candle to one fucking day of actually talking to her. The flustered, less professional, overtly female version one simple encounter had turned her into, that is.

She was still poised, as always, knowledgeable, and completely on top of her tasks and obligations. But her looks lingered longer—when she forgot to think about being awkward—and her humor lived at the surface, just at the tip of her quick-witted tongue, instead of buried under layers of propriety and boss-employee relations.

Put simply, I looked different to her, and, with her hair swept up off of the smooth, slim column of her neck and her eyes bright with mischief, she sure as fuck looked different to me.

"Mr. Brooks!" she called, fiery and peeved that I wasn't listening to her with full attention.

"Kline," I corrected, thinking about the way she'd sounded singing about her pussy and the faces I thought she'd make while I finger-fucked it, and then waited for her to agree with popped brows.

"Fine," she consented. "*Kline.*"

God, I needed to hear her say that while she came.

I smiled again and fought the urge to adjust my tightening pants under my desk.

"Good."

She didn't seem nearly as amused. I forced my mind to the mildly professional side of its coin when she crossed her arms over her chest and tapped a toe on the tile. After years of keeping every exchange with employees above board, I'd never felt such a blatant need for betrayal by my eyes. They wanted to be bad. They wanted to be *really* bad. And my stupid cockblock of a brain wouldn't let them.

"Look, I trust you." Her feathers unruffled slightly. "Do I want to know that the deal went through? Absolutely. Do I need to know the details and question your every move? Not so much."

She unwound her arms from her chest.

"In fact, I'm headed to L.A. tonight, and I need someone to hold down the fort. Can you handle it if I tell everyone to report to you?"

Her spine straightened involuntarily, outrage at having to be asked tensing all of the muscles around it. "Of course I can."

I studiously ignored her irritation.

"I'm not expecting you to solve every issue that comes your way. Just keep the ship afloat and the piratelike crew members from setting her ablaze."

"Done."

She traced a circle on the front edge of my desk, and I could practically *see* her effort to be casual. "So you're, uh—"

She tucked an imaginary strand of hair behind her ear. Not a single one had been out of place.

"You're headed to L.A., huh?"

I bit my lip in victory. She was asking because she wanted to know. She *wanted* to go out with me, she just hadn't accepted it yet.

"Yep."

"Oh…okay. So, um—"

"Quick trip," I said, letting her off the hook. "Just a couple of investor meetings and then right back to the East Coast. I'll be back in plenty of time for Friday night."

"That's cool," she muttered, clasping her hands together like she didn't know what to do with them.

I had a few ideas, but most of them came from the brain downstairs. And I didn't think she'd be extremely welcoming of them at this stage of the game.

"Georgia?"

Her attention jumped from the floor straight to my gaze. The vivid depths of her eyes' blue, swirling with a heady mix of excitement and uncertainty, nearly knocked the wind out of me.

"I'm looking forward to it."

"Looking forward to it?"

"Friday night, with you." Her clasped hands turned white with pressure, and a blush colored the apples of her cheeks. "I wouldn't miss it."

Her face softened briefly, overwhelmed by a powerful look of longing. Fifteen seconds later, when determination replaced it, her sweet jaw flexing under the pressure, I wasn't sure it had ever existed.

In contrast to the harsh hue of her features, her voice was nothing more than a whisper. "Are you sure this is a good idea?"

I considered her question carefully instead of firing out some bullshit answer. I knew the reason she was asking, and it wasn't trivial. I was her *boss*, and for all she knew, I had plans to fuck and forget. There were no guarantees that anything would really bloom between us, and we'd both feel the fallout. She was an asset to my company, and I signed her checks. Everyone would argue she had more to lose, but I wasn't as sure.

Cynthia in HR would ride my ass for a decision like this—because, regardless of the absence of an actual no-fraternization policy, interoffice romance was *always* messy, especially when one of those employees was the boss. She knew it as well as I did, and I might have even known it better. But as I sat there looking at Georgia's face, my big fucking desk in between us, the only thing I could think about was being closer, standing next to her, escorting her as I walked with a hand at the perfect swoop of her lower back—*smelling the sweet curve of her neck and nibbling it with my teeth.*

Maybe I was blind, but as far as I could see, it was the best goddamn idea I'd ever had.

Her gaze followed me as I stood up and pushed my chair back, circling the desk and settling my hips into it a mere foot in front of her. She wanted to move back, I could see it, but she held her ground anyway, ready to listen to whatever I had to say.

I crossed my feet at the ankles and clasped my hands together in front of my thighs.

"I get it."

Her bottom lip rocked as she chewed at the inside of it. My vision locked on to the movement like a heat-seeking missile. With effort, I forced my eyes back to hers.

"I get why you're nervous, and I get the kinds of things a leap of faith could cost you. All I can promise is that I won't be a prick."

Surprised eyebrows ate up half of the distance to her hairline.

"Whatever happens between me and you, Kline and Georgia, is a completely separate entity from what happens under the umbrella of Brooks Media between Mr. Brooks and his Director of Marketing. My employee is efficient, well liked, and boasts a seasoned track record of success. Mr. Brooks has seen it, paid attention to it, and appreciated it for a while now. But Kline..." I laughed. "Well, that guy's been an idiot."

A small hiccuplike laugh bubbled up her throat and right out of her mouth before she could stop it.

"Because Georgia Cummings is a beautiful, smart, intriguing woman, and until yesterday, he hadn't seen her at all."

"Good God," she muttered to herself.

I smiled wholeheartedly, with nothing held back, and felt my heart jump in my chest when her eyes flared like she noticed.

"Kline *is* like Mr. Brooks in some ways, though. He *hates* to be stupid. And now that he knows, he's not too keen to be stupid ever fucking again."

She swung toward me on instinct, the movement excruciatingly slow and too fast to consider all at once. I grabbed her hips, squeezing them too hard, I knew, but I couldn't help it. The thought of leaving my mark on her skin had my hands clenching again.

Heat settled in my palms and shot straight to my crotch as I caught a whiff of all that was her. A mysterious mix of fruit and flowers, her scent stabbed me right in the fucking chest like some kind of olfactory voodoo doll.

I slid my hand up her side with little finesse before cresting her shoulder and forcing it into the tresses of her bright red hair at the back of her head.

Her eyes were open and searching and a whole lot frightened, but her lips moved toward mine with purpose. My fingertips flexed in her hair of their own accord, and a cross between a whimper and a moan caught right at the top of her throat.

"*Kline*," she whispered emphatically. The puff of her hot breath on my lips was enough to push me right over the goddamn edge.

"Knock knock," Leslie called *as* she was pushing open the door.

The two of us shot apart like Leslie's arrival was a hell of a skeet shooter and we were the clay pigeon. At the sudden release of so much sexual tension, I would have sworn shattered pieces of me littered the room.

My heart beat at double its normal speed, and Georgia's cheeks were the color of cherry Kool-Aid. Though, given the fact that *Kline* had been milliseconds away from eating *Georgia* alive, I'd say *Mr. Brooks'* and *Ms. Cummings'* level of faux composure was impressive.

"What do you need, Leslie?" I asked, straining to make my voice sound even, but she was clueless. Most of her attention focused inward, on herself, rather than the things going on around her. I swore it was the first and only time in my life I'd be thankful for that kind of woman.

CHAPTER 9

Georgia

It had been one of those days where staying in bed and calling in sick would have been a better option than actually participating in life. Kline Brooks left his new intern, Leslie, under my watchful eye while he flew out to L.A. for the day to schmooze investors and impress potential advertising clients for TapNext.

I was certain she had been sent straight from Hell. The devil might as well have wrapped a big red bow around her neck and attached a note.

Dear Georgie,

Have fun with this one.

Love,

Satan

I'd seen more of her tits today than I had of my own in the past month. Either she had a severe body temperature control issue or she didn't wear a bra. I didn't care who was setting the dress code policy; nipples would never be considered business casual.

Why Kline had hired her was a goddamn mystery at this point. And I hadn't even brought up her predilection for selfies. Her social media was busier than a Las Vegas escort during March Madness. Which I guess was fine—if only she'd put the same amount of work into her actual job.

Finally at home, I settled into my favorite pastime—sweatpants, a bag of sour cream and cheddar potato chips, and a DVRed episode of *Keeping Up with the Kardashians*. Despite the ridiculousness that this family had made a fortune off reality television, I still found myself recording every damn episode. It was a true mind-suck of valuable time and brain cells, but I couldn't deny my consistent guilty indulgence. What could I say? I was a *true* American—enjoying every trashy reality show produced for my viewing pleasure and shit-talking them the next day.

Kim had just declared that *women wearing the wrong foundation color is, like, the worst thing on the planet* when my phone rang.

Incoming Call Kline Brooks

What in God's name does he need now? He should've been on a plane headed home from L.A. His absence was the exact reason why I would have five pounds worth of potato chips on my hips and ass tomorrow morning. Two days ago, I would have told you he'd put stars in my eyes with swoony almost kisses and confidence in my ability. Now, after a visit to the depths of incompetency hell, the blush on my feelings had more than worn off.

That cocky, demanding bastard damn well knew what he had been doing when he'd asked me if I could handle being in charge.

After five rings' worth of muttered curses, I decided to put him out of his misery. "Good evening, Mr. Brooks. What *else* can I assist you with today?"

His hearty chuckle filled my ears. "I thought we were past the Mr. Brooks bullshit?"

"Yeah, not after today we're not."

"Rough day at work?"

Rough day? Was he serious? I was still trying to scrub my brain free of the moronic comments Leslie had made all day. "Your new intern is a gem. Quite the asset to the company, I might say. It's amazing how many selfies one woman can take in a fifteen-minute stretch, and yet, she can't seem to make a single photocopy in the same amount of time."

"I know she's got some time management issues, but she's a good kid, Georgie." There was a smile in his voice.

"After today, I honestly have no idea how you've gotten anything done for the past two weeks." I strived to be the type of woman who didn't judge other women by their brainpower, but Leslie made the Kardashians look intelligent.

"Are you concerned about my workload, sweetheart?"

Sweetheart? I hated that something as simple as Kline calling me sweetheart made my heart flip-flop inside of my chest. But it did. *Stupid heart.* The damn thing didn't have a clue. I cleared my throat, ignoring my body's reaction to his sweet sentiments. "Of course not. Why would I be concerned when *you're* the one who hired her? Plus, *you're* the one who continues to let *your* intern make a mockery of her job responsibilities."

"Is now the right time to tell you Leslie is a friend of the family? Her dad asked for a favor and I obliged. Plus, I've got Dean keeping an eye on her."

"Oh, so you're making Dean do your dirty work. I see how it is. That explains his bitchy mood today. I was worried Prada went out of business."

Kline laughed.

Good God, that laugh. It was crazy hot and had my body reacting in all sorts of dirty ways. "I'm kind of sad you didn't have Leslie reporting to Meryl."

"Meryl would have had my balls," he teased. "I've seen that woman make grown men cry. Hell, I've had to wipe a few phantom tears of my own. Plus, you asked for it."

I was two seconds away from giving him a telepathic beatdown when his voice turned warm and soft like honey. "Thanks for dealing with Leslie. I really appreciate it."

Did he just thank me? I pinched my arm just to make sure I wasn't dreaming. "Shit, that hurt." I winced.

"Everything okay?"

"Yeah. Just…stubbed my toe," I tossed out. "Sooooo…did you just call to see how truly awful my day was? Or is there something you actually need?"

"For starters, I wanted to make sure we're still on for tomorrow night."

I sighed. "Even though you threw me under the bus and have expressed little to no remorse, I'll be there. But it has nothing to do with you and everything to do with the delicious ten-course meal I know will occur."

"Duly noted." He laughed. "If their food isn't to your standard, I'll make it up to you. Dinner anywhere. Your choice."

"That's easy. BLT Prime."

"The steakhouse in Gramercy Park?"

"You betcha."

"Swanky digs." A low whistle left his lips. "Consider it a deal. I'll take you there Saturday night."

"Slow your roll, buddy. I haven't agreed to a second date yet."

"Yet," he retorted with a flirtatious tone. "Haven't agreed *yet*. And if it makes you feel better, you can think of it as more of a deal than a date. An *I'm sorry for leaving you with Leslie* kind of thing."

When had the tables turned? This wasn't the Kline Brooks I had grown accustomed to. He was the quiet, reserved, yet frequently demanding boss who made a point to keep me on my toes. Our interactions consisted of cursory emails and business meetings to assess my current game plan for Brooks Media's promotions strategy.

This playful, charismatic man requesting my presence at dinner dates and effortlessly turning me on in his office was a complete stranger. I couldn't deny my enjoyment out of seeing this side of him, but dear God, it was completely knocking me off my game. I felt like a fish out of water, floundering for an equally charming response.

And seriously, when had I started wanting to appear enchanting to the enigmatic Kline Brooks?

I cleared my throat. "Mr. Brooks, w-why did you call me?"

"Ms. Cummings, why are we being so formal tonight? I thought we got past the formality bullshit."

He was probably right. *I'd say it happened around the time he pulled my hips into an impressively unprofessional erection in his office two days ago.*

"Okay, *Kline*," I agreed with a mouthful of sass. I didn't really want him referring to me by my middle school joke of a last name anyway. "If you're not calling to chat about work, why are you calling me?"

"I actually need a favor. Are you busy?"

"No, not really. I'm just sitting here…" I paused, reaching for the remote and turning down the volume. Even though we were past "formalities," my boss didn't need to know about my reality show obsession. "Just sitting here reading through emails."

He chuckled into the phone. "I'm sure those emails can wait until tomorrow. I'm in a bit of a bind. Can you turn on ESPN?"

"ESPN?"

"The Western University-New York State game is on. Thatch and I can't get the fucker to stream on the plane. I *need* to know what's happening."

Thatcher Kelly, the ever-mysterious financial consultant of Brooks Media. He worked as a contractor, providing expertise for several companies, or so I'd heard, but no big money decision within Brooks Media happened without him. I'd heard his husky voice and boisterous personality on several conference calls. Even received emails with his signature sarcasm. But I'd never met the man. Hell, I'd yet to successfully locate an actual photo of him. All of his social media accounts were private and most had some random sports-related profile picture.

"This is life or death here, Georgia," Kline interrupted my thoughts. "Thatch is a big New York State fan, and I've got five on the fact that his Tigers are no match for the Mustangs."

I scrunched my nose up. "So…what exactly do you need me to do?"

"I need you to give me the play-by-play for the next twenty minutes until we land."

"Isn't there anyone else you can bug? I'm probably not the best person for the job." The last football game I'd watched had been the Super Bowl where Janet Jackson's nipple had made its television debut, and I could honestly have told you more about her areola than the game. I literally knew zilch about sports, especially football.

"Please, Georgia." He rasped his words, confusing me by making me think about sex. "I'm begging you."

I held in my answer until I knew I wouldn't stutter. "You owe me. Big time."

"Anything you want, sweetheart."

The promise of his double meaning oozed from his voice, but I ignored him, grabbed the remote, and switched the channel. "Okay, it's on."

CHAPTER 10

Kline

Thatch waved his arms manically, trying to get an update. Our personal flight attendant flashed him a look of distaste, but with one quick wink, her contempt turned into consideration. I didn't have much to my name that said *billionaire*, but the private plane sure did. With the amount that I traveled and the necessary fluctuation in timing, it was just easier.

When his attention came back to me, I flipped him off, putting Georgia on speaker. "What's the score? How much time is left? Who has the ball?" I rambled, desperate to know if Western University was pulling through. Fucking Thatch wouldn't let me live it down if New York State won this thing. It was a nothing game—early season, Thursday night, and unquestionably obscure teams. But Thatch could turn anything into a competition, and he'd created this rivalry out of thin air years ago.

She gave us the rundown in succinct, inaccurate terms, but I got the gist of it.

Fourth quarter. Tigers were winning.

I cursed.

Thatch shouted, "Victory is mine!"

I'd honestly never seen a guy that big Riverdance.

"All of this for five measly bucks?" Georgia asked.

Thatch's loud, boisterous laugh echoed inside the cabin of the plane.

"No, not five *dollars*. A little more than that..."

"Five hundred?" Her voice was incredulous. I pictured Georgia's nose scrunching up in that adorable way of hers.

"Actually..." I cleared my throat. "Five grand."

"Five thousand dollars?" she shouted.

Internally, I cringed. Hell, externally, I cringed.

I probably sounded like a pretentious asshat. Betting exorbitant amounts of money on sports was not my usual M.O. "It's Thatch's fault. He won't take no for an answer and never bets anything less than a grand. He could be the poster child for gambling addicts everywhere. His only redeeming quality is that he actually knows how to invest his profits."

Thatch's smile mocked me. He knew what I was doing, exaggerating his faults to help minimize my own.

"Whatever you say, Mr. Moneybags."

Yeah, she definitely thought I was an ostentatious dick.

"Georgia girl, give me an update. What's going on?" Thatch schmoozed, laying it on thick just to get a rise out of me.

"Uh..." she mumbled, trailing off for a brief second. "Boobear just tackled somebody."

"Boobear? Who the fuck is Boobear?" Thatch mouthed in my direction.

I shrugged. "Who just got a tackle?"

"Boobear. He plays on the orange team," she repeated as though it made sense. "Oh no, I think Boobear is hurt."

It took some serious thinking, but I finally decoded the mystery. "Do you mean *Boudmare?*"

"Yeah, that's him. His nickname is Boobear."

"The commentators are calling him Boobear?" I asked, fighting a smile.

"No, I nicknamed him Boobear. He looks like a giant teddy bear. He's so cute!"

"Oh, dear God," Thatch groaned.

"Oh, thank goodness. Boobear is back up and on his feet. They're lining up again. White team has the ball. The big guy in the middle chucked it to the thrower guy. He threw the ball… really far…" She trailed off, and then the line went silent.

"Georgia?"

Nothing.

"Georgia!" I strived to grab her attention.

"What?" she snapped.

"The ball was thrown…*where?* What happened?"

"Coca-Cola threw it a bunch of yards to Stuart Little. They're lining up again near the touchdown box."

Coca-Cola? Stuart Little? Who in the hell was she talking about?

"Who is she talking about?" Thatch mouthed, arms wide in frustration. "I fucking knew we should've called Wes," he whispered, pacing the aisle.

"Help me out here," I said into the phone. "Who is Coca-Cola?"

"The quarterback on the white team."

"You mean Cokel?"

"Yeah, that's him."

"Is she fucking nicknaming the players?" Thatch boomed in disgrace.

"Uh-huh," she responded over what sounded like a mouthful of chips, not an ounce of shame in her tone.

I couldn't even get pissed at her. She was too fucking adorable. I glanced over at Thatch. He was wearing a figurative hole in the aisle carpet and practically pulling his hair out. I grinned. Even though I hadn't a clue what was happening in the game, watching Thatch's upset come to a crescendo was worth it.

"Touchdown!" she whooped. "Coca-Cola to Howie Mandel!"

Translation: *Cokel to R.J. Howard.*

"Fuck yes!" I cheered.

"Son of a bitch!" Thatch shouted.

"Go Wild Horses!" Georgia put in.

I chuckled. "That's right, sweetheart. The Mustangs are going to pounce on Thatch's pussy Tigers."

While my best friend was cursing up a storm, Georgia commentated the game for the rest of our flight. She added ridiculous nicknames for every player, called running backs' stutter steps *Icky Shuffle* steps, and gave her overall opinions on which player looked the most cuddly (Boobear, of course), the meanest, the nicest, etc. It was an endless list and I damn near forgot there was five grand and a long-standing rivalry between Thatch and me on the line.

Once we landed and were sitting with beers in our hands, watching the final five minutes of the game in the airport bar, I still kept Georgia in my ear.

I couldn't help myself. This woman whom I'd seen handle an entire boardroom full of cocky sons of bitches without batting an eye was crazy adorable. She was tough as nails and hotter than sin. And Christ, she was hilarious. I wanted more of her. A lot fucking more.

"Sorry your flight got delayed on the runway, but I'm glad you guys got home safely."

"Me too," I replied in half-truths, taking a swig of beer. I wasn't even remotely upset about the extra time I'd spent talking to her. "So, is it safe to say that Georgia Cummings is now a Western University fan?"

"Uh-huh." She giggled. "They kick ass."

"Next year, you'll have to come to a game with me. It's insane."

"Kline Brooks, are you still trying to plan a second date before we even go on a first?" she teased.

I laughed. "You'll find I'm a determined kind of guy."

"Ain't that the truth." She yawned. "Well, that's my signal to get my tired ass in bed. I guess I'll see you in the morning."

"Good night, Georgia girl," I said, stealing Thatch's endearment.

"Night," she whispered, ending the call.

I set my phone on the bar and downed the rest of my beer. "Ready to hit it?" I asked Thatch, tossing money down on the bar.

He just shook his head, sighing heavily. "Glad you got time for precious pillow talk during the *fucking game.*"

I patted him on the shoulder. "Don't worry, sweetheart. I think Boobear will be healthy and ready to play next season."

"Fucking Boobear." He chuckled with another shake of his head. "Even I can't deny that's hilarious."

CHAPTER 11

Georgia

It was Friday—the big date night with my boss—and I was sitting on the subway, heading home from work a little early. Nerves were starting to get the best of me. My brain ran through a thousand possible scenarios of how the charity event with Kline would go. Most of them were awkward and ended with me doing something outrageous. It was my M.O. I had a serious propensity for word vomit. A certified foot-in-mouth expert.

I needed someone to talk me off the proverbial ledge or else I'd end up faking the flu and backing out last minute.

Cassie was a no-go. She had just boarded a flight to Seattle to photograph an up-and-coming football star who'd signed with the Seahawks. My beautiful, spunky best friend had made a name for herself as a freelance photographer. Her photos had graced the pages of The *Times*, *Cosmopolitan*, and even ESPN. It seemed her lens had a knack for hot men flexing their muscles. Shocker, huh?

My mother was a hell-no. Ever the sex therapist at heart, she'd probably offer her sage advice of rubbing one out pre-date to stave off nerves.

My finger hovering over the TapNext icon, I finally said, "Screw it." Maybe **BAD_Ruck** could make me feel better about this situation. We'd been chatting back and forth over the past few days, and despite the absurdity of our introduction to one another, I was really starting to like the guy. He was funny, laid-back, and could give good flirt. I spent a crazy amount of my day wondering what he was like in person. Did he really look like the guy in his profile? What did he do for a living? Where did he live in New York?

We hadn't shared any intimate details of our personal lives, a la *You've Got Mail*, which I preferred at the present time. We weren't living in the dial-up internet era of Kathleen Kelly, and it was a different world. For me, all of her dangers were magnified by a thousand—and she was worried Tom Hanks was a serial killer! These days, there was a show called *Catfish*. It seemed like people got off on it now more than ever. And, although Ruck was quite charming in our online conversations, I wasn't convinced he wasn't a complete weirdo in real life.

Funny how that didn't stop me from messaging him.

TAPRoseNEXT (2:15PM): Ruck? Come in, Ruck? I need someone to talk me off the ledge.

BAD_Ruck (2:16PM): We're talking proverbial ledge, right?

TAPRoseNEXT (2:16PM): Yes. Don't worry, I'm not literally standing on the ledge of a skyscraper.

BAD_Ruck (2:16PM): That's good news. So, tell me, why are we flirting with proverbial death?

TAPRoseNEXT (2:17PM): I've got a date tonight. I'm nervous. And freaking out. Big time.

BAD_Ruck (2:17PM): And here I thought I was the only man

in your life. You wound me, Rose.

TAPRoseNEXT (2:18PM): Get over yourself. I would lay money on the fact that Mr. Charming himself has a date tonight too.

BAD_Ruck (2:18PM): Maybe.

TAPRoseNEXT (2:19PM): My point exactly. Now, help me out here.

BAD_Ruck (2:19PM): Okay. Let's start with the obvious. Why are you nervous?

Why was I nervous? That was the big question. I stared across the aisle, watching an older woman working on a crossword. The tip of her pen ran across the empty blocks as she tried to think of a four-letter word for 15A. "_____ comes trouble!"

Here comes trouble. Apt phrase for my present state. My mind had been shouting this from the second I had agreed to a date with Kline.

God, I was definitely freaking out over a bunch of things, and one thing, in particular, stood out the most.

TAPRoseNEXT (2:20PM): For one, I work with him. If things end up badly, I'm worried it could cost me my job.

BAD_Ruck (2:20PM): Ah, the old coworker conundrum. Did he ask you out? Or did you ask him out? And is it forbidden in your employee contract?

TAPRoseNEXT (2:21PM): He asked me. And I have no earthly clue. Was that something I was supposed to actually read?

BAD_Ruck (2:21PM): Okay. Different tactic. Does he normally date women he works with?

TAPRoseNEXT (2:22PM): No, never. Either that or he's a super sleuth about it. I'm not personally the office gossip, but I know someone with an ear to the ground.

BAD_Ruck (2:23PM): If he asked you out, and you've never seen him date any of your colleagues, he's probably thought this through. How long have you worked with him?

TAPRoseNEXT (2:23PM): A couple of years.

BAD_Ruck (2:24PM): And in that time, has he ever seemed like the kind of man who lets his personal life affect business?

TAPRoseNEXT (2:25PM): Actually, no. Picture of professional. Business always comes first with him.

BAD_Ruck (2:25PM): Then what's different now?

TAPRoseNEXT (2:26PM): I honestly don't know.

BAD_Ruck (2:26PM): Smart money says it's you, Rose.

He had a point. Kline Brooks had never given me any reason to doubt the decisions he made. He wasn't a player. He didn't make a show out of fucking anything in a short skirt and pair of heels that sashayed around the office.

Leslie was a perfect example. The girl was gorgeous and made a job out of flaunting her curves for the world to see. And I'd yet to see Kline act anything but annoyed with her—no salacious glances or devilish intents flashing across his eyes. He was ever the professional when his new intern was around. Most days, he was doing everything he could to push her off on someone else.

But my dating Kline equaled us getting to know each other on a more personal level. If one date turned into more, then eventually, he would know *other* things about me. Things I wouldn't normally want my boss to know.

TAPRoseNEXT (2:27PM): Can I be frank with you?

BAD_Ruck (2:28PM): I guess. I'm surprisingly partial to Rose.

TAPRoseNEXT (2:28PM): I said frank, not Frank, Ruck.

BAD_Ruck (2:29PM): Have you ever not been frank with me?

I laughed, startling the pen out of the crossword woman's hands.

"Sorry." I cringed, leaning forward and picking it up from the aisle.

"No worries, honey." She took the pen from my outstretched hand. "Two words for puppy amuser?" she asked, grinning.

"Chew toy," I answered.

"Aha! You're right! Thank you!" And that was that. She dove right back into her crossword, tuning the rest of the world out.

I replayed past convos with Ruck in my head. I tended to be pretty open and honest with him, maybe a bit too much. The other night I had kept him up until one in the morning discussing why most men thought anal sex was a good idea.

He'd ended the conversation with, "I'm not going to speak on behalf of all men, because let's face it, there are some real morons in my gender. But for me, when I really want a woman, I want to claim every part of her."

See what I mean? He gives damn good convo.

That response made me instantly jealous of the woman Ruck had set his sights on. Even I couldn't ignore the sexiness of Ruck going caveman and wanting to claim every part of her, whoever she was. *Lucky bitch.*

TAPRoseNEXT (2:30PM): There's another reason I'm nervous.

BAD_Ruck (2:31PM): Okay...

BAD_Ruck (2:32PM): Are you going to freely give this reason or is this an invitation to pry?

TAPRoseNEXT (2:33PM): Ugh...

BAD_Ruck (2:34PM): Do you have a foot fetish you're trying to hide?

TAPRoseNEXT (2:34PM): No. I don't even like my own feet, much less anyone else's.

BAD_Ruck (2:35PM): An ex-boyfriend's name tattooed across your lower back?

TAPRoseNEXT (2:35PM): I do not have a tramp stamp!

BAD_Ruck (2:36PM): Hairy back moles?

TAPRoseNEXT (2:36PM): I'm a lady, Ruck. I'm smooth everywhere.

BAD_Ruck (2:37PM): Damn, Rose. Stop talking dirty to me. We're trying to talk you off the ledge, remember? Not push me out onto it.

TAPRoseNEXT (2:40PM): I'm a virgin.

BAD_Ruck (2:41PM): An anal virgin?

TAPRoseNEXT (2:42PM): No. A certified, my-pussy-has-never-been-penetrated virgin.

BAD_Ruck (2:44PM): Jesus.

TAPRoseNEXT (2:45PM): That's sweet, but we don't have time to pray right now.

For what seemed like an hour, I watched the text box bubbles move as he gathered a response.

BAD_Ruck (2:48PM): This scenario deserves a prayer. Hell, it deserves an airplane banner with the words, "Get your shit together, men, because dreams can come true. There are still gorgeous, sexy, intelligent women out there who are saving themselves for the right guy." Christ, I think you might be the last twenty-something virgin in New York.

The last twenty-something virgin in NYC? *Gah.* That did *not* make me feel better. That made me feel a hell of a lot worse. I sounded pathetic.

TAPRoseNEXT (2:50PM): That's one crazy long banner. And thanks for the vote of confidence. I feel even worse about it now. I'm not a total prude, by the way. I've been with men. I know what a penis feels like in my mouth. I've just yet to find the right penis I deem worthy of sex.

BAD_Ruck (2:51PM): You're killing me right now. Do you

even realize how rare you are, Rose?

Now, I do. I was the last twenty-something virgin in New York! I might as well have offered up my vagina to the Museum of Natural History. Surely, it would be shown in the fossils display. I could already picture it, right beside Tyrannosaurus Rex's teeth.

The Last Virginal Vagina in New York.

Georgia Cummings 1990-2080

Died happily in her Chelsea apartment, surrounded by all sixteen of her tabby cats.

TAPRoseNEXT (2:53PM): Yeah, I'm the last single virgin in NYC. I might as well start stocking up on cat food because my future is looking very glum at the moment.

BAD_Ruck (2:54PM): Rose. Listen to me. This is not a bad thing. You're funny, intelligent, and obviously beautiful. And you're confident enough to know what you want and how you want it. Your confidence and self-respect are sexy as hell.

TAPRoseNEXT (2:54PM): Well, when you put it that way, I sound really awesome.

BAD_Ruck (2:55PM): Because you are. So, tell me why your sexual history is even factoring as a problem in your mind?

TAPRoseNEXT (2:57PM): My experiences in telling a guy I'm a virgin have never ended well.

The reactions I received were not usually great. I either became a challenge, where getting into my pants became their sole purpose in life, or treated like some pariah, as if my virginity was a problem that needed a solution. Sometimes, I wondered if it would be easier telling a guy I had crabs.

BAD_Ruck (2:58PM): I can imagine. Most of us are just grunting cavemen.

TAPRoseNEXT (2:59PM): Exactly. And I can't help but wonder what would happen if I told this guy I'm a virgin. He has potential. He could end up being more than just one date. I'm just worried if I tell him, I'll end up being a challenge instead of something more.

Wow. Even I was surprised by that response. Did Kline Brooks really have the potential to be something more?

BAD_Ruck (3:01PM): If he's worth your time, he won't see you as a challenge. Of course, he's going to be silently thanking God you're willing to give him the time of day, but he won't make a one-eighty and just focus on trying to get in your pants. And from what you've told me, he doesn't seem half bad. He apparently knows how to separate his personal life from business. And he doesn't have a reputation of screwing all of the women in your office. This isn't the New York norm.

Everything he said was true. Kline's track record was a good one. He wasn't plastered all over Page Six with a different woman on his arm. He wasn't known as some playboy. He was just Kline—handsome, attractive, and all-business Kline Brooks. Which only made me more curious what he was like outside of the office.

TAPRoseNEXT (3:04PM): So, let's just act like you're him for a second. When would you want the whole "I'm a virgin" bomb to be dropped?

BAD_Ruck (3:05PM): Before it got to the point where our clothes are off and I'm sliding a condom on.

TAPRoseNEXT (3:05PM): LOL. Obviously.

BAD_Ruck (3:07PM): If you're asking me when to bring it up…I don't really have an answer for you. It should come up organically. You know how dates go. Eventually, the whole sex topic does come up. Your being a virgin isn't a fucking crime, so don't feel like you have to confess it the second the date starts.

TAPRoseNEXT (3:07PM): Good point.

BAD_Ruck (3:08PM): Feel better?

TAPRoseNEXT (3:08PM): Consider me officially off the ledge.

BAD_Ruck (3:09PM): Fantastic. Good luck tonight.

TAPRoseNEXT (3:10PM): Thanks, Ruck. Enjoy your date with whomever the lucky woman may be.

BAD_Ruck (3:11PM): Dirty talk and a compliment in one convo? You're too good to me. And listen…

TAPRoseNEXT (3:12PM): LOL. Yeah?

BAD_Ruck (3:12PM): If all this advice turns out to be shit, I might be able to help you out with the cat acquirement. I know a guy.

TAPRoseNEXT (3:13PM): And that's my cue to officially end

this convo. Bye, Ruck.

BAD_Ruck (3:12PM): Bye, Rose.

I hopped off the subway way uptown, and instead of heading to my apartment, my legs strode for the one place that always helped take my mind off things. It was a quarter after three. I had four hours to get my hair done, get ready, and meet Kline at the event.

If there was one thing I was good at, it was choosing a kick-ass hair color to suit my mood.

And if there was one thing Betty, my hair stylist, was good at, it was fitting me in last minute. She was a genius when it came to color and cut. If I told her blonde, she'd find the perfect shade to match my skin tone and have me trimmed, dyed, and out the door within two hours.

Hmm… From red to blonde? That might be the best idea I've had all day.

CHAPTER 12

Kline

"Nervous." I shook my head. "I can't believe I'm fucking nervous."

I guess Walter *was* having an effect on my life like my mother had predicted. Although, I highly doubted me talking to myself was what she'd had in mind.

That was what this was, though. It had to be. The illusion of someone being there, *listening*, and fooling me into saying all of my rambling thoughts out loud rather than reciting them internally.

Long and unkempt, his whiskers flowed freely from beneath his nose, and in keeping with his old man status, stuck out haphazardly from his kitty eyebrows. His white-rimmed eyes rooted me to the spot with their contempt, and the subtle stripes in his fur did nothing to soften his appearance.

"This is your fault," I told him, his wolflike ears mocking me with every word.

One uninterested lick of his lips is all he gave me in return.

"What? Nothing to say? No support?"

He licked his paw and wiped his face before turning abruptly and sauntering out of the room, holding his tail pointedly straight in the cat version of a middle finger salute.

"Thanks for nothing, asshole," I shouted after him.

Jesus.

I shook my head as I stepped in front of the mirror to adjust my tie. This was a whole new level of low. Not only was I talking to the fucking cat; I was *yelling* at him.

Tonight had my stomach on edge in a way it hadn't been since I'd given Tara Wallowitz my first kiss behind the gym after our seventh-grade dance. She'd had braces and I'd been drowning in all my awkward, barely-a-teenager glory. Two sets of fumbling hands, an overaggressive tongue, and a cut to my lips later, it was over.

I didn't foresee tonight with Georgia being like that at all, but the basis of my feelings was remarkably similar. Out of my element and thrown off by her initial lack of enthusiasm, I'd put in a lot of effort over the last couple of days to turn it around and smooth the way for tonight's date. But now I was invested. I *cared* how tonight went. And that hadn't been the norm in a long time. I felt a little like I was walking into a set-up with no tools to escape the consequences. That wasn't cool. MacGyver was cool, and he always made tools out of whatever he had. I'd have to do the same.

"Mr. Brooks?" my intercom squawked.

I grabbed my phone from the counter and jogged the five steps to press the button.

"Yeah?"

"Your driver's here."

"Thanks."

I snatched my wallet and keys off of the front table and slid out the door without looking at myself in the mirror again. I'd already spent far too much time questioning my tie color.

I was *not* the kind of guy who carefully considered every element of my outfit. Tonight was the closest I would ever get to contradicting that.

"Frank," I greeted as I approached the car, reaching a hand out to shake his. On days like today, I couldn't help but notice how much of his time I monopolized.

"Mr. Brooks." His greeting was warm, and he had a face to match. A smattering of wrinkles at the corners of his eyes pointed to a life filled with laughter, and the gray of his hair hinted at the possibility of a daughter or two.

"I wish you'd call me Kline," I said with a smile, knowing it would never change.

"I'm sorry, sir."

I shook my head and gave him a friendly slap on his shoulder with the hand not clasped in his. "Don't be sorry. I'm the one who should apologize—dragging your ass all over town all day and night."

"No trouble at all, sir."

I chuckled again. "This makes twelve hours in this shift, right?"

"Yes—"

"And you've still got the rest of the night to go?"

"It's no trouble, Mr. Brooks."

A nod was all I could give at the time, so I did. It was a gesture that made it possible to get on our way, to get to the benefit, and to get busy letting Frank off the hook. I'd embellish the not-nearly-enough gesture with a fatter-than-expected tip on the bill later.

I slid into the car and Frank closed the door behind me. I unbuttoned the coat of my tuxedo and pulled at the lapels to make it stop feeling like it was choking me.

As Frank climbed into his seat, he spoke again. "Another stop, sir?"

Forced to give an answer I didn't like, I shook my head. "No. Straight to the benefit."

He nodded and pulled the gearshift into drive. "Yes, sir."

I'd been hell-bent on picking Georgia up like a proper date, but apparently, on this matter, she had a closer relationship with the devil. Refusal was too kind a word to describe her reaction when I had suggested my driver would pick her up. In fact, she'd looked like the suggestion was more revolting than stepping in dog shit.

And I understood to a point. I personally hated taking the car, preferring immeasurably to take the subway and people-watch. I didn't even mind walking fifteen blocks on a nice Manhattan day.

But certain aspects of my life demanded the car. It kept me on schedule during the day, on time to the office, and never late to meetings. Without the motivation of someone like Frank waiting on me, and the desire to respect his time, I'd have been late everywhere I went.

I liked to wander too much, experiment with new spots in the city and observe people as they met and chatted and said goodbye.

Human behavior was fascinating, and I found the more I studied it, the easier it was to manage all of my people-based businesses.

I glanced down at my phone, feeling guilty for checking it on my way to my first date with Georgia, but at the same time, not being able to help myself.

Nothing. All quiet.

My conversation from that afternoon with the mysterious Rose burned in my mind. I hated the fact that any woman would feel like being a virgin was something to be ashamed of or even be embarrassed to talk about it. But I was also a man, and fuck, it wasn't a stretch to understand why. I could feel myself becoming more and more irrational the longer she'd talked about it, even knowing that she'd come to me for honest advice.

I'll be *honest*. I had to *advise* my dick to calm the fuck down.

Very scumbag-like of me, I supposed, but I was convinced hearing or seeing the word 'virgin' or 'anal' or 'sex' fired some kind of hormonal response in the heterosexual male mind.

Maybe it fired it in the homosexual male mind too, but I didn't have any firsthand experience to confirm.

Photographers lined the entrance as we pulled up to 30 Rock, a well-known skyscraper in New York City and home to several entities, including NBC Studios. For me, on this night, it was the Rainbow Room I wanted, an iconic restaurant on the sixty-fifth floor and host to the benefit for Mount Sinai Kravis Children's Hospital. The fundraiser was being held by an outside organization made up of the well-meaning wealthy. I wished they'd spend less money on the event and donate it all to the fucking hospital, but the truth of it was that *this* was what it took to entice people into donations and make it feel worthy of their money. Schmaltzy entertainment, expensive food, and an evening out.

I was here to hand over a check, make my mother happy, and enjoy the evening with Georgia, the level of importance of each not relative to their order.

The dog and pony show passed by in a blur, camera flashes and shouted questions melding and mixing together as I covered my eyes and stepped inside.

Security for the event had taken over two of the elevators, and a small line trickled from the doors of each all the way back to me.

I scanned the crowd for Georgia, hoping to find her sooner rather than later, but, after several sweeps, came up completely empty. It was one of the perils of coming separately, I supposed, but I didn't want her to feel awkward or alone while she waited for me.

A check of my watch confirmed that I was on time, and the line was moving fast. I'd be up there to look for her in no time.

"Macallan on the rocks, half a lime on the side, please."

The bartender confirmed my order with a nod, turning to the glass shelves behind him to grab my scotch. It was fifteen minutes past eight, forty-five minutes later than our agreed upon time, and still no sign of Georgia. I was beginning to think she might have stood me up—hoping that she had, rather than something having happened to her—when Stacey Henderson sauntered up to me and leaned her body into my space with an elbow at the bar.

"Where's your date?"

I grabbed my scotch and the lime as the bartender set it down in front of me, squeezing the juice into my glass before handing the carcass back to him with a smile and a nod. Plucking a napkin from the top of the stack, I wiped the remaining juice off of my palm.

"Well, hello to you too, Stacey." I turned to her in acknowledgment, but my body did it under protest. It feared the effects of cross-contamination if it got too close.

"Your mother told me you already had a date. That's why you couldn't come with me."

"I'm aware. What I wasn't aware of was the fact that she had arranged a date with you in the first place. Don't you think that's the kind of thing you should be asked directly by a man?"

She waved the thought away like a pesky fly.

"If you're not here with someone—"

"I am," I interrupted.

Her eyes narrowed while mine searched the room nearly desperately, and my brain tried to conjure up an excuse. My face and body portrayed an outward calm.

"Where is she, then?"

"The restroom. You know how you ladies are," I patronized in the name of inserting frivolous, vaguely-insulting conversation into a still-civil exchange. As much as Stacey Henderson was asking for a big 'go fuck yourself,' the Mount Sinai Kravis Children's Hospital was not. "Always running to the restroom to touch up something or other or to relieve your peanut-sized bladders."

Stacey scoffed rather indelicately, an effect of too much alcohol too goddamn early in the benefit, and I winced, fearing the turn of events when no one returned from the restroom.

Then, out of the crowd emerged a frazzled—but *stunning*—Geor-

gia. Red framed her body from breast to foot, the tight material clinging to her in all the right places. Her tan skin peeked out of a cut-
out just below her chest, and a matching blood red painted her lips
and nails. The only thing missing red was her head, her now blonde
locks cascading and curling down and around her slim shoulders and
damn near robbing me of the ability to think.

Worry from her late arrival ravaged her face as she approached
the two of us without pretense or fear.

"Oh my God, Kline, I am so sorry I'm—"

"It's okay," I cut her off, stepping pointedly around Stacey and
pulling her into my arms for a hug.

"I'm just glad you're here," I whispered softly into her new hair.
Stacey groaned audibly in begrudged response before grabbing her
high-priced clutch from the bar and stomping away like a petulant
child.

"Who was she?" Georgia asked, leaning back and glancing over
my arm as Stacey dragged ass away.

"*That* was a day-spa-loving version of my cat."

Her nose scrunched up adorably as she tried to make sense of
my words.

"Would you like something to drink?" I offered, escorting her the
few steps back to the bar with a hand at her back. I felt the warmth at
my palm all the way in my dick, the need to touch her having been a
palpable thing all day long.

She smiled, and it lit up her face and mine. "Can I say 'God yes'
without sounding like a lush?"

One side of my mouth hooked up in a grin. My cock said she
could say 'God yes' anytime she wanted, but thankfully, my mouth
said, "Sure."

I looked away long enough to grab the bartender's attention and
then turned back to her.

"You look beautiful."

She started to smile but stopped herself, the skin between her eyebrows pinching slightly.

"I'm an asshole. I can't believe I'm so late. I mean, I *can* believe I'm late," she rambled. "Just not *this* late. This is a new low for me."

"You're always late?" I asked, trying to distract her from the late arrival and learn more about her instead.

"Yes. Every day of my life. Well, to everything other than meetings with you." She winced again. "The work you, at least."

"Don't worry," I promised with a grin. "Kline won't say anything to Mr. Brooks."

"What'll you have?" the bartender asked, tossing a napkin up on the bar for the anticipated glass.

Georgia looked to me in question.

"No." I waved her off and lifted my glass. "I'm good. Just got one. You go ahead."

I glanced down the line of her back as she leaned over the bar. Wide straps criss-crossed to form cut-outs in the fabric of the back as well, and smooth material hugged the curve of her hips and ass. Her body petite but curvy, I wanted to run my hands all over that fabric.

God, she looked gorgeous. It was almost unreal.

She turned to me, holding a glass of wine she had obviously ordered at some point during my ogling.

"Sorry," I apologized through a tight throat. "I was…"

She raised an eyebrow pointedly, a knowing grin on her face. "Staring at my ass."

"Yeah." I nodded. "That's exactly what I was doing."

She laughed.

"It's a really fine ass, though. And your hair…"

She grabbed a strand of it self-consciously, twisting it around her finger. "Oh. Yeah. I have a thing for dyeing my hair. I'm not sure why, but I tend to change it like a hobby. Red or blonde or sometimes—"

"Georgia?"

She finally took a breath. "Yeah?"

"I meant what I said. You look beautiful. Own it."

"Thank you," she whispered, but her face relaxed.

From there on out, she seemed herself: funny, sometimes awkward, but mostly at ease.

We worked the room, schmoozing all of the people who needed it and small-talking with the others. Unable to help myself, I kept a hand on Georgia all night.

Her hand in mine, my palm at the small of her back, a set of my flexing fingers on her perfect hip. Anything to touch her. Anything to keep her in close proximity.

Finally done with my obligations, I asked her something that'd been on my mind all night.

"Would you like to dance?"

She seemed surprised. "You dance?"

"With you, yes."

"I swear," she whispered with a shake of her head. "Do you secretly have one of those things on your wrist that Coca-Cola wears?"

I grinned in confusion.

Her eyes searched mine like I held all the power, a sheen of fear coating them with moisture.

Only then did I realize she meant the quarterback's playbook cheat sheet.

I took her cheek in my palm, smoothing a thumb over the apple of it softly.

Apparently, when it came to Georgia Cummings and tonight, I'd been doing just fine.

"Come on," I coaxed, setting my drink down on a nearby table, pulling her onto the dance floor with me, and pressing her body right to mine.

Hands clasped together, I pulled them into my chest and wrapped my other arm tightly around the curve of her hip.

Her eyes followed mine and mine followed hers, a closed loop of exploration into each other. The moment picked up speed as the band played a sweet and melodic tune, and the rest of the room faded completely away.

My chest felt tight with anticipation of what was to come—right now, in this moment, and beyond, as I gave myself over to getting to know this amazing woman.

Our weight shifted from foot to foot and our hips swayed, very much moving but, at the same time, fighting with everything we had to stay stagnantly lost in that moment.

Without thought or delay, I leaned in, touching my lips to hers for a full second before I felt the tension leave her body and her eyes fluttered closed.

Tentative but bold, her lips began to move under mine, exploring on their own rather than waiting for my invitation.

I abandoned her hand at my chest immediately and sought the solace of her hair instead, entrenching my hand and using its leverage to pull her lips even closer.

A sigh bounced from her mouth to mine as I focused on her bottom lip, pulling it between my own and sucking ever so slightly.

She tasted like the sweet cherry notes of her wine, and my tongue shot out to lick up another drop. When the tip of her tongue touched mine, everything else was lost.

Time.

Space.

All sense of propriety and appropriateness for a crowded dance floor at a Children's Hospital benefit. My hand left her hip, circling around on a path straight for the cheek of her ass.

When the corners of her lips tipped up despite their connection to mine, I knew I'd never experienced *anything* sexier than a woman unable to withhold a smile while we kissed.

"*Kline*," she whispered, pulling away and smiling without inhibition.

Just the way she said my name had me groaning.

"God, I know. Not the time." I pulled her close to me and practically dragged the two of us off the dance floor. The band had started to transition into an old Grand Funk Railroad song, "Some Kind of Wonderful," anyway. In the haze of my peripheral vision, I could see other couples head in the direction we'd just come, and amongst the shuffle and swing of their active bodies, our lip-locked, fully intertwined ones would have been even more obvious.

I grabbed Georgia's wrist lightly, and her pulse thrummed and fluttered under the tips of my fingers. The feeling made my grip tighten minutely as I turned her to face me.

Her hair hung in a veil around her face, but I could actually *feel* our chemistry in the air between us.

When I pulled her body flush with mine, she tipped her chin so that she could look straight into my eyes.

Her signature blue eyes were shining with emotion, but something else wasn't right.

She was still beautiful, but her face—something was different. Her lipstick-smeared lips looked to be twice their normal size.

"Um, Georgia—"

"Georgie," she corrected while looking up at me sweetly. She fluttered her lashes coyly, but I barely even noticed. I couldn't look away from her mouth.

"Right. Georgie." I steeled myself. "Listen, I know this is a weird question, but you wouldn't happen to have had some light work done, would you?"

"Work?" she asked, oblivious.

"Yeah, you know. *Work.*"

She shook her head and smiled a little, clearly still in the fog from our kiss. I wished I was. "I don't know what you're asking."

I coughed to clear my throat and wiped the building sweat from my brow. This wasn't a good idea. Asking women questions like this was never a good idea.

Maybe I should just pretend not to notice.

"Kline?"

Shit. Were they getting bigger?

"I don't know," I fumbled. "Some kind of lip filler that has a de-layed reaction, maybe?"

"Wip fiwer?" She tried again, her nose scrunching with the effort. "Wip fiwer. Wipppp fiwer."

Concern blanketed my face and hers turned distraught.

"Oh, sit. Sit sit sit."

"Sit?"

"Not sit. Siiit." She dropped her face into her hands. "Sit."

"Ohhh," I said in realization, picking her face up out of her hands to find her lips and the palms that had just touched them swelling at an alarming rate. "Shit, Georgie."

"Exacwy."

"What's happening? What do I need to do?"

I moved to grab some ice out of my forgotten glass, and her eyes followed me and then widened exponentially.

"Sit, Kwine! Is where wime wuice in where?"

"Wime wuice?"

"Wime wuice!"

"Oh! Oh, yeah. Shit. Shit! Yeah, there's lime juice in there."

"I'm awerwic. I nee benedetto. Benedwetto. Sit! Benedwiwww."

"Benadryl!" I shouted, victorious. Like it was some kind of game. She looked disgusted.

"Right. Sorry," I apologized, turning my attention back to sur-veying her and putting my focus back on her health. "Jesus, it's bad, Georgie. Do we need to go to the emergency room?"

"No." She shook her head, eyes determined.

Her lips looked like cartoons. I panicked at the thought of her throat closing up with the same fervor.

"Please. Let me take you to urgent care or something."

"No, Kwine. Wet's wust wet ouw of hewre. Benedwiwww."

"Right. Benadryl." I grabbed her hand and dragged her toward the elevator without looking back. No way was tonight going to go down in history as the night I fucking killed a woman with one kiss.

I shoved through the crowd that had gathered there without apology, and Georgia shielded her face from their scrutiny. The doors propped open with my foot, I ushered her in and hit the button for the lobby as fast as I could before holding the 'close door' button with excessive force. When they finally shut, I pulled Georgia's gaze from the floor with a gentle finger at her chin.

"I'm so sorry, Georgie."

"Is wit bwad?"

"It isn't good," I answered vaguely. "Please, let me take you to the hospital."

"No," she refused, taking some of the sting out of it by offering a smile. I mean, her mouth didn't smile—it was too swollen—but there was visible happiness in her eyes. "I'm owkay. Pwomise. Wust nee Benedwiw."

The doors opened on the ground floor, and I peeled out of there like a drag car, Georgie in tow.

"Swow down, Kwine," she ordered, tugging on my hand and nearly tripping on her dress.

"I'm sorry," I apologized, knowing I wouldn't be able to beat the panic back enough to slow down to her pace.

She smiled again, but it didn't last long. It turned right into a shout when I swept her off of her feet and into my arms and took off at a jog again, dialing Frank as I did.

Two rings and he answered.

"Mr. Brooks?"

"I need you to meet us at the Rite-Aid on the corner!"

He wasn't used to me shouting, but he sure as hell didn't question it.

"Yes, sir."

One look at Georgie's face, and I started running faster.

For the first time in ten years, I didn't have the first clue what I'd done with my phone after ending the call—and I didn't care one bit.

CHAPTER 13

Georgia

"Here." Kline slid back into the car and handed me a brown paper bag with what I could only assume was Benadryl.

"Tanks," I whispered, offering a small smile.

He furrowed his brow, lips fighting a wince.

Shit. How bad is it?

Seeing as it was my first date with Kline, I knew this wasn't an optimal situation. In a matter of a few minutes and one perfect, sexy kiss, I had gone from smiling and offering up charming, flirty responses to sounding like I was talking around a wiener in my mouth.

Lime juice had sabotaged me. It had been years since I'd come in contact with the allergy-inducing demon. And the last time, it was *way* worse. My throat had started to close up because I had ingested it, whereas this was just contact swelling.

Swallowing a few times, I confirmed my throat was breezy and clear.

But the way Kline was trying *not* to react to my appearance?

Well, that had me rummaging through my purse and getting my compact out. Flipping the clasp, I opened the mirror, coming face-to-face with something that could nauseate horror movie enthusiasts. Bright red blowfish lips consumed my face. The skin was stretched so tight I feared something might burst.

Bottom line: It was bad. Real fucking bad. Kylie Jenner's mouth on steroids bad.

"Ah ma gaw," I gasped, tongue still swelling by the second.

I glanced at myself in the mirror again, which was a big, fat mistake of epic proportions. The swelling seemed hell-bent on consuming my entire face.

"Tis is ba! Tis is so ba!" I grabbed the paper bag off the seat and pulled it over my head.

On a Britney Spears' scale of embarrassment, I had proverbially flashed my beaver to millions of people.

For the love of God, the inflammation is going to my brain. I can only think in celebrity speak. My allergic reaction had turned me into Leslie.

"Georgia, please, don't hide your pretty face." Kline removed the paper bag, staring back at me with serious concern.

Pfffffft. Pretty? All forms of pretty had fled the building the second I had contracted elephantiasis of the face.

I averted my eyes from his and focused on removing the cellophane wrapping from the Benadryl. "Somonabith," I cursed, fumbling with the childproof cap.

He gently took the bottle out of my hands, detaching the cap with ease, and handed it back to me. "We need to get you to an emergency room. St. Luke's is just around the corner."

Oh, hell no. Out of all of the emergency rooms in New York, I was not going to *that* one.

Well, unless my reaction gets worse—then I'd reconsider. I'd face the embarrassment and my brother's incessant teasing for a shot of epinephrine over not breathing at all. I'm not a complete moron.

I shook my head frantically. "Ma brudder. Nob way."

He scrunched his brow up in confusion.

"Nobe. Nob hobitals."

My brother Will was finishing up his ER residency at St. Luke's, and I knew for a fact he was elbow deep in a twenty-four-hour call shift. If I walked into his ER looking like this, I'd never live it down.

"But—"

"Uh-uh. Nob habbenin'," I cut him off, resolute.

And to solidify my decision, I tipped the bottle of Benadryl to my goliath lips and knocked back as much as I could.

"Shit! Georgia!" Kline grabbed the bottle from my hands, panicked. "That's too much. Way, way too much."

I shrugged, reaching for the discarded paper bag and pulling a pen from my purse.

No ERs needed, I'll be fine, I wrote, holding it out to him.

He frowned. "I'm really worried."

I promise, I've been through this before. The Benny will do the trick.

I reassured, hating seeing him so anxious.

His mouth offered a wry grin. "Benny?"

I nodded, my neck doing its best impression of a bobblehead doll. It was safe to say, the antihistamine was kicking in.

Yeah, Benny and I go way back. I promise I'll be fine in a few hours.

He assessed my face. "Pretty sure you drank way too much Benny."

I shook my head, hiding my lips with my free hand.

Just stop looking at me until the Benny kicks in. I'm sorry this is the worst first date ever.

He took the pen out of my grip and pulled the bag into his lap. His hand moved in fluid motions as he scribbled something down and then slid it back to me.

~~**Just stop looking at me until the Benny kicks in. I'm sorry this is the worst first date ever.**~~
This is the BEST first date ever.

"Thank you for coming with me tonight." He offered a smile—a real smile, not the *I'm trying to smile, but holy shit, you look bad* kind of smile he was showcasing before. "And, Georgia." Kline touched my cheek. "Even with an allergic reaction, you still have the power to take my breath away. You're gorgeous, sweetheart. Swollen lips and all, you're still gorgeous."

I stared back at him, speechless. There was still so much I didn't know about Kline, but my gut told me, at the root of his soul, he was a good man. A sweet, kind, and undeniably good man.

Despite the lime juice fiasco, I'm glad I'm here too.

My eyelids started to feel heavy, my lashes blinking past the fog. I leaned my head back on the seat.

"You okay?" He wrapped his arm around my shoulder, tucking me into his side.

I wasn't vomiting and I could still breathe, so I muttered, "Uh-huh," as I nuzzled into him. "Jus a lil sweepy."

The pull to go comatose was strong. In the back of my mind, there was a tiny bit of rational thought wondering, *Am I going to overdose on Benadryl?*

Before the urge to sleep snuffed out all the light, I grabbed my phone from my purse. Pulling up my text conversation with Will, I attempted to shoot him a message.

Me: WELLY IM BENNY
Delete.
Me: WELLIUM ODOR
Delete.

Slowly, but surely, my fingers got their shit together and autocorrect stopped trying to make me her bitch.

Me: WILL CAN AN OC GIVE A BENNY!*&

There. Perfect.

If he thinks I'm in trouble, he'll call me. Otherwise, no big dealio, was the last thought before Benny took over and said, "Goodnight, Georgia."

"Georgie. Georgie." A hand nudged my shoulder. "Wake up, Georgie."

"*Fuuuuuuuuuuck.*" Someone cursed under their breath.

I opened my eyes, blinking past the blurred vision. Peeling my face off leather, I sat up, finding a concerned Kline staring back at me.

"Thank God. Are you okay?" He touched my cheek.

Mmmmmmmmm. That feels nice. I had the urge to purr into his palm and beg him to scratch my belly. All of a sudden, being a cat sounded like the best idea I'd ever had.

"Meow?" he asked, all four of his eyebrows scrunching together.

"Huh?"

"Did you just say meow?"

"*Meowww... Meowww...*" I tested it on my tongue. My lips felt funny. "Yeah, I think I did." I nuzzled into his palm. "Keep petting me, Kline. I might actually start purring soon."

A deep chuckle vibrated his chest. My head moved of its own accord, leaning forward and resting against his hard pecs. For real, Kline Brooks had pecs. Hard-as-fuck pecs. Mmm. Nipples. I wondered what his nipples tasted like.

He adjusted in his seat, his hand resting at the nape of my neck. "Georgie? We need to get you upstairs. I think you might've had too much Benadryl."

Me thinks so too. Suggested dosage, schmagested mosage.

"Hahaha. Mosage."

My body rocked like he was shaking his head.

"I think I'm high."

He chuckled again, pec-pulsation caressing my cheek.

"Now I remember why I loved Mary Jane so much in high school."

"I'm going to carry you out of the car, okay?"

"We're in a car?" I sat up straight, releasing his perfect chest from my cheek's assault. "Whose car?"

"This is my regular car, sweetheart. Frank drove us. Are you ready?"

I glanced at his crotch. "Oh, I had no idea we were already headed in that direction. I guess this date went pretty good, huh? We're headed for naked time. That's gotta be a good thing." My hand stroked his thigh, savoring the feel of muscles sheathed by soft material. "I bet you're fuck-hot naked."

He grinned, grabbing my hand and pulling it to his lips for a soft kiss. "How about we get out of this car and head up to my apartment?"

I nodded. At least, I thought I was nodding. I decided to nod a few more times just for good measure. You could never be sure about a nod. They could be tricky little things.

"Okay, wrap your arms around my neck. I'm going to carry you upstairs."

"Oh, yeah. Carry me, Kline. Carry me so good."

Big arms wrapped around my body, pulling me out of the car. Once I was airborne—swaddled up in strong muscles and delicious male pheromones mixed with sexy cologne—my voice decided to make its debut. If there was ever a time for a song, it was right now, while Kline carried me past a doorman and through a lobby I'd never seen.

"Wicky, wicky, wicky, beatbox! K-K-Kline looks like sex and he's so clean, clean!"

I'd always had a talent for freestyling.

"Wicky, wicky, wicky, beatbox! Big-dicked Brooks in da house! Can I get an Amen! Wicky, wicky, wicky, remix!"

"Georgia," Kline whispered through a laugh. "I need to set you down for a second while I get my keys."

My feet touched the ground and the hallway morphed into a dervish's wheel, spinning around in a hypnotic display of plush velvet rugs and cream-colored walls. "Whoa, settle down, hallway! You're outta control!" I reached for the wall, but he was quicker, gripping my waist and stopping my forward momentum.

"Here we go," he instructed, maneuvering me through the door and inside his apartment. "Let's get you settled on the couch and maybe get some non-alcoholic fluids in you."

I threw my body onto the leather sofa, nuzzling my face into the pillows. "Oh yeah, baby. Now, this is the kind of couch I'm talking about."

"Georgia." Kline's face was inches from mine, his long fingers settling below my chin.

"Hey, where'd you come from?" I asked, peeking out from my pillow fort. "I thought you were by the door. Man, you're quick. Are you working out?"

He smiled, blue eyes working their magic on my libido. *Li-bee-dough.* What a weird word. It sounded more courtroom than sex. *"I'd like the record to show he was badgering my key witness for a libido!"* See what I mean?

"Georgia, sweetheart," Kline summoned my gaze. And son of a hooker nut, there were those blue eyes again. Surely, they were trying to hypnotize my vagina. It was working, by the way.

Any minute, my panties would just, *poof!*, disappear into thin air.

"Have mercy," I whispered. "That smile, plus those eyes, it's like a sex cream sundae. I want two scoops."

A small laugh left his lips. "How about we start with a drink first? What sounds good? I've got water, tea, coffee?"

"I'll take the vodka. But on the rocks, please."

He shook his head, amused. "Vodka wasn't an option."

"It wasn't?" I tilted my head and realized things felt so much better with my head resting on the pillows.

"How about you just rest here while I get the drinks?"

"Yes, sir." I saluted him.

"Wait!" I shrieked before he even made it a foot. I had something to tell him, and I had to tell him *now*.

"Yeah, baby?" he asked, concern mixing deliciously with just a hint of a smile.

"You're the best kisser on this side of the Mississippi. NO! The best kisser in the whole entire world!" My voice turned grave. "I'm talking, I've never had better *in my life*."

Any concern disappeared as though it'd never been there.

"Yeah?" His blue eyes twinkled like actual glitter. Like he went to Michael's, got a jar of it, and then poured it in his irises.

"Ohhh, yeah," I agreed before reaching out and yanking him back to me with a fist in his shirt.

A chuckle rumbled his chest as I pushed mine to it tightly and slammed my lips to his without apology. They were just so soft and plump and *mmm, that groan tasted good*. I took what I wanted, exploring and plundering his mouth even though my face wouldn't seem to fucking cooperate. I shoved him away softly, ordering a needy "Thirsty!" in someone else's squeaky voice.

He shook his head and smiled, retreating without a word.

His footsteps moved farther away, toward the land of drinks, I was sure.

My fingers moved to my face, tapping my nose, and then my cheeks, and then my lips. Oh my, these things were bigger than I remembered. I grabbed my boobs just to see if other things had doubled in size.

Damn, no such luck.

If I was Goldilocks and this was the three bears' apartment, this room was too fucking hot.

Relocation was needed. My feet flopped onto the floor. Heels were kicked off across the room, clanking against the wall. Once I got my sea legs in order, I tip-toed into the hallway.

Peeking into the room at the end of the hall, I found a king-size bed summoning me.

"Oh, yes. Come to mama!"

I cannonballed into the bed, fluffy comforter and pillows bouncing around me.

After a few body rolls from one side to the next, I found that it wasn't the room that was stifling my temperate vibe; it was my clothes. Too many clothes.

How'd I get so many clothes on?

I stood at the foot of the bed while my numb fingers worked at the zipper of my dress. It took a bit for me to figure out the zipper was just for show. Someone had superglued me into it. *Geez Louis-a May Alcott, the price we women pay for beauty.*

My hands tore at the front of the dress until the initial rip echoed inside the room.

"Now, that's what I'm talking about."

I got down to my skivvies and decided even those were not up to par for the bed. Call it a superpower, but I could sense when a bed wanted me naked. The king had spoken, and naked was his final offer.

No one could deny the glorious feeling of rolling around naked under a soft sheet. My face met the pillow, and then my nose felt it was the perfect time to sniff the delicious Kline Brooks aroma embedded in the material. God, he smelled good. Like clean laundry and man soap and *I'm going to fuck him.*

Boy, that escalated quickly.

The Benadryl had become my truth serum. I wanted to sex him. I wanted to hand him a valentine that said, "Be my cherry popper," and spread my legs as far as those babies would go. I knew valentines were only meant for a particular holiday, but this felt like an exception to the rule.

"Georgia?" Kline's voice moved down the hallway.

"I'm in here!" I called back.

His tall frame moved through the doorway, finding me luxuriating in the bedding.

"Comfortable?" he asked.

"Oh yeah, baby." I patted the spot beside me. "Come join me. I don't know whose bed this is, but hells bells, it's wonderful."

"It's my bed." He chuckled, setting two glasses on the nightstand and sitting on the edge.

I sat up, holding the comforter to my chest. "This is your bed?"

He nodded, eyes moving to my bare shoulders.

"Well, I'll be damned. I'm a fan of your bed. Big fan. The biggest fan."

His eyes moved around the room, searching for something. His jaw dropped when whatever he was looking for came into view. "Are you naked?" he asked, swallowing hard enough to make his Adam's apple bob.

"The bed made me do it."

"My bed made you get naked?"

"He's a real pervy bastard, but who was I to argue?" I shrugged, the comforter falling to my waist.

Kline's spine stiffened, averting his gaze toward the floor.

I touched his shoulder. "Everything okay?"

"Uh-huh." He coughed out a laugh.

"Is one of those for me?" I nodded at the table.

"Please." He gestured toward the glasses. "Help yourself."

"Only if you stop looking so uncomfortable."

That caught his attention, his curious eyes meeting mine. "Uncomfortable?"

"Yeah. You look really uncomfortable. I insist that you take your shoes off and sit back on the bed."

He ran a hand through his hair. "Georgia, I'm not sure that's such a good idea."

"Of course it is, you silly, gorgeous piece of man meat!" I got to my knees, forcing his body to lie back on the bed. Straddling his hips, I stared down at him. "See what I mean? It's so comfortable down there, isn't it?"

"It sure is something." His gaze raked down my completely bare body, going darker with each second that passed.

While he made himself cozy, I grabbed a glass from the nightstand and took a satisfying drink. "This vodka is delicious. Not very strong, though."

"That's because it's water."

"Hmmmph. Well, look at that."

Kline hesitantly gripped my waist. "I think I should grab you some clothes to wear to bed."

My mouth formed a pout. "Do you not like seeing me naked, Kline? Naked time is fun time."

He shook his head and muttered under his breath, "*Dear fucking Lucifer.*" He cleared his throat. "Shit, Georgie. I don't think I've ever seen anything better than you naked. And *God*, I want naked time to be fun time. I want it really fucking bad."

"Well, then what's the big rush? I'm starting to understand all the fuss about nudist colonies. There's a lot to be said for being naked, Kline. I think you should try it." I moved my hands to his belt, slipping the metal from the prongs.

"This probably isn't a good idea." He stopped my progress before I made my way to his zipper.

I looked up at him, my ass resting against Kline's better half—

his bigger, thicker half. The one that seemed to wholeheartedly—or *wholecockedly*—disagree with him. "I think you're wrong. I think you think this is a really good idea." To emphasize my point, I rolled my hips against him.

Jesus. His dick.

Wait, that sounded a little sacrilege.

Kline. His dick.

There, that was better.

"Kline," I moaned, rubbing my clit against him. "This. Feels. So. Good."

"Shit," he groaned, his fingers digging into my hips. "We shouldn't be doing this, but *fuck*. You're gorgeous and naked and *wet*. So fucking wet. I can feel you through my clothes."

"You make me crazy," I half growled like an animal. "I want to kiss you, lick you, suck you, ride you. I want to do *everything*. Right. Now." I leaned forward, pressing one pert nipple to his lips.

He sucked me into his mouth, his tongue flicking my nipple and urging heat to flush across my skin.

"You have the best tits, Georgia. The best fucking tits." He moved to the other breast, kissing and sucking and licking me into a frenzy.

"God, yes. Keep doing that," I begged.

He gripped my chin, pulling my face to his. His lips crashed against mine. We were a delicious mess of tongues and lips and hips grinding and hands groping.

"You're too perfect," he whispered against my skin. "I can't get enough of you."

"I want you to have all of me," I urged. "I want you inside of me, Kline. God, I want it so bad. Christopher Columbus the fuck out of my pussy prideland!"

"What?" he asked as he stilled.

The words ran through my head enough to know I'd screwed some sort of pooch by alluding that my pooch had yet to be screwed.

"What?" I repeated back, attempting, and failing, to be the absolute picture of aloof.

His fingers held my hips still. Blue eyes stared deep into mine before shutting closed.

"Kline? What's wrong?"

His gaze met mine again. "We can't do this, not like this."

"Of course, we can," I disagreed. "I'm naked. You're hard. This seems like the perfect time for screwing. It's like Marvin Gaye himself put us in this moment and whispered, 'Go ahead and let's get it on.'"

A grin kissed his lips. "God, you're adorable," he said, biting back a laugh.

"No." I pouted. "I'm sexy and naked and ready to fornicate."

He quirked a brow. "Fornicate?"

"Penetrate?" I offered, hoping it sounded more enticing.

"Baby, I'm losing my mind over how sexy and beautiful you are, but I'm also trying to be a gentleman here. You're a little under the influence, remember?"

I frowned, mentally counting the amount of drinks I'd had throughout the night.

"I didn't drink that much."

"I'm not talking about alcohol."

My eyes went wide. "Did we do drugs?!"

His grin consumed his face, dimples peeking out and saying hello. "Calm down," he said, humor in his voice. "We didn't do drugs. Not in the illegal sense. But *you* had a crazy amount of Benadryl."

"Oh, I forgot about that."

"So, Benny girl, I think we should press pause on this fantastic moment—because you can bet that sexy ass of yours I want to revisit this—and let's throw some clothes on you and find something a little less tempting to do."

I thought it over for a second. "Do you have any pizza?"

A wry grin creased his mouth. "You want pizza?"

I nodded. "Pizza and Netflix. We'll save the chill part for later."

Kline lifted me off the bed and onto my feet as he sat up. "How about you rummage through my closet and find something you like and I'll order us one?"

I pressed a soft kiss to his lips. "Deal."

As I turned for the closet, his hand met my ass, spanking a high-pitched squeal right from my lips.

"Hey!" I shouted, turning toward him.

He shrugged, smirking like the devil. "Can't expect a man to ignore a perfect ass shimmying around in front of his face."

"I was *not* shimmying."

"Baby, you were shimmying. But don't worry, I was definitely watching and enjoying the show."

I ignored him, striding—*okay, sashaying*—into his walk-in closet, where I enjoyed a few moments to myself to swoon over the whole "Baby" sentiment.

There may have been jumping and silent screaming. Who knows? Maybe I even buried my nose into his dress shirts and put myself in a momentary Kline-induced coma?

But I will tell you this.

The pizza was fucking delicious.

CHAPTER 14

Kline

Confused and sleepy, Georgia stumbled out of my bedroom and into the hall, the light from my sun-beaten bedroom windows backlighting her in the doorway. My shirt hung off of her tiny frame in a bloblike shadow and covered her completely, but the image of her naked body underneath was burned on my brain from having it straddling me last night.

She'd been out of her mind, completely out of control, and most of all, irresistibly fucking adorable. She made the term hot mess look good, and the rambling thoughts of her Benadryl-influenced mind would stick with me forever.

Honestly, I didn't know if I'd ever met someone funnier—and I knew a whole lot of brilliantly funny people.

"I feel like someone buried me alive last night and I spent all twelve hours trying to claw my way out."

I smiled apologetically.

She stopped to lean on the wall at the mouth of the hallway, putting the tips of her fingers of one hand to the skin of her forehead.

"I'm so sorry about last night," I told her.

But I wasn't sorry. Not really anyway. The only thing I regretted was that I should have taken her to the goddamn hospital in spite of her protests. It could have turned out so much worse. My Catholic roots were a little rusty, but I'd dust off the old prayer playbook to thank the big guy for keeping an eye on this one.

Inching her way into the room, she settled on the other end of the couch and pulled her knees carefully into her chest, stretching the cotton of my t-shirt to cover them.

"Fucking lime juice," she muttered into her knees, the skin of her now normal lips teasing the soft knit of the fabric before looking up at me. "Scotch with lime juice, really? Who even drinks that?"

I leaned back into the couch, stretching an arm along the back and propping my feet up on the coffee table in front of me to keep from reaching out and running a finger along those lips.

"Ernest Hemingway drank scotch with lime juice."

She chewed the recently healed skin nervously, and I could imagine what she was thinking. Trying to assess how she felt about waking up here, with me, at the same time she considered what I said. She seemed genuinely intrigued that I'd know something like that, but she warred with herself when it came to concentration on it. "Really?"

I laughed, explaining, "Well, I never witnessed it for myself, but I read it once somewhere, yeah."

A smile crept into the corners of her mouth and brightened the blue of her eyes. And the maroon of my shirt already had them blazing.

Moving her eyes from the couch to the kitchen, down the hall and back again, she asked, "What is this place?"

I pinched one eye in winklike confusion, attempted to survey the scene from her point of view, and then answered the only way I could. "Uh, it's my apartment."

"*Your* apartment?"

"Yeah." I shook my head. "Why did you say 'your apartment' like it's infested with bed bugs?"

"No!" she denied vehemently in surprise. "No, it's nice. It's just…"
Silence lingered where words should have been.

"It's…" I prompted. "What?"

Her cheeks puffed out slightly with the sour taste of her thoughts, and I could see her run the scenario of saying it out loud through her head more than once.

"*Georgie*. It's what?"

"*Normal.*"

A laugh slipped out. "Yeah, well. So am I."

And it wasn't *that* normal, I thought a little bitterly. It had a doorman, for fuck's sake. I was a single guy. What the fuck did I need a penthouse with six bedrooms for?

I didn't want Georgia to think I needed some big apartment. I wanted her to *get* it.

"No," she disagreed. "*You're* Kline Brooks."

I just shook my head, trying to find the right words to describe how much nothing my fucking name meant to me—and how very little it should mean to everyone else.

"Trust me, that name doesn't mean nearly the same thing to me, my relatives, or any of my friends as it does to other people."

She untucked her knees from my shirt, stretching her long, tan legs out on the couch toward me and crossing them at the ankles. Unable to resist, I reached down and rested the palm of my hand on her bare shin.

She watched it happen and paused for just a few seconds before looking back up and into my eyes. She forced serenity over her features, but discomfort lived just under the surface. It wasn't that she didn't want it; she just felt awkward because it had been unexpected.

"What's it mean to your family?"

"I don't know." I searched my mind for the best way to put it, ignoring her minor discomfort and running a thumb along the skin of her calf casually. "A guy who eats way more pizza than he should and has sweaty feet and a grumpy cat who hates him."

"Meowwww," Walter said on cue, hopping up onto the arm of the couch and startling her.

"Oh!"

"Speak of the devil."

"Hi?" she prompted.

"Walter."

"Hi, Walter," she cooed, turning her upper body and rubbing his back from head to tail.

He purred and nudged into her. "Meowwwww."

"Sure," I scoffed. "Bond with the pretty girl. How fucking predictable."

"Was he here last night?" she asked haltingly.

I bit my lips to stave off the urge to go into detail. "Uh…yeah. The two of you had quite the lengthy conversation." They had. Georgia and Walter had bonded over pepperoni pizza and reruns of *Friends*. She sang "Smelly Cat" to him no less than fifteen times.

The snooty motherfucker purred for every single one of them.

She nodded as if that made sense. "He seems like the friendly sort."

I scoffed audibly.

"Maybe that's your problem," she suggested simply, scratching behind his ears like they were old lawyer friends there to co-prosecute my trial. "You're being kind of an asshole to Walter. He responds to kind words and soft touches."

"Are you kidding me?!" I nearly yelled, pointing to myself and then back at my grumpy old cat wildly. "I'm not the asshole! *He's* the asshole! I tried to bring that cat around to me for weeks. I'm just treating him how he treats me now."

Walter leaned into her as if scared. That fucking cat con-artist!

"Aw, it's okay, Walter," Georgie swore sweetly, tucking his kitty face between her hands and rubbing their noses together. "I'll protect you from the bad, scary man." Her face turned conspiratorial, an eyebrow arching up menacingly to match the traitor-cat, as she looked me in the eye again. "I know how you feel. He tried to poison me last night!"

"I didn't poison her," I told him calmly, going along with this crazy conversation for some reason. "I ordered the same drink I've been ordering for ten years, and then I gave her the best kiss of her life."

Georgie's playful eyes jumped to mine and turned serious. Panicked even.

"It was not the best kiss of my—"

"Uh-uh-uh." I tsked with a wave of my finger. "Don't lie now, Benny. I know it was the best kiss of your life for a fact."

"And how do you claim to know that?"

"Because last night you told me so yourself."

She gasped. Walter hissed in camaraderie.

"Right before you kissed me again—"

Her cheeks flushed with embarrassment, and everything about her posture said she was two seconds away from sprinting straight out the door.

But I knew there was more, and I gave it to her, sliding a gentle hand from her shin up to her knee as I did. Walter jumped down and trotted off in protest, but we both ignored him.

"And they were both the best kisses of mine." I decided not to focus on the fact that beyond those kisses, she'd given me much more— including a naked lap dance. With the way her skin burned red about the kisses, I thought the trauma of the rest might make her actually combust.

She opened her mouth just to close it again and forced a visible swallow down her throat. I gave her the time she needed, the time to process my words and run them through a cross-check with her emotions.

I'd had all night, listening to her and enjoying her, to prepare for the blow. She hadn't.

Just when I thought she might actually say something in return, her phone started to play the opening beats of "Freek-A-Leek" by

Petey Pablo.

It was horrendously endearing.

I had Thatch to thank for that kind of music knowledge myself. It used to be one of his favorite songs in our much wilder post-college days.

She jumped up in a hurry, pink hitting her cheeks with embarrassment.

"Sorry. For the awkward ringtone and the interruption—"

"It's okay," I consoled with a smile and a wink. "It would have been way more awkward had Shonda, Monique, and Christina called you last night at the benefit." Her eyes widened in shock.

"Me, it doesn't bother so much. I'm actually *looking for the goodies*," I teased, referencing another one of Petey Pablo and Ciara's masterpieces I knew she'd recognize.

And it worked, surprising her so much that she almost didn't make it to the kitchen to answer her phone before it stopped ringing.

I really wasn't much of a mystery, but she was convinced I was.

With the way I craved her company, I planned to enroll her in the accelerated education program and keep her there until she had me mastered.

CHAPTER 15

Georgia

The terrace door clicked shut as I answered Will's call. "Hey, stranger, I'm surprised you're awake right now." Elbows resting on the banister, the sounds of an already popping Upper East Side hustled and bustled below me. "Rough call shift?"

"The ER was hopping last night." Will's raspy, exhausted voice filled my ear. "From the random text I got last night, it appears you had an interesting evening. Night on the town with Cass?"

"Huh?" I tilted my head to the side. How on Earth would my brother know about my night?

"Oh, come on, Gigi." He chuckled softly in my ear. "Have you checked your text messages?"

My face twisted into utter bewilderment. "Text messages?"

"You sent me a text message. To which I did attempt to respond, but honestly, I didn't have a clue what in the hell you were talking about."

I tried to recount last night's events, but my brain still had a residual Benadryl fog.

"Check your messages."

I tapped the screen, putting Will on speaker, while I scrolled through my text conversations.

Me: WILL CAN AN OC GIVE A BENNY!&*

Will: I'd like to buy a vowel, Pat.

Will: Gigi? Hello????

Will: Your Masturbation Camp PTSD is flaring again, isn't it?

Will: You're going to be so fucking sick in the morning.

Will: Seriously, text me if you need anything. I'm pulling an all-nighter in the ER.

Masturbation Camp. My adolescent nightmare that Will won't let me forget about.

Since my mother was a sex therapist, my introduction to sexual health was not the norm. Three days after my thirteenth birthday, I got my period. While most mothers took their daughters to the drug store to buy pads or tampons, my mother signed me up for Camp Love Yourself.

Before your mind wanders to weird and disturbing places, I should explain that we weren't sitting around naked, diddling ourselves to Justin Timberlake music videos.

It was a two-week summer camp focused around teaching teenage girls about sex education, as well as encouraging girls to explore their sexuality in a healthy and safe way. Which explained why my older brother called it "Masturbation Camp."

My empowered and liberated mother was a strong advocate for

Camp Love Yourself and their pro rub-yourself stance. "A few rounds of masturbation a day keeps the babies away, Georgia Rose. It's proven that you're less likely to give in to your teenage hormones if you're exploring your sexuality through healthy, self-love methods."

Needless to say, my experience at "Masturbation Camp" had been about as horrifying and awkward as you'd expect.

It had taken me a good three years to get past the emotional trauma from sitting around a campfire, singing "Kumbaya" with counselor Feather (yes, that was her legal name), while she encouraged us to roast vagina-shaped marshmallows for s'mores. This was one of those life moments where, even ten or fifteen years down the road, I was still wondering if it had really happened.

"Seriously, Wilbur? How many years are you gonna hold on to the Masturbation Camp bit?"

"Forever," he responded, laughing. "That shit will never get old."

I sighed. "You're the world's worst older brother, you know that?"

The insult deflected off of him with ease.

"So, what in the hell were you up to last night?"

Glancing down at the text messages between Will and me, memories from last night hijacked my brain, taking it hostage.

The dance. That kiss. My lips. Benadryl. Kline's bed.

My jaw hit the terrace, my eyes going wide in shock. The details were hazy, but the basics stood out enough to worry me.

Did I really get naked in his bed last night?

"Gigi? You still there?"

Moments and snapshots from twelve or so hours prior flooded my head. *"I'm sexy and naked and ready to fornicate."*

"Oh, no." I covered my mouth with my hand.

"What's wrong?"

"Bye, Will."

"Hey! Wha—"

I ended the call. I didn't have time for his shenanigans or the hour-long physician's lecture that would have occurred had I told him about my allergic reaction. No doubt, Will would've been furious I didn't go to the emergency room last night.

This moment required an immediate call to Cassie. The line rang three times before she answered, her voice drugged with sleep. "It's kind of early, Wheorgie."

Forgoing pleasantries, I dove right into my current situation, highlighting the main points. My ramble lasted a good three minutes, only pausing to take a quick breath between run-on sentences.

"So, what you're telling me is that your date with Kline started off great, until you had an allergic reaction and your face ballooned up like a blimp? And then you chugged a bottle of Benadryl, got naked in his bed, and attempted to hand him your lady flower, but you guys just ended up eating pizza instead?"

"It sounds even worse when you repeat it back to me," I whined.

"Where are you right now?"

"I'm in his apartment, standing outside on the terrace so he can't hear me freaking the fuck out."

"And you stayed at his place last night?"

"Yeah, I woke up in his bed this morning."

"Did he try to usher your ass out of his bed the second you woke up?"

I shook my head. She didn't respond.

"See, the way phone conversations work, is that you actually have to say the words out loud."

"You're such a pain in the ass," I retorted. "And no, he didn't try to push me out of bed and send me packing. He was actually pretty sweet."

"I'm not sure what the problem is, then."

"Are you serious?" I shouted. "I'm mortified, Cass! I pretty much made a fool out of myself last night! I don't even—"

"Hey," she interrupted my rant.

"What?" I snapped back.

"Take a breath and think this over," she coaxed, her voice cool and calm. "Sure, things didn't go as planned, *but*…you're still at his apartment. He's not acting weird. He didn't try to shove you out the door. Right?"

I nodded.

"I'm assuming you're nodding your head, so I shall continue," she said, amusement highlighting her voice. "You have two options here, Georgie. You can either grab your shit and make a beeline for the door and continue to stew in your mortification back at our apartment. Or you can get some tits and go in there and demand a re-do."

"A re-do?"

"Demand you finish that amazing kiss. Or, you know, turn that sexy lip-lock into something else. Something more *orally* challenging."

I ran through my options. I could either let self-doubt rule my brain or walk back into his apartment and show him what a confident, self-assured woman looks like when she's ready to take what she wants.

"You're right," I agreed, steadfast in my decision. "Embarrassment can go fuck itself. It's time for a re-do."

"That's my girl."

"I love you, Casshead."

"Love you too," she responded, a smile in her voice. "Now, stop wasting time and go in there and kiss the hell out of Big-dicked Brooks."

"Okay, that's my cue to end this call," I teased. "Have fun snapping pics of muscly men."

"Oh, the fun has already been had, my dear. I plan on having even more fun tonight, *without* a lens in front of my face."

I smiled, my nerves finally at ease. "I miss your crazy ass."

"Miss you too, sweet cheeks. Call me later and let me know how things went."

"You got it."

"But make sure it's tomorrow because I'm about to be balls deep in my best impression of a rodeo queen. The Italian Stallion—"

"I'm hanging up now!"

Her laugh was the last thing I heard as I tapped end on the call.

Turning for the door, I stopped mid-step, my eyes meeting my reflection in the glass panes. I did a quick once-over, taking inventory of my current state. My hair was a little askew, pulled up in a messy bun. My legs peeked out from beneath Kline's Harvard cotton tee. My ass was covered by a pair of white cotton boy shorts. It wasn't my sexiest of days, but I didn't look awful. And surprisingly, my lips had gone back to their normal size.

I sniffed the collar of his t-shirt, and despite the clean scent, remnants of his cologne managed to linger on the freshly laundered material. *God, he really did smell good.* Kline just might have been my very own aphrodisiac.

I wanted him. And I was hell-bent on taking what I wanted.

Walking through the doors, I left any inkling of self-doubt on the terrace, finding him shirtless, standing at the sink of his master bathroom. His perfect ass was clad in boxer briefs and nothing else, wide shoulders on display, muscles stretching as he brushed his teeth. His biceps flexed as he finished up, turning off the sink.

His body was perfect. Defined with just enough bulk. Smooth skin sweetened the deal, leading from his muscular shoulders to his defined pectorals. I wanted to trace the lines with my tongue. He didn't shave or wax his chest like guys on magazine covers. No, Kline Brooks was a *man.* A beautiful, sexy man with a natural smattering of dark hair on his chest. His abdomen was defined with ridges and hard lines that led down into a glorious V, and a soft, just barely noticeable trail of hair paved a path from his belly button to territory I'd have had to remove his boxer briefs to see.

I wanted to lick that happy trail, spend some time there, make a fucking day out of it.

My body was getting way too excited over the possibilities.

Cool it, Georgia. Slow your horny roll.

I wanted a re-do of our first kiss, not the beginning of a porno flick.

Cornflower blue eyes, with the tiniest bit of yellow lining the contrasting black pupils, met mine in the mirror. "Everything okay?"

I nodded, moving toward the sink and plucking his just-used toothbrush from the holder. Without hesitation, I made myself at home, putting a glob of toothpaste on the bristles and going to town on cleaning my teeth.

Kline watched with amusement.

"You don't mind, do you?" I asked after two circuits on my top teeth.

"Not at all," he responded, smirking. That perfect ass of his found the edge of the sink as he continued to observe.

"I need a favor," I stated, turning off the sink and wiping my face with the hand towel.

"Favor?"

"Uh-huh. It's a mighty big favor, but there's a possibility it will benefit you greatly."

"I'm all ears, Benny girl." He winked, amused with my new nickname. Though I was less impressed with his creativity than he was, I still felt a tingle.

"Do you have an iPod dock anywhere in the apartment?"

His gaze turned intrigued. "In my bedroom, on the dresser beside the terrace doors."

"Perfect," I said over my shoulder, walking that direction.

He followed me, sitting on the bed, while I set my phone in the dock and found the perfect re-do song.

The Drifters' "Some Kind of Wonderful" filled the room.

"I know this wasn't the song we heard after our dance," I pointed out, shrugging, "but it's my favorite 'Some Kind of Wonderful.'"

"Hmm, I don't know. The first version seemed pretty good to me." He tapped his chin thoughtfully. "I can relate to the lyrics."

I put a hand on my hip. "Is that so?"

He nodded. "I think most men come to a point in their lives where the concept of one right woman above all other things seems logical—warranted, even."

I swooned. Head, heart, stomach—my entire body was in on it.

"Well, this is *my* show, so this is our some kind of wonderful for right now."

Kline grinned.

My bare feet moved across the soft carpet, stopping once my knees tapped his. "Stand up, please." I gestured with my hand. "I want a re-do. I want to finish what we started, *before* you tried to kill me with lime juice." A teasing smirk crested my lips.

"I did not try to kill you," he said through a chuckle, getting to his feet. "But, I *am* saying yes to the favor."

Blue-tinted tenderness gazed down at me, while strong hands slipped under cotton, finding the curve of my hips.

"I'm sorry I ruined our date last night," I whispered.

"You didn't ruin anything."

I cocked a disagreeing brow.

"Georgie, I had an amazing time." He touched my cheek, warmth spreading across my skin. "And I'd do it all over again. Allergic reaction and Benny high, I'd still do it all over again. You're pretty damn adorable when you're buzzing on antihistamines."

Good Lord, I can only imagine the kind of crazy things that were coming out of my mouth last night...

Self-doubt could be a real tricky bitch. Even when you thought you had her under control, she found a way to creep back in, making you analyze everything. Despite my earlier confidence, I had reached that moment.

"Please, don't remind me of anything I said or did. I have enough embarrassment stocked up to last a lifetime." I groaned, burying my face in his bare chest.

Kline consumed me in a hug. He held me for a long moment, shouldering my mortification. Lips found my ear and whispered, "Do you want to know something?"

"What?" I asked, my voice muffled against his skin.

"I'm glad you're here."

"Really?"

"Yeah, Benny girl, and now, I'm ready for our re-do."

I leaned back, staring up at him. The man I'd come to know as Mr. Brooks, CEO and well-known mogul of the online dating industry, was morphing into someone different. He wasn't just the serious man whose life solely revolved around business. He was funny and sweet and lived in the moment. He wasn't the flashy, ostentatious billionaire I pictured living in a million-dollar apartment. He was practical and humble, so damn humble. He was someone I wanted to spend more time with. He was someone I could see myself *falling* for.

He wasn't Mr. Brooks anymore. He was Kline, the man I wanted to take a *real* chance on. It shocked me how little time it took to recognize the difference.

I slid my hands up his back, savoring the feel of his toned and smooth skin. Gripping the nape of his neck, I rocked my feet forward, standing tippy-toed. Desperate to feel his mouth on mine, I made the first move, slowly, softly, pressing my lips to his and coaxing a kiss from him.

He responded with fervor, sliding his tongue across my bottom lip and then slipping it inside my mouth to dance with mine. In a matter of seconds, our kiss turned heated, hands groping, tongues clashing. Kline gripped the cotton material covering my skin and removed it from my body, tossing it haphazardly across the room.

My breasts pressed against his chest as he pulled me closer. I moaned into his mouth when his hands met the curve of my back, sliding to my ass and slipping under my boy shorts. He gripped my bare skin for a beat before slipping his hands back up the curve of my spine, leaving my underwear back in place in his wake.

It was a crazy-hot move.

"Get on the bed, Georgie," he demanded, turning our bodies and guiding me toward the mattress.

I lay back, staring up at him. Uncertainty started to sneak in. I was worried he might expect more out of this moment than I was prepared to give. But the way he was looking at me—it was enough to make me forget my own name. Light blue eyes took in every inch of my exposed skin, darkening closer to navy by the second.

I couldn't think about anything else besides him touching me.

He rested his hands beside my head, body hovering above mine. His tongue licked a line down my jaw, to my neck, until his lips were sucking a sensual path between my breasts.

"Now, *I* need a favor," he whispered against my skin. "Let me taste you, sweet girl." He sucked a nipple into his mouth, his skilled tongue eliciting panting breaths from my lungs. "Let me taste every inch of this perfect body. Let me hear what you sound like when you come."

"Yes. God, yes," I whimpered.

He grinned against my skin, fingers sliding down my stomach until they found my boy shorts, slipping them down my legs and off my body. Strong hands gripped my thighs, spreading and baring me to his heated gaze.

"You are so beautiful."

He kneeled between my legs, slipping a finger between my lips and sliding through my arousal. "You're soaked and so fucking soft. I want to lick up and down every part of this." His finger traveled the slit and flicked the clit at the top for emphasis. "I'm hard just thinking about how good you'll taste."

Nerves started to fill my stomach with second thoughts. He didn't know I was a virgin. And I knew, even though I was really into him, I wasn't ready to take that kind of step. "Kline," I whispered, my voice too shaky and quiet for him to hear.

"Now this is the kind of pussy a guy can get along with," he said, flashing a wink in my direction.

And just like that, his playfulness washed my worries out to sea.

"Just how good of friends are you?" I asked.

He smiled. The bastard.

"I know *her* really well."

My eyes narrowed, and he smiled harder.

"But it's the kind of friendship built on trust and respect, and I *never* have more than one friend at a time."

God, this man. He didn't even know how good he was for me.

"That's good to hear because this pussy doesn't have more than one friend at a time either. And she demands respect and trust before letting anyone *all the way in.*"

"Duly noted." He ran his tongue up the inside of my thigh. "Let the record show, I'm the kind of man who doesn't rush things. I like to take my time and savor every moment, *every single inch.*" He moved to the other leg, repeating the same sexy-as-hell move. "And, Georgia?"

"Yeah?"

He slipped a finger inside of me and out again before sliding it into his mouth. He moaned audibly and closed his eyes. "You're going to melt on my tongue."

Holy hell.

"I think I'm already melting," I whimpered, my head falling back on the bed.

"No, baby, you haven't even started to melt yet," he whispered, moving his tongue against me.

God, it felt so good. So fucking good.

I swallowed my moans, gripping the sheet for support. It was intense. My orgasm was building far quicker and stronger than anything I'd experienced. My legs and hips shook as he sucked my clit into his mouth, his tongue working me into a frenzy.

But he didn't let up.

He gripped my thighs, keeping me spread wide for his ministrations.

My fingers found his hair while my hips moved of their own accord, grinding against his mouth, riding his tongue.

This was the hottest round of oral I'd ever received in my life.

He repeatedly built me up, only to slow things down when I got too close.

He wasn't racing to get me off; *no*, he was savoring every second. He told me how good I tasted and how hard he was just from watching me slowly lose control. He told me how sexy I was and how he never wanted to stop.

"Please, Kline. Oh fuck, please," I begged. I didn't even know what I was begging for. I wanted him to get me off—*badly*—yet I never wanted this to end.

"My greedy girl." He sucked harder and my back bowed off the bed.

"Oh, God," I moaned.

"Do me a favor, Georgie. When you come, don't hold back. I *need* to hear your sounds."

"Yes. Yes. Yes," I chanted, too consumed with the orgasm about to pull me under. Hell, he could've asked me to put on a top hat and sing the "Star Spangled Banner" when I came. I would've agreed to anything in that moment. Though, that might have made things a little more awkward.

He grabbed my breasts, caressing the pliant flesh possessively, while his mouth pushed me toward the edge.

My eyes rolled back, gasping breaths escaping my lungs.

"Say it," he demanded.

I moaned, moving my hands to his hair and gripping the strands for leverage. My hips had a mind of their own, grinding into this face with reckless abandon.

"Fucking *say it*, sweet girl." The sexy growl to his voice was enough to push me over.

"Yes! Kline! I'm coming!" My body lost control—legs shaking, lungs gasping for breaths. My pulse roared in my ears.

I didn't just melt. I *dissolved*. And I gave him my sounds. I'm not sure *what* sounds, but I remember shouting, "*This is the best orgasm of my life!*" at some point.

I'm pretty sure I lost consciousness for a moment, only to be stirred when strong hands cradled my body, adjusting me on the bed so my head rested comfortably on the pillows.

My eyelids fluttered opened to find a smirking Kline staring down at me.

He pressed a kiss to my mouth. "Thank you. That was the best orgasm of my life too," he said softly against my lips.

His mouth crested into a wry grin as he stood, adjusting himself in his briefs. He was hard and standing at attention, making his appearance the hottest, most obscene thing I'd ever laid eyes on.

"Now, I think it's time for breakfast. Eggs and bacon sound good to you?"

I glanced down at his crotch, shocked by the nonchalant tone of his voice. His dick was saluting me, yet he didn't seem the least bit affected by his current *situation.*

"But you're, uh, hard." And I mean fucking hard. That soldier was ready for all-out war.

"Seems to be a common occurrence when you're around." He winked and walked toward the doorway, only to shout, "Meet me in the kitchen, Benny girl!" over his shoulder as he strode out of the bedroom.

Did he just…? He did, didn't he?

Orgasms never helped my eloquence with words, but Kline Brooks was a giver.

Like whoa.

This wasn't the norm. We'd all been with the norm. The guys who would only go down on you because they were expecting some sort of oral exchange. Once you'd gotten your rocks off, they were flashing slanty-eyed glances toward their dicks, waiting for you to return the favor. They'd do everything just short of shoving their crotch in your face. They'd rattle off options like an auctioneer: *Blow job? Hand job? Just hold it for a minute? Let me hold your tit while I jerk off?*

They might as well have had flashing neon arrows pointing to their pants or, better yet, taken out a piece of paper and drawn a "here is my dick" treasure map, just in case we might have forgotten where the male member was located.

But Kline hadn't done that.

He'd straight up licked me into an orgasm and then said, "Thank you."

He had thanked *me* for letting him go down on me.

I'd never claimed to be a genius, but I was pretty sure Kline Brooks had just *wham, bam, and you can thank me, ma'am*ed me.

It was the sexiest fucking thing I'd ever experienced.

CHAPTER 16

Kline

Uncomfortable was too cushy a word to describe the kind of hell I was in right now. Hard and engorged, my ax was ready to chop some fucking wood, and because of the redistribution of blood flow, my brain was having a hard time explaining why it couldn't.

It wasn't that I didn't want to, that was for goddamn sure. But Georgie's overall discomfort was easy enough to read. I knew she'd enjoyed my mouth on her—I doubted as much as I had—but she would have reciprocated out of duty or expectation. And honestly, the first time she sucked my cock, I wanted it to be because she *wanted* to. Because she couldn't fucking stand not to.

Gripping the base tight through my underwear, I fought to stop the pulsing and bring it even a little bit of relief.

When the fiery depths of hell felt more like the heat of Death Valley, I rearranged myself into the best position and got to work digging out a skillet to make some omelets.

Eggs, turkey bacon, and cheese, I lined the basic ingredients up on the counter and put some cooking spray in the bottom of the skillet. Poised to crack the first egg directly into the waiting heat, I had a flashing memory of Georgia's swollen face last night and panicked. The egg nearly slipped from my hand, a completely graceless juggle the only thing that saved it.

I needed to do an allergy rundown with her before I even considered preparing any kind of food products.

I rounded the counter to ask her, but stopped abruptly in my tracks when she came sauntering out of my bedroom naked. She was like a new woman, confidence and determination fueling her stride as she ate up the distance between us.

My dick backtracked, immediately swelling with the excitement I'd spent the last several minutes trying to calm.

"Georgie?" I asked as she beared down on me, wondering what was on her mind while my dick prayed whatever it was would end in some form of attention.

She didn't say anything as she planted a hand on my naked chest and pushed me back until the top of my ass hit the edge of the island counter.

The heat of her palm scorched my skin and the look of her body did the same to my eyes. I couldn't focus on one place, my eyes bouncing and bounding from one glorious part of her to the next.

Everything lost focus when she sank to her knees, the room around me blurring so badly I nearly passed out.

"Georgie," I called again, hoping she'd give me something to ease my mind. A look, a comment—anything to put my racing thoughts at ease enough that I could do nothing but enjoy whatever she intended to do. I didn't want to be the guy who said the standard, "You don't have to," at the same time that I was thinking, *Oh yeah, you do* inside—because that was how it worked. But I did want some kind of reassurance that neither of us would regret this.

Finally, her eyes met mine, and she licked her lips as she shoved her hands into the waistband of my boxer briefs, sliding them down with her palms flat against my skin the whole way.

Fuckkkk. Me.

"Mmm," she hummed in anticipation, leaning forward and taking the whole head in her mouth. Just like that. *Right in her fucking mouth.*

Gun to my head, that moment, my cock would have been known as The Grinch. Because that fucker up and swelled to twice its size in the matter of a heartbeat.

"Good God," I breathed, my neck craning back in ecstasy.

She hummed at that, the vibration in her throat coating my skin along with the wet and warmth. I put my hands on the counter to stop from gripping her hair.

This ride was hers, and I was merely a passenger. So many times, women play to what they think a man wants, defaulting to him rather than owning their ability.

I'll let you in on the fucking secret—absolutely nothing I could ask her to do would be as good as letting her surprise me.

She slid her mouth down as far as it would go and back, leaving a coat of moisture behind. The chilled air tingled the skin she unsheathed and shot straight to my tightening balls.

Her hand must have sensed it or something, shooting out to cup them at the perfect pressure, just between timid and crushing, rolling each of them between her fingers like a goddamn sac expert.

My legs started to shake, but I fought it, scared she'd stop to ask if I was okay or if I needed to change positions.

A swirl of her tongue at the tip later, she took me inside again, pushing the flat of her tongue against the underside and tapping it in a rapid rhythm. Up and down she worked me, adding her free hand at the base and mesmerizing me with a frenzy-inducing twist.

My mind raced and blanked at once, knowing the cum was coming and working overtime to find the faculties to actually tell her.

"Baby," I groaned, finally letting my hand shoot out to grip her hair. I pulled it up with a jerk, but took care not to be too rough or startle her.

Her eyes fucking destroyed me when they met mine, eating me alive with the same intensity as her mouth. She was swallowing my fucking dick like it was her last meal and she'd had a goddamn choice of the whole menu.

I couldn't hold back anymore.

"Oh shit. Oh *fuck*. I'm gonna come. *Ahhh*, God."

She sucked harder instead of letting go, pushing me to get there faster with a strum of her fingers at my balls.

I didn't think I usually came that fast, but the surprise had everything fucked. My stamina, my mind—my ability to form complete sentences. Gone.

When the last jerk subsided, she soothed me with her tongue, sliding her loose hand up and down the shaft slowly.

"Mmm," she moaned again, nearly knocking me on my ass. "You taste good too."

I would never, *ever* be able to look at this woman without remembering this moment. Not for my entire life. I was fucking sure of it.

I was equally sure, as one of her greatest fears centered around being able to maintain a professional relationship with me in a work environment, she would *not* want to hear that.

She got to her feet slowly, but I sped up the process, grabbing her by the hips and slamming her naked body directly into mine. My slowly softening cock rested between our bellies, and my lips sought hers.

I fought the primal urge to eat her alive, though, teasing her tongue with mine in a sweet dance of thank-you instead.

I wanted her to feel cherished and fucking appreciated. Her bottom lip swelled in my mouth with the pressure of my suction, so I soothed it with my tongue immediately upon its release.

She moaned in my mouth, hard and deep and needy, and I took it as my completely ass backwards cue to break the kiss. My hands had already found their way to her ass, and I knew if I didn't stop now, I'd end up pushing her into something she really *wasn't* ready for.

"Go put on a shirt, baby," I ordered softly, and then offered, "Take a shower if you want to."

The shy girl was just under the surface, clearing the fog of lust, and I knew she'd much rather succumb to it in the privacy of my room or the shower than have to live through it in front of me.

I pressed a soft peck to the corner of her lips and inhaled the smell of the skin of her cheek with my nose. *Subtly sweet like a rose surrounded by apples.*

"I'll finish making breakfast," I said into her skin before pulling away. "You're not allergic to anything other than lime juice, are you?"

She smiled slightly before shaking her head.

"Good. I'll turn the bacon and eggs into omelets, then."

"Kline?" she asked, ignoring my rundown and sliding her hand up my neck to the juncture of my jaw. My throat tightened and my pulse beat double time as her thumb brushed the line of it.

"Yeah, Benny?"

"Thanks." One soft kiss to my lips later, she turned and retreated to my bedroom and all I could do was watch as she went, my boxer briefs still twisted around my ankles.

I was fucked—really and truly fucked—when it came to Georgia Cummings.

"Omelet's ready," I called through the closed bathroom door after making a quick stop in my closet to put on a pair of jersey shorts until I showered. I was still sticky with the evidence of Georgia's performance, so I opted to go commando underneath them until I could rectify it—this billionaire's apartment only had one bathroom.

I expected her to call something back through the door, but she opened it instead, stepping into the doorway and nearly into me with wet hair, a towel around her body.

With a mind of its own, my hand reached out to wipe away the lingering drop of water on the top swell of her breast. She shivered.

I felt downright needy for more contact. Hugs, hand holding—I didn't give a fuck. I just wanted to touch her, and I wanted to do it all day.

"Spend the day with me," I blurted.

"Kline—"

"No," I interrupted. "Don't say no."

She smiled, a tiny laugh coating my skin as she tilted her head to the side just slightly. "I wasn't going to."

"Good," I breathed in relief.

"But I do need to go home first. I need clothes. Preferably ones that fit and don't smell like you." She held up a hand before I got defensive, admitting softly, "It's distracting."

"Fine," I agreed easily, countering, "But I'm going with you. Last time I let you arrive separately, you were forty-five minutes late."

Her face pinched in annoyance.

I leaned forward and pressed my lips to hers, smoothing it away just as fast. Without moving back, I spoke my parting words right against her lips. "Any other time I'd be patient, baby, but today, when it comes to spending time with you, I find I'm a little less willing to wait."

CHAPTER 17

Georgia

"Cokes from a vending machine? Hot dogs from a vendor? What's next, Mr. Spontaneity?" I nudged him with my shoulder.

He shrugged, taking the last bite of his mustard and relish-covered dog. "I didn't really have a plan. I just wanted to make sure you spent the day with me."

Night was settling over the city, streetlights glittering the pavement with their soft glow. We had spent the day riding the subway and making stops at random. Kline would ask me a question and my answer was what decided our next stop.

Favorite place to relax? A stroll through Central Park.

Favorite childhood memory? Feeding ducks at the Brooklyn zoo.

Dinner was outside of MoMA, after we had spent most of the evening browsing Picasso's sculptures and Jackson Pollock's beautiful landscapes. He had kissed me slow and deep, fogging my brain with memories of this morning. Kline waited until he had me good and turned on, then pulled away, nonchalantly asking what sounded good for dinner.

The horny side of me quickly responded, "Well, I *really* enjoyed breakfast this morning."

"You want bacon and eggs again?"

"No," I answered, standing on my tiptoes and kissing a sensual path along his jaw. Using my teeth to tug at his earlobe, I whispered, "That wasn't my favorite part of breakfast."

And that's how we ended up at a street vendor outside of MoMA, ordering hot dogs. The cheeky bastard had made sure to order us footlongs, adding, "Just trying to get the size right."

He found a bench, pulling me down into his lap. "Let's eat, Benny girl," he said, kissing my forehead and setting dinner in my hands.

I ate my footlong, enjoying every second of being in his company. Pedestrians meandered past us. Taxis sped by in their usual hurry. But the world didn't exist in that moment. I was too busy savoring every soft kiss to my cheek and handsome smile flashed in my direction.

"This might have been better than breakfast." I took my last bite, moaning.

He tickled my ribs with his free hand. "I never pegged you as a liar, Ms. Cummings."

"Who said I was lying?" I winked.

"You got a little something, right here." He wiped a drop of ketchup from the corner of my mouth, sucking it off his finger and waggling his brows. "Always so fucking good."

I laughed, shoving his shoulder playfully. "All right, dirty boy, what's next on the agenda?"

Helping me to my feet, he grinned. "I've got an idea, but I need to know if you're ready to be a little wild."

"How wild?" I questioned, a sassy hand on my hip.

He tossed our empty bottles and napkins in the trash.

"Crazy, insane kind of wild." His eyes turned serious. He grabbed my hips, guiding me toward a vacant alley and gently pushing my back against a brick wall. "Can you handle getting a little crazy with me?"

I nodded, smiling up at him.

He pressed a kiss to mouth. "Are you sure, Benny girl? Because I can't have you chickening out last minute."

"Are you calling me out?"

"Are you too scared to take the challenge?"

I bit his bottom lip, my teeth tugging playfully. "I'll take any challenge you throw my way."

"Is that so?"

"You bet your tight ass it is."

"I've got fifteen dollars *and* a striptease that says you'll chicken out."

"I'll see your bet and raise you an orgasm."

His mouth met mine again, his tongue slipping past my lips. He kissed me passionately, sliding his hands into my hair and taking control. His lips coaxed a moan from my throat, only to leave me disappointed when he pulled away, smirking like the devil.

"Game on, baby." He grabbed my hand, leading me back onto the sidewalk. "Oh, and I want you wearing heels. Sexy fucking heels that'll blow my mind."

I giggled, shaking my head. "You better prepare yourself because I'm demanding Channing Tatum-like dance moves. I'm talking pelvic thrusts and lots of grinding action."

We took the subway until Kline ushered us off at Midtown East. Ten minutes later, we were standing in front of ONE UN—a prestigious hotel in the business of catering to the rich and famous.

"Are we schmoozing with diplomats tonight?"

He chuckled. "No, but we're definitely going to get a little wet."

I raised a curious brow as he led us through the lobby and to a bank of elevators hidden on the eastern side of the facility.

The ride was quick, and once we reached our apparent destination, we hopped off and walked hand in hand past a reception desk. A twenty-something-year-old girl glanced up from her laptop, offering a simple, "Enjoy your workout," and resumed typing. She didn't question our motives, seemingly oblivious to the fact that we were basically breaking in to their facility.

I started to get a little nervous as Kline led me through a locker room. He held open a glass door, ushering me toward an indoor pool. The water was enticing, lights still on and glowing beneath the clear water.

"Uh?" I asked, glancing around.

We were the only ones there, but a white sign with big red letters instructed us why.

No one permitted in the pool area after nine o'clock.

It was half past ten.

The sign also stated, *Members only pool. Police will be contacted in the event this rule is violated.*

Hefty warning for an indoor pool, right? Yeah, but remember, this hotel wasn't just any hotel. It was adjacent to the United Nations Headquarters. When I'd joked about schmoozing with diplomats, I hadn't been kidding.

Kline took off his shoes and socks, setting them on a chair.

"Uh, what are you doing?"

"I'm getting ready to hop in the pool," he responded, unbuckling his belt. "You're joining me, right?"

"Pretty sure I don't have a bathing suit." I glanced down at my attire—jeans, a cotton tank top, a light cotton sweater, and brown leather flats.

"But I thought you said you wanted to be a little wild?" he asked, amusement in his voice.

"Yeah, but…" I paused when he unzipped his jeans and slid them down his legs.

"But…what?" He looked up, his eyes filled with a playful edge.

"We're not even supposed to be in here," I whispered, even though no one outside of the pool could hear me. "And you want me to what? Go for a dip in my bra and panties?"

He shrugged off his shirt. "You could always go without."

My jaw dropped. "You want me to skinny-dip? In a pool that we're not even supposed to be in?"

"Are you getting ready to chicken out?" Kline taunted. His gorgeous body was on full display, only boxers covering his muscular thighs.

"No," I retorted.

He cocked a brow. "Are you sure? Because it kind of looks like you're ready to jet."

I narrowed my eyes.

"Get ready to strip, baby." A grin covered his lips. "And don't forget the heels."

His smug confidence had me changing my tune. I wasn't usually the type of girl to break rules, but I also wasn't the type of girl to back down from a bet.

My stubborn side won the battle for supremacy.

I kicked off my flats and moved toward the pool. My jeans, cardigan, and tank top were removed in quick fashion and discarded onto an empty chair. "Get ready to pay up." I strode to the deep end, staring at his amused expression from across the water. I unclasped my bra and shimmied out of my panties, tossing them in his direction. With a sweet, devious little smile, I said, "Remember, I want lots of pelvic thrusting action," and then dove into the pool.

After savoring the warmth of the water, I broke the surface, resting my arms on the ledge, and grinned back at Kline. "Put your money where your mouth is, Brooks."

He laughed, sliding off his boxer briefs and turning around. He started humming a striptease beat, glancing at me over his shoulder and grinning playfully. Kline proceeded to pelvic thrust, his hands resting behind his head and his grin turning cocky with each punch forward, not an ounce of embarrassment on his face. He was visibly enjoying himself, loving the growing smile on my lips, and he was crazy adorable yet insanely hot at the same time. I watched his tight ass and muscular thighs flex with each circuit. He kept it up until my giggles turned loud and uncontrolled.

He dove into the pool, slicing through the water in succinct maneuvers. He moved toward me, his hands finding my hips and signaling him that he had reached his target.

When he broke the surface, his face hovered mere inches from mine. Water dripped from his eyelashes, down his cheeks, and clung to the very tips of his spiky wet hair. "Are you ready to shove twenty-dollar bills in my g-string?"

"Eh, maybe *one* dollar bills?" I teased.

"One-dollar bills?" he asked. "Baby, I recall a lot of pelvic action back there."

"Yeah, *but…*" I sighed "…I didn't get the full-frontal experience."

He laughed, shaking his head. "I'll make note that you're a fan of full frontal."

I smiled, my cheeks damn near bursting with amusement.

He wrapped his arms around my waist, moving us in the water. It rippled into tiny waves around our bodies. "You know what you're not a fan of?" he asked, brow quirking.

"Small wieners?"

His chest vibrated against my skin, laughter spilling from his lips. "Besides that. I'm well aware you've got an appetite for nothing smaller than a footlong."

I giggled, savoring his teasing smile. "Tell me, Brooks, what am I not a fan of?"

"Emergency rooms."

I tilted my head to the side, perplexed.

"You were really fucking adorable last night, slap-happy and high on Benny, but before you got to that point, I was worried." His forehead touched mine. "I wanted to take you to St. Luke's, but you're pretty damn stubborn."

The look in his eyes warmed my stomach. I couldn't imagine, didn't want to imagine, the kind of shape I had been in last night. I could recall bits and pieces here and there, but for the most part, it seemed like a hazy dream. It had been our first real date. We barely knew each other outside of work, yet Kline hadn't hesitated to take care of me. He hadn't freaked out or gotten embarrassed that his date looked ridiculous. Because, let's face it, I'd looked insane. Like someone had given me botched plastic surgery kind of crazy.

Last night, Kline hadn't been focused on anything but making sure I was okay.

And it was apparent, he really was worried.

Those were not the actions of a man whose intentions were less than genuine.

He was different from anyone I had ever met, in the best way. In the span of forty-eight hours, he had somehow gained a large part of my trust. I wasn't skeptical or scrutinizing his every word; I was merely enjoying feeling safe and cherished in his presence.

"My brother is an ER resident at St. Luke's. He just so happened to be working a twenty-four-hour call shift last night," I explained.

"*Oh*," he said, understanding in his voice. "Now it makes sense."

"Yeah," I said, shrugging. "He's my older brother. My only sibling. And even though my lips were about to consume my face, no way in hell was I going to give him that kind of ammunition." If I thought Will still bringing up "Masturbation Camp" was bad, my arriving in his ER looking like a blowfish would have made that never-ending joke look easy.

"Do you have any siblings?" I asked, curious to know more about him. The short amount of time we'd spent together outside of the office had me realizing every preconceived notion I'd had about Kline was dead wrong. Hell, his small, quaint apartment was evidence of that. It truly was not the kind of flashy, extravagant place I'd pictured him living in. Sure, it was nice, but it looked more like a place I would live in, not someone who had grossed nearly a billion dollars last year with just TapNext alone.

He shook his head. "Only child."

"What are your parents like?"

"My mom is a meddler, but she means well. She's actually the reason Walter is at my apartment."

"Don't you dare say anything bad about Walter," I teased, pointing my finger at him.

"You try living with that asshole for a few weeks and see how it goes."

"He is *not* an asshole. He's a big, fluffy sweetheart," I defended my feline friend, fighting the urge to grin.

Kline scoffed. "Yeah, he is. He's the world's worst cat."

"Stop talking about my buddy Walter like that!"

"I'll be more than happy to gift him to you. I can have his shit packed up and ready to go tonight," he challenged.

"Tell me more about your parents." I laughed, choosing to change the subject before I ended up with a new roommate.

"My father is an old school Irish Catholic who loves beer and offers a constant supply of dad jokes. Even though they drive me crazy sometimes, Maureen and Bob are pretty wonderful."

There was a soft kindness in his voice that showed how much he adored his folks. "What about your parents?"

"My dad is a sweetheart, but he's a total ballbuster. He has to be to keep my crazy mother on her toes."

"Crazy mother?"

"My mom is a sex therapist. She's just about as quirky as it gets."

"*Sex* therapist?" he asked, smirking. "I did not expect that one."

"It's not really a common profession."

"Wait…your mom's last name is Cummings, right?"

"Yes." I nodded, already knowing where he was going with this. "Dr. Savannah Cummings is my mother, the sex therapist extraordinaire. As if it wasn't hard enough growing up with Cummings as your last name."

"No wonder you're so good at blow jobs," he teased.

I shoved him away, mouthing, *Pervert.*

"Only for you." He chuckled, pulling me close again. Our bare chests were pressed against each other. Water droplets slipped down my skin, and my nipples hardened instantly.

"Do you even know how sexy you are?" His eyes met the curve of my breasts peeking above the waterline. Strong hands slid from my hips to my ribs until they moved around my back and caressed my ass. "Baby, you drive me fucking insane."

My heart tripped. He'd called me *baby*. Sure, he had said it before, but this time, it had just rolled off his tongue with such ease. It was a reflex, *instinctive*. I felt like we were really trying this, trying *us*.

I brushed my lips against his. We weren't kissing at first, just teasing, breathing the same air. I could smell the chlorine on his skin, the hint of sugar on his lips from the soda we'd shared earlier. I saw my reflection in his pupils, eyes wanton and needy.

"I don't think I'll ever get enough of you." He parted his lips, pressing his mouth to mine. "I'll never get enough of these perfect cherry lips." He opened his mouth, sucking on my top lip, my tongue.

Heat pulsed in my lower belly, my heart racing in anticipation.

Kline moved his mouth down my neck to my collarbone and across the curve of my breasts.

I felt the shape of him against my hip, hard and prominent. I reached down to take him into my hand, but he was too quick, gripping my ass and lifting me out of the water and onto the edge of the pool.

He spread my thighs, gazing up at me with wet lashes and hooded eyes. "How many fingers does my wild girl need?" His mouth met my hip, sucking with a force that reddened my sensitive skin.

I had never been so turned on in my life. My body thrummed, blood thundering in my veins, getting off on the illicitness of our location.

And I ached. God, I ached, desperate for more than just his hands. I wanted his mouth on me again.

"Or does she need more? Does she need my lips and tongue to give her what she really wants?"

My head fell back, and I gripped the edge of the pool to hold myself up.

"*Tell me.* Tell me what you need."

"Your mouth," I moaned, sliding my legs over his shoulders. "I need your mouth on me."

He licked a path down my belly. "Hold on tight, baby. This is going to be fast and you're going to fucking *explode.*"

He ate at my pussy until my body was strung tight with the need to come. I tried to hold out, tried to let the intensity build, but Kline's mouth was too talented, too fucking good at seducing a climax out of me.

In the distance, heavy footfalls moved toward us. Keys jingled against a hip. I didn't know where or what or who or how those noises were occurring, my mind stuck somewhere between *suck me harder* and *make me come.*

"Shit," he mumbled, taking that delicious mouth away from where I needed him the most.

"N-N-No," I stuttered out my frustration, but it didn't matter. Kline's hands were wrapped around my waist, yanking me into the water.

My head spun, shocked from the sudden change in position.

"Shh," he quieted me, nodding toward the entrance.

My eyes grew wide in horror, realization setting in. The footsteps, the keys, they were coming from the other side of the door. The very doorknob that was being turned.

Fuck. I was going to get arrested for not only breaking and entering, but for public indecency too. The police were going to be called while my body still throbbed between my legs.

"I got you." He held me tighter. "Hold your breath, baby. We're going under," he instructed, just before sliding us toward a darkened corner and submerging us under the water.

I shut my eyes, held my breath, and prayed to God we wouldn't be seen. Surely, I wasn't going down like *this*, naked in a pool with my boss's cock pressed against my belly.

It really was a fantastic cock, but that was beside the point. Shit was about to hit the fan.

Kline's lips found mine and I felt his smile against my mouth.

Devious bastard.

Trailing his fingers down my belly, he found the spot where I was still slippery and hot. He didn't waste any time, two fingers sliding inside of me while his thumb rubbed my clit.

Seriously? How was he even thinking about getting me off at a time like this?

But did I stop him? *Nope.* My heart pounded in my ears, the needy, orgasm-driven side of me too focused on what he was doing. I wrapped my legs around his hips like the true hussy I was. If we were going to be Bonnie and Clyde tonight, I sure as hell was going to enjoy the ride.

A few seconds later, he floated us to the top, our heads peeking above the waterline, our lungs dragging in much-needed air. The coast was clear, the mystery person no longer in sight. The lights were off, the doors were shut, and Kline was still finger-fucking me, seemingly unfazed by our almost arrest.

"Sweet, dirty, *wild* girl," he whispered in my ear, picking up the pace. "Even when we're thirty seconds away from getting arrested, you still let me slip my fingers inside your pussy. You like this, don't you? You love being bad just for me." He licked the water from the curve of my breasts.

I moaned, my teeth finding his shoulder and biting down.

"Yes, just like that. Christ, baby, when you catch fire, you motherfucking *burn.*"

Hot damn, Kline Brooks was a certified, class-A, deserves-the-major-award dirty talker. His words served their purpose, pushing me straight over the edge and spurring my brilliant response.

"*Ho-ly fuck.*"

CHAPTER 18

Kline

Monday night rugby practice was gearing up, but my mind was still on the weekend—laughter and sexiness and a Benadryl-fueled trip through an allergic reaction. The mixture of all three had me smiling to myself.

Georgia Cummings was quickly becoming one of my favorite people. She made me feel high on life and like the world's biggest idiot all at once.

Curiosity about Rose's weekend was the only thing that kept me from thinking about how close I'd come to never experiencing what I had for the last week. Because I wouldn't have traded the last seven days for anything, even if it were to come to an abrupt end tonight. The memories would have been worth it.

Take note, friends. Don't close off any one section of your life from possibility. Fate gives us chances, but we're the ones who have to take them.

A touch of the icon brought the TapNext app to life. Realization swallowed me with an unexpected sense of accomplishment. This thing was my baby. I'd nurtured it, grown with it over the years like a close friend. I'd watched it make mistakes, veer off the path to greatness, but I'd pulled it back and I was proud of what it'd become. A place where people could find almost anything. A place where people who were lucky found something worthwhile like I had.

BAD_Ruck (6:15PM): Hey, Rose. You busy? I'm just curious how the date went. I didn't get to check in with you over the weekend.

I stared at the message window, waiting to see if she would reply. I was just about to give up waiting when the little bubbles popped up on the screen.

TAPRoseNEXT (6:17PM): If avoiding contracting bubonic plague from the passenger next to me can be considered busy, then sure. I'm just on the train on my way back from work.

BAD_Ruck (6:17PM): And the date?

"Put your phone down, K. Everyone is waiting on us," Thatch shouted.

I looked up to find the team captains still in the middle of the rugby field, known as a pitch, chatting, but I tossed my phone down anyway. Any amount of dawdling would only be cause for Thatch to publicly bust my balls. As my best friend of more than a decade, he had too much ammunition and a specially made gun for the job.

I broke into a jog for extra measure, joining the group of no-good assholes I called my teammates. Sponsorship wasn't necessary for obvious reasons, but we played the league on the straight and narrow, using businesses to sponsor the team like everyone else. I'd volunteered Brooks Media, but with a dating site being one of the main focuses of the company, that had resulted in a resounding, "Veto!"

Instead, Wes's restaurant, BAD—a fucking joke of a name for all the success he had—was our sponsor and earned our team as a whole the moniker "BAD Boys." But because everyone thought they were fucking cute, that wasn't enough, and the trio of Thatch, Wes, and I were forever dubbed the *Billionaire Bad Boys*. It was there to stay. Trust me, I'd been trying to shake it for years.

"We're skins," John announced to the informal huddle when he came back from the captains' meeting.

"Fuck," Thatch breathed, rolling his head in distress for some reason.

"What's the matter, Thatch?" Wes asked. "Afraid one of the boys is going to pull out your titty ring?"

"Blow me, Torrence."

"Torrence?" I questioned, feeling a wrinkle form between my eyebrows.

"It's a *Bring It On* reference," John remarked casually as he stretched out his hamstring by pulling his heel to his ass, as though it wasn't weird that he'd know that.

When I turned my curiosity from Thatch to him, he piped up again.

"What? Kirsten Dunst is in the movie, and she's fucking hot." He added, "And I have a younger sister," when the group was slow to buy in.

"How *is* your sister, Johnny?" Thatch asked with a smirk.

John's eyes flashed brightly before turning to stone. "Eighteen, motherfucker."

Thatch turned to me, and I could practically *see* what was coming. He didn't actually want to bone John's little sister. Not even a little.

"What's that he said, Kline?"

He might have been a manwhore, but Thatch fucked *women*—not girls just starting to make the transition. What he wanted was to poke at one of John's pressure points just enough to make him explode.

I trained my face to look serious and held in a laugh. "I think he said she's legal, Thatch."

John lunged and my humor finally broke the surface. I grabbed his shirt with both hands and shoved him away playfully while Thatch busted out in hysterics beside me.

"Relax, John," Wes coaxed. "Thatch doesn't need your sister to fill his pussy punch card. He's got all the tramps he'll ever need right here in Manhattan."

Thatch tsked. "There's no card, Wes. My dick is not a Value Club."

"It sure fucks in bulk," John threw in, eager to even the score because of some running feud between the two of them. We were all well-off, grown-as-fuck men, but you'd be surprised by how similar we were to a group of teenage girls sometimes.

"And how would you know, Johnny? Got a camera in my bedroom?" Thatch snapped back.

"All right," I called, babysitting like usual. "Drama club is over, assholes. Let's go play rugby. Focus all of that energy into your attack, for fuck's sake."

"You're the one who can't manage to make it past halfway without getting tackled and steamrolled into the ground," Wes pointed out. He laughed as he said it, though, continuing the teasing vibe by wrapping his arm around my shoulders and walking out onto the field with me.

"At least I manage to touch the ball every once in a while," I jabbed back, shoving him away and jogging to the other side of the pitch.

At this point in the season, practice consisted mostly of scrimmages, dividing into two teams and trying to outplay each other. I was just glad that when we split up, Thatch was usually on my side. He might have acted like a clown from time to time, but the dude was one big motherfucker and had been known to do some permanent damage when he tackled you. I liked to walk without a limp, and if I was going to be told I couldn't have kids one day, I sure as fuck didn't want testicle mutilation to be the reason.

I shook out of my daydream when the ball slammed into my chest, a smirk ghosting Wes's lips from the success of his unexpected pass.

I took off at a run, dodging a defender and reaching the half-way line. Pain shot through my waist as another defender made hard contact. I tossed the ball underhanded and toward my back, the only direction allowed for a legal pass in rugby, and tucked my arms to my chest to take the impact of the fall without breaking a wrist.

"Jesus," I groaned, shoving Tommy off of me as quickly as I could in order to rejoin play.

"Lay off the cookies, Tom," I shouted as I ran toward the ruck my teammates had going.

"Weights!" he yelled back. "I think when you said cookies, you meant weights!"

And fuck, by the way my spleen throbbed, Tommy just might have been right.

I slammed my body into the linked shoulders of Thatch and Wes, pushing them forward over the loose ball and helping the group gain momentum in the fight upstream against the defenders. Thatch fought for control in front of me, and I nearly took an elbow to the face in the process.

Rugby was a rough game, and when my organs felt like they might fall out or a limb ached like it might fall off, I wondered why I did it.

But then the ball was in my arms again, tossed underhand and over his shoulder by Thatch, and I remembered without question—the adrenaline, the thrill, the all-out expulsion of a week's worth of tension, stress, and aggression.

I was convinced a little extracurricular rugby not only kept me in prime physical shape, but it also kept my mind at peace and on an even keel. I could only hope that as my physical health started to sub-side with age, my need to vent would dwindle along with it.

The weight of three bodies hit me at once as I was crossing the try line, but Thatch had them off in no time to celebrate the score. I was barely on my feet before the choreography started, Thatch firing off shots from his crotch like a semi-automatic weapon, the men of our team playing into his antics by hitting the ground one by one as he fired off "rounds." As the scorer of the try, I was the only one who'd earned the privilege to stay on my feet.

I laughed and high-fived my teammates before jogging back across the pitch to do it all over again. Practice had just started, and now that I'd scored, my body was ready for more abuse.

I ran for the train just before it was set to depart, sliding through the doors in just the nick of time. Starving and ready to be home, all I could think about was getting there, showering, and ordering a pizza.

As my tired ass met the surface of the seat, I took a moment to be thankful for the lack of pregnant women and elderly. I was worn the hell out, but I wasn't a prick. The rest of these fuckers could fend for themselves.

I wiped some of the lingering sweat and mud from my face with my towel and pulled my phone from my bag.

A message sat waiting from earlier.

TAPRoseNEXT (6:18PM): Gah. The date. The date was amazing. And then it was pretty fucking traumatic.

BAD_Ruck (7:52PM): Traumatic??? Am I going to need to hunt this guy down?

TAPRoseNEXT (7:54PM): No, he's great, I promise. It wasn't traumatic because of him. He's...I don't know, Ruck. I've got this gut feeling that he's some kind of wonderful.

The corners of my lips started to curve, some weird, unconventional but meaningful relationship between us forming and instilling genuine happiness in me. But before the smile cycle could complete, utter disbelief washed over me in a wave of tsunami-like proportions—the conversations we'd had, the things she'd said. Work relationships and awkward yet somehow easy conversation. The way Rose, despite my more than infatuation with Georgie, managed to make me feel.

None of it made sense, not one single piece of it, until all at once, *it did.*

No fucking way.

The doors of the subway opened, and I didn't even hesitate, shoving my way through the throng of people without apology or remorse. I didn't even know what fucking stop we were on, but I ran for the stairs with single-minded abandon, taking them two at a time and reaching the top on a leap.

New Yorkers scoffed and jumped out of the way, burning me with their dirty looks and judging eyes. The yellow of a cab shone like a beacon in front of me.

I ran for it without thought or pause or respect for my surroundings. The heavy leather of a handbag may have even grazed my shoulder in a glancing blow, but I didn't care. Words thrummed in my head in time with the memory of her heartbeat, building and buzzing around my brain until I almost couldn't stand it. The not knowing, the unlikelihood—it was all too much.

"The Winthrop Building. Fast as you can go," I demanded abruptly to the cabbie, but he didn't bat an eye at my brusque delivery—grunts and commands were the nature of more than half of New York City.

I dug in my bag for my wallet and fished out the first bill I came to. With a swift thrust, I dropped it through the plexiglass window and jumped out while the last notes of his screeching tires still rung in the air.

Pigeons panicked and people swerved as I wove my way through them, and a woman strummed a guitar on the corner.

The building was locked after hours, but being the CEO afforded me access to the keyless entry code on the main door. Until today, I could honestly say I'd never broken in to my office building before.

Sixteen smashes of the elevator call button, another code, and a fidgety ride later, I stepped off onto the fifteenth floor in all of my sweaty glory and strode straight for Human Resources.

The lights were dimmed, and once again, the outer door to Cynthia's office door was locked, but nothing could stop me at this point. Not a lock and certainly not my morals.

I ran to my office at a near sprint and around the back of my desk, yanking drawers open one by one in search of my old master key that opened all of the individual office doors. I hadn't had a need for it in years, so it took me several minutes of digging through pounds of junk to find it.

Priority for tomorrow: My desk needed to be fucking reorganized. *Stat.*

Mud under my fingernails from practice, I clutched the key tightly and jogged back down the hall.

With a turn and a click, I was in, moments away from officially violating half a dozen privacy laws.

I breathed a sigh of relief when the drawer of the filing cabinet slid open with ease, laughing maniacally to myself before trailing into words.

"Of course it's not fucking locked. It's not like she was expecting a *fucking psychopath* to break into her office and dig through it."

Like fluttering wings, my fingers shuffled through the labels, knowing Cynthia followed an unbreakable filing system. Nothing was ever out of order or place, and finding it would be easy enough.

Not knowing the actual wording of the label challenged me a little bit, but it wasn't more than five minutes before I was pulling it out of its spot and cracking it open.

Tracing the lines of the employee names, I ran my finger down the page, muttering through last names until the one I wanted stood out in stark relief.

"Cummings, Georgia." I slid it across the page in some kind of slow-motion daydream until the other column sealed my fate in undeniable bold text.

TAPRoseNEXT.

Some Kind of Wonderful.

CHAPTER 19

Georgia

Gary clicked to the next PowerPoint slide, stating something about the cost effectiveness of *blah blah blah...* Who knows what he was talking about by that point? We'd been in the meeting for over two hours, and I was seconds away from losing my cool.

My stomach growled its irritation.

I glanced at my watch and noted it was five minutes past three, which meant it was five minutes past my daily scheduled sugar fix. I had a Greek yogurt and a leftover piece of cherry cheesecake sitting inside the break room fridge with my name on it.

Conclusion: Someone needed to end this or I was going to end Gary.

It was Thursday afternoon, and it'd been five whole days since I'd had any real private interaction with Kline. We'd texted a lot, snuck a few minutes to chat and say hello here and there, and even had lunch together twice, but he'd been unbelievably swamped with work and activities and I was still one hundred percent determined to keep a professional relationship in the office. The combination of all that crap had put the kibosh on substantial alone time. And let me tell you, the memory of last weekend had my anticipation riding at an all-time high.

Gary plodded over to his laptop, tapping around on the keys. The man moved like a turtle. He was a genius when it came to numbers, but a moron when it came to social cues. While everyone in the room was moments away from falling face first into a coma, he appeared to think we had all the time in the world to discuss more goddamn numbers.

I was numbered the fuck out.

"And if you'll just give me a minute here," he mouth-breathed, licking his lips and clicking away. "I'll pull up another spreadsheet that documents how effective we've been in narrowing down our target ratios for the last financial quarter."

Jesus Christ in a peach tree.

My stomach roared its impatience. Hunger pangs. Crazy, loud hunger pangs. It's a mystery no one else heard it over Gary's droning.

The flash of a text notification caught my eye.

Kline: Was that your stomach, Cummings?

Okay. Obviously, *someone* heard them.

The handsome bastard was sitting beside me. Honestly, I had no idea why he was subjecting himself to this meeting. It was solely for my marketing team. I glanced at Kline out of the corner of my eye, scratching the side of my face with my middle finger. His body jerked noticeably with the effort to conceal his laugh.

Me: It's 3:05pm, Brooks.

Kline: Ah, right. Georgie's snack time. What was I thinking?

Me: I don't know, but if you don't end this soon, I will murder Gary with my pen.

Fighting a smile, he subtly nodded his head in understanding as he set his phone down on the table. My eyes trailed to his forearms—sleeves rolled up, hard muscles and thick veins on display. To quote Uncle Jesse, *Have mercy.* If I hadn't been so damn hungry, I'd have happily sat through this tedious meeting just to gawk at those glorious arms. They were a beacon of muscly man delight.

Gary chuckled, seemingly entertained by himself. His monotone voice penetrated my daydreams about Kline's forearms, officially popping my Big-dicked Brooks fantasy bubble.

I tapped my pen against my notepad. *Shut Gary up. Now.*

Kline knew it was a warning. He flashed a secret grin, eyes crinkling at the corners. God, his eyes, they were this flawless shade of blue—so bright, so vibrant. Montana-sky blue.

I'd started to make a game out of nicknaming Kline's eyes. Those ever-changing blue retinas could be Montana-sky blue one day or, like today, M&M's blue. But that probably had more to do with the starvation setting in than anything else.

Mmmmmmmm, M&M's. I'd have devoured a bag of that candy-coated chocolate goodness.

"Fantastic work, Gary," Kline interrupted moments later. "I think we can all agree we've gained valuable information on Brooks Media's projections for the fiscal year."

Everyone in the room nodded, agreeing far too enthusiastically.

I *knew* I wasn't the only one dying a slow death with each Power-Point GoodTime Gary put on the projection screen.

Gary started to respond, but Kline stood up from his chair. "Go ahead and send the materials out to the rest of the team. That way all departments within Brooks Media can see how they've contributed to another fruitful quarter."

"Oh, okay, but—"

"Really great work, Gary." Kline patted him on the back, not giving him an inch. "I think we can officially say, successful meeting adjourned."

My coworkers scattered faster than roaches when light flooded the room. I followed their lead when I realized Kline would be tied up with Gary for a few more minutes. My stomach couldn't wait. I damn near sprinted to the break room, all kinds of ready to dig into my snacks. Would I start with my yogurt and then move on to the cheese-cake? Or would I just go for it and dig into the cherry cheesecake first?

The world was my oyster, baby.

"Uh oh," Dean announced, walking out of the break room. "It's a quarter after three and Georgia isn't eating?" he teased, making a show of glancing between my face and his watch.

"Yeah, GoodTime Gary gave a go at murder by numbers in our quarterly marketing meeting. If Kline hadn't cut it short, I think I would've staged a riot."

"Well, I'm sorry to tell ya, cupcake, but inside there isn't any bet-ter. Ivanna Swallow is on her selfie break and she has *blowregard* for anyone but the spoon she's currently sucking yogurt off of for Insta-gram's sake."

I groaned.

"Head down, don't make eye contact, and you should be fine." He grinned, slapping my ass as he walked past me and down the hall.

Leslie was sitting at one of the break room tables, doing exact-ly what Dean said she was doing—taking a selfie of a spoon in her mouth. She could probably describe her life in a series of hashtags.

Hashtag, my spoon is so sexy.

Hashtag, my lips bring all the boys to the yard.

Hashtag, my life's goal is to be a walking bonertime.

"Hey, Leslie," I tossed over my shoulder as I headed for the most important thing in the room. The fridge.

"O-M-G. You're, like, never going to believe how adorable people are."

My phone buzzed in my hand. Thinking it might be Kline beg-ging for a rescue, I let my heart overpower my stomach and paused to look. No message from Kline, but the TapNext icon was aglow with a message from Ruck. He'd been messaging me in a steady stream ever since Monday night, and I had to admit, he never failed to amuse me.

BAD_Ruck (3:11PM): Lizards or Birds?

Lizards or fucking birds? Jesus.

The sadistic bastard had talked me into this little game by starting it with normal choices. Pillows or blankets, candy or pizza—he'd been getting a real kick out of asking me which thing I'd rather have in bed with me. *You can only have one,* he'd say. With this kind of choice, the decision was a struggle for a different reason.

TAPRoseNEXT (3:11PM): Neither, you lunatic.

My stomach growled, reminding me that I didn't have time for Ruck and his random get-to-know-you choices right now.

Opening the fridge, I started searching for my snack-time loot. I didn't respond to Leslie, knowing full well she'd just prattle on. If Gary was the prime example of not understanding social cues, Leslie was the girl who didn't care about those cues. In her hashtag and selfie-driven mind, *everyone* wanted to know what she had to say.

For fuck's sake, where is my food?

"Seriously," she called, completely oblivious that I'd left a two-minute pause for a reason. "People are, like, so cute. I just ate a turkey sandwich named Gary, and now I'm eating a yogurt named Georgia."

I stopped mid-rummage and slowly stood, glowering at Leslie over the fridge door.

Her answering grin told me that my eyes weren't *actually* shooting out death rays.

"How cute is that?" She held up the half-eaten cup of yogurt. *My* half-eaten cup of yogurt.

"People are naming the food in the break room. I just *can't even.* It's totes adorbs." She went back to wrapping her crazy-huge lips around the spoon that was feeding her *my fucking yogurt.*

It had to be severely unhealthy to want to kill two of your co-workers in the same day.

I took a deep breath, counting to ten in my head.

One-Don't-Kill-Leslie

Two-Don't-Kill-Leslie

Three-Don't-Kill-Leslie…

By the time I reached ten, my hands felt less stabby.

"Hey, Leslie?" I asked through gritted teeth.

"Uh-huh?" she responded, mouth full of yogurt.

"So, that turkey sandwich named Gary was actually just Gary's turkey sandwich. He wrote his name on it so no one else would eat it."

She cocked her head to the side like a confused puppy. "But what about the yogurt named Georgia?"

I fought the urge to shout, inhaling and exhaling another cleansing breath. "The yogurt wasn't named Georgia. I wrote my name on that yogurt because I brought it in. It's *my* yogurt and I planned on eating it today."

She stared back at me, her pea-sized brain visibly processing my words.

The wheels were turning; slowly but surely, they were turning.

"*Ohhh,* my bad." She held out the half-eaten yogurt container. "Here, you can have the rest of it. I'm already so full from eating that turkey sandwich and piece of cherry cheesecake."

Wait a minute…

Piece of cherry cheesecake?

I glared the fuck out of the food-snatching idiot for a good minute before turning for the door.

"So, like, I'm just going to eat the rest of it, okay, Georgia?" was the last thing I heard as I stormed out of the break room and straight for Kline's office. Since he had hired her, I figured it would be a nice gesture to let him know housekeeping was going to need to branch out into crime scene remediation.

His door bounced off the wall with a bang. Kline raised an eyebrow, his expression confused yet curious behind the large mahogany desk. "Everything okay?"

"Nope." The door slammed shut, courtesy of my stiletto-adorned foot. "Everything is not fucking okay."

I strode around his desk and planted my ass on the edge, forcing him to push his chair back to allow room for me and all of my bristling glory.

"I need housekeeping's number. They're going to need to bring a body bag tonight. Figured it'd be nice to give them a heads-up."

"A body bag?"

I nodded. "For Leslie."

He crinkled his forehead, but I guess apprehension did that to a person. "Come again?"

"She's fine," I reassured. "Well, right now. She won't be fine later."

He tilted his head. "What's happening later?"

"I'm going to kill her."

"Any particular reason you're plotting her murder?"

"She's eating everyone's food, including *mine*! She ate my cheesecake and my goddamn yogurt!" I gestured wildly, flinging my hands into the air. "Do you know why she's doing this?"

Kline shook his head. The hint of a smile kissed the corners of his lips.

I pointed my finger at him. "Don't even think about smiling right now."

He held up both hands. "I wouldn't dream of it. I'm taking this very seriously." He forced his mouth to the side, trying to hide another smirk, and his voice turned almost offensively diplomatic. "Why is Leslie eating everyone's food?"

"She thought people were being *totes adorbs* and naming the food."

Blue eyes lit up with amusement. "Leslie didn't realize the names on food meant it belonged to someone?"

"Today, she enjoyed a turkey sandwich named Gary. And a yogurt and piece of motherfucking cheesecake named Georgia. She thought it was *like, the cutest thing ever* how her coworkers were naming food. She's too dumb to live. Literally."

I saw the second he couldn't hold back laughter. A grin had cracked the secret code and covered his entire face—his eyes, lips, and cheeks were all lit up with hilarity.

Like a boiling pot, it worked its way up his throat and spilled right over, coating me with its vibration. If I hadn't been so pissed, I might have acknowledged its ability to turn me on.

"This isn't funny! Your intern is a dumbass! All she does is take selfies and eat my food! Why haven't you fired her?"

"Baby," he cooed condescendingly. "She's just an intern. How picky can I be? She's not costing the company anything."

"Not costing anything!" I very nearly shrieked. "She just cost me my goddamn cheesecake!"

Kline shook his head with a smile and started to turn his leather chair in the other direction, away from my glaring eyes, but I was too quick, damn near jumping on top of him. "Don't even think about it!"

His strong hands gripped my hips and finished the job.

In an instant, his laughter was gone, a look of pure, unadulterated longing taking its place. For two days, we'd practically crawled all the way inside each other, we'd had so much physical contact, but it'd been a long time since then.

For a few moments, all we did was stare at each other. I was straddling Kline's lap, his muscular thighs forcing my legs to spread that perfect amount. Only a few measly inches kept me from finding out if he was as turned on as I was. And judging by the look on his face, if I pressed my hips to his, I'd hit the cock landmine.

"Dessert named Georgia?" He caressed the sliver of skin that was exposed above the waistline of my skirt. His lips were near my ear. "I'm certain this is something I wouldn't be able to stop myself from *devouring*."

Oh, my...

His hands disappeared under my flowy skirt and gripped my ass, pulling at the cheeks to open me farther to him. Only a minuscule piece of lace was separating his fingers from touching my bare skin. Kline's hips ground into mine, and I had to swallow the moan threatening to spill from my lips. He wanted this as much as I did. The evidence was hard and ready between my thighs.

My breathing turned ragged, heart pounding inside my chest.

I loved seeing this side of him. The all-business, Armani-suited CEO getting messy and wild, *with me*. His reserved side morphing into a man possessed by passion and desire. I felt possessive, wanting to be the only woman who could affect him this way.

I should've been freaked out over the idea that someone could walk into his office and find us in this precarious position, but all I could think about was wanting him to push himself against me, harder, rougher. Good God, I wanted more. So much more.

His lips moved from my ear to my jaw to the sensitive, toe-curling spot on my neck. His teeth just barely scraped at the pulsing vein, and a shiver rolled down my spine. If he kept this up, I'd end up doing something I shouldn't. Like unzip his pants and offer up my V-card as tribute.

Get it together, Georgia.

"Kline?"

"Don't worry," he whispered against my skin. "I won't let this get out of hand."

But he didn't disentangle us. *No.* He did the complete opposite.

He kissed me hard, delving deep enough to brand me, while our tongues tangled in an inferno of want and need and crazy desire.

Sliding a hand up my blouse and underneath my bra, Kline brushed his thumb across my nipple.

I moaned into his mouth, biting at his bottom lip.

"Fuck," he breathed, still cupping my breast.

I sucked at his tongue as my hips circled his, savoring the feel of his cock pressed against my pussy. Even though we were both fully clothed, I could practically feel every inch of him. And hot damn, there were a lot of inches.

He pulsed upward and my pussy clenched in empty agony.

"Oh, yes, yes, Kline, yes," I whispered, my head falling back.

Our ragged, wanton breaths were the only sounds filling the four walls of his office.

"You're driving me wild." His hand covered mine, moving it down to cup him through his slacks. "I want you so fucking bad."

Self-control was nowhere in sight as I went for his belt, fingers sliding against the cold metal of his buckle. The only thing that mattered was touching him. More of him. *All* of him. I wanted Kline hard and ready and bared in my needy hands.

"Mr. Brooks, your four o'clock is here. Should I send him back?" Pam's voice echoed from the intercom.

We froze, startled by the interruption.

"Christ," Kline muttered, his eyes clenched and forehead pressing against mine.

My cheeks turned a terrifying shade of red once realization set in. "I-I should probably leave," I stuttered, attempting to un-plaster myself from him.

"Hold on." He gripped my hips, stopping my momentum. He leaned forward, one finger pressing the intercom to respond. "Just give me a minute, Pam. I'm just finishing up signing some contracts for Georgia."

I was thankful he still had enough brainpower to think of an excuse for me to be in here. Telling Pam that he needed a minute to remove his Director of Marketing from his dick wasn't the best scenario for either of us.

"Hey," he whispered, cupping my cheeks. "Don't freak out."

"I'm not freaking out."

"Are you sure?" He smirked. "Because that deer-in-headlights look you've got going on says otherwise."

I glared. "That's not the look I'm giving you."

He mimicked my wide-eyed stare before his face morphed into a teasing grin.

"Excuse me for being a little freaked out that someone could have walked in and found us going at each other like a couple of horny teenagers. Speaking of which, you should probably let me up."

He massaged my ass. "Only if you promise to let me finish dessert later."

Dear God, what was he trying to do to me?

I couldn't hide my smile. "You're trouble. Big fat fucking trouble." I shoved at his chest and proceeded to remove myself from his lap. Straightening my clothes, I glanced down at his disheveled attire. "And you look ridiculous. Like some woman was in here mauling you with red lipstick." My crimson lips were branded across his face and neck.

It was absurd, but mostly just fuck-hot.

He stood, flashing that sexy smirk of his while I removed my lipstick smudges with my fingers. I adjusted his tie and patted him on the chest. "Don't work too hard, Mr. Brooks."

As I turned for the door, he spanked my ass, earning a small squeal of approval from my traitorous lips.

"Don't worry, I'll save up my energy for later, Ms. Cummings."

Outrageously sexy bastard. I was certain he'd be the death of me.

"Wait." He grabbed me before I could take another step, pulling me toward him, my back against his chest. His breath was warm on my neck. "I'm not letting you out of this office until you agree to another date. A weekend date."

"Like a whole weekend?"

"In the Hamptons, with me."

"You have a place in the Hamptons?" I asked, then realized what a stupid question that was. Kline wasn't a flashy kind of man, but he had made more money from one business deal than most people make in a lifetime. Hell, he could quit working today and would be set for the rest of his life.

"Yeah, baby." He kissed my neck, teasing the sensitive skin with his lips. "So, you'll go?"

I turned in his arms, gazing up at him. He was business Kline laced with a little messy wildness from our earlier tryst behind his desk. The adorable grin cresting his mouth had me smiling in return. "What do I get out of it?" I teased.

His grin grew wider. "You want terms and conditions for a weekend getaway I'm asking you to join me on?"

I nodded. "Sounds about right."

"You're like a little shark when it comes to business." He pressed a kiss to my forehead, chuckling against my skin. "I'll make sure you have a good time. So good you'll be doing a reenactment of my bedroom…and the pool. Who knows, maybe it'll be like both combined."

"Draft the contract, Brooks, but remember, I'm holding you to these terms."

"Wonderful doing business with you, Cummings."

CHAPTER 20

Kline

When the GPS told me I was two blocks away from Georgia's apartment on Friday night, I pulled over and put the car in park. My phone had just buzzed in the cupholder with a message, and I knew I wouldn't be able to answer it once I picked her up. Ignoring the blinding red light on my mail icon, I swung my thumb directly over it before landing on the TapNext app.

> **TAPRoseNEXT (7:04PM): HE'S GOING TO BE HERE ANY MINUTE, FOR CHRIST'S SAKE. CALM ME DOWN BEFORE HE TAKES ONE LOOK AT ME AND RUNS IN THE OTHER DIRECTION.**

A smile overwhelmed me as my chuckles bounced around the echoey interior of an otherwise empty car. She was so fucking cute, I could hardly stand it.

> **BAD_Ruck (7:06PM): Calm down, sweetheart. Let's start slowly by eliminating the shouty capitals.**

TAPRoseNEXT (7:07PM): FUCKING FUCK FUCKERS. Okay. FUCK. Okay, I think I'm good now. Move on to step 2 (the coddling).

I bit my lip and shook my head, smiling like a crazy person.

BAD_Ruck (7:08PM): Good job. Also, creative swearing.

TAPRoseNEXT (7:08PM): The calm is wearing off, Ruck.

BAD_Ruck (7:09PM): Okay, okay. Coddling. Got it. This guy is still talking to you after spending all that time with you last weekend and invited you on a weekend away, right? He sounds smart enough to appreciate a little nervous energy. Everything is going to be fine.

Okay, guys. I know. I can feel you judging me. But let's talk this over.

I knew not telling her that I knew she was Rose, and that I was Ruck, was bad form.

I did, really.

It'd been a few days since I found out, and I should have told her *immediately*.

But God, as twisted as it was, I was having too much fun. Georgia was different with me online, no pretense or fear of saying something to her boss that he couldn't unhear, the safety net of anonymity weaving the protective web that it did for a lot of people.

As easy as it was to be someone else online, it was equally easy to be yourself, no expectations or trepidation blinding the true artwork underneath. Knowing Georgia in both places, without her knowing that I knew, was one of the most remarkable experiences of my life. She was the same yet different—honest and open and unafraid of re-crimination. She wasn't afraid to send me messages about freaking the fuck out. She was just her, and I liked getting to be on the receiving end of twice the interaction. She was still scared to wear out her welcome with Kline Brooks. I couldn't fucking welcome her enough. This gave us the best of both worlds.

I even found myself sending her more goddamn messages as Ruck, just to be able to enjoy what she might say. I pushed the envelope, trying to get her even more comfortable with me, even knowing that, in her mind, she was splitting her affection between two men.

It was fucked, but I knew if *she* could forgive *me*, her actions wouldn't be an issue in the slightest. Love, lust, and attraction were base instincts. They were simple and finite and somehow still infinitely complicated. She liked Ruck because *he* was another dimension of *me*.

So as much as it didn't make sense rationally, it made heart-sense. Call me a hopeless romantic, or maybe a fool, but to me, that was all that mattered.

Stowing my phone in the console, I put the car back into drive and pulled away from the curb. Cute brick-front brownstone buildings with iron-railed stairs lined the sides of each street, mature trees casting their shadows every fifty feet. Dusk threatened as the sun made its descent, already hiding behind buildings despite its place just above the horizon.

And my heart? Well, it just about beat right out of my chest.

Georgia sat on the stoop of her building with her arms crossed on her knees and her suitcase at her feet as I pulled up.

Her hair was wild and unkempt, curling just enough that I knew she'd probably showered and left it to dry on its own. Clothed in jeans and a simple sweatshirt with just barely a trace of makeup on her face, she was still the most beautiful thing I'd seen in just about forever.

Eager to put her racing mind at ease, I pushed the gearshift into park, turned the key to off, and jumped out to round the car before she even made it to her feet.

Adorable and wondering at my hurry, her teeth dug into the skin of her lip and her head tilted just slightly to the side.

I watched her as she watched me, a fire lighting her gorgeous blue eyes just as I pulled her directly into my arms and sealed my lips to hers.

"Mmm," she moaned, melting into my frame and wrapping hers around my shoulders. I licked at her tongue and her lips, sucking the taste of her into me as I slowly released.

"Kline," she whispered, overwhelmed.

My eyes shut on their own and my forehead met hers, and I breathed her in until my lungs burned only a little.

"I missed you."

She smiled and pushed her nose deeper along the side of mine. Her voice was barely audible.

"You saw me today at work."

I shook our heads together, lips and noses and foreheads touching the whole time.

"Not like this."

"No," she agreed softly, placing one simple kiss to the corner of my mouth before pulling away. "You're right. It wasn't like this."

I took a step down to grab her suitcase but kept a squeezing hand on her hip.

"You ready?"

Her face was alive and at ease, excitement lining the corners of every angle as she nodded. I couldn't help but return the sentiment.

"Mount up."

She raised a brow, but I just winked, moving to the back of the SUV and lifting the hatch to load her bag.

Looking it over from back to front, she seemed to notice the car for the very first time.

"This is your car?"

I looked at her in question.

She rolled her eyes at my implication, since I was very much accessing said car and the likelihood that I had stolen it was remarkably low.

"This is my *rental* car. I don't own a car."

"You don't own a car?" She was incredulous.

"Baby." I laughed, biting my lip to summon my patience. "I live in Manhattan. For business, I have a driver because you're not the only one with the ability to be late. For everything else, I walk, take a taxi, or ride the subway. If I need to go anywhere outside of the city, I rent one. Simple as that."

"But this is a Ford Edge," she pushed stubbornly, still not getting it.

"I know," I joked. "I sprung for the SUV since I've yet to get a handle on your luggage habits." I jerked my head to the back and slammed the hatch. "Just the one bag. I'll stick to midsize from now on."

"*Kline.*"

Rounding the rear, I walked back to her, leaned my back into the car, grabbed her hips, and pulled her body into mine.

"Baby. I can see you're struggling to get this, but I swear it'd make sense if you met Bob."

"Bob? Of Bob and Maureen?"

I nodded. "The one and only. Bob Brooks, my dad and the biggest influence on my life."

Wrinkles formed on her nose as she grinned, so I kissed it.

Pushing the wild blonde hair back from her face, I trailed one finger along her jaw and then dropped it.

"Let go of who you thought I was…who you think I'm supposed to be. Be here with me now." I grabbed her hand and pushed it to my chest. "*Feel* me."

Her free hand shot to my jaw and stroked it, eyes bright in reaction to my so-obviously-messy emotion.

"I promise, this is who I am, and if you let go of what you thought you knew, you'll get it. You'll get me. I *know* it."

I sounded desperate because I was. Desperate for her to be the woman I thought she could be. Desperate for her to let go of the *bil-lionaire* experience and just be with *Kline*.

"Okay." She sealed her lips to mine and the tip of her tongue ventured into my mouth briefly. An answering tingle ran down the length of my spine. "I'll let go of it all." She pecked me on the mouth once more. "Promise."

"Good," I said before slamming my mouth to hers again. A slow groan rumbled in my chest a second later at the feel of her soft tongue. With effort, I forced myself to extract my mouth from hers. "Plus, nothing humbles a man more than cleaning Walter's litter box. I swear the little fuck flicks shit outside of it on purpose."

She shook her head with a dreamy smile and bit her lip to stop herself from making fun of me. It didn't matter what I did. She'd forever be on Walter's side of this war.

"Now get your ass in the *Ford Edge*, and let's get out of here. I'm ready to have you all to myself for the weekend."

"Yes, sir!" she joked with a salute before reaching for the door. I wrapped an arm around her waist at the last second, swooping her off her feet and swinging her around to put me between her and the car.

She bristled, but the icy edges of her attitude melted as soon as I winked and popped open the handle myself. "What kind of a man would I be if I didn't open the door for you?"

"The kind that fill the streets of Manhattan."

I just shook my head and smiled, waiting patiently for her to climb in.

"Right. You're not those guys."

"Ahh," I teased. "Now she's getting it."

She grabbed the inside handle of the door and pulled it closed as she spoke. "Get in the car, Kline."

The door slammed in my face and I laughed. "Yes, ma'am," I mouthed through the window, rounding the hood and climbing in.

"To the Hamptons!" she shouted.

I shook my head, fired up the engine, and pulled away from the curb with an enormous smile on my face.

An hour and a half or so into the drive, she started to fidget. And I don't mean a little movement here or there. I'm talking, for a few seconds, I feared she was having a seizure.

"What's up, Benny?"

"What?" Her gaze jerked toward me in surprise.

I glanced from the road to her and back again. "You literally look like your skin is in the process of *attacking* you. What's up?"

"I just… I have to tell you something."

Her tone was serious, and her nerves were beginning to eat her alive. I didn't want to be presumptuous, but I had a feeling I knew what was coming. Our intimacy had been on a steady advance from the moment we'd collided, melding together and racing for the finish line like one entity. We were on our way to a weekend alone, and the relevance of her sexual inexperience had to be beating her over the head with a bat at this point.

"So tell me, baby," I coaxed gently, trying to walk the line of someone who didn't know what was coming and someone who absolutely did, having heard it *twice* already, and was prepared to answer in a calm, respectful manner. If it hadn't been for the blunt conversation *Ruck* had had with *Rose*, *Kline* would have never realized that *Georgie* had already told him in a Benadryl-fueled rant.

Christopher Columbus her pussy prideland.

God, I'd laughed so hard about that when I realized how brilliant it had been.

"I'm…like…a…" *incoherent mumbling* "…virgin!"

I bit my lip and considered her words. I knew what she was trying to say, but a little *figurative* ice breaking never hurt anyone. *Literal* ice breaking—well, that hurt a lot of people.

"You want to listen to Madonna?"

I reached for my phone like I was going to search for the song.

"No," she huffed, adorably frustrated at having to gather the nerve to say it *again*. I didn't blame her. This was the fourth time in about twice as many days that she was admitting it to *someone*. That I knew of, anyway.

Turning in her seat, she forced herself to face me head-on. Her eyes sought mine, and I hated that because I was driving, I couldn't fully give them to her. I had no right to it, but that didn't stop me from being proud of her confidence.

When I found a straight stretch of road and glanced her way for more than a quick, passing beat, she spoke. "I'm a virgin." Crisp and calm, her voice managed to be matter-of-fact and silky all at once.

Did I mention I was proud of her?

Was that fucked up? I didn't mean for it to be. I was just happy to see her owning it—being proud of herself and her own choices instead of feeling like she had to answer for them. I wanted to yell out some kind of cry for all of the empowered females, but I thought that might seem suspicious.

So, I went with the only other thing I could think of.

"Okay. Cool."

Eloquent, right?

"Okayyyy," she repeated, adorably confused by my non-response. "Cool."

I'm sure she'd been expecting the usual questions.

How'd you manage that?

or

Are you, like, super religious?

or

What the hell are you waiting for?

As her lover, I had a right to know she'd never taken a sexual encounter to that level before, a warning of sorts to make sure I didn't make an assumption that affected both of us. But really, the rest of it was her business and hers alone. Sharing was a staple of every healthy relationship, but she got to be the creator of the terms and conditions under which said sharing happened.

"Kline?" she called, pulling out of my thoughts.

"Yeah, baby?"

"You don't have any questions? Or…I don't know. You're so quiet."

I *was* being quiet. Obviously, it was doing nothing but torturing her.

"I'm sorry, sweetheart, but it's not what you think."

"What do I think?" She raised a brow and I laughed.

"Okay, fair enough. I don't know what you're thinking. But I'm thinking you're a fucking brilliant, beautiful woman with the most delicious pussy I've ever tasted. I'll be lucky as fuck if you decide you wanna share more of it with me. But I don't fucking expect it, and I've done nothing to earn it. I'm guessing none of the other fuckers in New York ever did, and I don't mind one fucking bit."

"That was a lot of 'fucks,' Mr. Brooks."

I laughed and forced the tension in my shoulders to release. "I know. You got me all worked up. Thatch is usually the only one that can get me to utilize that many fucks in one thought process."

Her laughter rolled through me like a wave.

"God, Thatch. I hear all sorts of lore about that guy, but the only actual interaction I've had with him was when you called me on the plane."

"There's Thatch lore?" I asked, mystified and horrified all at once.

"Oh yeahhh." She laughed. "But most of it is from Dean, so I've taken any and all information with a very large grain of salt."

I laughed.

"Like, rock salt."

I shook my head, knowing Dean usually had a pretty good bead on the reality of things despite his juicy delivery.

"Ehhh. You can probably stick to the regular iodized kind. Thatch is a crazy asshole. Fun, though. And, occasionally, a good friend."

"Is he really that crazy?" she asked, insistent in the belief that he couldn't be as rowdy as people described.

As always with Thatch, examples of his depravity were plentiful, but one stood out above the rest.

"You know the scar on my abdomen?" I asked. "Lower right side?"

I glanced over in time to see her nod, eyes brimming with biblical knowledge. "It's completely plausible I've noticed it."

A smile arrested my features.

"Well, I owe its existence to Thatch and one of his half-baked ideas."

Waiting for an explanation, she settled farther into her seat.

"One night during our freshman year of college, he got this idea that stair surfing on our mattresses on the icy courtyard steps could be the next big campus activity. Three broken fingers, one bloody nose, and a tree-branch-impaled abdominal muscle later, I decided I didn't want to be a part of the sales pitch."

"You could have said no from the beginning," she suggested and I shrugged.

"What fun would that have been?"

I flipped on my blinker and turned into the long gravel drive of the Hamptons house. This had been the quickest drive of my life with Georgia keeping me company, and the salty sea air clung to my skin as I rolled my window down to put in the code for the gate. The stars were brighter now that we'd left the city behind, and when I turned to look at Georgie, I found her head hanging out of her window with her face to the sky like she'd noticed.

"Georgie?" I called, fighting back a grin.

"This place is outrageous!" she all but shouted. "Have you seen the fucking sky? And the length of this driveway?"

I shook my head and laughed some more, pulling forward cautiously so she could stay in her happy place half in, half out of the car.

"I might have noticed it a time or two."

She sank back into the seat and shook her hair out of her smiling face.

"You should notice more. Like, a lot more. You know, every weekend or so. Anddddd, if you just happen to want some company," she said, feigning nonchalance, "I could *probably* fit it into my schedule. I mean, I'd be willing to check."

"I'll make note."

"Holy hell! Look at that house! It's adorable!"

I followed her eyes through the windshield, smiling so much my cheeks started to ache. The little bungalow wasn't ostentatious, but it didn't lack space either, and the wood-shank shingle siding had seen better days. The inside pretty much matched, but I was working on fixing it. Slowly but surely.

"I'm glad you like it."

She bounced in her seat.

"But you probably shouldn't like it too much. I'm fixing it up to give it to my parents, and I'll start to feel bad if you get too attached."

"Really? You're doing the work yourself?" If she had been a dog, I imagined her ears would have perked up.

I smiled and nodded. "Really. I had an electrician work on the wiring and Thatch and Wes have helped me a couple of times with the heavy lifting, but I've done most of it myself."

She slammed an open hand down on my thigh and squeezed, her expression deadpan.

"I think I just orgasmed."

I shoved the gearshift into park and reached for her neck at the same time. I rubbed my nose with hers and smiled before touching my lips to hers just once. "Please, Benny. For the love of all that's holy, hold on to that thought—and the easy trigger."

Bags inside the house, a quick dinner of sandwiches I'd picked up from Tony's deli and packed to bring along consumed, and wine in hand, Georgia demanded a tour of the house.

"I want to know every detail. What it looked like when you started, what you're in the middle of now, and what you see it being like when you're done. Don't cut corners, Brooks," she'd said.

"I intend to travel each and every curve in its entirety," I'd teased back salaciously.

She'd just laughed and shoved me down the hall we were currently walking.

She'd seen the completely redone kitchen, the room I'd tackled first. I'd known it would be an outrageously extensive job, as well as the heart of the house. Crisp white cabinets, light stone counters, and dark wood floors, I'd kept the character of the house but added a ton of modern twists and convenience.

"God, Kline. I still can't get over that island! It's freaking enormous."

"I know."

Twelve feet by twelve feet, it was nearly enough room to use as an elevated dance floor. Part of me worried that it was too much, but my reasoning was sound. Maureen and Bob Brooks lived their lives in the kitchen, hip to hip or one or the other relaxing at the counter while the other one cooked. I swore ninety-five percent of my childhood memories happened in that room.

"It's perfect, though. Like the epicenter of the house."

My chest tightened with an unexpected surge of pride and accomplishment. The fact that she understood made me feel validated in a way I hadn't even known I'd needed. I turned quickly, grabbing her hips and slamming her surprised and open lips to mine.

"Thank you," I said. "That's exactly what I was going for."

I almost couldn't handle the feeling of her answering smile.

"Watch your step," I advised as we stepped into one of the completely unrenovated bedrooms. The original wainscoting was the only thing I really wanted to keep, and it was acting more like a temporary storage room for supplies than a bedroom at the moment.

"This place is amazing," Georgie remarked in wonder. "It's almost like a time capsule."

"I know. It's nearly a hundred years old. Which was really fucking intimidating when I first started doing the work."

"I bet."

"Come on. Let me show you upstairs real quick and then we can watch a movie. I'm ready to cuddle."

"Kline Brooks, a cuddler?"

"Born, bred, and proud of it, baby."

She pursed her lips, scrunched her nose, and shook her head—Georgia's look of trying to figure something out.

"You almost never say what I'm expecting you to, you know that?"

I shrugged and nuzzled my face into her neck before touching my lips to the shell of her ear.

"Fine by me. As long as what I *actually* say is better."

She shivered and then touched her lips to my cheek. Sauntering toward the door, she looked over her shoulder as soon as her small body lined up with the frame. "You haven't failed me yet."

CHAPTER 21

Georgia

I slowly opened my eyes as Kline lifted me off the couch, cradling me close to his chest. I must've fallen asleep halfway through the movie. Only two glasses of wine deep, I hadn't been drunk, just a delicious mix of relaxed and sleepy—sated from resting by the fire and cozy from being wrapped up in his arms.

His eyes met mine as we moved down the hall, toward the bedroom. "I figured you'd want to be somewhere a little more comfortable than the couch." He gently set me on the mattress, pulling the covers back and tucking me in. After a soft kiss to my forehead, he whispered, "Go back to sleep, baby."

I watched him move around the bedroom—charging his phone, sliding off his jeans, shrugging out of his shirt, and turning off the lights. I wasn't sure I'd ever get used to how amazing Kline looked in just his boxer briefs. It should have been an offense to let a man who looked like *that* walk around without clothes. But I wasn't complaining.

If he is a crime, then by God, get the handcuffs ready, because there is no way I can resist him.

He slid into the bed beside me, oblivious to my awakened state and ogling thoughts.

Tonight had been so perfect. He was perfect—sexy, kind, funny, and so very sweet. He made me want things I'd spent a lot of time wondering if I'd ever have.

Under the covers, I slid toward him, moving my body on top of his.

His eyes popped open.

"Hi," I whispered.

"Hi." He smiled softly, wrapping his arms around my back and holding me close.

"I didn't really feel like sleeping." I brushed my nose against his.

"And what is it you feel like doing?"

I shrugged my shoulders as my lips nibbled along his neck. Kissing a path back to his mouth, I bit his bottom lip and then licked across the plump skin to soothe it better.

He groaned, gripping my hips and flipping me to my back. His mouth locked with mine as he kissed me, long and slow and deep—so deliciously deep. I gripped the strands of hair resting at the nape of his neck. I swallowed his breaths and savored the taste of him.

My body was getting more riled, almost restless, with each heady second that passed.

He pushed my tank top up and over my chest, grabbing my breasts. He sucked a hardened nipple into his mouth, teasing the peak with his tongue, until switching to the other and repeating the same delectable torture.

The pulsing ache between my legs was proof of how badly I wanted Kline.

And God, I wanted to *feel* him, *all* of him.

His mouth found mine again. "Tell me what you want." Our tongues danced. "I'll give you anything."

"I want you inside of me," I moaned against his lips. "I want it so badly." The need burned in a way it never had before—in a way I knew couldn't be otherwise extinguished.

His eyes met mine, searching. "You know I'll wait, right? I'll wait until you know you're really ready. There's no rush."

A tiny, self-doubting voice crept in. "You don't want to have sex with me?"

"Are you kidding?" A soft laugh escaped his lips. "Baby, I'm losing my mind over the idea of feeling you come on my cock. I'd say that's quite obvious." He playfully rubbed the proof against my thigh, spurring a giggle from my lips.

"But I'm not rushing you." He cupped my cheek, eyes tender. "You hold the power. You decide when it's right."

My hands found their way into his hair again, grasping the strands and pulling his face to mine. I kissed him like I'd never kissed him before. My mouth plundered his lips and tongue, taking what they wanted. I was out of my mind with feelings for this man. I had just told him I wanted to have sex, and he'd done the opposite of what I'd expected. He slowed us down, trying to make sure I was making the right decision for myself.

I didn't need time to think, because Kline *was* right. He was all of the rights.

And I wanted to give him another part of myself.

"I want this. I want this more than I've ever wanted anything in my life." I wrapped my legs around his hips, pulling him closer to where I was desperate for him. He settled between my thighs, his hardened cock pressing against me.

My body shook in anticipation. This moment was why I had waited so long to take this step. I wasn't naïve, expecting my first time to be beside a fire or surrounded by rose petals on a bed. I wasn't expecting cheesy lines of undying devotion or an engagement ring. I just wanted to make sure it was meaningful, that it was with someone I trusted, someone I cared about. And most importantly, I needed it to be someone who cared about me too, who wouldn't intentionally hurt me—not just physically, but emotionally as well.

Everyone had their own views on sex. Some people could have sex for the pure act itself. They could savor spending the night with a gorgeous stranger and have no lingering doubts or feelings nagging them the next day.

I had always been able to leave my emotions at the door when it came to an oral exchange. But when it came to full-on penis penetration, home run sex, I knew I couldn't approach it with that same mindset.

To me, intercourse was more intimate than oral. There was something about looking directly into a person's eyes while your bodies became one. I knew *that* type of sex had to be something more than just physical for me.

I trusted Kline so much, and I'd come to do it quickly. But I felt the way he cared about me with every kiss, every smile, every lingering touch. With him, it wouldn't just be sex. He was more than that to me. I truly cared about him. My feelings for him ran deeper than I was ready to admit. The intensity and depth of those feelings had awareness hitting me like a wrecking ball.

My heart was on the line here, and I had just realized how much I could lose.

Fear drowned my mind, spilling into my eyes.

"What's wrong?" he asked, assessing the uncertainty on my face, acutely in tune with my wavering thoughts.

"I'm scared," I admitted.

He stared deep into my eyes. "There's nothing to be scared of, Georgie. I'd never pressure you into doing something you're not ready for."

I wiped the worry from his brow. "I know that. Believe me, I know that."

"Tell me what you're scared of." His eyes were so earnest. "I'll do everything I can to fix it."

This guy. I swallowed around my heart in my throat.

"I'm scared because…it's so intense." I fumbled to find the right words. "I just…I feel like I'm falling too fast with you. It's scary as hell. I can't ignore the fear that, one day, I'll wake up and things will have ended badly between us. I don't want to associate you with hurt in the end."

He cupped my face, gazing down at me. "No matter what happens, baby, it will always be a good hurt for me. You make me feel alive. And I'll do everything I can to make sure it's the same goddamn experience for you."

That look. There was a gentleness in his eyes that let me know I wasn't the only one falling.

This wasn't going to be just about sex for him either. This was more. He and I were going places, and his look said, "I'm falling too."

And that look was why I reached for the nightstand to pull a condom from the drawer. The *empty* drawer.

His eyes followed me the whole way; I could feel them, but when I turned back to him, they were slightly pinched together.

"I thought there'd be condoms."

He laughed a little, just enough to ease the tension and make me start to smile.

"There aren't any condoms in the drawer."

"Obviously," I replied.

He smirked and rubbed at the skin of my waist. "I've never brought a woman here."

A comforting statement to all, but somehow I managed to turn it on its head, panicking slightly, thinking that things were going to come to a very abrupt stop. I didn't want them to. I was ready *now*.

"Please tell me you have condoms somewhere."

He smiled fully at that. "In my bag."

I shoved him off and jumped off the bed before running to his bag and rummaging through it without remorse. When the foil of the package met my fingertips, I took off in reverse, shoving him aside, resuming my position, and pulling him back on top of me.

He shook with silent amusement as he grabbed the condom out

of my hand, setting it on the bed beside my hip. But his mirth transformed quickly to heat as he moved his hands to my panties, slowly sliding them down my legs, pressing kisses down my body in their wake.

He removed his briefs, his thick erection popping free.

My eyes went wide for a beat, distressed by the size of him. It was one thing to take a cock of that magnitude in my mouth, but it was a whole other ballgame when that cock was going to be the first to slide into home. "Not gonna lie, I wish you were smaller," I blurted out before I could take it back.

Kline stopped mid-kiss, and his forehead fell to my abdomen as a few chuckles escaped his lips. I could feel his smile against my flesh. "No can do, Benny girl. I'm Big-dicked Brooks."

I stilled. "What did you just say?"

"Nothing." He laughed softly into my skin, his tongue sneaking out and licking around my belly button.

"Did you just say *Big-dicked Brooks?*"

"Huh?" He peeked up at me, amusement on his lips and his eyes feigning confusion.

My nose scrunched up. "Where did you hear that?"

"I can't recall the exact moment." He shrugged, playfully biting my hip. "But I really did appreciate the sentiment." Goosebumps dotted my skin as he slid his hand up my thigh, slipping his finger inside of me. "God, you're wet and I haven't even started with you yet."

A hot flush crawled up my neck, my lips parting on a sweet sigh when his thumb circled my clit.

God, if he promised to keep doing that, I'd call him Big-dicked Brooks any time he wanted.

"Remember when I had my mouth on you? How good it felt? How *hard* you came?" He licked my inner thigh while his fingers continued working me over. "In my bed, when I sucked on your pussy until you were begging me to let you come. At the pool when I had you spread so wide and my mouth devoured you even though anyone could have walked in and seen us. They could have seen my face between your legs while your tits bounced with each gasping breath that fell from your pretty lips. Remember that, Georgia?" He moved to the other thigh, sucking a soft bruise into my skin. "God, I can't stop thinking about how perfect you taste. How sexy you look, sound, *feel* when I make you come. I'm dying to know what you feel like wrapped around me."

I was getting so hot, so wet, just from his words alone. As he kissed a slow trail across my pubic bone, my body relaxed—legs opening up and arms falling to the sides.

"I'm going to make it so good, baby." His mouth moved to my clit, sucking and licking and caressing me into an orgasm. He didn't stop until my body quaked and my limbs turned lax and sated.

"Hey," he rasped, moving up my body and kissing me.

I moaned when I tasted my sex on his tongue.

This enormous sense of relief took hold, wringing the air from my lungs. I was thankful, so very thankful, that I had found him. Thankful that he was taking his time with me, making sure my first time was what I wanted it to be. I hoped he could feel it in my kiss, my touch, that this was more, so much more than I'd ever experienced. He was spinning my world out of its orbit, taking me to places I had never been.

I watched in rapt attention as he kneeled between my thighs and slid the condom on. He pulled back, pushing his hips forward and pressing the tip of his cock against my clit.

My eyes found his as he hovered over my body, his hands resting beside my head. His blue eyes glowed in the moonlight, tender and soft.

"You're beautiful," he whispered against my lips, deepening our kiss.

Hips pressed into mine, he started to slip inside of me. The pressure built to the point of pain as he slowly, so very slowly, slid deeper. He didn't rush, didn't hurry to claim me, just took his time. He pushed himself a little farther, then stopped to kiss me until my body let go of the tension and relaxed into him.

My eyes glazed over, overwhelmed by the intensity—not just of the deed itself, but of the feelings that passed between us. Tiny inward gasps accompanied my every breath.

Once he broke the barrier, pain consumed me and forced an involuntary whimper from my lips. I was sure he could see it on my face.

His eyes turned remorseful as he caressed my cheek.

I wanted to remove that look from his face.

"More, Kline. Don't stop." I wanted this. Of course, there was discomfort, but there was also a perfect ache starting to build inside of my core with each small thrust of his hips.

"God, you're so tight. So wet. So perfect. I'm losing my fucking mind." His lips found my neck, sucking and licking and placing little bites across my skin. Every word eased an ounce of discomfort. Every kiss, suck, and lick eased two.

"Baby, move with me," he encouraged.

My muscles relaxed and I lifted my legs higher to my sides, allowing him to slide in farther.

He groaned.

A hiccupping breath escaped my lungs.

I needed more. I wanted Kline as deep as he could go. I rolled my hips, pulling him all the way inside of me. We both cried out. The sensations were overwhelming—his cock fully sheathed by my heat, my thighs pressing against his hips.

I let out a raspy moan, whispering, "God, this feels so good."

"Fuck yes it does." He kissed my jaw, my cheek, the corners of my lips.

My hips pushed up of their own accord, unconsciously telling him I still needed more. This is what it felt like to want to crawl inside a person—to be a part of them. It made me greedy; every inch he gave just made me want another one even more.

Kline moved in an easy rhythm, careful of my sensitivity but not lacking in intensity. He started to pick up the pace when I begged him to go deeper, harder, faster. He sucked savagely on my neck, growing uninhibited and frenzied, only to slow down again, finding my mouth and giving me soft, drugging kisses.

My hands explored his body, moving down his arms, his back, his ass, savoring the flex and strain of his muscles as he thrust.

"You okay, baby?" he asked, sweeping a few damp strands of hair from my forehead.

"I'm more than okay."

"Fuck, Georgia, you look so perfect like this. Here. Under me." His eyes turned fierce and determined, like he wanted to make me lose control, completely turn my world on its head.

My body started to shake as he sped up, only to whimper in taut frustration when he slowed down again.

"Do you trust me, baby?"

I didn't even have to think about the answer.

"Yes. God, yes. I trust you."

"I want to show you how good it can be when there's no rush." He kissed me, sucked on my lips, my tongue, stealing every one of my sounds into his mouth and swallowing them greedily.

And God, I loved his hoarse noises, how he kept telling me how beautiful I was, how good this felt, how hard he was. I loved how he took control and knew the exact way to drive me wild.

"I want to do this for hours and hours, but fuck, you're too much. It's too much." He shifted his pace—lazy morphing into quick and hungry. "Tell me how good it feels," he ground out, pressing his face into my neck. His voice was demanding, but he wasn't chasing my climax so hard for himself. He was doing it for me.

All I could do was nod, too consumed with desire to answer. I gripped his ass, my nails digging into the toned flesh.

"Good, because I'm going to make you feel even better," he swore. "I'm going to make you lose your fucking mind."

He slid out of me, spurring a distraught moan to slip past my lips.

He gripped my thighs and moved his face between my legs before I could stop him. His mouth consumed me—sucking and licking and tonguing at my pussy until my orgasm started to build at an explosive pace beneath my skin. Warmth spread across my body, a thin sheen of sweat following its lead. Unintelligible words escaped my lips as I started to come.

"That's my wild girl. Let me watch you catch fire," he said, continuing to take me over the edge.

I squeezed my eyes closed, mouth falling open, body bowing off the bed. I didn't just come. I screamed, exploded, burst into flames.

Time. Location. *My name.* Those things didn't exist, my senses too consumed by what Kline was doing to me.

He moved back up the bed, gripping my thigh and pushing my knee to my shoulder, spreading me wide open for his straining cock. He pushed inside of me with ease and started fucking me deep, dragging in and out at the most mind-blowing pace.

He propped himself up on his hands, staring down at where he moved in me. "Fuck, it's so good."

Moving one hand between us, he rubbed my clit. "I need to feel you come around my cock."

"I don't think I can. It's too much already."

He didn't let up, determined. "Yeah, baby, you can. Come on my cock."

I whimpered.

"Let go."

I was his instrument and he had mastered the skill of making me sing. My body arched into his touch, my hips rocking faster with his. "Kline… I… Oh… God…"

"Fuck yes, give me one more." His eyes focused on his hand moving over me, his cock sliding in and out.

I closed my eyes, my mind drowning in pure sensation.

My thighs quivered, my pussy tightening rhythmically around

him, and my hips threatened to cramp up from the strain. A surprised cry escaped my lungs as I came hard and fast. My head was thrown back into the pillow, and I gripped his ass, pulling him forward while he rocked into me.

His eyes squeezed shut, lips parted as he chased his own release. His hair was mussed up, sweat wetting his brow. And God, his eyes, they were fierce and hooded with his impending climax.

"I want to feel you come." I gasped, dragging my nails down his back. I needed to see him lose control, needed to feel his body when he came.

He stared down at my breasts that were moving with the force of his thrusts. His skin was sweaty and perfect, and I wanted to lick it off with my tongue. And when he looked up and met my eyes, I watched him lose control.

The moment felt like a dream—everything slowing down so I could imprint every second on my brain. His mouth moved in slow motion with each soft grunt, each guttural moan. And his movements echoed that I was seeing the real thing.

This was real. *We* were real. My feelings, his feelings, even though they hadn't been said out loud, they were real. Deep down, I knew—he was it. My person. My soul's infinitely interesting counterpart.

"Let's stay here, wrapped up in one another until the sun burns out," I whispered into his ear, once his body had stilled and my burning lungs had cooled enough to fill with breath.

He lifted my chin, staring into my eyes. My heart latched on to billowing blue and refused to let go. "I know you're not ready to hear what I'm feeling, but just know, for me, tonight was *more*. It was *everything.*"

I closed my eyes, letting his words wash over me.

This moment would last forever. No matter what happened, I'd never forget the look in his eyes, the sound of his voice, and the feel of him claiming every part of me.

CHAPTER 22

Kline

I woke with a start, the brief confusion of my surroundings passing quickly enough that my hands slid across the sheets in search of Georgia's warm, sweet skin within seconds. The hunt for heated skin turned up nothing but cold cotton.

I lifted my head and opened my eyes to continue the search, and the mid-morning sun filtering in through the glass windows highlighted her clothes from last night, strewn across the bench beneath the bay window. Sitting up to get a better visual perspective, I blinked the sleep from my eyes and scanned the room thoroughly, but still came up empty.

With my sense of sight foiled, the others engaged, and the sound of her voice echoing from down the hall turned my short bout of panic into pride. Beautiful and brilliant, the unpredictably vivacious woman down the hall had chosen me to share last night with.

Her voice wasn't as pretty as the rest of her, though, the familiar, high-pitched, nails-on-a-chalkboard tune of her unrecognized song bringing a smile to my face. And it was *loud*. So loud—and unexpectedly inviting—that I got out of bed and threw on a pair of boxers to find out what she was up to.

Striding down the hall, I found her in one of the bathrooms. The door open and her body in motion, her back was to me as she slid a paint-covered roller across the wall and danced at the same time. Her voice boomed inside the small, confined room, and a Mary Poppins-like accent emphasized her tone. I'd never heard the song before, but I couldn't tell if that was because I didn't know the band or that she was only singing every third word.

In disbelief that I'd found her making her own episode of something on HGTV so early in the morning and without cause, I leaned against the doorframe and just watched her, drinking her in. Blonde hair sat on top of her head, curls cascading from a messy bun. She was a mess, earbuds in with her phone tucked into the side of my boxer briefs, and her black lace bra was the only other article of clothing covering her petite and curvy frame.

Her perfect little ass shook back and forth as she danced in place, painting the wall to the rhythm of whatever offbeat music filled her ears.

I crossed my arms across my chest, smiling at her obliviousness to my presence. She was painting the room the wrong color, smearing the light shade of blue I had decided I hated weeks ago all over the unfinished walls, but I didn't care. She could paint the entire house this godawful blue—as long as she did it in her current uniform, and I got to watch. Bob and Maureen would have to learn to love it, because every time I saw it, I'd think of this—of her, of last night, and of this perfect, simple moment.

I couldn't help but think, if I only made bad decisions for the rest of my life, at least I had made one really good decision with her.

Asking Georgia out was the smartest thing I had ever done. Period.

She turned to soak more paint onto the roller, and her hands flew to her chest, droplets of blue streaming across the room and staining everything in their path.

"Christ, Kline! You scared the bejeezus out of me!" she shouted, the accent of the band still hijacking the normal lilt of her voice. She removed her earbuds, letting the cords fall past her hips.

"My apologies, love," I said, mimicking her English brogue.

Her cheeks turned pink, an embarrassed smile cresting her full lips. "Sorry, I've been listening to English rock bands all morning."

I grinned. "You sound like a young Julie Andrews. It's pretty fucking adorable."

Georgia giggled, setting the roller down. She bounced around the room like a pinball, pouring more paint into the tray. Her excessive energy level piqued my interest.

"Did I wake you? God, I really hope I didn't wake you up. I was up by five, and I couldn't fall back asleep so I put on a pot of coffee. I watched Home Shopping Network for about twenty minutes and walked through the house, and then I saw the room and I figured why not make myself useful, right? So, yeah, I saw you had already painted one of the walls this color blue, so I decided to finish the job. Are you still tired? Hungry? I can make some more coffee if you want some?" Her words were strewn together in one giant, fast-paced, run-on sentence.

I tried to recall the last time I'd seen her take a breath.

She fiddled with bright blue painter's tape while tapping a persistent foot against the squeaky hardwood floor.

I cocked my head to the side. "How much coffee have you had, sweetheart?"

She shrugged. "A few cups. I guess I lost count after three...or maybe it was four?"

My eyebrows popped in understanding.

"Anyway, what do you think? Are you happy with the color? I think I like it. It's cheerful. Serene. Hopefully, your mom will like it. I guess her opinion would be the most important one, huh?"

I nodded. "I think she'll love it," I lied. "Have—"

"Fantastic!" she exclaimed, before I could ask her if she'd eaten anything. Her mind was like a damn hummingbird's wing, flitting around from one thought to the next faster than the naked eye, or in this case, ear, could process.

She grabbed the roller again, sliding it into the tray, and resumed her painting with more-than-necessary focus.

"So, last night…it was…did you…" She glanced over her shoulder, eyes uncertain, and before I could offer a reassuring smile, her gaze was back on the wall, her arm sweeping up and down in quick succession. Her feet fidgeted a few times until she just blurted out, "I had a really good time last night!"

And the light bulb went on.

Normally, I could get a pretty quick read on someone's headspace, more quickly than this, but after waking up to find her painting my house, her beautiful mouth moving a mile a minute, I was a little off my game.

Georgia was nervous. And about a pot of coffee deep into the caffeine jitters.

She seemed uncertain if I'd enjoyed last night, which was insane. First time or not, Georgia Cummings knew just how to sexually woo a man.

A tight, hot pussy was just the beginning because the rest of it was what I would remember. The shake of her body, the gravel in her voice. The way her words turned into moans, and those, in the fiery inferno of her orgasm, gave way to nothing but enraptured silence. Her eyes held mine, and her heartbeat was my second favorite part of her chest.

Nirvana was the only way to describe it.

I knew she felt it along with me then, and I knew, deep down, she knew it now, too. I just needed to remind her.

I moved to the shower, turning the nozzle and letting the water warm up.

She glanced over her shoulder at the squeal of the pipes. "What are you doing?"

"Just want to make sure the plumbing is still good in here," I lied. The only plumbing I cared about was hers.

I smiled in reassurance. She kept the suspicious face but turned back to her task.

Once the water hit a good temperature, I moved toward her, wrapping my arms around her waist, and whispered into her ear, kissing the soft skin of her neck.

"Hey, guess what?"

"What?" She shivered but didn't stop painting.

I kissed her jaw and stepped back, holding my hand out. "Let me borrow that roller for a second. I have a little trick that makes it easier," I lied again.

She shrugged, handing it to me. I set it down in the tray, glancing at the shower and noting the steam rising from the floor.

Perfect.

It was time to take this situation into my own hands. I grabbed her hips and tossed her over my shoulder before she could stop me.

"Kline!" she squeaked as I strode toward the shower, the top fragments of her bun tickling the skin of my thighs. She smacked my ass and back as I stepped under the showerhead, water drenching us both.

"Holy shit!" she shrieked as the water soaked into her skin and very few clothes. "What the hell!"

Chuckling, I set Georgia on her feet and ignored her glare. I reached around her back with a flourish, popping the clasp on her bra and dragging it off her arms and down until it landed at our feet. She was a vision, wet, waiting, and wearing nothing but my briefs.

"I enjoyed last night." Her uncertain eyes warmed just slightly. "So much that I feel compelled to thank you—" I paused and licked my lips with a wink. "And this perfect fucking pussy." Her eyes widened, but I didn't wait, sliding down her body, kissing between her swinging breasts, her belly, until I reached the waistband of my underwear.

"Kline?"

"Shh," I said into her skin, pulling a tiny section between my teeth. "I'm a little busy right now."

She shook as I slipped the briefs down her legs and pressed my mouth against her pubic bone, licking the water from her skin. "God, Benny girl, last night, you blew my fucking mind. It's safe to say I want to do that with you for the next one hundred years. It was the best goddamn sex of my entire life."

"Really?" she whimpered.

"You. Were. Perfect." My lips trailed down her inner thigh.

Her legs were trembling, her hands sliding into my hair and tugging desperately.

"Did you enjoy last night?" I prompted, putting the ball back in her court. "Was it as good for you as it was for me?"

"God, yes. Last night was perfect," she moaned, her head falling back thanks to my suction on her pussy.

Sweet like candy, I feasted on the taste of her until her inner muscles tried to take possession of my tongue.

Goddamn, I wanted that pussy to milk another part of me.

"How sore are you, sweetheart?"

She shook her head 'no,' but her eyes said 'God, yes.'

"I need to feel what it's like to be inside you again. I want to feel that pretty pussy squeeze the cum out of my cock."

"Yes," she moaned. "Please. Now."

I picked her up and wrapped her legs around me tight, moving us down the hall and into my bedroom before tossing her wet body onto the mattress. My sheets would be soaked, but fuck if I cared. I grabbed a condom out of my bag, tearing the package with my teeth as she watched from the bed.

"So, I guess this means there really weren't any painting tips?" she teased, biting her bottom lip.

"It's all about the strokes, baby," I said, flashing a devilish grin as I slid the condom on, stroking up and down my length to punctuate that statement.

I crawled onto the bed, moving between her legs. She gripped my ass as I held her thighs, my fingertips branding her skin, and spreading them wider until the tip of my cock nestled against the one place I *needed* to be.

"Now, Kline. God, I can't wait any longer," she begged. Her hips pushed up, urging me closer.

The second I pushed inside of her, we both cried out, losing ourselves in each other and chasing *each other's* pleasure.

I spent the next two hours using my cock and mouth and hands to reassure Georgia that sex with her was the single best thing I'd ever experienced, and she gave every second of that time to confirming it.

Hands down, motherfucking *nirvana*.

CHAPTER 23

Georgia

"Windows up or down?" he asked, cranking the engine and putting the gearshift into drive.

Reality started to set in. We were headed back to the city, and I knew I'd miss being wrapped up in my perfect Kline bubble. No responsibilities, no plans, just us, lazily enjoying the entire weekend together.

"Down, please." I wanted to smell the ocean one last time. The day was beautiful, sun shining brightly and only filtered by the occasional fluffy white cloud strolling past its glow.

He rolled down the windows then leaned over the console, grabbing two pairs of aviators from his glove box and handing one to me.

"Such a gentleman." I smiled, slipping them on and tossing my hair into a messy bun.

"For you—" he rested his hand on my thigh, squeezing gently "—always, baby."

As we drove onto the main road, the Hamptons house slowly diminished in the passenger mirror and an unexpected surge of melancholy consumed me. I was going to miss that beautiful, rustic house.

If I could've made a Pinterest board of my perfect home, that place would be pretty damn close. Once finished, I bet it would exceed my wildest dreams.

I was still in awe that Kline had bought a home for his mom and dad. And it wasn't a brand new house, which he could obviously afford. It was a home he was filling with love and care and thoughtfulness by fixing it up himself.

Everything I had assumed about him had been dead wrong.

He'd rented a Ford Edge, for goodness' sake. Nothing against that vehicle—I'd have been more than happy to drive one around—but it wasn't the type of car you'd see a man with his kind of money drive.

A Range Rover? Definitely.

But an economy, mid-size SUV that he'd *rented*? Hell no.

He was so damn humble and endearing and *practical*. Every new facet of his personality I discovered, I adored. Kline was one of the most intriguing people I'd ever met.

"I'll drive. You handle the music. Sound good?" He handed me his phone, iTunes already pulled up.

I nodded, scrolling through his playlists and choosing Young the Giant's "12 Fingers." It was the perfect song for this kind of day. I hung my hand out the window and savored the unseasonably warm wind that caressed my skin. After slipping off my flats, I moved my feet up to the seat, knees finding their way under my chin. Catching sight of each mile marker we passed, I felt a twinge of sadness as the distance grew between us and that gorgeous beach view.

I glanced at Kline out of the corner of my eye. He was softly singing the words, tapping out a beat on the steering wheel. He looked delicious—aviators, two days' worth of scruff, handsome mouth set in a soft grin. I wanted to eat him with a spoon.

A swell of emotions tightened my chest as our weekend replayed in my mind.

It had been perfect. *He* had been perfect. Kline hadn't rushed. He'd been attentive and careful and made sure my first time was good for me. And it had been. That night had been more than good. It had been *amazing*.

He made me feel crazy, in the greatest, most overwhelming way. It was hard to describe. Hell, it was hard to even put it into words without saying things I wasn't quite ready to say.

Just… God, this man… He was *everything*.

I felt like I was on the best roller coaster ride of my life. In the beginning, when everything started with us, I had hesitantly hopped in, mind racing: *What the hell am I thinking? Is this a good idea?*

The guy I'd known at work was a fair, honest, friendly guy but not one I'd ever considered. But then, it had been too late to back out because I'd been moving—*we'd* been moving.

We'd been climbing and whirling and twisting all crazy, and my thoughts had immediately shifted. *I'm pretty sure I'll survive, because how many people fall out of roller coasters, right?*

But I didn't really know because I'd never really paid attention to theme park statistics.

Shit, I had never really been into riding roller coasters.

Until Kline.

Every corkscrew and curve was exciting. I was enjoying every nerve-wracking minute, and I started to just let go and trust. I started to truly believe that as scary as it was, I was right where I needed to be.

Then, there was that "holy shit" turn when the bottom would drop out and my stomach would fall to my feet, but I was soaring again and screaming and laughing because I had made it. I was *alive*, and this—Kline and me together—was the most real, amazing thing in my life. And the ride slowed just a little bit, and the turns and twists were more like reverberations of the really crazy ones from before, but I was fine with that.

I was happy with everything.

And when I pulled into the place where I had started, I felt changed—overjoyed, enlightened, and knowing, without a doubt, I was right where I'd always wanted and needed to be.

In the craziest explanation, that was what he made me feel.

Complete. Alive. Amazing. The same but somehow very, very different.

The song switched to The Used's "Smother Me." The lyrics and the slow, silky beat had me looking at Kline again, drinking him in.

He sensed my eyes, glancing in my direction and smiling. One hand left the wheel, reaching for mine and entwining our fingers.

I laid my head back on the seat and just enjoyed, savored, greedily soaked up this little moment. I memorized every second, locking it up tight with the rest of my Kline memories.

We'd made a lot in a short time, but they were good ones. Every single one.

Before I knew it, Kline was hopping out of the driver's side and opening my door. The drive had been nice and we'd made good time. He'd held my hand the entire way, his thumb caressing my fingers. We didn't talk much, just silently enjoyed each other's company.

Sometimes, words don't need to be said. Sometimes, simply enjoying someone's company, just having them beside you, just being in their presence was enough. Plus, my inner monologue had said enough for the both of us.

Since we had spent the majority of the day packing and driving, I was going to stay the night at his place. We'd take the rental car back on our way to work and get into the office a little later than usual.

That was definitely one positive for dating your boss. If he wanted to take you away on a long weekend in the Hamptons and demanded you go into work a few hours later than normal, who were you to argue?

"Let's leave the bags," he said, taking my hand. "I'll grab them later."

He handed his key off to the valet and led me into the lobby and onto the elevator.

"Did you have a good weekend, Benny?" he asked, pushing the button for his floor.

"Eh." I shrugged. "It was okay."

"Just okay?"

I nodded.

He stalked toward me like he was a predator and I was his prey, and he caged me against the wall. "Are you sure about that, baby?"

"It was *pretty good?*" I stared up at him, fighting the urge to smile.

"I have a feeling you're trying to get me riled up." His kissed the corner of my mouth. "Is that what you're doing?"

"Is it working?"

His hand slid into my hair, gripping the strands. "That depends. What kind of reaction were you hoping for?"

"One that includes taking off your pants."

"I think that can be arranged."

His mouth was on me, kissing me hard, making my moan echo in the small confines of the cart.

My hands were all over him, touching his chest and stomach and then sliding up his back. I was about two seconds away from mounting him inside the elevator when the bell dinged, signaling we'd reached his floor.

He didn't waste any time, picking me up and wrapping my legs around his waist as he carried me out, grabbing my ass.

We were a mess of kissing and groping as we reached his door. It took him three tries to fit the key into the lock and open it. We tumbled into his apartment. He kicked the door shut. My back was pressed against the wall as he continued to kiss the hell out of me.

"Kline? Is that you?"

We stopped, glancing toward the female voice coming from the living room.

"Shit," he cursed, untangling us.

My feet hit the floor and Kline discreetly adjusted my shirt.

I looked at him, confused. What the hell?

"My mom," he mouthed just as she rounded the corner.

Panic hit me. I was about to meet his mom. Kline's mom. She was here, in his apartment. And two seconds ago, I'd been about to hump him in the elevator.

I mean, what were the odds? Friday night, Kline had popped my cherry, and today, I was meeting his fucking mother. I felt like I was in the Twilight Zone.

Deep breaths, Georgia. You can do this. You can get through this without looking like a moron.

"Kline, darling! We didn't know you'd be home so early," she greeted, moving toward her son and giving him a hug. His mother was beautiful—dark hair that was cut into a bob, bright blue eyes, blinding smile. I was starting to see where Kline got his looks.

"Uh, hi, Mom." He cleared his throat. Scratched his cheek. "Just out of curiosity, how did you get in my apartment?"

"The spare key you gave us."

"You mean my *emergency* key? The one I gave you just in case I lost mine or managed to lock myself out of my apartment?"

"Yeah, that one." She nodded and smiled, not catching his drift in the slightest.

Kline sighed, scrubbing a hand down his face.

"Kline, my boy!" A tall, handsome man walked toward us. He was a distinguished kind of handsome, with salt and pepper hair and glasses covering his brown eyes.

Oh, shit! His dad is here too?

"Hey, Dad," Kline greeted.

The two men hugged, clapping one another on the back.

His dad's focus turned to me. "And who is this gorgeous woman?"

"Bob, I was just about to ask that," his mother added, almost insulted that he'd gotten to it first. It caused a hint of a smile to spread across my face.

"This is my girlfriend." Kline wrapped his arm around my shoulder, tucking me into his side. If it hadn't been for the panic over his parents, I might have focused a little harder on the use of the label 'girlfriend,' jumped up and down a couple of times—that sort of thing.

"Georgia, these are my parents, Bob and Maureen," he begrudgingly introduced us. I had a feeling he was peeved their unexpected visit had put a damper on our little moment in the elevator.

I fought my normal urges to shout something awkward and completely inappropriate.

"Oh, hi! I'm Georgia! Your son took my virginity this weekend! You really did a great job with him! He sure knows how to please a woman!"

Yeah, don't worry. I managed to keep my foot-in-mouth syndrome under control.

"It's a pleasure to meet you both." I shook their hands. "Kline has told me so much about you."

"Oh, she's very pretty, Kline," Maureen murmured, winking at her son.

"Can't deny that," Bob added. "Looks like you're finally slowing down and enjoying yourself."

"Thank goodness!" his mother agreed. "It's about time our baby boy took some time for himself. He works too hard." She looked at Kline. "You really do, honey. You work way too hard."

Kline started to say something, but his father was already chiming in. "Definitely works too hard. You look good, son. And I have a feeling it has a lot to do with this pretty lady here." Bob nodded in my direction.

I felt like I was in the middle of a tennis match, moving my head back and forth, back and forth, just to keep up with their constant chatter. They were pretty adorable, to be honest.

"So, what brings you guys here, to *my* apartment, on a *Sunday*?"

"Your father still hasn't fixed my washer. And I needed to throw a few loads in," Maureen explained, giving Bob the side-eye. "But don't worry, I went ahead and did all of your laundry while I was at it. And

I cleaned your bathroom. It was a mess, Kline Matthew," she scolded.

He chuckled, shaking his head. "Thanks, Mom. I really appreciate it."

"Well, it was the least I could do. But really, Kline, between that and the litter box, I nearly fainted. You should think about getting a maid or something. Georgia shouldn't have to see that."

Pretty sure the last time I was here, what his bathroom looked like was the very last thing on my mind. The bedroom? Yes. Kline naked? Hell yes. But the cleanliness of his toilet? Yeah, not so much.

"Only one of those things is even remotely my fault," Kline grumbled under his breath. It was one of those moves where you want to stick it to a person by saying what you're feeling, but you don't *actually* want them to hear you.

I tried really hard not to laugh.

"How was the Hamptons?" Bob asked as we made our way into the living room.

"Fantastic." Kline encouraged me to sit down on the couch before settling beside me. "We had great weather."

"Had you ever been to the Hamptons, Georgia?" Maureen asked.

"A few times, but not since I was a teenager. It was nice being by the coast. Honestly, it makes me want to live there permanently."

Kline grinned at me, gently squeezing my thigh.

"What'd you rent for the drive, son?" Bob asked.

"Ford Edge."

"Sensible vehicle. Not my first choice, but I guess you didn't want to pick Georgia up in a Focus, huh?" He chuckled, smiling at Kline. "How was the gas mileage?"

"Pretty good," Kline answered. "Twenty-eight miles to the gallon."

"Not too shabby." His dad scrunched his lips together, nodding his head.

The whole practicality thing was really starting to make sense.

"Darling, have you offered Georgia anything to drink?" his mother whispered, but loud enough for me to hear. "I'm sure she's parched from the drive."

Before I could decline, Kline was pulling me to my feet.

"Come on, let's get you something to drink."

"I'll take a beer, son!" his dad called out to us as we walked into the kitchen.

"She's so pretty, Bob," Maureen whispered to her husband, giddy. "Do you think they're having s-e-x?"

"Christ, Maureen, I hope to God our son is having sex by now. He's thirty-four years old. If he isn't, I've screwed up somewhere along the way."

"Shh," she quieted him. "Keep your voice down. And stop talking like that."

"Pretty sure they can hear everything you're saying, Maur. You've never been too good with the inside voice." His father didn't even attempt to keep his volume down.

"Do you think they are, Bob?"

"By the way they looked when they walked in the door, I'd say they were about two seconds away from s-e-x-ing."

If they hadn't already shown me approval, I'd have been burrowing myself into the floor.

The second we got into the kitchen, Kline was lifting me onto the counter and standing between my legs. He gripped my thighs.

"Sorry for the ambush," he said, his eyes apologetic.

"It's not like you planned it. Anyway, I really like Bob and Maureen."

A relieved grin covered his lips. "They really do mean well. My mom can be a bit of a meddler, though. I'm sure that was apparent the second we walked into my apartment and found them making themselves at home."

I laughed, nodding. "It's okay. Once you meet my parents, you'll realize you have nothing to worry about."

He pressed a soft kiss to my lips. "I look forward to it, baby."

"Do you think we'll have s-e-x tonight?" I teased, waggling my brows.

"God, I was praying you hadn't heard them," he groaned, dropping his head to my chest.

I laughed, lifting his chin up to meet my eyes.

"I'm glad you're finding this hilarious."

"I can't wait until we have s-e-x again," I whispered.

Kline's face cracked, a smile consuming his perfect mouth.

"I hope you put your mouth on my p-u-s-s-y, too."

"If I put my c-o-c-k in your mouth, will you stop spelling shit?"

I nodded, my mouth twisting into a devious smile.

He tickled my ribs, urging giggles from my lips.

"Stop it!" I whisper-yelled, squirming away from him. "Now, stop being so damn ornery and get me something to drink. I'm parched."

He rolled his eyes, turning for the fridge.

I stayed on the counter, swinging my legs and watching him rummage around for refreshments.

"Hey...psst..." I tried to get his attention.

Curious blue eyes peeked over the fridge door.

I cupped my mouth with my hands, whispering, "You have the best c-o-c-k."

CHAPTER 24

Kline

"I just realized maybe I should have chosen a more profession-al meal. Something delicate." Georgia rolled her eyes with a self-deprecating smile and took a sip of wine.

Professional. *Ha.* These days, professional felt like nothing more than a fancy name for a distant memory. I was so wrapped up in her, my eyes were practically staring straight down the barrel of my ass-hole.

It didn't feel remotely natural, but it sure as fuck didn't feel bad either.

"You're not a delicate professional. You're a take-charge, no-bull-shit kind of woman. If Glen would rather watch you eat a salad than a steak, he can go fuck himself."

"Kline!"

"Well, he can. Don't worry about anything other than being your-self and the contract. Fuck the rest."

It had been two weeks since our trip to the Hamptons. We were at a dinner meeting with Glen Waters, President and CEO of Flowers-First, to button up an exclusive contract with them that I hadn't been crazy about—until Georgia had outlined all of the guaranteed cross-advertising they were contracted to do.

Full disclosure, I still wasn't one hundred percent sold. But Georgia Cummings was a smart, efficient employee, and that wasn't even my dick talking. He got a vote, I supposed—not worth denying it— but that wasn't the basis of my decision. My confidence in her ability was what had brought us to this meeting.

But the flower market share on TapNext alone was gargantuan, and I didn't like giving any one entity the entire pie. Contracts were airtight for a reason, but swearing yourself to one person professionally was just ripe for a fucking.

Glen better have some real unicorn and rainbow type bullshit planned for ad content or I am going to derail this train before it even gets out of the station.

"Sorry about that," Glen apologized as he approached the table. He'd left to take an "important" phone call. It happened from time to time, so I understood, but he rubbed me as one of those people who *thinks* he's hot shit and irreplaceable. Everyone is replaceable in business.

Some people like me, or Georgia, or maybe even Glen, could be an asset, but we sure as fuck weren't necessities. Businesses needed competence, patience, and drive, and plenty of people had those qualities.

"No problem," Georgia appeased easily, obviously feeling like telling him to go fuck himself a little less than I did.

"Now, we were just starting to dive into the specifics when you got pulled away," she began, steering Glen back to the prize. I sat back to watch.

"We'd be looking at a twelve-month exclusivity in exchange for majority placement in each of your ads: television, radio, and print. In general, our website makes up twenty percent of the online daily flower market alone. Brooks Media would contractually reserve the right to approve any and all ad content that references or deals with us."

God, she was something.

Every word she spoke made it clear—business didn't need specific people, but love and relationships sure did. I was starting to realize my specific person was her.

I checked back into reality just in time to find Georgia looking to me in question. Of course, I'd missed the question.

Glen, the helpful bastard, filled me in, though. "Don't you think she'd look sexy in one of the ads, Brooks?"

"No," I answered simply, hoping he'd drop it. We'd just gotten started, and I wanted to believe he was just trying to get into her good graces by complimenting her—inappropriate in both context and manner, but a compliment all the same.

He laughed and gestured at my girlfriend.

"Sex sells. You know this."

I did. Sex was a huge share of marketing in the U.S. specifically. But there was a whole slew of creative ways to use it, and they didn't include Georgia.

"Your whole market is sex, and this girl would *sell*."

I clenched my hand into a fist under the table but worked to keep my voice and demeanor steady. I even managed a completely unfriendly smile. "No, Glen. Georgia is an executive and an asset within the company. What she *isn't*, is *sex* to *sell*."

"Kline," Georgia whispered. My anger was building and she wasn't oblivious to it.

"Oh, I see," Glen said with a nod. "Her sex isn't for sale because she's already sexing the boss." He reached out to brush the loose hair off of her shoulder. "Good move, sweetheart."

My mind raced with a thousand scenarios of how I could strangle this motherfucker from across the table. *Shit.* I shoved back my chair and fished in my pocket for money at the same time. Rage bubbled and boiled under the surface, singeing the lining of my veins, but I didn't give in to the scene. He wanted that. He'd pushed the last straw to try to get a rise out of me and draw attention to himself because he knew the contract was already swirling the drain.

Guys like Glen were snakes, slithering around until they found the perfect opportunity to pounce. He wanted a physical reaction, one that would land me in handcuffs and balls deep in lawyer's fees. But I wouldn't be a party to it.

He was the coward, not me. Instead of facing his poor, pathetic, unintelligible business decisions head-on, *like a man*, he'd sexually harassed my girlfriend.

"The deal's dead, Glen," I declared, throwing the money down on the white linen tablecloth. "Contract's destroyed. Any future opportunity to do business with Brooks Media and any of its subsidiaries extinguished. And you've lost a powerful business ally, and instead, gained an enemy."

I pulled out Georgia's chair and forced her to stand.

"Kline—"

"Georgia, let's go."

She nodded, grabbed her clutch, and followed, but I could tell she wasn't happy.

And that made fucking two of us.

Frank sat at the curb waiting, and I opened the door and ushered Georgia in without delay.

"Mr. Brooks," Frank said as he jumped to attention in the driver seat.

"My apartment, Frank."

"Yes, sir."

Georgia tried several times to meet my eyes, but I couldn't return the favor. I was too goddamn angry. At Glen, at myself, and a little at her. I hated the last most of all.

I expected her to call to me. Tell me to look at her. Something.

But the more my anger stewed, the more her own built. When I glanced her way, she was staring out the window and grinding her teeth, the curves of her nails cutting into the skin of her palms every few seconds.

The ride remained silent and tense and didn't break until the door to my apartment slammed shut behind us.

I tossed my wallet and keys onto the counter and pulled the tails of my shirt out of my pants. As I loosened my tie, Georgia geared up for battle, turning to face me and slamming her tiny purse down on the kitchen table with force.

"I can't believe you!" she seethed.

"Me?" I asked in disbelief, four fingers pointing to the outside of my chest and raging heart pumping under the surface.

"Yes, you! That was a multi-million dollar deal. Access to ads we don't have to pay for for twelve months!" She shook her head. "I've been working on it for the better part of six months! And you threw in the towel because you were a jealous boyfriend."

"Fuck that, Georgia!" I yelled, and she jumped. It was the first time I'd ever raised my voice at her, and it felt just awful enough that I hoped it was the last. But she needed to hear this. "I didn't screw shit. That deal was menial at best from the beginning, signing away our lives to *him* for an entire year. And the way Glen conducts business is bullshit."

"I'm a woman, Kline! Sometimes I have to play the game a little differently than you."

"That's horseshit."

She jerked back, and her face flushed red with anger.

"The moment you lower yourself to playing into fuckwits like Glen is the moment you've already shot yourself in the goddamn foot *and* leg."

"I had it under control."

"You didn't have shit," I spat. "He was *touching* you. There is no-where, not one single place, where that's appropriate in business, man or woman."

"Kline—"

It would be bad enough that I'd interrupted her, so I forced my voice to calm. "You are a brilliant woman. When someone notices your beauty and belittles it like that, you tell them to fuck off, and you do it immediately."

"I was trying to—"

"No," I interrupted again, pulling my tie from my neck and tossing it next to my keys, softening my voice even further. "You're right about a lot of things, a lot of the time, baby, but about this, you. Are. Wrong."

Anger lined every angle of her body, the way she stood, and the expression on her face. But she didn't say anything. She knew I was right. She knew she hadn't been on her A-game, and she was fucking pissed about it.

Pissed that women had to be in that position in the first place.

Infuriated that she hadn't held her ground when he'd pushed.

She could carry that anger for the whole night for all I cared. In fact, I hoped she did. Stewed on it. Learned from it.

I didn't mind one fucking bit as long as she got the hell into my arms.

"Be angry," I told her. "But, please, for the love of God, do it while you're touching me."

Two fuming steps ate half the distance between us, and I closed the rest, pulling her face to mine with a clutch of her jaw.

Buttons scattered as she ripped my shirt wide open and pushed the destroyed fabric from my shoulders. Heat ran down my spine like a bullet out of a gun, burning a track all the way down and gripping my balls at the bottom.

I could feel them tighten in excitement, and an aggressiveness I didn't know I possessed surged through my veins in accompaniment.

As soon as the tattered fabric cleared my fingertips, my hands went straight for her ass and around, down the backs of her thighs and back up the inside, bringing her skirt with them. Scratching lightly, my fingernails tested her skin before the urge to grab overwhelmed me. Skin bunched and moved with the pressure before forming a perfect shelf below her ass where my hands could live.

I lifted her with ease, forcing her legs up and around my hips with pressure at my pinkies, and strode for the bedroom. She wrapped her arms around my shoulders to ease the pressure on my own and redistribute it perfectly to my hard-as-fuck cock.

Uninhibited, she ate at my lips, sucking one and then the other between her own and running her tongue along the seam of them.

A groan rumbled in my chest and her breath came out in pants, but that didn't slow either of us. Time versus pleasure was a race, the culmination of both right on the edge with no chance of stopping. I wanted her more than I wanted to breathe, and when she threw her head back, let go of my shoulders, and ripped her shirt over her head, she confirmed I wasn't the only one.

"Suck on them," she ordered, thrusting her tits in my face and reaching behind her back to unhook her bra.

With my hands at her lower back to hold her steady, I didn't delay or disappoint, pulling one cup down with my teeth before she could find the clasp.

Little nibbles and sucking kisses, I tortured every inch of skin, burrowing my face in the bottom swell and biting it enough to make a mark.

She yelped slightly, but it morphed into a moan as she pulled the scrap of fabric down her arms in between us and threw it to the floor of my bedroom.

With my back to the bed, I fell to my ass, unwilling to abandon our current position or circumstances. Her knees sank naturally into the mattress at my sides, and the newfound freedom of my hands made me test the weight of her perfect tits in each one.

"God, Kline," she whimpered. "They ache." She let out two short pants as my tongue swirled the tip and sucked it deep into the warmth of my mouth. "*I ache.*"

"Make it better, Georgie," I dared after releasing her pink nipple with a pop.

Always up for a challenge, she didn't hesitate, backing off of my lap in an instant and unbuckling the belt at my waist. Her tongue flashed out and tasted her own lips as she did, heady arousal running so hot in her blood that she couldn't stop. I nearly lost my fucking mind.

Belt undone, she made quick work of the button and zipper and shoved her hands inside before I could make a move to reciprocate with her skirt.

Jesus Christ.

The feel of her hand diving in to grab my dick without remorse or hesitation nearly made me come in my pants.

"Georgia," I whispered, and her bright, fiery eyes jumped to mine with desperation.

She'd been pouring all of her angst and uncertainty from the meeting into this—*into us*—and I didn't mind. But at the same time, I wanted her to feel what was coming from me. My jealousy, my rage—*sure*—but mostly my fucking disgust at listening to someone treat her like anything less than the smart, beautiful, goddamn goddess of a woman she was.

"Come on, baby. Climb on. Fuck me until it only hurts good."

She finally shucked her skirt and I did the same with my pants, toeing off my shoes in the process. She didn't bother, keeping her heels on her feet and climbing on top of me again.

I reached to grab a condom from my pants, but she slid down on my dick before my fingers even met the fabric.

"*Fuuuuuck.*"

"Oh yeah," she agreed, emphatic. "I'm going to."

"Condom," I reminded her, grabbing her hips to slow her already building speed.

She just shook her head with a smile, a halfway distant look in her eyes suggesting she didn't even understand what the fuck she was doing.

If I thought for even a second there was a chance I'd hurt her in some way or give her some kind of a disease by taking her without a condom, I would have stopped her.

But I knew for a fact I wouldn't, and if there were other consequences, like an unplanned pregnancy, I'd literally run myself ragged to make it worth it for all of us.

Because *good God*, I did not want to interrupt or ruin this show.

I eased my grip on her hips just enough that she could move freely and she took advantage.

She found her rhythm quickly, her tits swinging deliciously and the plump cheeks of her ass cradling my thighs and balls with every stroke down.

Her hair fell down and around her face, and her breath came out in staccato pants. I'd never seen a woman take hold of her pleasure so thoroughly. She squeezed me internally with every stroke, touched the skin on my chest like she couldn't get enough—*connected*—and yet, she worked me with the focus of someone doing nothing but chasing their own pleasure.

A smile swallowed my face as her pussy did the same to my cock. Up and down she went, her thighs shaking more and more with each stroke.

"That's it, sweetheart."

She was getting close now, and her fingernails were digging half-moons into the skin at my chest. I grabbed a handful of flesh at the sides of her hips and held on, saddling up and getting ready for what was to come.

When a moan exploded from her chest, I lost any pretense of control. A clap of sound cracked the heavy, sex-filled air as I reddened the skin of her ass with one hand and plucked at one of her perfect nipples with the other.

"Ride that cock, Georgia."

Her pussy clenched.

Fuck yes.

"Make it yours," I demanded, pushing her to take it to the next level. With an ab curl, my mouth lunged for her untortured nipple and sucked it with a pop. Her pussy grabbed me again, and this time was slow to let go. "Fuckkkkk. God, this cunt. It's gonna make *me* yours for fucking ever."

And it was. That and her mind and her single-minded determination to redefine herself—to redefine her evening's decisions—in one dominating ride on my cock.

If this was how we fought, I'd fight with her forever.

CHAPTER 25

Georgia

"Honey, I'm home!" Cassie yelled. A familiar echoing thud filled my ears as she dropped her bags to the floor. "Where in the hell are you?"

"In here!" I called from the bathroom. My lashes fluttered as I tried to apply mascara without poking my eye out. I liked makeup, loved when someone helped me apply my makeup, but I wasn't very good at doing it myself. Which was why if Cassie—the makeup guru—wasn't around to help me get ready, I stuck with the basics.

"Aw, isn't this sweet," she said, resting her shoulder on the doorframe. "My little baby is all grown up, applying her own makeup and shit."

"I even got my period last week, Mom," I tossed back, my voice monotone. "I think I'm officially a woman."

"What in the hell are you doing?" she scoffed, watching my reflection in the mirror. "Are you trying to remove your eyelid with that brush?"

See what I mean? Makeup and I weren't all that great of friends.

Lipstick? Sure.

Blush? Yeah, okay.

Even mascara I could manage.

But anything else, I was pretty much incompetent.

"Give me that before you detach a retina." She snatched the eye shadow brush from my hand.

I scrunched my nose. "What do you know about detached retinas?"

"I dated an optometrist like a million years ago and there was—" She stopped midsentence, taking in my narrow-eyed expression.

"*Okay*, if you want to be specific about it," she amended. "I *banged* an optometrist a few times."

"That's better. Keep going," I urged her.

"Well, there was an incident, and he freaked the hell out about my eye. Mumbling something about a detached retina."

"Do I even want to know details?"

"If you don't want to hear about how Wally's giant penis poked me in the eye while he was com—"

"Yep." I held up my hand, laughing. "I'm much better without."

"I'll tell ya one thing." She smirked, resting her hip on the sink. "Wally was my first uncircumcised penis."

I stared at her.

"What?" she asked, shrugging. "I felt like I was playing with one of those toys from the '90s. You know, the ones filled with water that would slip through your hands. I wasn't prepared for the foreskin." She looked off into space, thinking about God only knew what. "But once I got the hang—" She stopped, taking in my wordless expression.

Of course, internally, I was cracking up, but I knew Cass. Believe me, I had to disengage before she went any further. Because if she continued, we'd all know far too much about Wally.

"Geez, tough crowd," she muttered, fiddling with my makeup and finding her choice in eye shadow color before gesturing to my eyes. "This color is all wrong, by the way. You have gorgeous blue eyes. You need something that'll make 'em pop."

She motioned for me to sit down.

I plopped my robe-covered butt on the closed toilet seat and waited patiently for her to work her magic.

"I was trying to do a smoky eye," I admitted.

"Yeah, but these dark tones are all wrong," she said, moving toward me with a color palette in hand. "You can do a smoky eye, but you need neutral tones. Otherwise, you're just going to hide that spectacular blue."

"Close 'em," she instructed, brush held up close to my face.

I shut my eyes, sighing in relief. My best friend was home. Sure, we'd still managed to chat nearly every day through texts and short phone calls, but it wasn't the same. Four weeks was a long fucking time.

"I missed you."

"I missed you too," she responded, a smile in her voice. "I'm happy you were actually going out and having fun while I was gone."

"What's that supposed to mean?" I peeked at her out of my left eye.

She flashed an *are you serious?* look.

"I go out," I disagreed. "I go out all the time. I party like a freakin' rockstar!"

"Yeah." She snorted. "A very poor rockstar, who isn't in a band anymore, and starts yawning by nine and just wants to be home drinking wine."

"I'm not like that *all* the time," I denied, laughing despite myself. "But seriously, you're never allowed to leave me again."

The brush swiped over my left eyelid in smooth, sure movements.

"I wasn't even gone for a month, and I'm here for tonight. Anyway, you were a busy little bee with your new boyfriend."

Boyfriend. It felt weird to hear someone else call him that. In private, we'd exchanged the boyfriend/girlfriend sentiment frequently, but we were still keeping our relationship very much on the down low at work. My choice, of course. Kline was more than ready to make us public to everyone, but I just wasn't in that place yet.

We had fallen into this relationship so quickly and I didn't want to be rash about letting my coworkers know I was dating the boss. I couldn't ignore that nagging thought in the back of mind that wanted to find a way to protect myself as much as possible if we didn't work out—and protect myself from the shrieks of Dean if we did.

There was no denying we were together, but in a way, boyfriend didn't feel like the right word for what Kline was to me. It was too small, too casual. In such a short amount of time, he'd become a huge part of my life.

The brush moved to my other lid, working a little quicker once Cassie had found her makeup-applying stride.

As I thought about Kline and me and everything we had together, a smile crept its way across my lips, until happiness consumed my entire mouth.

"Well, look at you, all smiley and smitten. By the looks of it, I'd say someone has got it bad."

My cheeks flushed hot.

"Are you blushing, Wheorgie?"

"No." My hands went straight to my cheeks. "I am most certainly not blushing."

"Of course you're not." She laughed. "Tilt your head back." She gripped my chin. "So, give me the scoop. What's the boss really like?"

"He's just… I don't know even where to begin." That smile was back, taking over my entire face—mouth, cheeks, even my eyes were crinkling at the corners.

"Dude, tone down the cheesy grin or else I'll screw up your makeup."

I laughed, despite myself. "Sorry, I can't help it. I really like him, Cass."

She paused for a second and my eyes opened, meeting her intrigued stare.

"What?" I asked, starting to feel self-conscious. "Does the smoky eye look stupid on me?"

She shook her head.

"Then what? Why are you looking at me like that?"

"Nothing. Close your eyes again so I can finish up. Other people need to get ready around here, you know," she teased, her hip bumping my side.

I did as I was told and enjoyed the luxury of having someone else do the tedious task of applying eye shadow and liner.

"You know," she whispered, "I think you're holding back on me. I think—actually, *I know*—this thing between you and Kline, it's a whole lot more than just like."

"I said I *really* like him," I retorted, my mouth staying in a flat line as she slid lipstick across my lips.

"I'm aware," she said, her voice tickled with amusement. "But I think there's another four-letter word rolling around in your brain."

"Fuck?" I deadpanned.

"No, but how is the fucking? Is it everything you dreamed of when you were holding on to your coveted virginity?" she teased.

"Eh." I feigned indifference. "I could take it or leave it." I pulled the corners of my lips down into a pout, hiding another cheesy grin.

She snorted, taking in my absurd expression—smiling eyes, frowning mouth, and cheeks about to burst at the seams. "So, what I think you're telling me is that he's better than you could have ever imagined? Your Big-dicked Brooks billionaire can bring it."

I shrugged, biting back a laugh. "Something like that."

"I knew it!" She fist pumped the blush brush. "I'm not one to say 'I told you so,' but yeah, I told you so!" Cassie danced around the bathroom, shaking her ass and laughing maniacally.

"All right, crazy. Less gloating, more fixing my makeup," I demanded, giggling at her antics.

"I feel like we need a kitchen dance party to commemorate this momentous occasion," she announced, still dancing around in the silent room.

Kitchen dance parties were our thing. We had been doing them since college. They were used for happy times, horrible times, and everything in between.

When Cass told her nasty professor to suck it? Kitchen dance party.

When I got the coveted internship I was striving for? Kitchen dance party.

A hot barista asked Cass out? Kitchen dance party.

The time I managed to do all of our laundry with four quarters? *Epic* kitchen dance party.

There were only three rules: Rotate who got dibs on the music selection. No boys allowed. And always bring your A-dancing-game.

Some of my fondest memories of college were with Cass, dancing around in our shitty apartment, singing our hearts out. God, this girl, she was my rock. My favorite person to vent to, cry with, and most importantly, laugh my ass off with. I wouldn't have traded her for anything.

"All right, sweet cheeks, you're all set," she announced, smirking down at me. "And your makeup is looking pretty damn fabulous if I do say so myself."

I stood, taking in my appearance in the mirror. I touched my cheeks as I examined the gorgeous shades highlighting my eyes. She was right; neutral was better.

"Now, I didn't go crazy, just went with subtle and your signature bright red lips. I still wanted you to look like my Wheorgie." She winked. "You're gorgeous, friend. Absolutely stunning."

Without hesitation, I wrapped my arms around her, hugging her tightly. "Thank you. I love you so much, Cass."

"Love you too." She hugged me back.

We rocked back and forth a few seconds, until I whispered, "You really dated an optometrist named Wally?"

"Banged." She laughed, shoving me away. "There was no dating. His name was Wally, for fuck's sake."

I pointed at her, grinning. "You're a troll."

She was completely unfazed by this. "I'm fully aware. I will not make apologies for my need to judge men by their names."

"That is so weird. You know that, right?"

While some women judge men by their looks or clothes or money, Cass judged them by their names. It was one of her little quirks and it was off-the-wall bizarre, but downright hilarious. I'd seen her in action far too many times, a man asking her out or offering to buy her a drink, and her response always depended on one thing: his name.

The name was always the make it or break it in Cass's dating life scenarios.

"I know, but I can't help it. I can't bring myself to date, much less marry, someone named Wally or Toby or Cliff. Just—" She shudders. "Nope, no way. I'll never do it."

"I need to know how staunch you are on this mindset." My hand went to my hip. "Let's talk hypotheticals. What if Jude Law asked you to marry him, but his name was actually Morty Law?"

She grimaced. "Nope. Sorry, Morty. Take your adorable accent somewhere else."

"What about Angus Efron?"

A look of disgust crossed her face. "I don't care how much cheese he can grate on his abs. Not happening."

I stared at her for a few seconds, deciding if I really wanted to do it.

Cassie eyed me with skepticism. "Don't you dare." She pointed in my direction. "Don't even think about it."

I nodded, a mischievous grin spreading across my lips.

"Georgia," she warned.

"What if..." I smiled, tapping my chin. "Eugene Tatum—" she gasped "—was naked, asking you to marry him while grinding against you to 'Pony'?"

Channing Tatum was Cass's guy. He would always be at the top of her list. When *Magic Mike* had come out, we'd seen the movie not one, but two times on opening night because she was a total hornbag for him.

"I hate you." A hand towel was tossed into my face. "I'm going to forget you ever said that," she grumbled, striding into the hallway.

Of course, I followed her. This was too good of an opportunity to pass up.

"You know? I think Eugene looked hotter in *Magic Mike XXL*."

"Georgia!" Cassie threw her hands up in the air.

I leaned against the doorway as she rummaged through her closet. "What? I really think his stripteases were way sexier. Eugene can bring it. That's for damn sure."

"I will not let you ruin Tatum for me."

"I'd never—" I raised both hands in the air "—ruin the appeal of Eugene Fillmore Tatum."

"Oh my gawd!" She placed her hands tightly over her ears, la-la-la-ing to tune me out.

I laughed the entire way to my bedroom.

Standing in front of my closet, I was wavering between about fifty different options. I wanted to look cute—no, I wanted to look sexy. I wanted Kline to be eating…out of the palm of my hand. I swear that was where I was headed with that.

I needed a guy's opinion.

TAPRoseNEXT (5:30PM): Psst…Ruck…Come in, Ruck.

BAD_Ruck (5:32PM): Need something, Rose?

TAPRoseNEXT (5:33PM): Little black dress (open back) and red heels OR black leather pants and lace top?

BAD_Ruck (5:34PM): Neither. Clothes aren't needed in bed. Anyway, lace isn't really my style.

TAPRoseNEXT (5:34PM): This isn't the bed game. I need a guy's opinion on outfit choices.

BAD_Ruck (5:36PM): You meeting your Some Kind of Wonderful tonight?

TAPRoseNEXT (5:37PM): You bet ya.

BAD_Ruck (5:37PM): You're really into this guy.

TAPRoseNEXT (5:38PM): Are you asking or telling?

BAD_Ruck (5:39PM): Both.

TAPRoseNEXT (5:41PM): For your information, Mr. Nosy, yes, I'm really into this guy. I'm meeting him for drinks later. And I want a guy's opinion on women's attire for date nights.

BAD_Ruck (5:42PM): Which shows the least amount of skin?

TAPRoseNEXT (5:43PM): Leather and lace.

BAD_Ruck (5:44PM): That's the one.

TAPRoseNEXT (5:45PM): Really?

BAD_Ruck (5:47PM): Less is more when it comes to showing skin. There are certain parts of you he wants to be the only one to see.

TAPRoseNEXT (5:48PM): I said the dress had an "open back" not open crotch.

BAD_Ruck (5:51PM): Just trust me, Rose. This is sound advice. I promise.

TAPRoseNEXT (5:52PM): Okay, okay. Leather and lace it is. Big plans tonight?

BAD_Ruck (5:53PM): Maybe...

TAPRoseNEXT (5:54PM): Your own version of Some Kind of Wonderful?

BAD_Ruck (5:55PM): Something like that. Be good tonight, Rose.

TAPRoseNEXT (5:56PM): You too, Ruck.

A part of me felt bad for still messaging Ruck, but we'd fallen into this odd sort of friendship, mostly chatting about one another's dating lives. We never attempted to take things to another level, never tried to meet in person. It had become a sort of unspoken rule since we were both involved with someone else.

I tossed my phone on the bed and grabbed my favorite leather pants and lace blouse. It was black with three-quarter-length sleeves, and the top revealed just enough skin to show off a bit of cleavage.

The only other things I needed were the Dolce & Gabbana leather booties I'd found a week and a half ago in SoHo. They had been a secondhand purchase, and a splurge at that, but I loved them.

"Georgia?" Cassie called from the hall.

"Yeah?"

"What time are we meeting Kline?"

"Not until eight-ish. I figured we could have a little girl time beforehand."

"Harry Potter shots at Barcelona?"

"I'm in." The bar in question specialized in shots. One in particular came with fire and was famously known as the Harry Potter.

If you've never been to Barcelona Bar, add it to your bucket list. It's not the bar you hang out in all night, but it's definitely the place you stop by to get your night started off right.

My screen flashed with a text message notification.

Kline: 8pm at The Raines Law Room?

Holy hell. It was one of those bars that had a secret door, and if you don't know somebody, no way you're getting in. It was a very unlike Kline place to go.

Me: Uh…pretty sure I don't have VIP access there.

Kline: Well, don't worry, because I do.

Me: Kline flaunting his money around? Are you feeling okay?

Kline: Not flaunting. Just using it to our advantage. Anyway, Will was pretty persistent since he's never been.

I should've known my brother was behind it. If Will had Kline's money, he wouldn't have any damn money left. Good thing Will would earn a nice salary as a physician and be too busy taking care of patients to spend it all. Where I was more frugal like our father, he was impulsive like our mother—a true American consumer who could easily be talked into buying a new car or plasma screen TV on a whim.

And I mean all of this in the most loving way.

Me: Okay. Count me in. Cass will be with me.

Kline: Perfect. Meet me there at 8. I'll leave your names at the door.

Me: Okay, I'll let Will know.

Kline: No need. He's with me now.

Me: WHAT? Are you having a bromance with my brother?

Kline and Will had finally met over lunch last week in Gramercy Park. It had taken about one minute of introductions and they were quickly bonding over rugby, scotch, and awkward stories about yours truly. By the end of the meal, they had exchanged numbers and my brother had enthusiastically agreed to guest play for Kline's rugby team the following weekend.

Kline: I had to find one somewhere. Walter certainly isn't filling the position.

I smiled at his ongoing battle with his cat. Every day I witnessed or heard about something else.

Me: What are you accusing my best friend of now?

Kline: I'm not accusing him of anything. I recount the facts. I went to all the trouble of fixing him a fresh bowl of milk, in the dish he likes, mind you, and the grumpy bastard took one drink and spit it out in front of me.

Me: That's probably because you should really be giving him water, not milk. He's probably dehydrated.

Kline: You always take his side.

Another message came before I could send a sarcastic response.

Kline: Are you standing around in your bedroom naked?

Me: Don't try to change the subject.

Kline: I'm not. I'm merely moving on to more important subjects.

I glanced at myself in the full-length mirror on my armoire, fully dressed and about five minutes away from being ready to walk out the door.

Me: Yes, dirty boy. I am very naked.

Kline: Liar.

Me: I'll never tell.

Kline: I'll tell you one thing, I'm going to take your panties off with my teeth tonight. I promise you that.

Well, shit. That had me wishing the night out was just a night in…in Kline's bed, to be specific.

Kline: We're still going out, Benny. Finish getting ready. We'll revisit this conversation later.

Did he suddenly become a mind reader?

Me: In your bed, later?

Kline: My bed. My couch. The floor. Against the wall. Shower. When it comes to my version of later, the sky's the limit.

Me: See you at 8. I'll be the girl with red lips and sexy heels.

Kline: Tease.

Me: You know it, baby ;)

"Okay, you've got about thirty minutes to get ready. We're sup-posed to meet Kline and Will at eight. That leaves us with about an hour to grab a drink at Barcelona," I shouted from my room as I sat on the edge of the bed, slipping on my new shoes.

"Wait…Will is going to be there?" Her amused voice echoed down the hall.

Internally, I groaned, knowing full well where this was headed. "Yes, my brother will be there."

"I'm definitely going with the dress, then! And sky-high stilet-tos!"

"I hope you break an ankle!"

"Me too! That way Will and I can play doctor and naughty pa-tient!"

"You are not banging my brother, Cass! He is off-limits!"

"When you say bang…what exactly do you mean?"

"No touching my brother!"

This was an ongoing joke between us. Cassie loved telling me how hot my older brother was. She adored him, and he mostly treated her like his little sister, but every once in a while, she could get him to play along and tease me about the two of them hooking up.

The mere idea of them together had me cringing. They'd be like oil and water. Both were far too opinionated and outspoken. If they got together, my life would implode from their bickering.

Grabbing my silver-studded clutch, I walked out into the kitchen and got my purse in order. Phone, wallet, lipstick, and keys—that's all I'd need for the night. When it came to New York, you learned quickly that the less crap you had to carry around, the better.

Cass came strutting out a few minutes later, legs on full display beneath a form-fitting gray dress and black stilettos. She did a little twirl, grinning at me. "How do I look?"

"Tell me you have underwear on underneath that."

"Of course I do." She feigned offense. "I have a thong on, Georgie."

"Go back in there—" I pointed toward the hall "—and put on another pair. Something that covers your entire ass. When you're around my brother and dressed like that, you'd best be double bagging that shit."

She laughed.

"I'm serious!"

"I know you are. I'm serious too. I'm real serious about getting Will naked. I guarantee his body is—"

"All right, that's enough." I held up my hand. "You made your point. Are we even?"

She nodded, visibly proud of herself for one-upping me. "Yes, I will forget about the Tatum incident."

"Good." I grabbed my clutch and headed for the door. "Eugene would be proud of you."

She groaned behind me. "You're an asshole."

"Let's go get drinks!" I shouted, fist pumping my clutch in the air.

Cass and I caught the train and made it to Barcelona in record time. We hung out for an hour, chatting and laughing and dancing for a few songs to the house band. We were one flaming Harry Potter shot and a beer deep by the time we left to meet the guys.

The Raines Law Room was located in Chelsea, fairly close to my apartment. I had a feeling Kline had had that fact in mind when he'd given in to Will's demands, always trying to make things easy and convenient for me. I'd heard all kinds of cool things about the speakeasy bar, but it was my first time making an appearance.

Hesitantly, I rang the doorbell outside of the discreetly marked door.

"I feel like we're going into a top secret sex club," Cass whispered even though no one was around us. "Shit, now my hopes are up. I'm going to be so disappointed if we're at the right place."

I gaped at her. "Of all the places your mind could go, you're sticking with sex club?"

She shrugged. "I've never been to one."

"I'm pretty sure most people have never been to one."

"Guess we need to add it to our bucket list, Georgie."

"No," I responded through a quiet laugh. "That's not going on my bucket list."

"Speak for yourself."

The door was opened and an attractive guy dressed in a vest and tie answered.

I gave him Kline's name and, just like that, access granted.

In an instant, we were surrounded by silky music, velvety curtains, plush sofas, and dimmed lights. I felt like I had been transported back into the 1920s. Any second a girl in a flapper dress with a glass of gin was going to stroll past me.

Will had already spotted us, walking toward the entrance.

"Well, hello, Cassie Phillips," he greeted, a devilish grin on his face. He picked her up in a bear hug. The second her feet were off the ground, she squealed.

"Just so we're clear, I'm hating both of you right now," I teased, feigning annoyance.

He set Cass down and pulled me in for a tight squeeze. "Aw, don't get mad, Gigi. You know I love you the most."

"Why aren't you with Kline?" I asked, scanning the room.

"I had to make a pit stop in the bathroom. He's at the bar with one of his buddies."

"Buddies?"

Will nodded. "Have you met Thatch?"

I shook my head, more than ready to meet the notorious Thatch. I'd heard enough stories to understand he was an infamous jokester and a ton of fun to hang out with, but Kline and I had yet to get around to hanging out with him.

"Well, follow me, ladies." Will gestured toward the bar. "Your boyfriend's been wondering where you were. I told him you guys probably stopped for shots and dancing at Barcelona before heading this way."

"That sounds like nothing we would do," Cass disagreed, hiding her smile.

"Uh-huh," Will said, grinning. "I'm sure you didn't get Harry Potter shots and request the house band to play Britney Spears either."

I shook my head, biting my cheek. "Nope. Definitely didn't do that."

We totally did.

It had taken a round of beers for the band to play Cass's request, "I'm A Slave 4 U," but they'd done it, and we'd danced like fools. It was an ongoing inside joke when we went out together. If we were going to request songs, it had to be a cheesy pop song. We loved seeing the reactions of the patrons in the establishment when our ridiculous request started to play—annoyed, groaning, cursing our names—but like clockwork, by the end of the song, everyone would be singing and dancing along with us.

"Yeah, no way we did that," Cass agreed, laughing quietly.

As we walked toward the bar, I caught Kline's reflection in the giant mirror accented by liquor bottles. My gaze moved to the attractive guy sitting beside him and déjà vu hit me full force, damn near knocking me to the ground.

Holy shit.

I stopped dead in my tracks, holding on to Cass's arm in a viselike grip.

"What the hell?" She turned toward me, confused.

My hands shook as I realized why I knew the guy next to Kline. It was Ruck.

Oh, *no.*

Ruck was here and he was sitting beside Kline, chatting like they were the best of friends.

Oh. Fuck.

I pulled Cassie away from the bar.

Will turned toward us, hands pushed out in a *what the fuck?* gesture.

"I forgot I need to go to the bathroom!" I called over my shoulder, damn near dragging Cassie across the floor.

"Holy hell, what is going on?" she questioned as I pushed through the crowd.

I didn't answer her until we were safely tucked inside the ladies' restroom.

"Oh my God, Cass!" I groaned, my voice echoing in the dimly lit room.

"I'm so confused," she muttered. "What is going on?"

"I know that guy next to Kline."

"Because he's Kline's friend Thatch, right?"

I shook my head, pacing the confined room like a caged animal.

"Are you going to give me a hint here or do I need to keep guessing?"

"He's Ruck."

"Huh?"

"Ruck! TapNext Ruck!" I stopped, my arms flying out in front of me.

She tilted her head. "The guy who sent the Hunchcock?"

I nodded maniacally. "Well, it wasn't really his Hunchcock," I started to explain, but realized we really didn't have time for that.

"I think I'm still missing something? I'm not really understanding your panic here..." She paused, waiting for me to give an explanation.

"Well, I never really stopped talking to him," I muttered, feeling ashamed to admit it out loud.

"Excuse me?" she asked, her eyes popping out in shock. "You've been talking to him this whole time?"

I nodded.

Cassie shook her head like she couldn't process it.

"Listen, I'll tell you all of the details later, but you need to act like you're familiar with him."

"With who?" She was still not catching on.

"Ruck!"

"Wait...who's Ruck again?"

I was about three seconds away from pulling my hair out.

"Kline's friend, Thatch! That's Ruck!" I whisper-yelled.

"Okay, okay." She gripped my shoulders. "Just take some breaths, G. Everything will be fine."

I took a few cleansing breaths, calming my racing heart down.

"Just tell me one thing. Why do I need to act like I know him?"

I sighed, staring down at my feet.

"Georgia?"

"Because you're still my profile picture," I whispered in a rush, hoping she wouldn't understand.

She started laughing and shaking her head in disbelief. "Remember this moment." She pointed a finger in my direction. "Because you owe me. Big time."

I nodded. "Anything you want."

"When we get home, you're going to explain why you're still talking to other guys when you're very happy with Kline."

"I swear to you, it's not like that."

She quirked a brow.

"I promise. I really like Kline. I wouldn't do anything to jeopardize that. Ruck is dating someone. I'm dating someone. And we never make plans to meet in person."

"Okay, I believe you." Cass pulled me in for a hug. "Who knows? Maybe he won't even know it's you…well, me…fuck, this is confusing."

I groaned. "How do I get myself into these situations?"

"Don't worry, sweetheart. I've got your back. I'll distract what's-his-face while you and Kline enjoy a night out."

"Thank you."

She handed me my clutch off the sink and moved toward the door.

I glanced at myself in the mirror, making sure I didn't look as crazy as I felt. My makeup was still intact, not a hair out of place. All I needed was another drink, or five, to calm my nerves and I'd be good to go.

Maybe.

As I walked past Cassie, she whispered, "Just so you know, this is really screwing with my big plan of seducing your brother tonight."

I rolled my eyes.

She held the door open for me. "Don't worry, I'll save it for another night," she added, a smirk on her face.

"Good plan, you slutty turncoat."

"Heyyy," she slurred, hinting at less sobriety than I'd hoped for going into a situation like this. "I'm no fucking traitor and you know it. I'm getting ready to eye-fuck the shit out of this guy for an entire evening just for you."

"No," I corrected. "No fucking, eye or otherwise. Just talking. We're friends."

She smirked as we rounded the corner and the guys came into view.

"What's his name again?" she asked, her eyes glowing like the last embers of a dying fire.

"Thatch," I answered by rote, minutely horrified that another member of my work world knew I was a virgin—or that I used to be—even though he didn't know I was me...I was Rose. Whatever. "Thatcher Kelly."

"Mmm," she moaned, fluffing her breasts into an even higher elevation in the cups of her bra and licking her lips.

"I'd thatch that."

Fuckkk. I should have known. For Cass, it was all in the name. This was going to be one long-ass night.

CHAPTER 26

Kline

"This place is unreal. You come here all the time?" Will asked as we walked into The Raines Law Room, dim lights and old-style sofas filled to the brim surrounding us.

"Not really," I answered honestly, knowing it wasn't really the place but the actual *going* that was the problem. "This is really more Thatch's style." The vibe was chill, but the allure was the drama. "The cloak and dagger, the limited access."

Will laughed and nodded in understanding.

I turned from him to the room to finish what I'd already started. My eyes had scanned the crowded bar immediately upon our arrival regardless of my knowledge that such an exercise was foolish and futile. My Georgie would be late to our wedding, the birth of our kids, and her own funeral.

Wait. *What?*

I glanced at her brother, panicked that he could read my mind, but he must have seen something other than outright terror in my eyes.

"Don't worry, man. George'll be here eventually." He laughed.

"But if Cass is with her, they probably stopped at Barcelona Bar before even thinking about coming this way. That girl *actually* gives *no* fucks."

I nodded along as though I understood, but I was barely even listening.

I mean, I could almost understand the wedding thing. I was crazy about her, no ifs, ands, or buts about it. But the kids?

Jesus.

My thoughts were in a tailspin, headed straight for the harsh reality of a quickly approaching ground when my pinballing eyes caught on something unexpected and unwelcome. Loud, boisterous, and impossible to ignore, it was quite possibly the only thing that could have superseded my line of thinking at that point.

Shoving through the crowd as gently as possible, checking to see that Will was trailing along behind me, I sought confirmation of my new, much more immediate fears.

Bodies moved with ease, and flirty smiles bombarded me from several female angles. I didn't have eyes for any of them, though, and for the first time in weeks, it wasn't because of Georgia.

Thatch turned as I approached, a shit-eating grin topping his redwoodlike frame at the sight of me. "K-man! Fuck yes! Out on the town! I thought I'd seen the last of this," he spewed out in quick succession, the effect of being several drinks deep slightly loosening his already slack tongue.

Will smiled at his greeting, and I tried not to cringe.

I really didn't need Thatch to be there tonight. I'd stupidly believed I could keep being Ruck and myself without the gun going off in my face. I was wrong. This was what happened when people played with things they weren't responsible enough to handle.

The walls collapsed, or at least, they felt like they did, and my tie set out to strangle me. Will smiled and greeted Thatch happily.

I ran through the consequences of his presence and tried not to puke.

God, if I couldn't get him the fuck out of here quickly, I was in trouble. His picture was on my profile. *His* face was the one Georgia had been associating with Ruck.

What was already a goatfuck of dishonesty was setting up to turn into an all-out cluster.

I leaned forward and right to Thatch's ear, using the crowd noise as an excuse to keep Will out of the loop.

"You need to leave," I told him succinctly, knowing that if ever there was a time my girl would be less than forty-five minutes late, this was it.

He laughed and slapped me on the back.

"It's good to see you too, man. I miss you. I only get to see you at practice these days."

I shook my head in frustration.

He laughed some more.

"I'm gonna run to the restroom, guys," Will excused himself, fading into the crowd fairly quickly.

Thatch nodded and smiled, taking Will's leave as an opportunity to shit talk.

"But, really, I guess that's the same as always. It's just the reason that's changed, right? Instead of work, it's the mystic pussy."

"Thatch."

"I get it, man. Sometimes your dick just gets caught in the snare of a good snatch. Like a vise grip, am I right?"

"Thatch, listen."

"How is Miss Georgia? Almost done with your ass and looking—"

Eyes to the door, I only heard the first half of his sentence—thank God—because, just as I knew she would, the object of my affection walked in looking like sex on legs right then. Leather and lace and enough beauty to make me think my earlier panic about kids was actually the best idea I'd ever had. Her blonde hair was styled wild, just how I liked it, and I could see the blue topaz of her eyes shining from across the room despite their failure to meet mine.

And arm in arm with her? The face of *her* profile, a woman I could only surmise was the infamous Cassie Phillips. I'd heard a laundry list of antics and anecdotes featuring Georgia's best girl, but I had yet to have the privilege of meeting her.

Fuck.

The web of lies was starting to look more like a convoluted clusterfuck of *what are the goddamn odds?* We'd each put our friends as our profile pictures—a scenario I should have predicted but absolutely *had not*—and now, I had to sit through an evening where any second this mess could brilliantly blow up in my face.

Out of time and patience, I turned to Thatch in a flash, and when I did, I led with my fist.

"Ouch," he said through a smile, rubbing his shoulder teasingly.

"Fuck, Thatch, fucking listen to me."

He mocked me with wide eyes and cupped his hands around his ears.

I considered hitting him again, this time for real, but with a glance in the girls' direction, I knew I didn't have time.

"The girl in the picture from the TapNext profile, the one you took it upon yourself to—"

"Traumatize."

I nodded. "Right. Well, I've been talking to her."

"Behind the lovely Georgie's back?" he asked in faux outrage. Regardless of his mocking, I could tell he was curious. Talking to two women at once wasn't like me, and when it came to these "two," he didn't know the half of it. And I didn't have the fucking time or means to explain.

One quick glance showed the women and Will together, hugging and laughing and all too close to heading this way.

I closed my eyes briefly to gain patience. He'd have to wait to hear how twisted my truth had become because that talk required more than fifteen seconds and several glasses of scotch.

"I've been talking to her ever since, and she's here. She's getting ready to come over here, right now, and she's gonna be doing it with Georgie."

With her? Ha! Fuck! More like, it is her.

"Well, fuck me," he said with a smile, his eyes searching mine in an effort to figure me out.

"Your picture is on that profile. You need to pretend to know her," I urged.

He paused for a beat, but he couldn't miss how important this was to me. Whether he agreed or understood or wanted to play along, or not, Thatch would always have my back. When you pulled back all of the prank-pulling, shit-talking layers, he was unmistakably one of the best kinds of people. "Got it."

I took air all the way into my lungs for the first time in the last two minutes and turned to greet my girl.

But she wasn't there. She and her friend had disappeared, leaving only her brother Will in their wake.

As Will made it to us, shaking his head, Thatch leaned over and added with a whisper, "And all this after I gargoyle-dicked her?" He whistled low. "You must have more game than I thought."

"What's up?" I asked Will, pointedly ignoring Thatch and hoping my face managed to do the same.

"Who knows, man? Hell if I can understand women."

When he provided no further information, I was sure my eyes tried to crawl all the way inside his head.

"Oh," he said, turning from the bar to find my inappropriately intense gaze. "They're in the bathroom."

I nodded woodenly in understanding, and Thatch nudged me as a result.

"You gotta lighten up," he whispered, turning me to the bar and flagging down the bartender. "Order a drink, for fuck's sake, and calm down."

I nodded again because I knew he was right, and it seemed to be the only action I could successfully complete at the time.

"Macallan," I muttered, knowing he'd make sure my order got to someone who actually *made* the drinks. Ordering directly was too complicated for me right now.

"Yeah, man," he said, smirking. "I know you drink Macallan. Macallan and lime, every day, every night for years now."

The cords of my throat tightened in frightened reflex. "No lime."

"No lime?"

I shook my head, feeling the tension drain from my shoulders a little at the memory of my sweet, doped up girl. "Georgie's allergic."

"Well, shit. That's problematic."

I laughed. "Not really," I said, then clarified, "Not now that I know, anyway."

"Make sure to leave out the lime," Will interjected, coming up on my other side to join the conversation.

"I guess she told you?" I asked with a laugh.

"Eventually. I still don't think she told me everything, but now that Cass is here, I'll find out the rest."

"Cass?" Thatch asked.

"Yep. Cassie Phillips. I'd say she's like another little sister to me, but I'm not sure she's the kind of girl who *can* be a little sister."

Thatch's eyes flared with excitement, and my panic came back tenfold. "Wild?"

Will just laughed and jerked his head toward the approaching women. "You'll see."

I forgot about everything else as soon as I saw her again. Long legs, a sliver of tan stomach, and a nervous smile, she was so fucking beautiful, I literally couldn't take my eyes off of her.

I pulled her straight into my arms, put my lips to her ear, and breathed. "Benny."

Out with the words and in with her smell, I held her body to mine and kept it there until she started to giggle.

"*Kline.*" I struggled to remove my face from her hair and my hands from her hips, but she helped it along, turning her body to include her friend in the conversation and making my hand slide along the skin at her back. "This is crazy Cassie."

"Crazy Cassie?" Cass squawked. "Is that my given name now?"

"Yes," Georgia challenged adorably.

"Ohhh, okay then," Cass conceded with a gleam in her eye. "I see. I'm a little slow, but I get it now."

Her hand reached for mine and I took it without question, giving it two quick shakes. "Hi, nice to meet you," she said.

I smiled.

"I'm Crazy Cassie. You must be Big-dicked Brooks."

Thatch spewed his whiskey everywhere, coating us all with a layer of spit to complement the shock courtesy of Cass.

Georgie squealed and Cassie just laughed, and through the chaos my eyes met those of an amused Will. He raised his glass in a gesture of confirmation.

Wild.

And unpredictable and funny and completely apathetic.

Good God, the people in this party were going to make this one interesting night.

I hoped we all survived.

I grabbed some napkins from the bar and handed them to Georgie, watching closely as she wiped Thatch's half-drunk whiskey from her cleavage. She shook her head slightly to let me know she'd noticed, and I felt my face dissolve into an outright smile before I turned back to Cass.

"That's me," I told her. "It's a wonder your friend is still alive."

Thatch and Cassie burst out in hysterics as Georgie slapped at my chest and Will covered his ears playfully.

"Kline!" Georgie screamed.

"Come on, baby. Let's go sit down," I told her, scooping her into my arms before whispering in her ear, "My legs are tired from carrying this thing around."

"Kline!"

"It's a real problem, Benny."

"Kli—" she started to chastise again, but I didn't give her the chance. Sealing my lips over hers, I licked and sucked and nibbled out a real hello. The night had just started and the implications of my lies hadn't even begun to be realized.

But *God*, I'd missed her.

And right then, in my mind, that was all that mattered.

"Where've you been all my life?" I asked against her lips as our kiss pulled to a close.

She smiled just for me, lust and like and maybe a little bit of love lighting her eyes and reflecting into mine. She rubbed the bridge of my nose with her own as I settled her into my lap, finding a space on a couch by sheer miracle. Hell, for all I knew, someone had moved at the last second to avoid having me on their lap. I wouldn't have noticed.

"I've been—eeeep!" she squeaked as she was ripped from my arms.

For a full second and a half, I feared for every single patron, a hulklike rage overwhelming my emotions and tensing the seams of my clothes.

"Relax, K," Thatch teased, cooling my rage but stoking the fire of my aggravation. "Just rearranging the seating chart."

My eyes narrowed as he set Georgie down on the sofa across from me and pushed me back to sitting next to him.

My thoughts were nearly murderous.

"Sheathe your claws, buddy," he cooed in my ear. "You're gonna have to get over your tantrum because old Ruck here needs some information and there's no one else to give it to him."

Goddamn, I hated when Thatch was right. And I hated it even more when it meant Georgia's ass couldn't be in my lap.

I looked at her, across from me, and found startled eyes bouncing back and forth between Thatch and me. To her, we were both a significant part of her life. It felt weird and I felt jealous, but mostly, I just felt *bad*. Bad for lying to her and bad for putting her through the confusion she felt now.

The responsibility for all of it sat squarely on my shoulders, and believe me, I could feel the weight. The sooner tonight was over with, the better.

"Cassie, right?" I heard Thatch ask above the ringing in my ears.

"Yeah."

"You know," he pushed, clearing his throat. "You look familiar."

"You too, actually. You look very Ruckish or Rucklike or something."

I shook my head and glanced at my panic-ridden girlfriend. She couldn't see it like I could—she was too nervous. This was like watching a bad spoof film of Ruck's and Rose's lives where the blind were leading the blind. We would never have reacted like this to seeing one another. Not in a million years.

Thatch's laugh was boisterous, his body nearly falling into my lap with the action. Turning his face to mine, he mouthed "name" quickly. I had to fight the urge to sigh. If it wouldn't have been a spectacular failure and an embarrassment for Georgia, I would have told everyone to give it up right then.

Instead, I typed out Rose on my phone and showed it to him quickly.

"Rose!" Thatch practically shouted. Cassie nodded along while Georgie's eyebrows pulled unconsciously together. She was rightfully confused. "I thought that was you, Rose! I can't believe how beautiful you are in person, Rose!"

I discreetly elbowed Thatch in the ribs. "Say her name one more time and I'll kill you," I whispered through gritted teeth.

He grimaced and shut his mouth.

"What's going on?" Will asked, the spectacle apparently just as confusing from the outside looking in.

"I was wondering the same thing," I said, playing along.

"It, um," Georgia mumbled. "It seems like they know one another or something."

"Thatch and Cass?" Will asked, confused.

"Yeah," Cassie confirmed. "We've been talking online ever since he sent me a picture of his big, ugly dick."

Will jerked in surprise. "What?"

"It wasn't his," I interjected at the same time Thatch taunted through a smile, "Well, you've got the big part right."

Georgie's eyes came to me.

"Or so I've heard," I added.

She looked upset. "He talks to you about it? What…" She paused and swallowed. "About what they say?"

God, this was horrible. I hated this and myself and every-fuck-ing-body right now.

"No, baby. That's the only thing he told me," I assured her, digging my fucking grave a couple of feet deeper.

The urge to flee was strong, but we'd literally just fucking gotten there. To hell.

The Raines Law Room was definitely what hell looked like. The devil and fire and the roaring fucking twenties.

She'd confided in Ruck, and she felt badly about what that meant to her relationship with me. I could see it written in cursive, scribbled and scrawled all over her beautiful face as she warred with herself about not wanting me to know the things she'd told him and feeling like a liar and a cheat for having hidden something behind my back in the first place.

It made me sick inside, twisted the lining of my stomach and my intestines alike, and I just barely managed to stop myself from jetting to the bathroom for reprieve.

But my face was her lifeline in this situation, for as much as she feared being outed, every smile I gave her was a comfort. I refused to leave her on her own in this stormy sea to float and flounder.

Bottom line, Rose would have ditched Ruck ages ago if I hadn't twisted every conversation to my advantage. I was the guilty party here.

As Thatch started to flirt, I pulled my attention from Georgia long enough to tell him to pump the fucking brakes. One comment about her tits and the ruse would be roasted.

"Ruck and Rose are *friends*. Ruck's dating someone else, and Rose is a virgin for fuck's sake," I informed him. "Lay the hell off."

Wild eyes jumped to mine. I wanted to shove the words back in as soon as they escaped.

"Excuse us for a second," Thatch said with a smile, dragging me from the couch and over to the bar in a way no one else could.

My ass hit the stool in front of him and he leaned in menacingly.

"You better start talking, dude. I'm fucking dying over there in the name of *your* two-timing ass, and you can't take your eyes off of your girlfriend long enough to save me."

I shook my head.

"What the fuck is up? If that woman is a virgin, I'll freeze my fucking nuts off with one of those wart removers."

I grimaced.

"Yeah." He nodded. "Not a pretty fucking picture. So tell me, what's the real deal here?"

I considered it for a second, what it would hurt if I told him versus what he would hurt if I didn't. I decided I liked all of my bones like they were. And anything I told him to keep to himself, I knew he would.

"Georgie is Rose, not Cassie. But she doesn't know I know that, and she doesn't know I'm Ruck."

"Jesus." He put his face in his hands and rubbed at his temples. "You don't pay me enough for this level of complication."

"Yeah, well, you're not here as an employee. You're here as a friend. And I didn't invite you, if you'll remember. I tried to get you the fuck out of here *before* they got here."

"All right, all right, I get it. You and Georgie need to leave or something. I can't keep this shit up, but I can't abandon you either."

"Noble of you."

"Duh, dude. My character is top of the pyramid."

I shook my head and scrubbed a hand over my face.

Realization flooded him in a surge, like the swelling of a tide. "Wait a minute. Does this mean Georgia girl is a virgin?"

I tried not to give him anything, but my face must have conveyed some kind of confirmation.

"Oh holy hell, K."

"Thatch—"

"But she's not anymore, is she, you dirty dog?"

"Thatch—"

"Kline?" Georgia asked from behind Thatch timidly. My tongue made a valiant attempt to choke me. The conversation, the circumstances. All of it was fucked, and a timid Georgia was the last fucking straw.

My girl was a fucking shark, and I was completely over anything that made her feel any different.

"Hey, baby," I greeted her from around Thatch, leaning out to make sure my eyes met hers.

"Is everything okay?"

With one last look to Thatch that conveyed *just* how important his eternal silence was, I was up, moving toward my woman to the slow beat of the house band.

I was done with the secrets, done with the space, done with the whole scenario of the night, and nothing made me happier than dragging this woman out onto the dance floor when she least expected it.

"How about a dance, Benny?"

Her eyes cruised the room, but I made her walk as she did, a warm palm at the small of her back allowing her to lead but still guiding the way.

"But no one else is dancing."

"I like being the first," I teased as I pulled her around to face me and planted her square in my arms. She blushed furiously.

"*Kline.*"

"I'm selfish," I admitted through a smile. "I don't want to share you anymore."

The color in her face drained to white, the transition from blush to blanched one of the fastest I'd ever witnessed. Immediately, I regretted the words despite their validity. She didn't need any more evidence to build a case against herself in the court of Georgia's opinion.

Lips to hers, I apologized the only way I could, loving her on an endless loop of licks and swoops and tongue to tongue connection.

She hummed right into my mouth, the rightness too powerful to be contained in silence.

My fingers in her hair, I rubbed at her jaw with my thumbs and sank every ounce of myself into her. I didn't worry about Thatch or Cass or Will or anyone else, and for a couple of minutes, neither did she.

I'd never been this consumed. Not in my entire life, not by anything or anyone.

Wrinkles formed in her little button nose as she pulled back, her delicate hands loosening my tie just enough that I could breathe again.

Relaxed by the music or me, Georgia finally felt comfortable enough to address the night.

"It really is a small world, huh? People crossing paths and never realizing that they already had…or maybe they should have sooner."

Complicated and twisted, she spoke of herself and me and Rose and Ruck and everyone else all at once. But the answer was simple to me.

"The world is small, baby. But love is large. Big enough that coincidence occasionally rubs elbows with opportunity."

"Where'd you get that?" she asked. "Ernest Hemingway again?"

I shook my head and pressed my lips lightly to hers briefly.

"That one's all me."

I lived in her eyes as she searched the depths of mine, swimming in the pools of blue and fighting to stay there. I was so deep in her, deep in this, entrenched in the muck and lies, and I still felt high.

High on her, high on us, and high on everything I wanted us to be. The wedding, the kids, the happily ever after. I thought it because I wanted it. Every minute, every hour, every day, I wanted her to be mine.

I was in fucking love with her.

And I needed to show her.

"Let's get out of here," I pleaded softly, rubbing the tip of my thumb along her perfect bottom lip.

She could feel my desperation, a tremble running through her from the crown of her head to the tips of her toes. Her gaze jumped to our seats, and I followed to find Thatch and Cass deep in flirtatious conversation and Will missing.

I scanned the room ahead of her, finding him at the bar in conversation with a woman and pointing him out.

"They're all busy, Benny," I coaxed. "Come home with me."

I expected her to survey them again, but instead, her eyes just found mine.

"Okay, Kline."

Okay.

All it took was a little love making to turn that okay into a repeated *yes*.

CHAPTER 27

Georgia

I was straddling the line between asleep and awake. My eyes were still shut, but the morning sun rested against my face. Kline's arms were wrapped around me, holding my back to his chest. Big spoon, little spoon, we fit perfectly.

My mind replayed last night. The bar. Finding out Kline's best friend Thatch was actually my TapNext friend, Ruck.

Talk about a twisted kind of irony.

When I'd seen Thatch's reflection in the mirror, a million emotions had steamrolled through me, but the biggest, most palpable one had been disappointment. That in itself had my gut clenching from guilt. That emotion made me feel like I had done wrong by Kline.

I couldn't deny chatting with Ruck had become one of the highlights of my day. He was funny and sweet and charming.

And the more I thought about it, the more it didn't really make sense.

Thatch was a nice guy, but he was also very different from the man I pictured as Ruck. He was boisterous and seemed to have a propensity for using the word fuck…*a lot*. In all actuality, he was Kline's version of Cassie. They were both crazy opinionated, a bit impulsive, and often tossed out humor in otherwise serious conversations.

Nothing like the Ruck I had come to know. But then again, it was the Internet, and just because we chatted often didn't mean I *really* knew him.

But I knew Kline. Despite the awkwardness of last night, it had still been a good night because of him. It was becoming a theme. If he was there, I was happy.

My own little Kline and Georgia movie played behind my lids. I curled into him more, keeping my eyes closed, and watched.

I saw us dancing on our first date, and the way I couldn't stop smiling when he kissed me. His eyes, worried and concerned, when I was having an allergic reaction to lime juice. The way he looked that morning, sleepy and handsome and *mine.*

I saw us walking through New York, holding hands, and taking it all in together. I saw him at the pool, playfully taking off his boxers and turning around, dancing for my entertainment.

I saw us in the Hamptons and the way he'd looked when he'd been inside of me, moving and kissing and loving me. And then, him laughing the next morning when I tried to feed him burnt toast and told him it was supposed to be that way.

The way he'd often sneak into my office, shut the door, and pull me into his arms.

All of the inside jokes and secret smiles that we shared.

We weren't just boyfriend and girlfriend, we weren't just lovers, we weren't just *one* thing.

We were *all the things.*

I was back in the present, blinking sleep from my eyes. I turned in his arms and took him in. The way his chest moved with each soft breath. The way his eyelashes separated into tiny points near the corners of his eyes. I brushed his cheek, fingers sliding past the tiny freckle near his ear.

My mind raced while my heart sped up, pounding in an erratic rhythm. And then, heart and brain collided, becoming one in the way I felt for him.

The bedroom was silent, only the faint sounds of the city filtering past us, but in the stillness, I could still hear it in the way my breath quickened. I could see it lying beside me—jaw slack and eyelashes resting against his cheeks.

And I could *feel* it. God, I could feel it.

I was in love.

I was in love with Kline.

Leaning forward, I pressed my lips to the corner of his mouth, silently saying, "I love you," against his skin.

He mumbled something, but otherwise, barely budged.

Looking at his handsome face, blissfully content in sleep, I knew what I had to do.

Scratch that—I knew what I *wanted* to do.

I didn't want this whole "Ruck" situation hanging over my head. I wanted to move past it, and most importantly, I wanted to move forward with Kline.

Sliding out of the bed as quietly and smoothly as possible, I threw on one of his t-shirts and headed into the kitchen to grab my phone out of my purse. I dialed Cass's number as I stepped onto the terrace and shut the door behind me.

She answered on the fourth ring. "What in the fuck time is it?"

"I need you to take over my TapNext account."

"Georgia?" she asked, her voice scratchy with sleep.

"Of course it's Georgia. Who in the hell did you think it was?"

"An asshole who decided to call me at…" She paused, and the sounds of sheets rustling filled my ears. "Eight in the morning. Jesus, Georgie, couldn't you have postponed this conversation for about four more hours?"

"I couldn't wait. I have to fix this, Cass. I feel like the worst person in the world."

"What? Why?"

"God, I'm such an asshole. Why did I do that? Why did I keep talking to Ruck when I knew the possibilities I had with Kline? I feel like I've been emotionally cheating on him the entire time."

"Georgia—" She started to respond, but I was already chiming in, too damn worked up to stop.

"In some weird way, I think I was invested in Ruck. Not even close to how I feel about Kline, but still, I liked talking to him. I wanted to talk to him. And you know what the worst thing is? When I found out Ruck was Thatch, I was fucking disappointed. It felt like a letdown."

"Shut. Up," she groaned. "You didn't cheat on him. You were just chatting with someone, *as friends*. This is not something you need to feel guilty about."

I stayed quiet, mentally chastising myself for being so stupid.

"Georgia. Did you ever make plans to meet up with Ruck?"

"No," I said, shaking my head. "Never."

"Did you ever tell him you love him or want a relationship with him?"

"Of course not."

"So stop berating yourself over this. It's pointless, and honestly, completely unwarranted. You haven't done anything wrong, sweetheart. You've been completely faithful to your boyfriend."

I took a calming breath. "You're right. I was completely faithful to him."

"Okay, great. I'm so glad we have that settled. I'll call you later."

"Cass," I warned. "Don't you dare hang up on me!"

"I'm so tired, Georgie," she whined. "Why won't you let me sleep?"

"Because I need you to promise you'll take over my TapNext account."

She let out an exasperated sigh. "Why would I want to do that?"

"Because you love me."

"Just unsubscribe from the damn thing," she muttered.

"I don't want to be a complete asshole to Ruck. And I felt like you guys hit if off last night."

"You're talking about Thatch, right?"

"Yes, Thatch. Your face is the one on my profile anyway. And you can just take over and act like it was you the whole time."

"This is a little weird, G."

"I know, but I don't really know what else to do."

She was right. It was bordering on insane to have her take over the conversations, but it felt like the best option. That way, Ruck wasn't left in the dust, and hell, maybe Thatch and Cass would be an interesting little matchup.

I'd just wait to mention all of the random jokes and personal shit I had divulged to Ruck at a later time. Like never. I had a feeling once he started chatting more with my crazy, beautiful, and smart best friend, she'd eventually just be Rose to him, without him knowing there was ever a difference.

It had to work, right?

She was still quiet and I wasn't sure if she actually fell back asleep or was mulling over her options.

"Cass?"

"Yeah, okay," she agreed. "Send me your login shit. I'll message him."

"Really? Oh my God! You're the best!" I squealed.

"I'm not doing this for you, Wheorgie. When I said *I'd Thatch that*, I meant it. I have a feeling that man is a beast in bed."

"Seriously—" I started to say, but the line clicked in my ear.

A word to the wise: never call Cassie before noon. I was lucky I'd managed to keep her on the phone as long as I had.

I don't know how long I stood out on Kline's terrace, elbows resting on the banister, eyes staring off into the distance. I watched the clouds move in, covering the sun and filling the sky with an impending sense of doom. Lightning flashed in the distance.

But the city, it still moved below me, still hustled and bustled and never quit showing off its boisterous personality.

"I missed you in my bed." Warm arms wrapped around my waist. The smell of his soap and clean laundry and Kline assaulted my senses.

I sighed in contentment, resting my head on his shoulder.

"What are you doing out here?"

"I had to call Cassie," I admitted, omitting the details about the actual conversation. Even though I still felt guilty about the whole Ruck thing, I decided it was best to leave it in the past. No good would've come from me rehashing it with Kline. Because at the end of the day, he was who I wanted. The *only* man I wanted.

"And now you're just standing out here, watching the storm roll in?"

"Something like that."

"God, you smell so good." His nose was buried in my neck, inhaling for a brief moment, until he rested his chin on my shoulder.

I turned in his arms, interlocking my hands high, around his strong neck.

Playful blue eyes stared back at me. He swept my hair off my shoulder, moving his lips to my neck, and then my ear, cheek, before he leaned back, taking in my attire…or lack thereof. A rogue hand slipped down my side, gripping my thigh. "And you're standing out here in nothing but my t-shirt. I think you need to come inside, baby."

My lips found his, placing sweet kisses against his smiling mouth. "Are you trying to have your wicked way with me?"

He slid his fingers up my thigh and brushed across the one place I ached for him. "I'd say I'm not the only one trying in this scenario." He bit my bottom lip, tugging on it until I moaned. His hands moved to my ass, lifting me up and urging my legs to wrap around his waist. Kline was hard beneath his boxer briefs, and the second he was firmly pressed against me, I whimpered against his mouth. And then, he was kissing me deeper, coaxing my lips open and tangling his tongue with mine.

Candles melted when you lit them.

I melted when Kline Brooks kissed me.

Into. A. Puddle. Of. Pliant. Swoony. Mush.

His mouth was my own personal brand of perfection. Every soft caress of his lips against mine only made me crave him more. I doubted I'd ever get tired of this. Him. Us.

My breathing sped up, his touch sparking every tiny nerve ending inside of me. His hands, God, whenever they were touching me, I was losing my mind.

I shuddered against him.

He felt it, smiling as he kissed me.

Thunder filled the air as the sky opened up and started to pour over the city. The wind caused drops of rain to slide into the terrace and onto us.

He didn't break our kiss, whispering against my mouth all of the dirty things he wanted to do to me as he did. My hair was wet and his t-shirt stuck to me like a second skin, but I barely noticed, too consumed by him. My hips moved of their own accord, desperate for the hardness he was so graciously offering against me.

"Fuck, you're perfect," he growled. Yes, he actually growled. I always thought the growl was bullshit, a mythical unicorn put into romance novels, but the guttural noise that came from his lungs proved me wrong.

He moved us back inside the apartment, kicking the door shut with his foot. We were walking across his bedroom one second and then tangled on his bed the next, our mouths never leaving one another.

I giggled against his lips as my ass bounced on the mattress.

Kline pulled back, staring down at me as he moved the wet strands of hair plastered to my cheeks.

I shivered against him. I couldn't help it. Having him this close, wrapped around me, completed me in some odd way. I'd never felt this before, for anyone. And it scared me to think I could have messed this up by never agreeing to that first date or meeting Ruck in person.

I could have lived an entire life without getting to feel *this*.

His eyes turned concerned. "What's wrong, baby?"

"Nothing." I swallowed down my emotion and distracted him with my lips. "I want you," I whispered against his mouth.

He grinned, purposefully taking in my soaked attire. "Is that why you're doing your best impression of a wet t-shirt contest?"

I bit my lip. "Am I being too obvious?"

His large hands caressed my breasts through wet cotton, thumbs brushing across my nipples.

"I've never been to a wet t-shirt contest, but is it normal to grope the contestants?"

He waggled his eyebrows. "This judge does."

"What else does this judge do?"

He leaned forward, sucking my nipple into his mouth and licking around the sensitive peak. I felt the warmth of his tongue and the cool wetness from his t-shirt all the way down my body and between my legs.

My fingers found his hair, gripping the strands tightly as he moved to my other breast.

"I think I need to enter these contests more often," I said, moaning.

He glanced up, shaking his head. "No one else is ever going to lay eyes on this perfect fucking body." He held my hips and pushed his pelvis against me, spurring another moan from my lips. "No one else will get to hear your sounds or watch your lips part when you're losing control." He nipped at my bottom lip and then trailed his mouth across my jaw to my neck, until his breath was hot and seductive by my ear. "But, if you promise to be in my bedroom, you can do it any goddamn time you want."

"Deal," I whispered. "Now, less talking and more getting me naked and fucking me until I forget my name."

"Fucking you until you forget your name?" His eyes turned heated, mouth curving into a devilish grin. "I think I can work with this."

And believe me, he did. I had praised Mother Teresa, Jesus, Buddha, and was calling myself Oprah by the time he was finished blowing my mind.

CHAPTER 28

Kline

"I'm sorry," Georgia apologized for the twenty-ninth time as she knocked on the door to her parents' suburban New Jersey home.

"Baby, it's fine. I want to meet them. Didn't I tell you I wanted to meet them?"

"Yes, you did. But I don't think you meant *this afternoon*."

I had to laugh at that. It was true, when I'd had Georgia wrapped around me in bed this morning, I hadn't envisioned meeting her parents only five hours later. But when her mom had called on FaceTime that morning and Georgia had run away to take the call in private, I hadn't been able to resist popping in for a hello.

"It's my own fault. You told me not to show my face on the call," I reminded her.

"I know. It is your fault. Maybe I'm mad at you."

"You're not," I disagreed.

"Okay," she conceded. "I'm not. Honestly, I'm just sorry that when Savannah makes demands, I can't turn her down."

"The power of a mother's guilt trip is compelling. Trust me, I'm familiar. I'd love to bottle it and use it at the office," I consoled just as the door swung open to a man with slightly wild hair that grayed around the edges.

"Georgie!" he called, engulfing her in a hug and pulling her through the door. He nuzzled her hair and breathed her in for a good five seconds before his eyes met mine and turned hard.

"Who's this clown?"

"Dad!" Georgia chastised, her cheeks going cherry with mortification.

I couldn't help but smile. In his most laid-back tone, her dad had thrown the ultimate insult my way. No warm-up or pretense or gestures of fond small talk. This was a man who cared about one thing in this scenario—his daughter. I liked him immediately.

"Kline Brooks," I introduced myself, offering my hand.

"Dick. Dick Cummings." He shook my hand with fervor, purposely trying his damnedest to crush my fingers.

Dick Cummings? Thank God Thatch wasn't here. He would have had a field day with that one.

"His full name is Richard," Georgia's mother interrupted, forcing her way into the open doorway. "I'm Savannah, by the way. It really is a pleasure, Kline."

"Stop with the formality shit, Savannah. If the man can't handle that I'm Dick Cummings, then he's not the right man for our Georgie," he retorted, eyeing me with slanty eyes. "Does it bother you, Kline?"

"No, sir," I answered, fighting the urge to laugh. I literally hadn't even set foot inside of the door to their house yet, and a full-length daytime drama was rounding its way into the second arc of the storyline.

"Son." He patted me on the shoulder, nudging the girls out of the way and pulling me inside.

"When you've got a last name like Cummings, you can either be a chickenshit, or you can grow some balls and roll with it. That's why I go by Dick and I had my son go by Willy for most of his life. Hell, Georgia's lucky we didn't name her vagina," he said through a laugh.

"Plus, it's pretty fucking enjoyable to watch someone squirm when they meet me." He grinned, big and wide, his eyes turning jovial. "You handled yourself well. Much better than the other idiots Georgie's brought home. I like you already."

"Jesus, Dad." Georgie sighed. "Think you can tone done the F-bombs for now? It's not even five p.m."

"No siree, Bob. You're in my home and I'll do anything I damn well please. If I want to walk around in my underwear all night, I'll fucking do it," he responded, unfazed. "Anyway, like you should talk. Last phone conversation I had with you, you were ranting about 'the *fucking* subway.'"

"And five o'clock is an antiquated schedule associated with alcohol, Georgia. The fucks have always been given free rein," Savannah put in.

Georgia's parents were a trip. I was having a hard time keeping my smile in check.

"Come here and give me another hug," her dad ordered. "I've missed you, baby girl."

She flashed a pointed look. "Only if you promise not to bust my boyfriend's balls all night."

"Deal." He grinned.

She hugged her dad, a genuine smile on her face, and then moved to her mom. Hugs and smiles overflowed the small space of the foyer. It was apparent she was close with her folks. I loved we had that in common.

"And Richard." Savannah tsked. "You know the no-pants rule doesn't start until after dinner."

He growled under his breath, wrapping his arm around his wife and whispering something I could only assume was full-on dirty into her ear.

"Later." Savannah giggled, a perfect incarnation of what I knew as her daughter's laugh, and slapped him on the chest.

He chuckled, waggling his brows at her, visibly amused with

himself.

"Why don't you two make yourselves comfortable and freshen up from the drive. There's fresh sheets on Georgia's bed and clean towels in the bathroom."

Dick abruptly turned for the hallway, striding toward the kitchen, muttering something about "the fucking grill."

Her mother still remained, smiling at both of us in a way that made me a little concerned about what would come next. "There's also a box of condoms on the nightstand," she whispered. "Feel free to put them to good use."

"Gee, thanks, Mom." Georgia sighed, tipping her red face to the ceiling in an effort not to meet my eyes.

"Anytime, baby girl." Savannah patted her cheek, smiling. "I'm just thrilled you're finally being adventurous with your sexuality."

This meet the parents visit was getting more interesting by the minute.

"Dinner will be ready in about fifteen minutes," she called over her shoulder, following her husband's lead.

The second they were out of eyesight, Georgia sagged against the door.

"I told you they were a little offbeat. Please don't hold it against me."

I grinned, pulling her into my arms, and avoided the urge to tell her that her definition of a little felt more like a lot. "I love everything about your parents."

Her eyes showed she was skeptical, but I spoke only the truth. I'd take a free spirit and a ballbuster over two sticks in the mud any day.

"They're *your* parents, baby. Believe me, I like them. Dick and Savannah are great."

"Yeah, they're *real* awesome. I mean, how great is it that my mother thought to put condoms in my bedroom, you know, just in case we decide to bang it out when they're two doors down."

"Very practical." I fought my smile, rubbing her shoulders to ease the tension in her muscles.

"Come on." She took my hand. "Let me show you my childhood bedroom. Who knows? Maybe my mother left a complimentary bottle of lube on the nightstand."

I stopped her before she could head up the stairs, pulling her tight against me, her back to my chest. "Like you'd even need lube when I've got my hands on you," I growled into her ear, then kissed along her neck.

"Okay." She let out a soft sigh, head falling to my shoulder. "Maybe we can follow the no-pants rule after dinner too."

"Wouldn't want to go against house rules," I added, smirking against her soft skin.

"We *are* guests," she said, lifting her chin and urging my lips to continue down her neck.

"Definitely wouldn't want to come across as rude." I nibbled along her neck a bit more, until I pinched her ass, earning an adorable squeal. "Show me your bedroom, baby."

The stairs creaked as we climbed, and pictures of Georgia and Will lined the wall. One of a toddler Georgia stood out in particular.

"Aw, look at your cute little—"

"Don't even say it!"

"What?" I asked innocently.

"I know you! I know where you were going, and we're *not* going to talk about the fact that my mother keeps a naked picture of me on the wall."

"I was just going to point out that your tushy then was nearly as cute as it is now."

"Kline!" she snapped with a finger in my face.

I threw her over my shoulder in a fireman's hold and slapped at said ass.

"Don't worry, baby. I'll pay special attention to it tonight. Especially if there's lube."

She shrieked and kicked as I ran up the rest and paused, throwing her to the hallway carpet at the top of the stairs and tickling her sensitive sides.

"Kline! Stop!" Her breath heaved. "Stooooop!"

When I removed my hands, she scurried up and out from underneath me, slapping at my shoulder lightly.

"What is it about being in a childhood home that makes a man act like a child?"

"Fun. Freedom." I smiled. "Memories."

"I just bet. Were you a bad boy in your youth, Kline?"

"Nope," I answered honestly. "As a boy, I didn't know enough to be bad." I waggled my eyebrows. "I'm much more convincing now that I'm a man."

She ran again at that, shrieking the whole way and trying to close her bedroom door between us. I played tug of war with the handle convincingly enough, reserving my full strength in an effort not to hurt her, before finally busting through and tackling her cackling form to the bed.

She turned her head to the left and sighed. "Ah. The condoms."

I pulled her eyes to mine and touched our lips together softly before rubbing my nose along the line of hers. "We didn't use one the night that we fought," I whispered. I hadn't even thought about it until now, too consumed by lies and love and the complicated mix of the two, but the box on the nightstand brought my oversight into stark relief.

She nodded.

"I'm okay with that in all the ways I can be. Are you?"

She nodded again, and a shiver ran through her body. I pulled her closer.

"I'm on the pill, and I trust you."

"I'll do every single thing I can to deserve that, baby," I promised.

She looked back over to the nightstand.

"I feel like we have to use a condom tonight because my mom put them there."

"Do you even know what you just said?"

"Kline!"

"Okay." I laughed. "Just tell her we used our own because she failed to get magnum."

Her body shook with laughter despite her stern face.

"Get cleaned up for dinner!"

"Yes, ma'am," I agreed with a wink, sliding my body all the way down hers and pushing my face to the front of her pants.

"Mmm." I inhaled. "I think I should help you clean up here. I'll lick up all of my mess," I promised, pledging my truth with a hand at my chest.

She just shook her head and smiled, sliding a hand into my hair and yanking up on my head. "Go get changed and throw some cold water on your face, you bad *man*, you."

I reached into my pants with a grin and adjusted my dick to a more comfortable position.

"I can't help it, baby," I teased. "It's the house's fault."

She shook her head again, climbing to her knees and pushing her lips softly to mine. She spoke softly right there. "What am I gonna do with you?"

"Keep me."

"What am I gonna do with me?" she whispered. "So lost in you."

I squeezed her tight and answered with a prayer.

"Stay there." *Forever.*

CHAPTER 29

Georgia

"Let me show you one of my favorite places in the house," my father instructed, leading Kline toward the garage. This was another one of his tests.

Hell, he'd been testing my boyfriend all weekend.

There had been the beer test. Dick had offered Miller Lite and Guinness. Kline had chosen Guinness, and my father had patted him on the shoulder, adding, "I'm happy Georgie didn't bring a light-beer, piss-drinking pussy into my home."

There had been the liquor test. Dick had offered him a martini. Kline had politely declined and asked if there was any bourbon or whiskey in the house. Dick's response: another pat on the back.

There had also been the pizza test. Last night, my mother hadn't felt like cooking, so Dick had handed Kline a menu from Pappadoro's—a mom and pop pizza shop up the street—and told him to order a bunch of pies for everyone. Kline had gotten another pat on the back when he ordered three large meat lover's supremes and cheesy garlic bread.

Sports. Cars. Politics. You name it, and Dick tested. Surprisingly enough, Kline had passed every one with flying colors. How'd I know this? The pat on the back, of course.

We stepped out into the three-car garage, and Kline immediately removed his arm from my shoulder, walking over toward one of my dad's cars.

"A 428 Cobra Jet Mustang. Wow." He let out a low whistle, eyeing my father's car with an appreciative gleam in his eyes. "She's a beaut."

"Probably my favorite person in the house." My father patted him on the back, chuckling.

"Bought her in sixty-eight. She's in prime condition. Engine was restored a few years ago."

"Tell me you kept the Low Riser cylinder heads," Kline added, moving around the car with his hands on his hips, his eyes plastered to the red paint of my father's most prized possession.

Sometimes, I wondered if he loved this car more than he loved his own kids.

"Of course I did."

"Thank God." Kline skimmed his fingers across the paint, light enough that he wouldn't leave a mark, and a giant smile consumed his face. "This, right here, was the game changer for Ford."

Dick stared at my boyfriend like he was falling in love. "She redeemed the Ford name in the factory of horsepower."

Kline nodded and glanced up at me, a boyish smile still etched on his handsome face. "Why didn't you tell me your father had this in his garage?"

I shrugged. "I had no idea you'd get such a hard-on for a car."

"Are you kidding me?" Kline laughed. "This is one of my favorite cars. Ever. My father's a Ford man, through and through. He'd lose it if he got his hands on this car."

"I think your dad and I would get along just fine," Dick said with a smile.

Jesus. I'd never seen my dad smile so much in my life. The pulsating vein in the center of his forehead, yeah, I'd definitely seen my fair share of that, especially when I'd missed curfew in high school. But this giant smile that had taken up residence on my father's face? It was so rare that it was almost creepy.

Dick Cummings was a pretty happy guy, but he didn't usually pass out smiles and giddy looks on a daily basis. Honestly, I think the last time I'd seen him smile like this, my mother had brought home three bags from Victoria's Secret.

"I'd let you take her for a spin, but I've gotta take her into the shop come tomorrow morning. She's having issues when I try to crank her."

"Mind if I take a look?" Kline asked.

By the sounds of their conversation, you'd think my dad's car was an actual person, a female, at that. Men were so weird.

"By all means." My dad gestured toward the car. He grabbed the keys from the hook and tossed them to him.

Kline hopped in the driver's seat and attempted to turn the engine. It didn't start, and I'd never claimed to know car sounds, but whatever abnormal sound was coming from the car couldn't have been good.

"See what I mean, son?" Dick asked, elbows resting on the driver's side window.

Son? One bonding moment over his car and my dad was calling him son. I was sure any minute he'd give Kline his blessing and tell my mother to start planning my bachelorette party. No doubt, Dr. Savannah Cummings would prefer picking out penis straws to floral arrangements.

If anyone bought me dicks for my bachelorette party, it would be my mother. Cassie would provide the liquor and gift bag filled with crotchless panties. Now that I thought about it, it was a wonder I'd stayed a virgin for as long as I did. I was surrounded by a bunch of horny floozies.

"Dick, I think it's the starter motor relay."

"Really?"

Kline nodded. "I can hear the high-load relay engaging. Mind if

I pop the hood and take a look at the engine?"

"Of course." My father stood back from the car as Kline hopped out and busied himself under the hood.

After a few minutes, my boyfriend was convinced he knew the issue and could fix it. And by the look on Dick's face, I was starting to wonder if *he* would be the one to marry Kline.

"I'm grabbing something to drink. You guys want anything?" I offered.

"I'm good, babe," Kline declined, while my father merely mumbled, "No," too damn entranced by what was going on underneath the hood of his car.

I walked out of the garage and into the kitchen, leaving them to their man time. Popping the tab on a can of Coke, I leaned my hip against the counter and took a gulp from the sugary soda.

To say I was shocked by the open-armed, constant-back-patting greeting my father had been giving Kline, would be the understatement of the century. My dad was never this nice to any guy I brought home. Growing up, it had been a common occurrence for Dick to clean his guns in the living room if he knew a boy was picking me up.

Sheesh. No wonder I'd fallen so fast for Kline's charms. He practically had my dad, the boyfriend ballbuster, eating out of the palm of his hand.

I walked past my mother's office, finding her typing away on her laptop. She paused, sliding her glasses to the brim of her nose. "What are you up to?"

"Nothing much. Dad and Kline are in the garage talking car shit." I shrugged, leaning against the doorframe.

"Seems like they're hitting it off."

"Pretty sure Dad's going to propose to my boyfriend before we head home."

"I hope he lets me plan his bachelor party," she joked.

See what I mean?

She smiled a wistful smile. "It's always been a dream of mine to jump out of a cake and do a sexy striptease for your father. The closest we ever got to that was when I—"

I held my hand up. "For the love of God, I do not want to hear about you and Dick doing the nasty."

"Georgia, sex is a normal human urge. It doesn't matter how old you are or how many kids you have, you'll still want to do it."

"Are you finished psychoanalyzing my views on human sexuality, Dr. Cummings?" I asked, raising a skeptical brow.

Her smile turned curious and I braced myself for the next question that would come out of her mouth.

"Speaking of sex, how are things with you and Kline?"

"I'm not talking about my sex life with you."

She pouted. "Oh, come on, sweetie."

"Nope." I raised both hands. "Not happening."

My mother cupped her mouth, whispering, "Last night, it sounded like things were going *really* good."

I groaned. "I get that you're a sex therapist and you're extremely open when it comes to talking about sex, but it's a little creepy you were eavesdropping."

"Actually, I wasn't eavesdropping. You were just *that* loud."

I gaped.

"I can't tell you how happy this makes me."

"You realize this isn't a normal mother-daughter conversation, right?"

"It's not the normal conversation society thinks we should be having, but I know it's the conversation we should be having. Just know, I'm beyond thrilled you've found someone who makes you happy in every facet of your life. Not just in bed, which I have to say, from the sounds of it, Kline knows what he's doing." She winked. "But it's obvious he makes you really happy. And anyone who can make my daughter walk around with a constant glow and a gorgeous smile is someone I hope she keeps around." She paused as I smiled, and she considered me closely. "He seems like a really good man, Georgia.

And he's extremely lucky he found you."

Although my mom was her own type of crazy, she was still my mom and I loved her. I'd always want her acceptance. And I'd definitely want her to like the man in my life.

I walked toward her, leaning down and wrapping her in a tight hug.

"I love you, Mom."

"I love you too, sweetie. I've missed having you home. I hope you'll start visiting more often."

"Consider it a done deal." I squeezed her tighter. "As long as you promise not to eavesdrop."

"Deal," she agreed, laughing.

As I walked out of her office, she added, "But seriously, sweetie. I was a little jealous. That orgasm must have lasted a good two minutes."

"Three minutes," I called over my shoulder. "It was three minutes and it might have been more, but I'm pretty sure I lost consciousness."

I heard her laugh the entire way to my bedroom.

The second I stepped into my room, I threw my body onto the bed, my back hitting the mattress, causing pillows to fall onto the floor. My eyes took in the many nuances of my childhood stronghold. My parents hadn't changed a thing since I'd left for college. Everything was as I had left it. Old pictures of prom and homecoming littered my desk. My graduation cap hung next to the door. And the pink and yellow flowered wallpaper still lined the walls.

It was hideous by all accounts, but it was still my room. The bedroom I had grown up in. The place I'd had sleepovers and gossiped with friends about our latest crushes. The place I'd had my first kiss with Stevie Jones, even though we were supposed to have been studying for our algebra exam.

Nostalgia was potent, filling my lungs and plastering a reflective smile on my face. So much in my life had changed from the day I'd grabbed my last suitcase and headed to college. I had a great job, amazing friends, and now…Kline. It was funny how two years ago, I'd thought of him only as my boss, refusing to see him as anything else, and now, he had become this fixture in my life, one I was starting to hope would be permanent.

The sound of a phone vibrating across the surface of my nightstand caught my attention. I picked it up, tapping the screen, wondering if Cass was getting ready to harass me about using the last of the coffee creamer and leaving a sink full of dishes before heading to my parents'.

The screen lit up with a TapNext notification.

TAPRoseNEXT: Hey you, how's your day going?

I tilted my head, confused. Why was I getting messages from my account? The one I'd told Cassie to take over?

Turning over the phone, my mind registered the case. Not the glittery sparkle one I'd bought a few weeks ago, but plain, old, simple black.

Kline's phone case.

Not mine.

Kline's.

I dropped the phone like it had caught fire. It hit the hardwood floor with an awful thud and I cringed, wondering for a brief second if I had broken his phone.

But then the shock of the entire situation took over.

If he…

Wait a minute…

Is this?

No way.

NO WAY.

I just stood there, staring down at the screen and the profile name **TAPRoseNEXT** glaring back at me. If he was getting messages from my TapNext account, then that meant…

I gaped, my eyes popping wide. Jesus Christ in a peach tree, did this mean that when I had been messaging Ruck, I had really been messaging Kline?

My heart pounded in my chest, erratically enough that I was a little concerned I might go into cardiac arrest.

Slowly, I bent down and picked up the phone. My mind warred between my options. I could either do the right thing and set the phone back down and act like I had never seen it, or I could swipe the screen, put in his passcode, and see if it was really what I thought it was.

The only reason I knew his passcode was because I'd had to retrieve a few emails for him while we were in the Hamptons. He had remembered he needed to check on a time-sensitive contract and just so happened to be elbow deep in soapy water and dishes. So, he'd told me the passcode, and I just so happened to still remember said passcode.

I scrubbed my left hand down my face while my right white-knuckled his phone. I was sure the correct choice was to act like I had never seen it, set his phone down, and walk away, but I needed to know if what I was seeing was real.

Which was why my fingers slid across the screen and pulled up the TapNext icon. I took one glance at his profile, and when the username **BAD_Ruck** met my confused gaze, I refused to invade any more of his privacy and immediately locked his phone, setting it face-down on the nightstand.

He. Was. Ruck.

My hands went into my hair, resting on top of my head, as I paced my bedroom. I felt like I couldn't breathe, the four walls closing in on me. I had been messaging Kline the entire time, without even knowing it. And he had been messaging me, but he didn't know it was me.

But wait, he *had* met my best friend. He knew her face was Rose's profile picture, but he hadn't known I was the one to put it there.

Irrational jealousy and anger started to build inside of my chest.

Had he still been chatting with Rose *after* meeting Cassie?

Fuck.

I picked his phone back up and quickly unlocked the screen again, pulling up the TapNext app within seconds. My heart threatened to thrash its way out of my body as I found the lone conversation in Ruck's message box.

I felt insane, completely off my rocker, as I found the last few messages and scrutinized the timestamps.

Relief robbed the breath from my lungs as I met the realization that the last message Ruck sent Rose had been *before* we had met up at The Raines Law Room.

Before he had met my best friend.

The edges of my anger, my jealousy, still shook my hands. I couldn't deny I felt betrayed over the fact that he had been chatting with another woman, while dating me.

But I breathed through it, slowly talking myself off the illogical ledge as I set Kline's phone back on the nightstand.

How could I be mad at him when I had been doing the exact same thing?

Of course, I was upset he had been chatting with another woman, not really knowing that woman was me. It hurt. A lot. But I couldn't deny it made sense. It made sense why we would continue to talk, even though we were dating other people. We were drawn to each other, in every possible way.

I was filled with this odd feeling of relief, but it was quickly pushed aside when I started to realize the consequences of my decisions.

My world had officially turned on its axis. I was in the *Twilight Zone* and playing the star role in a weird, modern remake of *You've Got Mail*. The only difference was that I wasn't Kathleen Kelly in this scenario. I was Joe Fox.

Holy. Fox.

And I had gone off script. I hadn't planned a big grand gesture where I would unveil it had been me the whole time.

No.

Not only had I given my best friend free rein to message my boy-friend, I had all but forced her to do it.

Holy. Foxing. Shit.

Finding my phone on my desk, I dialed Cass's number and went into the bathroom, shutting the door and sitting in the bathtub fully clothed.

"Hey, sweet cheeks, how are the parental units?" she answered, her voice too goddamn cheery for the shitstorm that was my life.

"Do not message Ruck ever again."

"Huh?"

I shut my eyes, resting my head on the edge of the tub. "I fucked up, Cass. I fucked up big time."

"Whoa, slow down, Susie. What's going on?"

"Thatch isn't Ruck. Kline is Ruck."

The phone was dead silent.

"Do you hear me?! Kline is Ruck!" I shouted, my voice echoing in the bathroom. I clamped my hand over my mouth, realizing anyone walking by my bedroom would be able to hear me screaming like a lunatic.

I listened closely for any sign I wasn't alone and was relieved when I didn't hear anything but my erratic breathing.

"Okay," Cassie started. "I'm officially confused, so please, spell it out for me in slow, clear sentences."

I rambled on for a good two minutes, giving her the step-by-step details of how I had discovered my boyfriend was Ruck.

"What are the fucking odds?" she asked, sounding just as shocked as I felt.

"I know. I should probably buy a lottery ticket today," I muttered.

"You realize what you've done, don't you?"

"Screwed up big time?"

"No, you catfished your boyfriend." She laughed. "Holy shit, G, he catfished you too."

"This is so messed up," I groaned.

"You're like two fucking catfish, sitting at the bottom of the lake, doing fish shit and stuff."

"Okay, enough with the fish," I snapped. "I'm freaking out here, Cass. What have I done?"

"You haven't done anything wrong," she placated me.

"Oh. M-my. God," I stuttered, panicked and overwhelmed over the entire fucked up situation. "How do I fix this?"

"Jesus, Georgia, relax," she sighed. "Stay calm. Act completely aloof. I'll send him another message and nip this crazy-town shit in the bud."

"What? What are you going to say?"

"For fuck's sake, stop panicking," she chastised. "I'll say something along the lines of 'I'm happily involved with someone else and I can't continue our conversations. Have a nice life.'"

Okay, that would work. It would put an end to the confusion. Rose would message Ruck, they'd stop chatting, and the world would be right again.

Would it work? And is this even the right way to handle this mind-fuck of a situation?

I warred with myself over pretending it never happened versus telling Kline the truth. But then I started remembering the many conversations I'd had with Ruck. My openness. My flirtation. Questions and commentary about *anal*.

Jesus. I cringed in embarrassment. The mere idea of talking to Kline about it had my stomach clenching in discomfort.

I just wanted to leave the whole Ruck and Rose debacle in the past. Truth be told, if I could've paid someone to bury it in a shallow grave somewhere in the depths of the Pinelands along with my stay at Masturbation Camp, I sure as fuck would've done it. Not that I knew anything about that sort of thing.

I sighed. "Could this be any weirder of a situation?"

"Well," she said, deadpan. "Considering he had foreskin, Wally sure put a weird spin on the old phrase 'Taking ol' one-eye to the optometrist.'"

"Old phrase?" I snorted. "I didn't even know that was a phrase."

"Savannah would be so ashamed of you right now," she teased.

That spurred a few giggles from my lips.

"Hey, I hate to do this, but I gotta scoot or I'm going to be late for my shoot," she updated. "Are you going to be okay?"

"Yeah, I'm good. Thanks, Cass. I honestly don't know what I'd do without you."

"Probably live a horribly miserable life trying to find your own way out of your crazy-ass situations."

"So true," I agreed, smiling.

After we hung up, I was so damn exhausted from the roller coaster of emotions that I stayed in the bathtub until I drifted off to sleep.

A throat being cleared startled me awake.

"Fully clothed, bathtub nap?" Kline asked, squatting down beside the tub.

"Would you like to join me?" I grinned and scooted over.

He didn't hesitate, squishing his large frame beside me and wrapping his arm around my shoulders.

"Fix my dad's car?" I asked, resting my head on his chest.

"Yeah. Pretty sure your dad thinks I'm a mechanic now, but honestly, it was an easy fix." His fingers found their way into my hair, running through the strands so softly I nearly purred.

"I think my dad is falling in love with you. He might propose marriage before we leave."

"Don't worry, baby. I won't let your dad steal me from you."

I laughed. "I'm not sure we're going to be able to fit that giant head of yours out of this house."

He wrapped both arms tightly around my body and slid farther into the middle of the tub, forcing me to lie on top of him. "There, that's much better."

"You're too damn big." I nodded toward his feet that were hanging over the edge.

"I thought we already figured this out, Benny. I might be Big-dicked Brooks, but your perfect, tight—"

I clamped my hand over his mouth, laughing.

He licked my palm, waggling his eyebrows.

"Gross," I scoffed, feigning disgust and wiping his spit on his own shirt.

He chuckled a few times and then his eyes turned soft and he brushed a few strands of hair out of my face. "I'm glad you brought me this weekend. I had fun meeting your parents."

I rubbed my nose against his. "Thanks for coming with me and being such a good sport. My mom and dad can be a little overwhelming."

"Your dad is a riot."

"He really likes you." I grinned. "That's huge, by the way. Dick doesn't like anyone."

"After you left the garage, your dad and I had an interesting conversation."

"What was it about?"

"I'll tell you, but you have to promise not to freak out or get embarrassed."

"I'm not sure I like where this is headed." My nose scrunched up in skepticism.

His index finger tapped my nose. "Just promise."

"Fine. I promise."

"Your dad asked me for a few tips."

"Car tips?"

Kline shook his head.

"I don't get it. What kind of tips?"

His eyes creased with amusement.

My jaw dropped to his chest. "Oh God," I whined. "Please tell me what I'm thinking you're about to say is not what happened."

"Apparently, your mother encouraged him to talk to me about

sex, particularly two-minute orgasms. I'll be honest, I have no idea why your mom thought I knew anything about that."

I shut my eyes and buried my face in his chest. "She heard us last night."

"What?"

"Well, she heard me last night."

"Oh, shit," he said before quiet laughter started vibrating his body.

I rested my chin on his chest, glaring at him. "Thanks a lot, asshole. You and your Jedi sex tricks had me screaming like a lunatic while my parents were two doors down."

"You didn't seem to be complaining about my Jedi sex tricks last night," he teased, grinding his hips against mine.

"Don't even think about it," I warned, poking him in the belly. "You will not get all frisky with me in this bathtub."

He waggled his brows. "What about in the bed?"

"No," I retorted. "I refuse to go into an orgasm coma again."

He tilted his head, an endearing smirk highlighting his lips.

"Well, not *ever*, just not here." I quickly backtracked because, yeah, no way in hell would I deny myself that kind of orgasm forever. I wasn't a crazy person.

He laughed, kissing my nose. "Whatever you say, Benny girl."

CHAPTER 30

Kline

As the plane throttled forward and took off down the runway, Georgia screamed like we were on a roller coaster, shrieking at every bump, lump, and wind gust.

"Jesus," I shouted over her squeals and rubbed at the meat of her thigh. "If I didn't know any better, I'd think you'd never flown before!"

We'd both been surprised by the trip, a last-minute meeting with a vendor that wanted to go live on our site ASAP. It didn't happen often, but when people jumped up and down and waved money around, we jumped back. This was one of those times and the reason we found ourselves San Diego bound this early in the day on the Tuesday after a weekend with her parents.

"It's different on a private plane," she yelled back, even though there wasn't a need. I'd only had to yell before to be heard over her screeching, but she wasn't concerned. And she didn't seem tired either. I, myself, was exhausted from a weekend filled with Savannah and Dick. And Georgia and my dick. Truly, the D was everywhere.

Gemma, my regular personal flight attendant, smiled happily from her jump seat. Thankfully, she seemed rather amused by it all.

"Baby, it's the same as a normal plane," I argued at a conventional volume. "Just smaller."

"No. Nuh-uh," she disagreed. "This is *not* like regular planes. Regular planes make you feel like a poor, desperate vagabond, willing to subject yourself to any treatment just to make it to your destination."

"What airline are you flying?" I laughed. "Third World Air?"

She shook her head and smiled before looking out the window again. "It's more whoopty or something," she tried to explain.

"Whoopty?"

"Whimsical. Roller-coaster-y."

I smiled and she laughed, throwing her hands up and pointing to her face in confirmation. "Fun!"

I leaned over and kissed the apple of her cheek. "I'm the fun part."

"You are," she agreed with my lie.

She was the fun. Hands down.

"You mind if I take a little nap?" I asked, knowing I'd need my business brain later instead of the current mush.

"Aw, Kline. My old man is tired, huh?"

I had to laugh as I nodded. "He is."

Her body seemed to deflate all at once as she laid her head on my shoulder. "I am too. I feel like I haven't slept in ages."

"We haven't," I pointed out. Weeks of courting and falling and fucking had taken its toll. "Just snuggle into me, baby. We'll both catch some shut-eye. We've got about five hours until we get there."

She didn't say anything out loud, just nuzzled the top of her head farther into my neck and crossed an arm over my body.

I breathed in the smell of her shampoo and rubbed the soft strands of her hair with my fingers. I wanted to stay awake and savor it, talk to her, laugh with her, soak more of her in. But the lull of the plane and the hum of the engine enhanced a pull into sleep that already needed no help.

With my eyes shut and heart full, I was mere moments away from a deep sleep when Georgia called my name.

"Yeah, baby?" I asked, my voice thick and sluggish with the impending doze.

"I've never been happier to miss sleep in my life."

Ditto.

"Just one room," I told the front desk clerk as she handed me our cards. My assistant, Pam, had, of course, made the arrangements, and she'd have had no way of knowing Georgia and I were following a one-room sleeping plan.

Personally, I didn't have even one fuck left to give. But Georgie cared. And I cared about what she cared about. It was a really mushy, complicated web of romance, but in the end, all that mattered was her.

"Yes, sir," the young girl agreed, taking the keys back and tapping away at the computer.

We'd gone straight from the airport to the meeting, and from the meeting to dinner. Thanks to one of the best plane catnaps I'd ever had, we had just enough time to spend another night *not sleeping* before Georgia had to be on a plane back home in the morning.

"Here you go," the desk clerk offered, handing me back a solitary key. "Room 554. The elevators are down the hall behind you and on the right."

"Thanks." I smiled and grabbed my small bag from its spot at my feet.

Georgia was already down the elevator hall, pacing the tile floor in front of them as she talked over the details of things she needed for tomorrow's meeting with Dean. As imperative as the phone call seemed on the surface, I had a suspicion it was more of an excuse to avoid awkwardly standing next to me at the desk than a necessity.

"Ready?" I asked as I came to a stop in front of her.

Her finger shot to my lips and pushed to say 'be quiet'.

"It was just Mr. Brooks," she said into the phone, rolling her eyes.

"No, I'm still in the lobby."

I went to speak, but she pushed on my lips harder. "Nope. The meeting ran really late and we still have a couple of things to go over before we call it a night."

I smiled. No one here was going to be calling it a night.

She shook her head in the negative and bit her bottom lip. My balls tightened immediately. Even they knew it was time to play.

"Georgie girl," I whispered mischievously. She shushed me and waved me away, pointing at the phone with wild eyes. She was just too easy.

"Come tuck me in," I teased, grabbing at her hips and backing her toward the elevators.

I pushed the up button to call the car and pulled her hips into mine. Hair loose from its earlier binding, she looked wild and willing and altogether too much like sex to stop.

"Dean, Dean," she called, obviously trying to break into his end of steady conversation. "You know, you've got this covered."

I smiled bigger. Pulled her breasts tighter to my chest.

"It was really just my neuroses calling. You're plenty competent to have everything ready on your own."

"Mm-hmm," I hummed, moving the hair off of her neck and sucking at her skin greedily.

She was dying to give me one of her signature, scolding *Kline!*s, I could feel it in her posture and staccato-timed wording, but with Dean on the line, secrecy won out.

"I know. I'll be sure to give Donatella Versace my recommendation, should I ever run into her on the street." She nodded at the phone, at something Dean said, a gesture he obviously couldn't see, and I swooned.

Hands down, Georgia Cummings was one of the most charmingly fascinating women I'd ever encountered. Dichotomous in nearly everything she did, I never knew which way was up or which version of her I would get. Awkward or easy, bold or shy, endlessly clever or laughably bumbling. Every time, day or night—work or play—I'd take any version I met.

"Hang up the phone, baby," I coaxed, pushing her gently into the open and waiting car.

"I'll see you tomorrow," she said into the line. "Yes, butt-fucking early." We both smiled like lunatics. "I'll see you then."

Finally, blessedly, she cut the call just as the doors of the elevator shut out the people.

I grabbed her hips, groping and squeezing at the top of her ass.

"God. It's about time," I teased, running my tongue along the closed seam of her lips.

"Fuck," she breathed as her head fell back and her hair hung well past her shoulders. I gripped the ends of it and yanked her throat open even farther.

"Ahh," she moaned, shoving her tit right into the palm of my waiting free hand.

"That's it," I cooed, circling her hard nipple with the tip of my thumb.

"Kline," she breathed. She could barely keep up with the rhythm of her pants.

"I can't wait to hear you say that again. On my face, on my cock…I'm gonna strip you down and sit you up on every fucking thing I can think of."

"God," she moaned as the doors opened on our floor. I scooped her up and into my arms, glancing at the sign that would tell me which way to go to our room.

Too fucking far from the elevator, at the end of the hall, I finally came face to face with our door. Georgia clung to me as I set her down to pull the plastic key card from my pocket. I couldn't wait to *make love* to every single inch of her petite body.

As the door clicked open and I slid our intertwined bodies inside, I knew without a doubt that was what this was.

Just lust was gone, like had grown, and love was positioned in Georgia's sumptuous mouth—right at the tip of my tongue.

CHAPTER 31

Georgia

"Just three more questions," Kline demanded, his voice raspy and sleep-filled.

We'd been at this game all night. Asking random questions to one another in between bouts of kissing that always ended in more. Crazy, sexy kind of more.

Best game ever.

But it was half past three in the morning, and I had a six thirty-five flight to catch. A contract meeting was sending me home today, and because he'd tacked on an additional meeting tomorrow morning with one of our regular investors in the name of efficiency, *today* meant *one day earlier* than Kline. *No need to make more than one trip,* he'd said. Now we had to face the consequences of that decision.

I hadn't packed a thing and needed a shower. As badly as I wanted to stay in bed, wrapped up in him, I had to get my ass moving.

I sat up, the sheet pooling around my waist. "You said that three hours and two orgasms ago."

"Two orgasms? I thought it was three…" He was lying on his belly, resting his chin on the pillow, his eyes locked on my bared breasts.

"If you can't remember the last one, I'm demanding a re-do."

A re-do. The bastard.

He licked his lips and moved his gaze from my breasts, to my waist, until finally making the slow circuit to my mouth.

Jesus. Kline flashing me smoldering glances during business meetings was dangerous enough, but this? That look. Those heated blue eyes. His sexy, bedhead hair. And that tight ass. It should be illegal.

"Stop smoldering at me!" I smacked his shoulder. "I have to get in the shower. I have a flight to catch, remember?"

He pounced on me, wrapped his arms around my body, and slammed my back into the bed before I could stop him. "Don't leave." His mouth found mine, his teeth tugging on my bottom lip.

"Stay here with me. Let me ask you questions and kiss these lips." He kissed me deeper. "And touch this perfect body." His fingers slid up my sides, resting below the curve of my breasts. "And put my mouth on you." He punctuated that statement by gliding those devious hands down my belly, until his fingers were touching me where I throbbed.

I'd never had marathon sex. Okay, before Kline, I'd never actually had sex. But I'd never experienced this feeling before. I'd never been so attracted, so turned on, so undeniably in love with someone, where the only thing I wanted to do was spend every day for the rest of forever touching him, kissing him, fucking him.

It was overwhelming. And amazing. And should have had me running for the hills. But when it came to Kline, I didn't want to run, unless it was toward his opened arms.

I trusted him. Cared for him. Loved him. I wanted him and only him. He was everything I'd always dreamed of, plus a million things I never even knew I wanted.

"Kiss me, baby," he whispered against my lips.

"I *am* kissing you," I retorted, my mouth still pressed against his.

"No. Fucking kiss me," he growled, his tongue slipping past my lips and making me moan. "I'll never get tired of this. I'll never *not* want this. With you. Only you."

"I'm going to miss my flight and it'll be all your fault," I whimpered.

"Fuck the flight. Fuck the meeting. Stay here and fuck my brains out." That devilish mouth moved to my neck and then my collarbone, sucking softly while his tongue licked along the sensitive skin.

My hands found his ass, tugging him toward me. "You don't play fair." My hips arched up into his, my body begging for him to connect us.

"With you, I'll never play fair." He pressed against me, the tip of his cock moving through my wetness. "I'll do whatever it takes to get you to keep doing this with me. *For-fucking-ever.*"

"We're gonna fuck forever?" I teased.

His laugh vibrated my skin. "Yes. Me and you. Fucking, kissing, groping, making love, *coming.* All the goddamn time. Forever."

"I want this in writing."

He moved away from me, rustling inside the nightstand and finding a complimentary pen clipped to a notepad with the hotel's logo written along the top. He tossed the pad across the room and put the pen in his mouth, removing the cap.

"Pretty sure contracts need paper…"

"Not this contract." He settled between my thighs again, eyes locked on my belly. The tip of the pen touched my skin and I shivered. "This is a different kind of contract, baby." Blue eyes peeked up at me, smirking.

The pen moved across my skin, but I couldn't see what he was writing, his messy hair blocking my view.

"Excuse me, sir, but what are you doing? Are you branding me?"

"Stop calling me sir. I'm trying to focus here and you're making me hard."

"You've been hard for the past eight hours. What's new?"

"You'd think you would have tried to help me with this difficult situation. Honestly, Georgia, I'm disappointed. You really need to work a little harder at this whole girlfriend thing."

I fought my grin. It was stupid that I *still* felt giddy over hearing him say girlfriend. I had officially reverted back to high school. But I didn't care. I loved that he made me giddy and girly and head-over-heels in love.

"Oh, so when I did that thing where I put my mouth on your dick and then didn't remove it until you came, that wasn't what a good girlfriend would do? I'm sorry I did that. I'll make a note to *never* do that again. Don't worry, baby, I'll learn from my mistakes."

"Now, wait a minute. Let's not get too hasty here," he backtracked, still focused on tattooing something on my skin. "I think you need to do that thing a few more times. Like every day, for the next five years or so, before I can really decide if I like it."

I grabbed his hair, pulling his head up so he looked at me. "You didn't like it?" I asked, my eyes narrowed.

"I can't really remember." He shrugged, fighting a smile. "Why don't you do it again and then it might help me give you a proper answer?"

"Oh." I feigned innocent understanding. "So, I should just put my mouth on your cock again? You know, slide it in real deep until it taps the back of my throat, and then suck *hard,* while I run my tongue all over you. Would that help? Or should I do something else?"

"No," he said, swallowing hard enough to make his Adam's apple bob. "You should do those things." He cleared his throat, his body's answer growing hard and straining against my thigh.

"All of those things you just said—yeah, do those."

My face cracked into a smile, amused by the strain in his voice and his, um, *yeah.* That too. I was definitely enjoying that reaction.

"Okay, all set. Per your request, the contract is in writing." He tossed the pen back onto the nightstand. He gripped my thighs as he kneeled on the bed between my legs.

"Now, let's get back to what you were saying before. I believe you said something about putting your mouth on me?" He smirked, waggling his brows playfully. "Or do you want me to just slide inside of you? Because I'm a big fan of this perfect pussy." He ground against me.

"The biggest fan, actually. No one loves this pussy as much as I do. Which is why no one else will ever see it, touch it, taste it. Consider me your orgasm donor for life. Any time, hour, second of any day, you need to come, I'm your guy."

I giggled. "Like my orgasm soul mate?"

I was rewarded with a smile. "Exactly like that."

He brushed his fingers across my belly and hip bone, where the pen's previous ministrations still had my nerve endings tingling. "This is the sexiest thing I've ever seen."

"What did you write?" My eyes followed his, to the place where his hand rested on my skin. "Move your hand," I urged. "I swear to God, if you drew a penis or—" I stopped mid-sentence, my gaze locking onto the straight and narrow lines of his masculine script.

My heart in your hands and you in my arms, that's all I'll ever need.

"I mean it," he whispered. "I mean every word, Georgia."

I looked at him, *really* looked at him, hovering above me, his hands now resting beside my head. His heart was in his eyes—tender, loving, *perfect*.

What simple words for such a profound declaration.

Kline had just laid it all out there. He'd just told me I had him. He was mine. His heart was in my hands. And all he wanted was *me*. And that would be enough for him.

"I love you," I said, my voice choking on emotion. "I love you so much, Kline."

"I love you, too." He kissed me hard, deep, and desperate. His lips, his touch, the way he made love to me, it told me everything I needed to know.

This was real, him and me. This was it. And the best part of that revelation was that we were both certain. Neither of us was in limbo, waiting for the other to catch up or decide if this was right. We were all in, both of us, in love.

Intense, life changing, forever a part of one another kind of love.

I handed my boarding pass off and walked onto the plane. I was beyond exhausted, my arms damn near giving out as I lifted my carry-on up and stowed it away. Kline had switched my seat without my knowing. Yesterday, he had seen my boarding pass on the nightstand and asked if I was in coach because the flight was overbooked. When I responded that I didn't want to take advantage of the company's budget, he told me to *never* book a seat in coach again.

I'd acquiesced with a sassy, "Yes, sir."

Apparently, he'd appreciated that answer because I had been generously rewarded with his talented mouth between my legs.

The second I arrived at the airport and got through security in record time—thank God, considering I was running thirty minutes behind schedule—I was called over to the gate, where an attendant instructed that I had been upgraded to a first class window seat.

He sure was one sneaky, adorable, demanding man when he wanted to be.

I clicked my seatbelt into place and grabbed my phone from my purse as passengers continued to board the plane and find their seats. Even though he was probably sound asleep, I decided to send him a quick text.

Me: Someone changed my seat. I'm currently relaxing in first class, enjoying the view from the window.

Kline: I think you should thank whoever did it with that really awesome thing you do with your mouth.

And I thought *I* had sex on the brain all the time. *Pervert.*
Me: When I figure it out, I'll keep that idea in mind.

Kline: If I told you it was me, would you make that idea a reality?

Me: I don't know…I'm an in-the-moment kind of gal. I'm not very good with hypotheticals.

Kline: It was me. I'll fit time into my schedule tomorrow night so you can properly thank me.

Me: Now that I'm in the moment, I'm not feeling all that into your idea…

Kline: Did I mention there would be an exchange? You thanking me, me thanking you kind of thing.

Me: Slot me in for tomorrow night at seven.

Kline: Sudden change in feelings?

Me: You presented a very attractive offer, Mr. Brooks.

Kline: Always a pleasure doing business with you, Ms. Cummings.

Me: Likewise…I miss you.

God, I really was a goner. It had only been an hour since I'd kissed him goodbye while he was all sleepy and adorable and begging me to stay, and already, my chest ached over the idea that I wouldn't get to see him again until tomorrow night.

Kline: I haven't stopped thinking about you since you left. I think you should quit your job. You should still be in this bed beside me and not on a goddamn flight back home.

Me: I'll let my boss know ASAP.

Kline: Good idea.

The third round of passengers started to filter down the aisle, heading through the curtains and into coach. I tapped the email icon, drafting a quick message to my "boss."

> From: Georgia Cummings
> To: Kline Brooks
> Subject: My Boyfriend's Requests
>
> Mr. Brooks,
> My boyfriend isn't too happy I'm on a flight instead of in his hotel room fucking his brains out. I'm requesting that this doesn't happen again. He's very upset.
> Sincerely,
> Georgia Cummings
> Director of Marketing, TapNext
> Brooks Media

> From: Kline Brooks
> To: Georgia Cummings
> Re: My Boyfriend's Requests
>
> Ms. Cummings,
> I am taking this concern very seriously. From now on, I guarantee any business trips you are scheduled to

attend, you will be booked in the same room as your boyfriend. I will also make sure there is plenty of time scheduled in throughout your day to allow you to fuck his brains out. And just because I feel terrible about this, I'm requesting you leave work early tomorrow and go to his apartment (his front desk probably knows you need a spare key) so you're there when he gets home. (I bet he'd prefer you to be naked and lying in his bed, too.)

Sincerely,

Kline Brooks

President and CEO Brooks Media

From: Georgia Cummings

To: Kline Brooks

Subject: I think my boyfriend will be very happy…

Mr. Brooks,

Thank you for your utmost concern. I will be sure to leave work early tomorrow and wait for my boyfriend at his apartment. I will also use your suggestion about my attire. Although, I think my boyfriend would prefer me to be wearing the sexiest pair of heels I own while I wait.

Sincerely,

Georgia Cummings

Director of Marketing, TapNext

Brooks Media

P.S. I'm crazy in love with my boyfriend.

From: Kline Brooks
To: Georgia Cummings
Re: I think my boyfriend will be happy…(YES, he will)

Ms. Cummings,
I think your boyfriend would love that. Actually, I bet
he'd insist on that.
Sincerely,
Kline Brooks
President and CEO Brooks Media

P.S. He's crazy in love with you too. For the sake of
everything that's right in the world, don't forget the
fucking heels tomorrow.

Eyes tired, I set my phone in my lap and rested my head on the
seat. My mind replayed last night, highlighting everything from Kline
stealing kisses between asking me my favorite bands, movies, and va-
cation spots, to him making love to me, over and over again.

My fingers touched my lips, hiding my ridiculous smile.

"I know that look," a woman softly whispered beside me.

My eyes blinked open, finding an older lady with salt and pepper hair and a rounded, smiling face in the seat next to mine. "You're
thinking about someone special, aren't you?"

"Am I that obvious?" I laughed, my cheeks flushing.

"Don't be embarrassed. Love is a beautiful thing when you find
it. It's something to be happy about, something to cherish, something
to wear on your face every single day," she said, genuine happiness in
her voice. "Is he a good man?"

I nodded. Kline's handsome face flashed in my mind. In that moment, I could picture every one of his smiles—happy, teasing, playful,
loving. It was an endless list and one that I wanted to memorize and

keep with me forever. "Yeah, he is. He's definitely one of the good ones."

"Is he your husband?"

"No." I shook my head. "He's my boyfriend."

She grinned, her cheeks puffing out in soft delight. "By the looks of your glow, I'd say you're headed in that direction."

Were we? My rational head wanted me to slow the hell down, but my heart was already picking out invitations and flowers. Even though we had just started exchanging I love yous, there was no denying I'd fallen hard for Kline. I was in so deep I honestly couldn't picture myself without him. *Ever.*

Before I could respond to her statement or ask her something about herself, she was adjusting in her seat, placing a pillow around her neck. "I wish you the best of luck, dear. I hope you and your wonderful man get a very happy ever after. Now, if you don't mind, I'm going to rest my eyes. I can feel my Xanax kicking in." She flashed an apologetic smile. "It's for the best, though," she added. "I'm a very nervous flyer."

She closed her eyes, and within seconds, soft snores fell from her lips.

I made a note to tell my doctor I was a nervous flyer too. The long flights I often took for business trips would have been much more tolerable with the magic that was Xanax. I'd much rather have slept through a four-hour flight than toss and turn without getting any rest.

"Sorry for the delay," a woman's voice filtered through the speakers. "We will be taking off shortly."

My phone buzzed in my lap, catching my attention.

It was a picture message from Cassie, with the words, ***"I'm so sorry, Georgia."***

Huh?

I tapped the photo and it filled the screen, zooming in so I could figure out what she was talking about.

It was a screenshot of a TapNext conversation.

TAPRoseNEXT (7:00PM): You're a very nice guy, but I can't continue talking with you anymore. I've gotten more serious with the man I'm seeing and this just doesn't feel right. I'm sorry. Good luck with everything, Ruck.

BAD_Ruck (6:45AM): I get it. I do. But I think we should meet in person, just the two of us. Please, Rose.

I white-knuckled my phone as I stared down at the screen in disbelief.

I don't think I breathed for an entire minute. I felt like someone had reached down my throat and pulled my heart straight out of my body.

My eyes closed of their own accord, my mind in self-preservation mode. My heart roaring in my ears, I took a cavernous breath and found the strength to open my eyes again, hoping—no, *praying*—I had missed something along the line.

But I hadn't. *I fucking hadn't.* The screenshot, Kline's response, it was real. One-hundred percent real.

I scrubbed a hand down my face, pressing into my lids to stop the tears wanting to spill down my cheeks. A shaky sigh escaped my lips as I tried to focus through the blurry mess of emotions.

His message was timestamped from this morning at 3:45 a.m. Pacific.

My throat constricted, cheeks straining in agony to stop myself from losing it.

I won't cry. I will not sob in front of a plane full of strangers.

This morning. He sent that message in between playfully asking me questions and making love to me. Or was it *faking* love to me? Because that was what it felt like now. I'd never felt so betrayed, so utterly devastated in my entire life.

The pain built in my chest, burning like I had swallowed hot coals. I was hanging by a thread, my free hand gripping the armrest in a pathetic attempt to hold myself together.

"Miss, we're about to take off. You need to turn your phone off now."

I pulled my eyes from the screen, finding a flight attendant with long blonde hair and a pink smile standing above me.

All I could do was stare at her. Honestly, I didn't even know what she was saying to me.

"Your phone?" She nodded to my hands.

I followed her eyes and realized what she was asking. "Oh, sorry," I mumbled, and with shaky hands, turned it off.

I felt like I was a passenger in a crash-and-burn landing, going from the highest high, only to be catapulted into the lowest of lows.

Memories flooded my mind.

The night at the Hamptons, when I had given myself to him.

I choked on a sob as a few tears slipped down my cheeks. I swiped at the liquid emotion, telling myself I could do this. I could get through this flight.

A man across the aisle glanced in my direction, his head tilted to the side in concern.

Oh, God, don't look at me like that! I wanted to scream at him. I did not want pity. I couldn't handle someone recognizing that I was falling to pieces. *That* would for sure make it impossible to hold this in until I was somewhere private.

Long, slow breaths were inhaled through my nose and exhaled from my lungs. I stared down at a nonexistent piece of lint on my pants, plucking at the material just because it was something to do, something else to focus on besides my heart falling out of my chest.

More memories drowned me.

Last night, with each kiss, each touch, each soft caress, he had silently been asking me to fall the rest of the way with him. And I had. I had followed his lead, and on the way down, he had made love to me until my heart was beating like he'd wanted it to. Like I'd wanted it to. My world had changed. Inside, my walls had fallen down and he was all around me. All I knew. All I wanted to know.

Kline had gone from being my boss to my best friend, my lover, and my intoxication until he let the needle break off in my skin. This wasn't a little cut that would scab over and flake off. *No.* He had cut me so deep I hadn't even bled.

The pain was so unbearable that all my emotions fled the scene. I switched from distraught—fighting the sob threatening to bubble up from my lungs—to robotic.

I didn't want to talk to him. I didn't want to ask him why, after the night we had shared together, he would still want to meet someone who *wasn't* me. Initially, when I'd found out Kline was Ruck, and he had been chatting with **TAPRoseNEXT** without knowing it was me, it didn't upset me. I looked at the entire situation with a rational, understanding head. Because I had done the same thing.

But the second I had met Thatch, the guy whose picture was on **Bad_Ruck's** TapNext profile, I'd known I needed to stop. I knew I wanted Kline. I knew I was falling in love with him, and I didn't want anything to ruin that. Which was why I had told Cassie to take the reins. Who would've thought that the whole time I was chatting with Ruck, I was actually talking to Kline?

It was the ultimate mindfuck.

Unfortunately for me, that mindfuck had just gotten a whole lot worse.

This was different from a simple response to another woman on an online dating profile. He was requesting to meet someone that wasn't me, someone he *knew* was my best friend.

What on earth did he think he was going to gain from that? Was he planning on being in a relationship with me while screwing Cassie on the side?

God, it didn't add up, didn't seem like the Kline I knew, but the proof was right in front of my face.

I felt so devastated. Knowing what we shared and all of the possibilities of what we could have been, why would Kline have risked that? In a matter of a few sentences, he had just ruined everything. Destroyed us. Destroyed me.

I felt sick. Nausea coiled my stomach, constant and unrelenting.

The minute the seatbelt lights went off, I made a beeline for the lavatory. My breakfast filled the small metal toilet within seconds. It took a good five minutes before I could stop dry heaving. I held myself up over the sink, staring at a woman I didn't even recognize. I did my best to clean up, splashing cool water on my face and rinsing my mouth out, before I made my way back to my seat.

God, I had never felt so cold, so fucking alone.

I didn't want to feel like this. I wanted the pilot to turn the plane around so I could talk to Kline. I wanted to forget that TapNext conversation had ever happened.

But I wasn't going to be that woman who couldn't step back and face the facts.

Even though it was going to kill me, I was going to be the woman who knew when to end things. The woman who could end a relationship with a man—even though she loved him—because she knew she didn't deserve to be treated like that.

He had told me he loved me, he had touched me and kissed me in ways a man would only do when he was in love. But while he had been doing that, he had also found time to request to meet another woman. These were not the actions of a man I wanted to be in a relationship with.

For the entire five-and-half-hour flight, my mind raced. Every memory was a picture in my head, his betrayal scratching across the surface of each photograph and tainting it forever.

I was fucking miserable, stuck on an old airplane with no Wi-Fi after finding out the man I wanted to spend the rest of my life with was going behind my back and requesting to meet other women on the side.

If he did that knowing it was my best friend, what else was he doing behind my back?

I knew it was crazy to go in that direction, but who could blame me?

Trying to talk this out with him was pointless. I could only take so much, and a nasty breakup would push me over the edge. I was afraid of what I might say to him. Hell, I'd have to hold my breath if I was in the same room as him, because breathing the same air meant breathing him in.

And my heart couldn't take any more.

I walked off the plane, my mind fogged with heartbreak and anger. I wanted to scream. I wanted to cry. I wanted to curl up in the fetal position and sleep for forty years.

Pre-life-altering screenshot, I would've sent Kline a text message telling him I had landed, but I didn't even bother turning on my phone. What was the fucking point? I had nothing to say.

Eventually, I found baggage claim and grabbed my suitcase.

I had options. Either I could let this drag me down and turn me into someone I didn't want to be, or I could find a way to get past this.

My decision was made and there was no going back to what we had.

There was no explanation he could give that would fix this, save us.

Steadfast in my choice, I hailed a cab and threw my bags in the back before the driver could even get out of his seat.

"Winthrop Building, Fifth Avenue," I instructed without a second thought.

When he pulled up to the building, I tossed money in the front seat and hopped out, grabbing my suitcases from the trunk. It was afternoon and everyone would be there. My coworkers would be roaming the halls. Dean would be waiting for me to attend the meeting.

Fuck.

No way could I handle sitting through a meeting. I had to go in, do what I needed to do, and get the hell out of there with as little interaction as possible.

I was striding off the elevator within minutes. I offered a few small waves to Meryl and Cynthia as I passed them in the hall before ducking into my office. Leaning against the closed door, I shut my eyes, biting my cheek to hold back the tears.

God, I didn't have time for a breakdown. I had about twenty minutes before Dean would stroll in, ready to escort me to the conference room.

I sat behind my desk and booted up my computer. My hands shook, and my foot tapped against the tile as nervous energy radiated off of me in unpredictable waves.

A letter of resignation was typed out at a quick, efficient pace. I sent a screenshot of the TapNext conversation to my email and printed it out.

And then I was walking down the hall, toward the one place I didn't really want to be.

"Oh, hi, Georgia!" Leslie stopped me as I rounded the corner. "Is Mr. Brooks back? I forgot to give him a few messages last week about some meeting…" She scrunched her eyebrows, her pea-sized brain trying to remember. "I think it was important, but, like, I'm not really sure."

"He won't be back until tomorrow."

"Oh." Her huge mouth jutted out into a pout. "Are you feeling okay? You look, like, really terrible today."

Wow. As if my day wasn't already fantastic.

I didn't even have the energy to form a sarcastic retort. I just nodded, because she was right; I looked like shit.

"Hey, do you mind going into Dean's office and letting him know that I had to go home? Tell him I'm sick and I'll call him later."

He would be crazy pissed at me but would understand. Plus, I was betting on the fact that Leslie would ramble on and on about my haggard appearance. It was the first time I could use her obsession with being the prettiest girl in the room to my advantage.

"Uh...*okay*," she begrudgingly agreed.

You'd think *I* was the intern in this scenario, asking my superior for a favor.

The second I stepped into Kline's office, my heart clenched. I glanced around at the familiar surroundings, taking everything in. Knowing I wouldn't last long, I pulled open a drawer on his desk in search of paper. My eyes got blurry when they caught on a photograph of us in the Hamptons resting on top of everything else. We were sitting on the porch, his arm wrapped around my shoulder. I was looking into the camera, grinning, while he gazed down at me, a soft, smitten smile on his lips.

What should have been a happy memory only made me want to throw up again.

I was starting to wonder if I ever really knew Kline Brooks.

I had to get out of his office and back to my apartment. The impending breakdown was sitting in my throat.

Slamming the drawer closed, I wrote out a simple note on the top edge of the screenshot Cassie had sent me, placing it on top of my resignation letter.

Walking out of his office and getting on the elevator, I was certain I'd never be the same after this. I knew getting myself to a place where I even felt like smiling was going to be the hardest thing I ever did. I knew there was no getting over Kline.

But I also knew I deserved better.

I'd find a new job. I'd find a way to move on.

And I'd be just fine pretending that I was.

CHAPTER 32

Kline

I shook the ice in my glass, watching as the cubes moved from side to side and melted into one another. One water droplet plopped from each surface to the next until it finally disappeared into the shallow amber liquid at the bottom.

I'd taken to drinking scotch on the flight to pass the time, the bouncing of my knee having grown old within the first fifteen minutes. Georgia was still on a plane too, having taken off precisely two hours and seventeen minutes ahead of me—according to the FAA—but every minute felt like a lifetime, and it took real concentration to keep myself from bombarding her turned-off phone with a stream of sappy messages.

Last night—the last few weeks of nights—had been the best of my life. Everything I'd worked for, built for myself, and strived to keep healthy felt like a drop in the life-bucket. Finding someone who made me anticipate each day and crave her company—someone who made me feel even more like me—well, that was what made a man realize the truth, *the importance,* in working to live rather than living to work.

I wanted my days to start and end with her, and I wanted the privilege to have even more of her in the middle.

Put simply, I was in love.

And it was irrevocably clear why I never had been before. *None of them were her.*

"Gemma?" I asked like the pathetic shell of a man I had become. I'd told Georgia I loved her, but it hadn't been enough. I needed some kind of confirmation. Some kind of peace. Some kind of promise of forever.

Gemma had the grace to smile. "She should be landing sometime in the next five minutes, sir."

I could have been the butt of many jokes, the object of numerous men's end-of-world postulation, but I couldn't find it in me to care. And it was clear I'd been feeling that way for the greater part of the morning.

Cutting short a meeting with Wallace Fellers, one of my biggest regular investors, and heading straight for the airport only to chase Georgia's plane across the country was not exactly precedented behavior.

The flight attendant's phone rang, and my head jerked up from my lap at the sound.

Gemma laughed as she hung it up and showed compassion for my pitiful existence by delivering the news from air traffic control immediately. "She should be on the ground, sir."

Phone in hand from the cupholder at my side, I scrolled to her number and dialed.

Two short rings gave way to her voicemail, and I hung up without leaving a message.

I knew it was crazy, dialing someone the moment the wheels of their plane touched the ground, obsessing over their arrival so valiantly in an effort just to hear their voice that I couldn't wait the five-minute security delay a Google search would imply.

But I was a very sick man, the first stages of love overwhelming my cells and multiplying by the minute. It was aggressive like most terminal cases, taking down one organ after the next until I had no choice but to succumb—succumb to the crazy, desperate lengths to make contact and the desire to swaddle myself in her presence and never unwrap.

I typed out a text instead.

Me: *After a few bribes and several heinous displays of my money and influence, I got the FAA to give me an exact schedule of your arrival time. Call me as soon as you can.*

Several minutes and an intense one-man conversation later, I added the words I should have included in the first place.

Me: *PS-I love you.*

When she didn't answer immediately, I knew I was one short step away from throwing myself off the proverbial ledge. I couldn't take it anymore. I had to do something else, be something else—if for nothing more than the sake of my poor, overexcited heart.

A nap. That was the only answer.

Determined, I sunk into my seat, reclined the back, and forced my eyes closed.

I pictured her smile and her hair, and as I focused really hard and gave myself over to the dream, I could even smell her perfect Georgia smell.

I woke hours later to the jolt of our wheels meeting the pavement of the runway. Gemma smiled and waved as my eyes met hers, and I jumped to pull my seat back to upright and grab my phone from the cupholder.

No messages showed on the screen, so I unlocked it to be sure, but no amount of hope could make the status change.

Nothing.

No calls. No texts. No messages from Rose. I checked each and every folder rigorously, searching for some phone-cyberspace loophole that'd robbed me of the one thing I desired so much.

But ten minutes and a mild case of carpal tunnel later, I still came up empty.

I prided myself on being a smart man, and something didn't feel right.

But I quieted my thoughts with the power of sheer will and unbuckled my seatbelt as we pulled to a stop.

She'd had a meeting to get to immediately upon landing, and as much as I'd bitched about her waiting for a later plane, she'd already had it scheduled to the very last possible minute.

With New York as her habitat, it probably took every ounce of concentration and a pledge of sainthood to make it there on time, in one piece, and with an inkling of schmooze left in the tank. She wouldn't have much left for me.

I moved to the front of the plane, re-strategizing on the fly and focusing on the element of surprise. I was here, in the same city, free to chase her down until the sun came up if I had to. She didn't know I'd flown home earlier than expected and keeping it that way would only amplify the reunion.

Jesus. *Yeah.* I liked the sound of that.

"Thanks, Gem," I said, giving her a genuine smile as she stepped to the side of the main cabin door to let me by.

"Anytime, Mr. Brooks."

I took two steps down the stairs when she called my name again. I looked back at her over my shoulder.

"She's very lucky, sir."

I shook my head and laughed.

"Me," I corrected, tapping my chest with a wink before scooting down the rest of the stairs to a waiting Frank.

He stood, holding an open door and wearing a smile.

"Mr. Brooks."

"Hey, Frank," I greeted. "Straight to the office, okay?"

I'd start at the beginning and work my way around the city until I found her from there. I couldn't wait to see her face.

"Yes, sir."

The lights of the office were dimmed enough that they rubbed off on my hope, but I headed for the back anyway. As long as I was here, I'd check my desk for messages and change into one of my spare shirts before heading for Georgia and Cassie's apartment.

I kept my pace to a near jog, but considering the strength of my desire to run, I counted it as a victory.

My door was cracked, the lamp at my desk illuminating the immediate surrounding space softly. My eyebrows pulled together at the sight, but I didn't slow my gait, striding for the beckoning light at a canter.

The surface was clear except for two loose sheets of paper. I shuffled them to the side in a hurry, grabbing for the tray at the back where Pam often placed my messages when the photocopy caught my eye.

It looked like a screenshot of a message window on a phone.

At the top, a few short strokes of delicate scrawl demanded my immediate attention.

Ruck,

Of all the people in the world…my best friend?
I hate that I still love you after seeing this,
but I can't be with someone who lies to me.
This <u>doesn't</u> hurt good.

Benny

One word bled into the next as I tried to make sense of the simple sentiment, but a mushrooming cloud of dread jumped and swooped, swallowing me whole.

Bold and cruel, the screen of the messaging page of the TapNext app taunted me.

TAPRoseNEXT (7:00PM): You're a very nice guy, but I can't continue talking with you anymore. I've gotten more serious with the man I'm seeing and this just doesn't feel right. I'm sorry. Good luck with everything, Ruck.

BAD_Ruck (6:45AM): I get it. I do. But I think we should meet in person, just the two of us. Please, Rose.

"No," I muttered, reading the words in a flash and reliving each of the seconds that led up to them and followed. "No, no, no, noooooo!" I screamed into the echoey silence.

So lost in the haze of new and all-encompassing love, I'd foolishly, faithfully believed I'd get the chance to straighten everything out in my time. Practiced, planned, and in a completely unmessy setting. That was what I'd been after, the meeting in person. I figured I could control the situation. She'd have the space to react and I'd have the chance to explain. I'd naïvely thought an in-person revelation could even be a little idyllic. But as I ran through the hours and the days I'd kept it to myself—the time I'd harbored my secret even after learning of our faux foursome with our friends—I knew I'd missed my chance.

Sometimes time is valuable, but it can also be your worst enemy. Because, no matter the root of my intentions, lies never led to romance.

This. This moment, this feeling.

This was hell.

I jumped into action, pulling the phone from the pocket of my pants and considering all the ways I could fix it. I was a fixer, a problem solver. *I could fix this.*

Couldn't I?

I fought the tightness in my throat, but it was potent in a way I wasn't prepared for.

I opened my text messages and typed out several drafts.

Me: Please, let me explain. I know it doesn't look good.

Delete.

I shook my head and scrubbed at my face, willing the right words to come.

Me: I love you. God, let me explain.

Delete.

Me: Georgie. Please talk to me. I've known it was you for a long time now.

Delete.

I opened the TapNext app and drafted a message to Rose.

BAD_Ruck (6:54PM): You've got this all wrong, Rose. I know who you are.

Delete.

Accusing her of *any* wrongdoing in this scenario was probably not a good idea.

BAD_Ruck (6:55PM): Remember the gargoyle dick, Rose. Not

everything is what it seems.

Delete.

Goddammit. This was definitely not the time to be a smartass, either.

None of it was good enough. No words powerful enough to convince the inconvincible.

My nose stung and my eyes burned and the screen of my phone blurred before my eyes.

I'd fucked up in a way I didn't know how to fix—didn't know how to *breathe* through the fucking pain.

Jesus. If I couldn't even put together a few fucking words that sounded convincing *to myself*, she was never going to believe me. *Not ever.*

"FUCKKK!" I screamed until fire raged in my throat and chucked my useless phone clear across the room and watched it shatter.

I punched at the top of my desk over and over until my hand developed a throb, pulling the pain and blood away from my pathetic pumping heart. Each thud enhanced the ache, and I prayed that somehow, someway, I'd find a way to make it end before the cycle purged my vital organs of enough blood to end me.

Time.

I needed it. Time to think, time to plan, time to understand what this was going to take.

Taking a deep breath and blowing it out, I pulled the sheet of paper over to expose the one beneath it and immediately lost my footing. I turned just in time, sinking to the floor with my back to the mahogany of my desk and clutched at the paper.

Her resignation letter, effective immediately.

She didn't want my hollow words or pleading looks.

My little shark had bitten the lines of contact clean through.

It was done. Done in a way that I wasn't remotely ready for. Done in a way that I couldn't even conceive.

Done in a way that would never actually be done, *not ever.*
This pain would haunt me for the rest of my life.

CHAPTER 33

Georgia

I gave myself twenty-four hours to wallow and cry and browse Reddit "my boyfriend is a cheating, cock-sucking, piece-of-scum dirtbag" threads. Okay, maybe they weren't really titled that, but I'd always enjoyed nicknaming shit.

And when I wasn't trolling Internet threads, I could've been found doing any of the following:

1. Crying. *A lot.*

2. Turning my phone on and off every five minutes, in hopes that Kline would attempt to contact me. He didn't, by the way. Not a text, a call, nothing but complete radio silence.

3. Re-watching the first four seasons of *Gilmore Girls.* If only we could combine Logan, Jess, and Dean to form the perfect man.

4. Eating all of our food. (Cassie was not happy about this.)

5. Taking one thousand BuzzFeed quizzes. I was a Hufflepuff, who should live in San Francisco and preferred NSYNC over Backstreet Boys. Chris Pratt should have been my celebrity husband, I'd have two kids, and my chocolate IQ was insane. Just in case you were wondering.

When BuzzFeed told me The Notebook was the Nicholas Sparks book that best described my love life, I gave it both middle fingers and shut my laptop.

If I was a bird, Kline Brooks could go fuck himself.

But you know what the hardest part was?

I still loved him. God, I loved him. I loved Kline just as much as I had before I'd seen that screenshot from Cassie. And this voice in the back of my head kept insisting something was off.

That Kline wouldn't have broken my trust like that.

Stupid voice. It was that kind of voice that made people stay in relationships with someone who didn't deserve them. I also gave that voice both middle fingers. Frankly, I was ready to give every-fuck-ing-body the middle finger. Misery loves company and all that jazz.

Day Two, Post-Kline-breaking-my-heart:

I had managed to get myself out of bed, shower, and make some phone calls to a corporate headhunter so I could find a new job. Sure, I'd slept in Kline's t-shirt that night and cried myself to sleep, but at least I was taking a step in the right direction. And it should be noted, I left my cell phone *on* and only checked for missed calls or texts every ten minutes that day.

Baby steps, folks. It was all about the baby steps.

Day three, Post-Kline-breaking-my-heart:

I woke up red-eyed and snotty but had several voicemails with possible job prospects and interview requests. One good thing out of the entire Kline mess, I had a killer résumé and other companies really wanted me on their payroll. I took an interview that day. It was a marketing position for an NFL team, popularly known as the New

York Mavericks. They'd had a recent change in management that had left them in dire straits.

I didn't know anything about football, but I knew marketing. When I sat down for the interview with Frankie Hart, the Maverick's GM, I reminded myself of that very fact. It didn't matter how much I knew about the game; all that mattered was if I could market their franchise in a way that was both profitable and creative.

I showed him slides of the successful campaigns I had done for Brooks Media. I asked questions about their current marketing outlooks and financial profitability. And then I showed Frankie the kind of ingenious skills I had by tossing out a few possible changes that would help build the Maverick name.

He loved my ideas. I left the interview feeling really proud of myself. And I hated that the first person I wanted to call was Kline. I hated that he had become such an important part of my life in such a short amount of time.

After drowning my hate and irritation in three beers and a plate of nachos at the bar up the street from my apartment, my headhunter called with a job offer. The New York Mavericks wanted to hire me and presented their offer with a generous salary and investment plan. I was shocked by their quick trigger. My experiences with getting a response from corporations was *never* this prompt. *But maybe football franchises are different? Who knows?*

I didn't waste time trying figure it out.

Immediately, I accepted the position. Even though football, or any sport for that matter, wasn't my forte, I was excited about the challenge, and honestly, I couldn't afford to sit around for months without a paycheck. Student loans and rent did not accept IOUs.

That night, I slid into bed and checked my phone one last time.

Still no response from Kline.

I clutched my aching stomach and forced my racing mind to sleep.

God, I missed him so much I felt physically ill from it.

Later that week, Cassie surprised me by coming home a few days early from her shoot in San Francisco. This was why she'd always be one of the most important people in my life. I needed her, desperately, and she didn't hesitate to rearrange her schedule to be my shoulder to lean on.

We ordered Chinese, gorged ourselves on chicken fried rice and crab rangoon, and lounged on the couch for a *Friday Night Lights* marathon on Netflix.

If anyone could brighten my mood, it was Tim Riggins, right?

Wrong.

I only got a few episodes deep before I was on the verge of losing it. The second I saw Lyla Garrity smile against Tim Riggins' mouth mid-kiss, the emotional dam was ready to burst.

"Are you okay?" Cass asked as I strode into the bathroom.

All I could do was shake my head. Because I was very far from okay. Probably the furthest I'd ever been from okay.

I stared at myself in the bathroom mirror, my legs trembling and hands gripping the sink like it would somehow give me the strength to fight my pitiful emotions.

Don't cry. He does not deserve your tears.

When that didn't work, I attempted to distract myself by peeing. But I quickly found it didn't serve as any type of distraction, because after about fifteen seconds, I was just peeing *and* crying at the same time. If you'd ever found yourself in that horribly tragic set of circumstances, you'd have understood it was the worst feeling ever. Not only could you not stop peeing, but you couldn't hold back the sobs. Pathetic was the only true way to describe it.

Cass found me in the bathroom that way—pants around my ankles and tears streaming down my cheeks.

"What can I do?" Her face was etched with concern.

"Nothing," I cried, shoving a clump of toilet paper against my nose. My elbows went to my bare knees—yes, I was still on the toilet—and my head was in my hands.

"Have you talked to him since?" She rested her hip against the doorframe.

"Nope. It's been a week and he hasn't tried to contact me. Hasn't called. Texted. Fucking tapped out Morse code. No skywriter or carrier pigeon. Nada. Zip. Zilch." I stared up at her, my chin resting in my hands. "He even knows I was out looking for a new job. How do I know this? Because when the headhunter called with the offer, he also mentioned my prior place of employment provided an amazing recommendation."

"But—" she started to interrupt, but I kept going.

"So, basically, Kline Brooks doesn't give a shit. He saw my letter of resignation. He saw the screenshot with the note I left him. And guess what? He never attempted to contact me. Plus, he was more than happy to give my future job prospect a glowing recommendation. Am I going crazy, Cass? I mean, was I completely deranged and thought Kline and I were way more than what we actually were?"

"No, sweetie," she responded. "I saw you two together and it was more than obvious he adored you."

"Then why did he want to meet up with you? Why did he want to meet up with my best friend?" I stifled a sob, pressing more toilet paper against my eyes. "Obviously, this is nothing against you, Cass," I muttered.

"I know, Georgie. And seriously, you don't have to apologize to me. This entire situation is fucked up, that's for damn sure."

I nodded, blowing my nose.

"How about you get off the toilet and maybe we can find something else to watch? It's safe to say Tim and Lyla are little too much for you at the moment."

"Okay," I agreed through a hiccupping breath.

"I'll give you a minute to get yourself together," she called over her shoulder, moving into the hallway.

I stood by the sink, washing my hands and face. I would not spend another night bawling my eyes out. It was just getting pathetic at that point. Obviously, what I'd thought Kline and I were, and what he'd thought we were, were two very different things.

The voice in my head tried to remind me of the way his blue eyes had looked the night he told me he loved me—tender, vulnerable, his heart resting in their depths.

I told that voice to fuck off. He wouldn't be the first man or woman in the world to profess love to someone they didn't really care about. Believe me, I had seen the threads on Reddit.

People did some horrible shit to one another. Relationships, that were otherwise amazing, could end on the worst of notes. That was not how I had pictured things happening with Kline and me, but that was life, right? Sometimes things didn't go as you planned or hoped they would. Sometimes bad things happened to good people.

Sometimes you just had to suck it up and move on.

I just hated that I missed him as much as I did.

I missed his laugh and his smile and his teasing comments.

I missed my big spoon.

As I wiped my face and hands off with the towel, I glanced down at my pants and noticed a giant grease stain in the crotch region. Normally, I would have just left it, but that night, I needed to *not* feel like the most pitiful person in existence.

I took off the sweats and headed toward my bedroom to grab a new pair of pants.

"Hey, Georgia, what do you think about *The Walking Dead*?" Cass asked from the other end of the hallway.

"Sure, why not?" I shrugged. Zombies seemed like a good, safe choice. How could I think about Kline when I was watching humans turn cannibalistic?

She started to turn back toward the living room but stopped in her tracks. "Hold up…are you wearing boxer briefs?"

Ah, fuck.

"No," I answered, covering my underwear. Well, Kline's underwear.

She flashed a skeptical look.

"Fine!" I threw my hands in the air. "I'm wearing Kline's briefs because I'm pathetic and I miss him and they smell like him!"

"*Smell like him?*" She fought the urge to smile.

"This isn't funny!" I groaned.

She held up both hands. "I never said it was."

I pointed toward her mouth. "Yeah, but you're about two seconds away from laughing your ass off!"

"Honey, you just told me you're wearing your ex-boyfriend's underwear because you miss him and they smell like him. *His underwear.* The material that literally cradles his balls."

"Oh, God," I whined, face scrunching into an agonized expression. "This is definitely a new low point in my life." I leaned against the wall, head falling back. "I'm so desperate for him that I'll take smelling like his sac over not smelling like him at all."

Cass moved toward me and immediately pulled me into a tight hug.

"It'll be okay, Georgie. I promise it'll be okay."

I sniffled back the tears, resting my chin on her shoulder and squeezing her tight.

"Do you want me to try to call him? Maybe it isn't what you think? Maybe he has an explanation?"

"Doubtful," I muttered. "He would have called. If there was an explanation, he would have called." I needed to say the words for myself just as much as I needed to say them for her. Her face reflected my misery perfectly.

"I just want to forget him, Cass. I just want to wake up and not have to go through an entire day of missing him and wishing things were different."

"I know, honey. I know. It'll get easier, but it's just going to take some time." She ran her fingers through my hair. "But you know what?

You're still doing your best to move forward. You went out and got a new job. You're not just sitting around and moping like most people would. I'm really proud of you."

"Thanks for coming home early. I really needed you."

"I will always be here for you. Even when you smell like ball sac," she teased, a smile in her voice, "I'll still be here."

I laughed and groaned at the same time. "God, I know I said they smelled like him but I didn't even really do a sniff check on these. I mean, Kline is usually a clean, well-groomed kind of guy, but for all I know, I'm wearing a post-rugby practice pair."

A quiet laugh escaped her lips. "How about you go take a hot shower while I make those amazing Ghirardelli dark chocolate brownies we have in the pantry? Then we can watch humans turn into zombies and eat one another?"

"I really love you."

"I love you too. Now go rinse the ball sweat off and meet me in the living room."

CHAPTER 34

Kline

A knock at my door picked at my already raging headache with an ice hammer.

"Yeah?" I asked, my voice heavily laden with days' worth of heartbreak and aggravation.

The door swung open and closed without delay, Thatch starting on one side and ending on the other.

"Good morning, my old, melancholy friend."

My eyes narrowed in a power-glare. He noticed immediately.

"Right. Not the time, I can see."

Definitely not. I shook my head.

"You're missing out, K. I've got some really fantastic new material I tried out on Gwendolyn last night."

I pinched the bridge of my nose and tilted it toward the ceiling.

Please, God, give me patience right now.

"All right, all right," Thatch conceded. "Not in the mood for Gwendolyn either. I get it."

I sighed.

"I mean, I have a hard time actually *getting* it, you know? I'm pretty much always in the mood for Gwendolyn. Or Amber. Or Yvette."

"Thatch."

"Definitely, Yvette. She does the best work with her tongue."

I had never been less in the mood for his teasing than I was right now. I wasn't sleeping, barely eating. I missed my fucking Benny. I didn't want to hear about any-fucking-body and I didn't want to listen to jokes.

Nonexistent patience tapped out, I scrubbed through the mess on my desk and shoved the bulleted proposal at him. I'd done my best to outline everything I was looking for it to say, but I was no goddamn lawyer. Neither was he, but he'd know what to do.

Wrinkles formed between his eyes as he concentrated and read.

"Are you serious right now?" Thatch asked, shaking the paper in front of him and looking deep into my eyes. He'd never looked at me that seriously. I was obviously scaring him.

"As a fucking heart attack," I confirmed.

"K—"

"Just do it!" I snapped, rolling my neck from side to side and blowing out a deep breath to calm down.

Fuck, I was tense. More so than I'd ever been in my entire goddamn life, and my nerves were shot. If people didn't start doing what I said, right when I said it, I was liable to lose my fucking mind.

He shook his head disdainfully, but either my totally fucked up head was playing tricks on me or the curve of his smile was growing with each pass.

"You are one crazy motherfucker, you know that?" he asked, his lips turned up in a full-on smile. I knew I wasn't making it up now.

I nodded a few times before the intensity of his happiness had me shaking my head. "Why are you smiling like a goddamn lunatic?"

"Because," he said in another uncharacteristic display of seriousness. "I'm fucking thrilled to see you this happy."

Happy? Was he high? I'd never been this fucking heartbroken.

"Dude, I've never been this miserable."

He nearly choked on a laugh. "Yeah, but see, that's the flip side. Crazy in love can only mean one of two things." He ticked each option off on his fingers. "Maniacally happy or butt-fuck desolate. It's one or the other, and it all hangs on the notion of said person loving you back."

He shook the paper in his hands. "I admire you. Fucking up but fucking doing something about it. *This* is what makes a man. Buried to shit in the weeds so he takes out a machete."

I cracked a smile for the first time in two days.

"Just make sure it doesn't take me four fucking years to cut my way out, okay?"

"I'll have the contract ready by Friday at the latest. There's some red tape, but you can thank me again for stopping you from caving to a structure with a board of directors. If you had, you'd have been fucked."

I shook my head.

He turned an ear toward me, cocked a brow, and waved a hand in invitation.

I rolled my eyes but played along. "Thank you, Thatch, for having the foresight to make it possible to make a last-ditch grand gesture in the name of love without being completely fucked."

He bowed slightly, tucking one hand to his stomach and the other to his back. "You're welcome."

My office phone ringing had me rounding the desk and meeting his eyes in question. He waved his permission.

"Brooks," I answered shortly.

"Kline, Kline, Kline." Wes tsked in my ear.

Jesus. I didn't know if I had the energy for both of them.

"This really isn't a good time, Wes."

"It never is—"

True enough.

"But I think you'll want to hear this," he taunted.

Like a starving fish, I took the bait on the line without question.

"What?"

"We just interviewed a new employee—"

Goddamn, everyone was making it their fucking mission to annoy me today. New conquests from one and new hires from the next, I had no desire to hear any of it.

"Wes—"

"Pretty little thing. Can't be more than five one, five two, but by God, she's got a body on her."

My stomach jumped with excitement and roiled with sick all at once. He sat silent on the line, just waiting.

"You saw her?"

"Nope, not me. She's in with the GM now. He wanted me to call and look into her references while she's in there, though, seeing as he liked the girl so much and didn't want to waste time getting an offer together."

The words burned my throat as I said them. "You're a fucking moron if you don't hire her."

"No kidding."

I'd never wanted to slit the throat of a friend before, but I guessed there was a time and circumstance for everything.

Thatch looked on as I worked hard to compose myself. Sure, I had a plan, but I had no idea how she'd react. I could very well still be royally screwed.

If that was the case, I still wanted the very best for her.

"Just...look out for her, okay?" My voice didn't even sound like my own, and Thatch looked away. The big fucking ox couldn't stand it either.

"You know I will, dude."

I nodded at the phone, too choked up to speak, and when it made me think of her, a single tear broke through the last goddamn barrier.

CHAPTER 35

Georgia

"**G**irl, it's pandemonium here! Where in the hell have you been? Do you even know what's going on?!" Dean shouted into my ear, not even offering a simple "Hello" or "How are you?"

I yanked the phone away from my face, my mouth contorting in pain.

Jesus, he was worked up about something. I could picture him pacing, his body vibrating with the need to tell someone whatever gossip he'd grabbed ahold of. If there was one thing Dean was great for when I was at...*yeah, that place I'd rather never speak of again*, it was keeping his ear to the ground and getting the down and dirty scoop on *everything*.

"Give me a minute, Dean. I'm trying to hear you over my ruptured eardrum." I sat down at my new desk, in my new office.

Even though it was a great job with amazing benefits, and the salary alone had me blinking twice when my eyes scanned the contract, it still didn't feel like home. I didn't have that sense of relief I had hoped for. I just felt...numb. I felt like someone had picked me up from my apartment and dropped me off in the middle of nowhere, without a lick of instructions or reassurance.

But I knew I could step up to the challenge and rock this job. I had learned from the best, a man who had started building his multi-billion dollar empire when he was a nineteen-year-old college student at Harvard.

Fuck you very much, Kline Brooks.

"Georgia," he said, ignoring my jab. "Listen. To. Me. Shit is crazy. I think everyone at Brooks Media is losing their ever-loving minds!"

Okay, that definitely caught my attention.

"W-what? Why?"

"Kline's moods revolve around colossally awful and biggest dick around. And *not* in the good way."

I blinked several times, attempting to process that information.

"Georgie? *Hell-o?* Are you still there?"

I swallowed past the shock. "Yeah, I'm here."

"Can you believe it? Kline Brooks, the man who rarely raises his voice and makes a point to be a gentleman, *no matter what,* has turned into the kind of guy his employees want to avoid at all costs. Talk about—"

I couldn't take any more. The last thing I wanted to hear was about Kline and his bad moods.

"Dean, I can't do this," I chimed in before he could continue. The mere thought of Kline had my stomach cursing me for eating a sausage biscuit from McDonald's for breakfast. "I just can't listen to this. I love you. I miss you. But I can't listen to anything related to Kline Brooks."

"Oh. My. Gawd!" he exclaimed. "My spidey sense told me something was off with your rash departure, but I brushed it off, figuring maybe you just wanted to see tight asses in spandex all day. And, girlfriend, I didn't blame you one bit for that. Hell, I would've done a whole lotta things—*emphasis on dirty*—that would've made them football boys blush to snag that job."

"I didn't take the job for the tight asses in spandex, Dean," I muttered.

"Well, I know that now! I can't believe I didn't see this sooner!"

"Didn't see what sooner?"

"You banged the boss." He sighed dramatically. "I am *so* jealous."

"Don't be." I snorted in irritation. "Kline Brooks might be good in bed, but he's even better at tearing your heart to shreds."

"Oh, no he didn't!" I literally heard his fingers give three quick snaps through the receiver. "What happened?"

"One day, when I don't feel like throwing up and crying when I hear his name, I'll give you all of the gory details. I just can't talk about it right now."

"Damn girl. I'm so sorry. It was that bad?"

"Times it by about a thousand and, yeah, it was that bad."

"If I wasn't wearing my new three-piece Gucci suit, I'd strut my ass right into his office and slug him."

That had me laughing. "You've never 'slugged' anyone in your life."

"That's only because I'm a bottom, sweetheart. The men in my life prefer me well-groomed and well-manicured. Slugging would mess up my pretty hands."

"*Wait*…you're a bottom?"

"Well…not *every* time, but yeah, I prefer to be ridden."

I grimaced. "Jesus. That's too much information for nine a.m."

"Pretty sure you asked, doll," he said through a laugh. "I miss having my little diva around. Tell me we can meet up for drinks soon."

"Definitely."

"And if you're curious and want to know what a certain some-one—"

I cut him off before he rehashed that argument. "Nope. Not gonna happen. But I will make time for you. Call me this weekend and we'll make some plans."

"Okay, lover. We'll chat later."

After we hung up, I busied myself with the one hundred pages of

Excel spreadsheets management had sent my way. I was finding out quickly the asshole who had run this position prior to me didn't give a shit about tracking expenses. The franchise would be lucky if their marketing investments broke even by the end of the fiscal quarter. No wonder he got the boot and they offered me the job at the drop of a hat.

Three soft knocks at the door grabbed my attention.

"Come in," I answered, glancing up from my computer.

A young man in his early twenties, and pretty much too adorable for words, hesitantly walked in. The Breakaway Courier logo was etched on his navy blue polo. His hands gripped a thick envelope.

"Georgia Cummings?" he asked, standing in front of my desk.

"That's me." I got up from my chair. "What can I help you with?"

"I've got an urgent delivery for you." He pulled a small black tablet from his backpack. "Mind giving me a signature?"

"Uh, sure…" I responded, slightly confused. "But are you sure this is for me? I wasn't expecting anything today."

"Definitely for you. I had strict orders to make this my next stop."

My brow rose. "Really?"

He nodded, holding the tablet out for my signature.

"Did they tell you who it's from?" I asked, signing and taking the package from his hands.

He shook his head and shrugged. "No clue, but apparently, it's really important."

"Okay, well, thanks."

I scanned the front of the manila envelope for a clue. Only my name and office address were written across the center, along with the words, *Urgent. Open and read immediately.*

"Have a nice day, Ms. Cummings."

"Thanks. You too," I mumbled.

My fingers slid beneath the lip of the envelope, breaking the seal. Still bewildered, I pulled out a thick stack of legal documents and skimmed the first page.

Business Purchase Agreement

This agreement is made on Monday, October 15th.

Between

1. Kline Matthew Brooks, Brooks Media, (the "Selling Party") and

2. Georgia Rose Cummings, (the "Buying Party")

This Business Purchase Agreement (this "Agreement") is made and entered into on Monday, October 15th, by and between, Kline Matthew Brooks, having its principal office of business at Brooks Media, 15 Fifth Avenue New York, NY ("Seller"), on the one hand, and Georgia Rose Cummings ("Buyer") on the other hand. Buyer and Seller are collectively referred to as (the "Parties") and are sometimes referred individually as a ("Party").

RECITALS:

WHEREAS, Seller is the owner of Brooks Media at 15 Fifth Avenue New York, NY, collectively, the ("Business").

NOW, THEREFORE, for and in consideration of the mutual covenants and benefits derived and to be derived from the Agreement by each Party, and for the other good and valuable consideration, the receipt and sufficiency of which are hereby acknowledged. Seller and Buyer hereby agree as follows:

Agreement to Sell:

Subject to and in accordance with the terms and conditions of this Agreement. Buyer agrees to purchase the Business from Seller, and Seller agrees to sell the business to Buyer. Seller represents and warrants to Buyer that it has (and Buyer will have) good and marketable title to the Business free and clear of liens and encumbrances.

Purchase Price and Method of Payment:

Brooks Media, all stock and investments, and corporations under the Brooks Media name are net worthed at 3.5 billion dollars, along with the ownership of one fluffy cat, Walter Brooks.

Buyer's price will include a 10:00 a.m. appointment at Brooks Media offices on today, October 15th. Buyer will give Seller fifteen minutes

of uninterrupted time to give an explanation to the Buyer. Once the
fifteen-minute time period is up, Buyer may sign the contract and
claim the title, CEO and President of Brooks Media, free and clear.

I stopped reading, staring down at the words in utter dismay.

He was selling—*no*—giving me his company? Just like that? Kline Brooks was just handing over his company and fortune for fifteen minutes of my time?

Oh, and he was tossing in Walter to, what, sweeten the deal?

What in the ever-loving kind of shit was this?

My knees buckled and I was thankful my ass was near the edge of my desk. I gripped the mahogany edge and tried to breathe through the intensifying tightness in my chest.

He had really, truly lost it. What did he think this would solve? Did he think I would just fall into his arms because he was worth over three billion dollars? That he could just buy me back with money?

Fuck. Him.

I would not be bought. *Never.*

He'd messed up. He'd ruined us. Our breakup rested solely on his shoulders, and I was more than ready to throw this stupid, insulting contract back in his face.

In. Person.

I grabbed my purse from my desk and stopped dead in my tracks as I reached the door to my office.

"Well, good morning," Frankie Hart greeted, flanked by a very attractive man who immediately had red flags raising in my mind. I knew his face from somewhere…

"Georgia, I'd like to introduce you to Wes Lancaster, the Mavericks' owner. He's very excited about—"

"*Wes Lancaster?*" I cut in, my jaw practically falling into my purse.

And just like that, the red flags turned to puzzle pieces as everything fell into place. I knew his face because I'd seen his picture, *in Kline's apartment.*

He was the Wes in the Kline, Thatch, and Wes trio. Which, *seriously?* Did they all have to be good looking?

"That's me." He nodded, a handsome smile consuming his stupid, perfect mouth. "Frankie's had nothing but good things to say about you. I'm excited to have you on board with our franchise."

I just stared at him. Speechless. Everything I thought I had earned in the interview went up in flames. I had a feeling I was only here because of Kline. How could I have been so stupid? No one got a call back after an interview that fucking quick, no matter how fast a company wanted to fill the position.

"Tell me, *Wes*, did you consult with Kline before the interview or after?" I snapped.

Obviously, I had lost it. I was standing there calling the owner of the Mavericks out.

My boss. I was calling my boss out on my first day on the job.

"Well…" He cleared his throat, visibly uncomfortable. "He told me I'd be an idiot if we didn't hire you."

I glared. At. My. New. Boss.

"It wasn't just because of him that we offered you the job. Frankie showed me slides from your previous marketing campaigns. He told me your ideas. And I loved them."

For some unknown reason, he seemed more concerned with calming me down than offended by my unprofessional behavior. Because, let's face it, I was being far from professional. So far, I had snapped at him, glared at him, and taken it upon myself to be on a first-name basis with him.

And I knew the reason why he wasn't acting insulted.

Kline motherfucking Brooks.

Wes caught sight of the contract balled up in my hand. "Obviously, we've come at a bad time, and I just remembered I had a nine thirty phone conference." He made a show of looking at his watch. "And it's already nine thirty-two. I better get moving."

Frankie's head tilted in confusion. "But…I thought that wasn't until noon?"

"Nope. It got changed." Wes shook his head. "It was a pleasure meeting you, Georgia," he said, ushering a confused Frankie out of the doorway. He pointedly glanced down at the contract before meeting my eyes again. "I've been friends with him for years because he's one of the good ones. Don't be too hard on him," he added before heading in the other direction.

First, Kline Brooks got me to fall in love with him, before breaking my heart.

Then he called in a favor to his best friend so I'd get a new job, before couriering over a contract to sign his entire business over to me.

Was this real life? Was he fucking joking with this right now?

The shock of meeting Wes was quickly replaced by anger.

I strode out of my office and didn't even bother telling my secretary I would be gone. Hell, with the floor show I had just provided my new boss, I'd have been shocked if they'd let me come back.

But I didn't even care to rehash that horribly awkward meet and greet in my head. I was solely focused on getting to Kline's office and letting him know how I felt about his offer.

Once my feet hit the sidewalk, I hailed a taxi and felt a surge of adrenaline rush through my veins because I was ten minutes away from shoving that ridiculous offer straight up his ass.

CHAPTER 36

Kline

"**I**n all the pining and whining you did over this chick, you failed to ever mention she was scary," Wes said into my ear.

I rolled my eyes. He'd had to listen to me talk about her for a fucking week. That was it.

"Scary?" I asked.

"Fucking *scary*. I wouldn't want to be you right now."

Hope bloomed and blossomed in my chest. "She's on her way?"

"Yep, as we speak. And she. Is. *Pissed*."

I smiled. God, I loved when she was fired up.

"How long ago did she leave?"

"Oh, about twenty minutes or so," he relayed in my ear as bedlam broke out in the office outside my door. I could see Dean running toward the office through the window, a look of pure glee on his face, and Thatch gave me the nod from the other side just as Georgia burst through the door.

She looked like Heaven and Hell and the sole reason for the constant ache in my chest for the last several days.

Hate and love and uncertainty all lined the edges of her face as she warred with herself at the sight of me.

I wanted desperately to pull her into my arms and feel the warmth of her seep into the cold of me, but I knew I had work to do before it was even a remote possibility.

I steeled my features and rounded my desk, leaning into the edge of it with the calm of a man who wasn't mere seconds away from coming out of his skin.

"Good, you're here."

Thatch slammed the door behind her and held it shut. Unable to resist, she ran to it, testing the effectiveness of all of his muscles with three sharp tugs. He didn't budge, one hand on the knob and the other still free to throw her a jaunty wave and a smile through the window.

She growled as she turned to me, stomping her foot in the most adorable way, and then made every effort to kill me with her eyes.

I put everything I had into not smiling and glanced at my watch. It almost worked.

"And for the first time in your life, you're on time."

She pinched her eyebrows together in question and didn't do it lightly. There was real anger there, harnessed between them. She was *raging,* and every single piece of her wanted me to know it.

I nodded to the tattered remnants of the contract, another victim of her wrath, clutched in her hand. "The meeting at ten?" I explained with the lilt of a question. "It was all outlined in the contract."

"Right," she scoffed. "The fucking contract. What kind of a sick fuck does something as mentally unstable as this? Your company?! The whole motherfucking company," she shouted and rambled. "An insane person. You've obviously lost all your marbles. Maybe *Walter* stole them, I don't fucking know."

She shook her head, her wild *brown* hair cascading and swinging and reeling me the fuck in. A handful of days without her, and she'd dyed it again.

She sure was something.

"What I do know is that if the meeting is at ten—" she glanced at her watch "—and it's nine fifty-nine, that makes me *early*."

I bit my lip and pressed my palms into the top of the desk to keep me there.

Her eyes shot to mine at the jagged sound of my whisper. "I'm so sorry, Benny."

Her slender throat jerked with a forced swallow.

"I know I fucked it all up," I admitted, working the edge of my tooth into my bottom lip to keep the pace of my words in check. I wanted to race and ramble like her, but I knew it wouldn't do me any favors.

"But I'm begging you to listen. Watch. Take it all in."

She shook her head and clenched her hands into fists.

"You don't have to change your mind," I offered—a desperate man clinging to whatever scraps he could get. "I want you to." I closed my eyes and prayed as I spoke. "God, Georgie, I want you to." When I opened them again, done with wasting any opportunity to see her, I made sure I didn't even blink. "But all you have to do is this. Be here for a few measly minutes. At least I'll get to fucking look at you. After that, you're free to go."

CHAPTER 37

Georgia

I shook my head, staring at the ground. I needed a reprieve from the havoc that pleading look on his face was doing to me.

"Please, baby, just five minutes of your time."

Immediately, I looked up, glaring at him. "Do *not* call me that."

He lifted both hands in the air. "I'm sorry, Benny."

I cringed. He knew what he was doing, the clever bastard, and that wasn't much better.

"Yeah," I spat. "Me fucking too. I'm sorry about a lot of things."

His face looked pained, but he quickly pushed the emotion down, forcing a soft smile onto his handsome lips instead. "Just fifteen minutes and then you're free to go. I promise."

"Promise?" I scoffed. "I've heard your promises. They're about as empty as my pathetic heart."

He couldn't hide that pain, couldn't push it down like he had before. His eyes creased at the corners, his lips mashed in a tight line. My chest ached as I watched him inhale a shaky breath.

I knew I wasn't being nice and I should have stopped, but I couldn't help myself. Awful words just kept flowing past my lips. Deep down, I wanted to throw knives his way until one of them stuck, cutting him as deep as he cut me.

"I know you're mad and you have every right to be." His voice was calm and composed and it only pissed me off more.

"I don't understand what this is going to help," I spat. "There is nothing you can show me that will change my mind, that will make me trust you again."

He ignored the tight lines of my body language—back stiff, fists clenched at my sides—and guided me to a chair. He gripped my shoulders, urging me to sit down. "Just a few more minutes of your time, Georgia. That's all I'm asking."

I sat, but I didn't want to sit. I wanted to be anywhere else but in that room with him. The simple touch of his fingers on my shoulders, his voice, soft and caressing near my ear, and those blue eyes, fucking slaying me with their pleading intensity—it was too much.

My heart was a rubber band and Kline was pulling too hard. Another glance into his saddened gaze, another tug on my emotions, and it would snap. I would end up doing something I regretted. And I'd be left with nothing.

Screw that. I wasn't going to be convinced. There was no amount of begging and pleading and lines of bullshit that would get me to change my mind. I'd stay strong. I'd watch whatever he wanted me to watch, and then I would leave. We'd both have closure that way.

Once this was over, I was going to be out of that door faster than I'd barged in.

He fiddled with his laptop until the projection screen came to life. I huffed.

Did he really have to make it this dramatic? I could have just watched it, whatever it was, on my laptop—even my phone.

He stood behind me, hands on my shoulders again, and lips near my ear. "I've only lied to you twice. The first time was when I didn't tell you I knew you were Rose."

My head jerked to look at him in surprise and disbelief, a nasty rebuttal on the tip of my tongue, but on the way around, my eyes caught on the video playing on the screen.

Security footage.

It took a minute to recognize the location, but it was Brooks Media's Human Resources. Cynthia's office, to be exact. My brows rose when a crazy person dressed in muddy clothes burst through her doors. He scanned the room until he found what he was searching for. In three quick strides, he was at her filing cabinet, yanking open the drawer and fingers sliding through the files.

The messy hair. The taut, tight muscles of his back, stretching and flexing. And that ass covered in shorts. I knew that body.

My breath caught in my lungs when the camera zoomed in, moving past his face quickly, but not too quick that I didn't recognize the jawline, especially the way it looked before he shaved, covered deliciously with two days' worth of growth.

It was Kline.

My mind tripped into realization that he was filthy and sweaty because he had come from rugby practice. Which also explained why no one else was in the office.

But why was he rummaging through Cynthia's files?

More importantly, why did I need to see this?

I caught sight of the timestamp in the corner. I counted the days in my head. It was a few days after our second date, where he had convinced me to go skinny-dipping at ONE UN. It was nearly eight-thirty in the evening and he was going through one of his employee's offices like a lunatic.

The camera zoomed closer, showing the file in his hands. I couldn't read the label on the edge quick enough before Kline was opening it, his finger tracing down the list of employees names.

The camera zoomed in again, blurry for a second before giving me a clear view. I watched his finger pause on one name.

Cummings, Georgia.

Then it slid across the page and came to a dead stop.

TAPRoseNEXT.

Adrenaline took over. My heart thrashed inside my chest as it furiously pumped the rush through my veins.

He knew.

He knew.

He knew.

It was the only thing my brain could compute.

He was in front of me, squatting down so we were at eye level. "The only other lie I've told you is that I liked you when I knew I was already in love with you."

My vision blurred, an unnamed emotion filling my lids.

Shock? Happiness? Relief? *Love?* I wasn't sure which. I was too overwhelmed.

But my heart, my heart knew what it wanted. It was on an escape mission, frantically trying to pound its way out of my chest, begging to return home.

I blinked, once, twice, three times. The room was clear again, and those blue eyes of his, they were staring at me, intense and pleading and so damn full of love I felt it bursting out of him and into me.

He'd known I was Rose. He had known since a few days after our second date.

Which meant, when he had messaged Cassie, he'd thought he was messaging me.

"W-why didn't you tell me?" I stuttered past the thickness in my throat.

His hand found mine, fingers entwining. "I should've told you. I know I should've told you, but I loved how open you were with me as Rose. I loved how you never held anything back. You were never afraid to tell me what you were thinking or how you felt."

He *would* think that. For the love of Christmas, we'd had a conversation about anal!

"I didn't want to lose that side of you until you were comfortable enough to be that way with me." A heavy sigh left his lips. "When I sent that last message, I thought I was sending it to *you*. I wanted to be open and honest with *you*."

He kissed my hand and then moved it to his chest. "This is yours. It'll always be yours." A frantic, erratic beat vibrated against my palm. "Please, tell me I haven't lost you for good."

I wanted to laugh. I wanted to smile wider than my cheeks would allow. I wanted to jump into his arms and never let go.

But I was scared. The remnants of the past few days had left a scar across my heart. I never wanted to feel like that again. I never wanted to feel so fucking lost.

"I love you," he whispered, his eyes staring into mine, deep and unrelenting. "I love you so much. Please tell me you feel the same."

No longer broken, his words stitched up that last remaining bit of my heart.

"Baby, say something." His voice cracked, desperation highlighting the edges. "Please, say something. Anything. Except for no. Anything but no."

God, he looked broken and defeated. I hated it. I didn't want him to be so sad, so anxious. I wanted him to laugh and smile and be the happy, charming, adorable Kline I had fallen in love with.

"You broke into my company?" I blurted out, trying to take him—take us—back to that place.

He paused, eyes searching mine. "Your company?"

I tilted my head, trying my damnedest to hold back a smile. "You wanted me to sign the contract, right?"

He nodded. "Yeah, I did." His eyes lit up, mouth quirking up at the corner. "But I want you to sign another contract too."

"What?"

He slid a small, black box from his pocket and went down on one knee.

My hand covered my mouth. "W-what are you doing?"

"You know what I'm doing." He gazed up at me, grinning. "Georgia, you are the only person I want to spend the rest of my life with. I knew it from the second you came barreling into my world with your rap lyrics and swollen lips and cute smiles and beautiful laughter. I knew the night of our first date, when you were buzzing on antihistamine and beatboxing about my huge cock, that you were the only woman I wanted. The only person that could make me happy for the rest of my life."

"I *beatboxed?*"

His grin grew wider. "Yeah, baby, you fucking beatboxed. It's one of my fondest memories."

My cheeks heated. There was no doubt in my mind, beatboxing took the cake over Masturbation Camp.

"God, you're so fucking adorable. I can't stand it." He laughed softly, fingers brushing across my cheek. "I can't let you go. I want you, with me, forever. My heart in your hands and you in my arms, that's all I'll ever need." He repeated the words he'd tattooed across my hip. "I said that then because I meant it, and I still mean it now."

Happiness and relief and love, so much love, it bubbled up past my throat and urged tears to spill past my lids. And when I smiled, I tasted the saltiness on my lips.

He brushed the tears from my cheeks with a soft stroke of his thumb. "Georgia Rose Cummings, will you marry me?"

I inhaled a hiccupping breath, smiling down at him.

And then I nodded my head a thousand times.

I was saying, "Yes, yes, yes," over and over again as he slid the ring down my finger and pulled me into his arms.

"I love you," he whispered into my ear.

"I love you too...*so much.*"

He brushed his lips over mine, kissing me soft and sweet, until his tongue slipped past the seam and danced with mine. His fingers slid into my hair, gripping the strands and tilting my head as he kissed me deeper, stronger, pouring everything he was feeling into that perfect kiss.

Kline Brooks had just asked me to marry him.

And I had said yes.

"Baby, will you beatbox your vows at our wedding?" he teased, face pressed against my neck, lips sucking softly.

"I want a prenup," I teased back.

He leaned back, his eyes meeting mine.

"See," I said, unable to stop the smile consuming my face. "I have all of this money now. And I own this awesome business. And I really need to start looking after myself. I don't think you're a gold digger, but—"

He cut me off with another kiss, chuckling against my lips.

"Does this mean you're agreeing to it?" I asked, feigning concern. "Because it's really important to me."

"I'll agree to anything you want as long as I get to keep you forever," he added, a mischievous smirk taking over his mouth. "But first, before we get into all the legalities of your money, we've got some more important things to do."

"Wait…you weren't kidding about signing your business over to me?"

"Fuck no. It's yours."

"Why would you—but that's—" I stuttered, jaw dropping. "Kline, that's ridiculous!"

"The only thing that's ridiculous right now is that we're still standing in this fucking office and not in my bedroom where I can take off that skirt with my mouth."

"Oh," I said, shocked by the sudden change in pace and my body's quick response to that specific pace. My nipples tightened under my blouse, and I was already throbbing in anticipation between my legs.

"Baby, don't get mad, but you're not going to be able to move fast enough in those heels."

"Huh?" I asked two seconds before I was airborne and thrown over Kline's shoulder.

"Kline!" I shouted, gripping his arms for balance.

"Just hold on, Benny," he said, chuckling, as he strode out of his office. One of his hands held tight to my skirt, keeping me covered and safe from flashing the entire office my ass cheeks.

"This is so embarrassing!" I shouted as we passed through the door and into the hallway where most of my former coworkers were gawking at us.

But he didn't care. He was a man on a mission, solely focused on getting us the hell out of there.

"Pam! Hold all of my calls! I'll be busy for the rest of the day!" he called over his shoulder.

"But I thought I owned the company?" I retorted, laughter spilling from my lips.

"I mean, hold all of Georgia's calls! She'll be too busy ri—"

I reached out, covering his mouth.

He laughed against my palm. His finger smashed against the elevator call button, practically breaking the down option.

He didn't waste any time, getting us on and off the elevator in what felt like seconds.

And then we were at his car, Frank opening the door.

Kline tossed me into the back, moving in beside me and telling his driver to get us to his apartment. He was itching with impatience, adding, "And don't worry about the cops. Just gun it. I'll cover the speeding tickets."

I loved that he was that anxious to get me alone in his bed. I loved that he was willing to put everything on the line to prove to me he was the man I had originally thought he was. I loved that he had proposed. I loved that he had carried me out of the office like a man possessed.

I loved him. God, I loved him.

I was so far gone on this man, I felt drunk from it.

I moved over to him, straddling his thighs, gripping his shoulders.

His eyebrows rose, blue eyes twinkling with intrigue.

"I can't wait," I whispered against his lips. "I need you. Right.

Now." My finger found the button for the privacy window, shutting it before Kline could refuse.

It was just the two of us in the back seat, Frank's eyes in the rearview mirror no longer visible.

"Fuck, I've missed this." Kline's hands found their way to the hem of my skirt, moving it up my thighs and over my hips. "I was afraid we'd never be here again."

"I've missed this too. I missed you so much."

His heady gaze moved up my body until they found mine again. "You're going to marry me?"

I nodded.

"You're going to move in with me?"

I nodded again, smiling this time.

His cock grew hard and strained beneath me.

"You mean, I get you, every day, for the rest of my life?"

"Yes," I said, a giddy laugh bubbling up from my throat.

"I get live-in Georgia. And beautiful, sleepy Georgia waking up next to me. And singing in the shower Georgia. And dancing around my kitchen Georgia," he rambled, eyes bright with excitement and adoration. "And I get—"

I stopped him with my lips, pressing my mouth urgently against his.

We kissed until we were out of breath, our bodies instinctively moving against one another.

"Baby," he moaned into my mouth. "Not here. Not like this. I want you in our bed." But he didn't stop kissing me, his perfect lips never leaving mine.

Our bed. I smiled, unable to control the love I had for this man.

He chuckled, pulling back to look at me.

"What?" I asked, a crazy, ridiculous smile still consuming my face.

"I love it when you do that."

"Do what?"

"Smile while I'm kissing you. It's like you're too happy to control it."

"I am." My cheeks burned, the goofy grin still intact.

He kissed my nose. "It's like I'm kissing a jack-o'-lantern."

I narrowed my eyes. "You calling me a pumpkin?"

"Yes." His teeth found my bottom lip, tugging gently. "Baby… Georgie…Benny…pumpkin. Mine. All fucking mine."

"Oh, no," I groaned, head falling back in defeat. "Not another nickname."

"Get used to it." He laughed, his tongue soothing the bite. "Remember? I'm Big-dicked Brooks, baby. And I'll call you whatever I want while I'm driving you crazy with my fingers…my mouth…my cock."

And then I was moaning. My eyes rolled back as he kissed down my jaw and sucked at the skin on my neck.

"God, Kline, I ache. I ache so bad right now," I whimpered when his hands slid up my thighs, fingers sliding my underwear to the side.

"Don't worry, soon-to-be Mrs. Brooks." I felt his grin against my skin. "It might hurt, but I'll always make sure it only hurts good."

EPILOGUE

Cassie

"Wheorgie, we need to go!" I exclaimed, grabbing our bouquets from the table and moving toward the door. We were sitting in the bridal suite, waiting for the ceremony to begin.

"Pretty sure you shouldn't be calling me Wheorgie on my wedding day," she retorted, her eyes still focused on the paper towel her pen was quickly scrawling across.

I stomped my heel, my flower-filled hand going straight to my hip. "Well, you're being a bit of a Wheorgie, considering you're going to be late for your big bridal entrance."

She held up one finger. "Hold on, I have to finish these."

I walked back over to her, glancing down at what she was writing.

"For real? You're writing your vows…like, three minutes before you're supposed to walk down the aisle?"

She shook her head. "No, I'm writing Kline's vows."

"He's too lazy to write his own vows?"

Talk about a broke-ass motherfucker, having his bride write his vows.

"No, we're writing each other's vows."

Oh, never mind.

"God, you guys are so cute that it literally makes me throw up a little in my mouth."

"Ew." She scrunched her nose. "Stop being so gross on my wedding day."

Three hard raps on the door startled us both. "Goddammit, Georgie! Get your ass out here. It's time," her father shouted from the other side.

"Just a minute, Dad!" she called back.

"Ah, shit. You've even got Dick mad," I teased.

"He's just mad because I'm marrying the man of *his* dreams."

We both laughed. It was one hundred percent the truth. Dick Cummings was in love with his soon-to-be son-in-law. He thought Kline walked on water. And after Georgia accepted his proposal, we later found out when Kline had asked her dad for his blessing, Dick had responded,

"Are you sure you want to do that, son? Georgie's a bit of a ballbuster."

Not, "You better protect my baby girl." Or, "If you hurt her, I'll kill you."

Nope. He had basically given him an out, or tried to keep Kline for himself, however you wanted to look at it.

"Finished!" She tossed the pen down and stood up, fluffing her dress. "How do I look?" she asked, taking one last glance at herself in the floor length mirror.

"Like the most beautiful bride I've ever seen." Because she did. Georgia was absolutely stunning.

She turned toward me, pointing an accusing finger in my direction. "Don't start. If you start crying, then I'll start crying."

"I'm not!" My face contorted into that awful expression you get when you're trying to hold back sobs.

"Goddammit, Cass!" Her eyes shimmered with unshed tears.

The processional music started to filter into the bridal room, and we both looked at each other with *Oh, shit!* expressions.

"Georgia! It's time!" her mother sing-songed from the other side of the door.

"Am I really getting married today?" she asked, bewildered, taking the bouquet of white lilies from my outstretched hand.

"Yeah, sweet cheeks, you're really getting married. My little, virginal best friend is all grown up. Marrying the man of her dad's dreams."

She giggled, flipping me the bird in a way only my best friend could pull off in a wedding dress. It was a beautiful dress—elegant mermaid cut with a small train. And it was simple yet blinged out with tiny clear crystals sewn into the bridal-white material.

Georgia had found it at a vintage store—*big surprise*—in Chicago, when we went there for a girls' weekend. It was Vera Wang, which was all Kline's doing. He'd made sure she spent a boatload of money on her dress, refusing to let her come back in the house unless she had drained at least several thousand dollars from their bank account.

Yes, *their* bank account. Even though she refused to sign his ridiculous contract and was adamant on keeping her new job with the Mavericks, he'd made sure to add her to all of his accounts right after she'd said yes. And he'd done this *without* the cushion of a prenup.

If that didn't tell you he was more than sure she was the one, I didn't know what would.

Before we walked out of the bridal suite, I wrapped her up in a tight hug.

"I'm so happy for you. You deserve all of this happiness and then some."

"I love you, Cass."

"I love you too. Now, let's go get you hitched!" I hooted, opening the door.

The wedding party was small, but it was perfect for them. Wes, Thatch, and Will were Kline's groomsmen, while Dean and I were Georgia's bridesmaids.

I walked down the aisle with Dean and took my place on the opposite side of the groomsmen. I couldn't help but notice the intrigued yet slightly salacious smile I received from Thatch. I assumed it was my tits' doing because my cleavage looked pretty damn fantastic in the little black dress Georgia had chosen for me.

And I didn't miss how delicious Thatch looked in his tux. I eye-fucked that Jolly Green Giant for a moment, moving from his brown eyes, to the broad shoulders filling out his jacket *like they fucking owned the joint*, to the noticeable bulge—not, *I'm the weirdo with a boner at a wedding* bulge, but *I'm packing* bulge—in his pants, and then back to his mouth.

Man oh man, those lips looked like they could do *things* (to my puss-ay).

Hey, cool your jets. It doesn't count as wedding inappropriate if it's in parentheses.

Seriously, I'd Thatch that.

The quartet of violins and harps Georgia hired for the ceremony music abruptly stopped. I glanced around, not sure what was happening. This definitely wasn't on her schedule.

Kline looked toward the side of the room and nodded at a woman with a guitar. She smiled, adjusted the microphone near her mouth, and started to strum a song that wasn't the planned "Bridal Chorus."

The crowd stood, turning toward the back doors.

And when they opened, there stood my beautiful best friend, her arm tucked into her father's, her mouth morphed into the biggest smile I'd ever seen.

Every wedding I had ever been to, while everyone was watching the bride, I always snuck a glance at the groom. When my eyes found

Kline's face, my heart damn near skipped a beat. Though a sight far more masculine, his smile mimicked Georgia's in all the ways that counted. He looked like a man who had just received everything he'd ever wanted. And it was obvious that everything was Georgia, walking straight toward him without looking back.

I had never seen a man look so in love.

The woman started to sing, softly playing her guitar, and that's when I put the pieces together. It was a slowed down, acoustic version of "Some Kind of Wonderful."

Their song. The song Georgia would always associate with Kline. And he'd done it, knowing how much that song meant to her, to them. Somehow, that sneaky bastard had arranged it on the sly.

It took every ounce of strength for me not to start crying. I was overwhelmed by them. My best friend and the man who'd swept her off her feet. They were happy. They were in love. And God, they were so perfect for each other. The world wouldn't be right if they weren't together.

As Georgia got closer, she was mouthing the words to the song, gazing at Kline.

And when she reached him, Dick hugged them both, and Kline pulled her into his arms. She whispered something into his ear and he nodded, his face pressed against her neck. And then he leaned back, staring down at his bride, and said, "You're so beautiful."

I'm pretty sure every woman in attendance swooned. I sure as hell did.

They stood before the minister, hand in hand, ready to profess their love and the rest of their lives to one another.

The minister greeted the attendants and proceeded to say nice, beautiful things about the happy couple. He was actually one of Dick's closest friends, which was probably a good thing, considering most of the people at this wedding tended to toss out the F-word more often than not.

And when the minister announced it was time for the vows, Dick cheered, "Hell yeah! Let's do this!"

See what I mean? Good thing he knew the kind of room full of morons he was walking into.

Kline pulled a neatly folded piece of white paper from his inside jacket pocket while Georgia slid the balled up paper towel out of her cleavage.

They handed each other their vows.

He glanced down at his tattered version and started laughing. "You finished these about two minutes before you walked down the aisle, didn't you, Benny?"

"I'll never tell," she said through a giggle.

He chuckled again. "God, I love you."

"It's not time for that!" Thatch yelled behind him. "Vows first!"

The crowd laughed.

"Okay, I guess I'll go first," Kline announced, unwrinkling the paper towel.

"Georgia Rose, I promise to trust you even when you deviate from our grocery list and convince me to buy six boxes of Dunkaroos and three bottles of wine I know you'll never drink.

"I promise to give you all of the love and support that I don't give Walter. Also, I promise to be nicer to Walter." He paused, glancing up at her and shaking his head with a giant grin.

"I'm not saying that."

She tapped the towel. "You have to. They're *your* vows, remember?"

He turned toward the attendants, letting everyone else in on the secret. "We wrote each other's vows, if you couldn't already tell."

"I warned you, Kline!" Dick shouted toward him. "Ballbuster."

"Daddy!" Georgia scolded. "There will be no talk of balls during my wedding ceremony."

The room filled with more laughter.

Once everyone settled down, Kline cleared his throat and continued, "He's a really good cat. The best cat. Man, I sure love Walter." He rolled his eyes, but said it nonetheless.

"I promise I'll never keep anything from you because there are no secrets between us. I vow to love you through the difficult and the easy. I promise to never put you or myself in danger. This includes me never drinking lime juice with my scotch ever again." He winked at her.

"I vow to never change from the amazing man that I already am. I promise to never lose my huge, strong, kind, and determined heart. I will never stop teasing you, making you laugh, or flashing smoldering blue eyes your way. I will always greet you with the smile that's only yours. And when it's just the two of us at home, I vow to only wear boxer briefs around the house. No matter what I'm doing, I'll either be naked or just wearing boxers." His blue eyes found hers, his brows waggling in agreement as a few women in the crowd hooted some catcalls.

"And I vow to listen, for as long as it takes for you to feel heard. I vow to be your unrelenting cheer squad on the days it feels too much. I vow to pick the important fights with you, especially when I know you're selling yourself short or not being treated with respect.

"I vow to spend the rest of our lives laughing, smiling, going on crazy adventures, and most importantly, loving each other through the good times and the bad. And if there are bad times, I promise the kind of makeup sex that has your blouse buttons hitting the floor."

And on the last sentence, he stared deep into her eyes. "I vow that I will love you, Georgia, every day, for the rest of forever."

Georgia sniffled a few times, and I handed her a tissue to wipe her eyes.

"Don't cry, TAPRoseNEXT," Kline whispered, brushing away a few tears. "You may have written those vows, but I'll stand by every last word."

She giggled at his sincerity, but I wasn't used to it, and therefore, found myself completely ill prepared. I dabbed at fresh tears with the back of my hand as she unfolded the paper in her hands.

"Kline Matthew, I stand before you today to become your wife." She paused for a second, looked up at him and then back at the paper. "I think everyone here knows that already, but I've got this feeling that you really wanted to hear me say it."

She turned to the crowd and remarked, "I'm not improvising." She turned the paper toward them. "It really says that."

Everyone laughed and he nodded. "Keep going, Benny."

She looked back to the scrawl of his words.

"From this day forward, I am yours and you are mine. I promise to remind myself of this most important fact every day and smile when you do it for me. I promise not to give up or run away when you make the kinds of mistakes that every man makes, and I promise to use my heart, rather than my ears, to really hear you."

Sweet cookies and dildos, this guy had a knack for saying the right thing.

"I promise to rap my way through our days and beatbox for you each night because it's times like those when I'm so..." She paused and glanced to the crowd. "I'm so...effing...adorable you can't even stand it."

Her amused eyes met his again. "You really wrote the F-word in my vows?"

He shrugged. "Adorable wasn't enough."

She shook her head, smiling, and continued, "I promise to keep you on your toes with my hair and my words and always stand up for myself with the backbone you love and expect."

"And, I promise to be late as often as I want because you'll always be waiting. But when it comes to lovin'—" Georgia stopped midsentence, giggling at her groom. "Kline, I'm not saying that in front of the minister."

"Baby, you have to. They're *your* vows, remember?"

She leaned forward, whispering something into his ear. His mouth twisted into a devilish grin and he whispered back.

Georgia turned toward the attendants. "Please feel free to cover your ears during this part."

She cleared her throat, cheeks pink, and said, "I'll come early and I'll come often because the power of Big-dicked Brooks compels me."

"I knew it!" I shouted. "I told you!"

Pffft. I knew my cockdar wasn't on the fritz.

Everyone in the crowd was a mixture of laughing, clapping, and wolf whistling.

Once we settled down, Georgia gazed at Kline like she would happily crawl inside him and stay there and said the rest of her vows.

"But most of all, I vow to love you with everything that I am, no matter the circumstances, because I know, from the very depths of my tiny, perfect being, that you will be there, doing your best to love me more."

And when the minister told Kline to kiss his bride.

He motherfucking kissed his bride so good it made *my* toes curl.

Thatch

"Congratulate me, boys," Kline toasted with a glass of scotch in the air, the happiest I'd seen the fucking sap in ages.

His body was here with us, but his mind and his eyes were on his boogeying bride on the other side of the dance floor. The space was fairly small. At least, this room known as The Greenhouse was. They'd rented out the entirety of The Foundry out of nothing more than necessity. Kline liked to think his life was boring and normal and that no one cared at all, but the truth was they did. They cared *a lot*. And keeping such an important event completely private was the only way to maintain his happy little bubble of make-believe.

"That," he said with a slightly tipsy gesture, "is *my* wife."

I laughed and slapped him on the shoulder, exchanging smiles with Wes behind his back. I raised my eyebrows in question, and Wes gave me a pursed-lip nod of agreement.

"Go get her," I urged simply, knowing he wanted to be with her a million times more than he wanted to stand here and shoot the shit with us.

And, regardless of what people might have thought they knew about me, that was fine by me. My oldest, closest friend had found it. Found *her*.

Always loyal and loving, I couldn't think of anyone who deserved it more than he did.

"Benny!" he yelled, pulling her attention from the crowd of women around her to him. "Make room on the floor. I'm coming for my dance!" The wattage of her smile was blinding.

I stood next to Wes and watched as Kline danced his way over to her, pulling her into his arms and handing off his drink to the first, unsuspecting free hand he came to so he could hold on to her with both hands. Hands to her jaw and lips to hers, he kissed her in a way that I felt all the way in my stomach.

"Good God, he's a goner," Wes remarked, sinking into the wall and tipping his drink to his lips.

"Yep," I agreed, thinking about the vows they'd exchanged during the ceremony.

"It's nice," I added without thought—because it was.

Wes laughed way harder than I thought was appropriate. "Jesus. Who are you and what have you done with Thatcher Kelly?" He morphed his face into what he thought was a good impression of me and mocked, "It's nice!" with a wobble of his head.

I punched him hard enough in the shoulder that he stopped laughing abruptly.

"Ow! Fuck, Thatch! Christ."

"It *is* nice," I told him again, further delving into the teachings of his lesson. "Take fucking note from your most experienced of friends. Multiple flavors of pussy are great, but what our fucking goner of a friend found is better."

He looked at me like he didn't know what to make of me.

"The two of them stood up in front of God and us and committed to each other forever with enough trust in each other to speak one another's words rather than their own. *That*, motherfucker, is love."

Powerful speech performed, lesson conveyed, I felt content with my message until Wes went and fucking ruined it.

"Jesus, fuck, The Foundry must be some sort of *Twilight Zone*. I don't even know who you guys are anymore," he teased, chuckling into his bourbon.

"One day, Lancaster, when it happens to you, I will remember this moment." I drained the rest of my drink and walked away.

Moving away from the bulk of the crowd, I sat down at a table that was mostly empty. My phone buzzed in my pocket.

I thought it might be the tattoo shop, checking in to see if I'd be there tonight, but instead, I found a number I didn't recognize.

Unknown: She's a lot older than you normally go for, but it looks like you've got a chance.

I looked around, wondering what the fuck whoever this was was talking about. Quickly, I typed out a message.

Me: Who is this?

A reply came almost immediately.

Unknown: Your mom.

I was no less confused, but hell if I didn't fucking laugh.

Me: WTF. Who is this?
Unknown: The hot bitch at the head table.

I looked up across the dance floor as the crowd parted in front of me. Cassie, the craziest bitch I'd ever encountered and Georgia's maid of honor, sat all by her lonesome at the wedding party's table, one leg cocked and her bare foot in the chair beside her. She popped her eyebrows in a mischievous challenge.

This chick had balls, sitting there by herself, just kicked back and relaxed with zero fucks given about it. Fuck, Cassie's balls might have been bigger than mine, and that was saying something.

Me: How'd you get my number?

Unknown: I have my ways.

Cryptic. Another message came right on its heels.

Unknown: But good luck with that pussy tonight.

I looked at her as she raised her glass in cheers and then looked at the area around me. Not even one prospective lay stood out in the nearest twenty-foot radius.

Me: What pussy?

Unknown: The silver-haired cutie beside you.

I looked to my left and then to my right, and what I saw had me smiling like a lunatic. Kline's grandma, Marylynn, sat clapping along to the heavy beat of the music and swaying back and forth. She was cute, but she was no less than eighty-five years old. I looked down to my phone and typed as quickly as my big thumbs would allow.

Me: You should be ashamed of yourself. This is Kline's grandma. But I'll be sure to tell her you find her attractive.

I shifted my gaze from the phone to her table as soon as I was done, but when the dancing crowd finally moved out of the way, she was gone. Gone from sight and gone from my phone, but she'd found a home somewhere else—stuck in my head.

THE END

Love Kline, Georgia, and the crew?

Stay up to date with them and us by signing up for our newsletter:
http://www.authormaxmonroe.com/#!contact/c1kcz

You may live to regret much, but we promise it won't be this.
Seriously. We'll make it fun.
And you really don't want to miss Cassie making good on her promise, right?
#IdThatchThat

Cassie and Thatch are coming for you in *Banking the Billionaire (Billionaire Bad Boys Book 2).*

CONTACT INFORMATION

Follow us online:

Website: www.authormaxmonroe.com

Facebook: https://www.facebook.com/authormaxmonroe/

Twitter: www.twitter.com/authormaxmonroe

Instagram: www.instagram.com/authormaxmonroe

Goodreads: https://goo.gl/8VUIz2

ACKNOWLEDGEMENTS

First of all, THANK YOU for reading. That goes for anyone who's bought a copy, read an ARC, helped us beta, edited, or found time in their busy schedule just to make sure we didn't write a pile of drunken chicken scratch.

We also have to thank ourselves for being awesome. Not *ourselves* ourselves, but each other ourselves. Max thanks Monroe, and Monroe thanks Max. We're not actually thanking *ourselves* like assholes. We both needed each other more than we probably ever could express, and we literally had the time of our lives doing this together.

Thank you, Lisa, for being funny and awesome and so freaking adaptable to our needs and requests. Your love for this book nourished it in a way that allowed it to grow into something better than the two of us could create without your input.

Thank you, Murphy, for whipping our shit into frosting. Or, you know, as close to it as possible. We love the finished product that we couldn't have created without you.

Thank you, Sommer, for creating the perfect Kline Brooks packaging. Hours have been wasted ogling rather than trolling through Facebook. We're happy with the change.

A special thank you to Colleen for being so gracious with both her time and sense of humor, laughing at our simple joke about not being her that we hadn't planned on anyone really seeing and further messing with our minds. We're still confused about how you wrote this book without us knowing it.

And last but not least, a HUGE thank you to our families, for allowing us the time and space and freedom from short-term household responsibilities that we needed to pull this off. They're the reason for everything.

All our love.

CPSIA information can be obtained
at www.ICGtesting.com
Printed in the USA
LVOW10s1749210218
567419LV00016B/1408/P